Connections

By: Anne Karin Elstad
Translated by: Iain Robertson

Table of Contents

Chapter 1

It is Sunday, 28th April,1940.

It has been an exceptionally fine weekend with weather reminiscent of summer rather than spring. A blue sky stretches high over the farms with their newly ploughed fields and sprouting greenery. The only thing disturbing the calm of this early Sunday morning is two German fighters flying low above the houses before they disappear over the fjord in the direction of the sea. People believe the planes come from Værnes. They have learned that the Germans have seized Værnes aerodrome.

During the morning a bank of clouds builds up over the sky in the west, making it look as if a powerful storm is on the way. These are black storm clouds, rising and falling. Some already know the truth; a couple of telephone calls have reached the village, and the news is spreading like wildfire. The town is under bombardment, and Kristiansund is burning.

That evening people from the village meet in the churchyard. The nights have now become shorter, and in the present good weather are not totally dark, more of a blue glow. The houses and the surrounding mountains stand out as black silhouettes against the sky, some still with snow on their summits. The people standing round, men, women and children are silent, as if round a grave. Women are in the majority because of mothers from the town lodging with their children on the local farms. Their husbands are not here, they are outside, looking at what they can see but cannot understand, which is like a crazy flame-red sunset out there in the west, a sunset which is dancing and never seems to stop. Above the sea of red light, there are clouds darker than the night sky. The men's faces are like white specks standing out in the blue darkness. Approaching them, what you can read in their faces is incredulity rather than anxiety, an incredulity which has characterised these last unreal days and weeks. Married couples who have never before been seen to touch now stand with arms clasped round one another. The youngest children are in bed, while the bigger and more grown-up among them seek solace with their mothers or fathers. Children who usually meet here for fun and games are silent. So very silent.

One man is standing apart from the group. There are not many of *them* here, but there is one, and he is well known to everyone. A farmer on one of the more prosperous farms in the district, he has, in countless conversations, aired his unshakeable belief in Hitler and, more recently, in Quisling. People have questioned him, made fun of him and ridiculed him, but have never really taken seriously the things he has said during these heated discussions. People have felt he thought of them as fools. Hallgrim Ås has always been a respected man in the neighbourhood, and his words would normally carry weight. Previously he was one of the few who voted for the Farmers' Party. He was also a council member for a number of years before ceasing to stand for election and then joining Quisling's party. He is quick-witted and a successful farmer, but he is also stubborn and has a strong will which not everyone finds easy to accept. And now here he is, standing together with his friends on the edge of the crowd, watching the disturbing action going on out there. As he leaves, he turns around.

- They should all go home. That is not a circus going on over there. And they must have heard that people are no longer supposed to meet like this. Yes, they should definitely go home.

But people no longer laugh at Hallgrim Ås. Words stick in their throats whenever he speaks. People are quite used to his sarcasm, but this is something new. Everyone catches a hint of hidden threats in what he is saying.

Once he is out of earshot, someone says:

- Hallgrim should watch out and not take himself so seriously. The Germans haven't beaten us yet.

These words lead to an uneasy mumbling before silence descends once more. No one can see any point in saying anything. But there is one man with his family following Hallgrim about. This is the shoemaker from Øra. Oh yes, poor chap, they say about him, he is easily led, and this they agree on. He is not much of a danger to anyone or anything.

Julie feels the warmth from Jørgen's arm over her shoulder and the weight of the child she is carrying. A feeling of anxiety grabs her. Krister is out there in what must be an inferno. Frightening images of all those who have not escaped in time appear before her eyes. She stands with her arm around Helene. Helge is standing right in front of her - he will soon be twelve and already reaches up to her chin. Jostein is here too; he is fourteen, too big to cling to anyone, but is standing so close to his father their shoulders touch whenever either of them moves. Jostein, Jørgen's favourite more than the others, works with his father whenever he has free time from school. Synnøve is here, too, together with Selma. Both are elderly and support each other.

- If there's one thing I'm happy about, it's that Erling and Kristoffer have managed to avoid all this, says Synnøve, her voice hoarse with tears.

Selma is weeping silently into her handkerchief.

- No, I can't take any more of this. We're off home, says Synnøve.
- It's a question whether there weren't more targets they shot at, Jørgen says so quietly that Julie can barely hear.
- Are you cold? Maybe you'd like to go home? he says.
- No, no, not yet.

Now she notices. It's just a vague feeling, a chill which is more than just the cool spring air. Is there not some distance between herself and her family and the rest of those present? Aren't the others clustering closer together? Is there a larger gap between them and the people from Storvik? Or is she just imagining this because she is not quite herself, so very tired as she is?

Under her arm she feels Helene shivering.

- I'm off home now, says Helene.
- Would you like me to come with you?
- No, you can stay here.

Can Helene have noticed the same feeling that she did? Maybe this is why she's leaving? Or can she have heard what Jørgen said when the two elderly women left? Helene would have understood what that meant.

- I'll go as well, she says and will take the boys home. They have school tomorrow.
- No, let them stay, says Jørgen - what they're experiencing here will stay with them and will give them far more than any school lessons can.

After a while the group in the churchyard begins to break up. It is the women who are first to leave, gathering together their children to take them home. They hesitate, for the sight out there still holds them fascinated. Jørgen sends the boys home, but he remains along with a few others. Midnight is drawing on, but that crazy light show in the west still continues.

- Someone asks: Is this never going to end? But apart from that they are just as silent as before, with the odd simple remark not requiring an answer swallowed up by the night.

Jørgen manages to recognise the fixed expressions round him, each person wrapped up in his own thoughts, just as he is.

- Aren't you worried about our boy? Julie asked as she left. Is he worried about Krister? Oh yes, he is, and it occurs to him that he has never done anything else but worry about Krister. If anything should happen to the boy, he would not be able to bear it. This is not because he does not love the other three children. No one can doubt that Julie is a good mother and that the children are the most important thing in her life, which is just as it should be. But her eyes never light up with quite the same pride and love as they do when she looks at Krister. This has become even clearer in the years he has been away at school in town. First there was middle school, and now it's the high school. During his weekends at home she is devoted to him and sees to it that there is always something extra on the table when he is present. When Krister suggests that she is overdoing things and that this could arouse jealousy in his brothers, she laughs it off and says she must allow herself a little extra for him since she sees him so rarely and that in any case there has always been a certain tension between Jostein and Krister. These two brothers are very different. Jostein is excitable while Krister is quiet and thoughtful. That they do not fight and quarrel more often than they do is almost certainly down to Krister. He is controlled, while Jostein is both excitable and challenging. This could be because of his red hair. Julie says that with that Jostein's temper could hardly have been any different.

Helge is different, for the most part like Krister, except that his hair is as blond as Krister's is dark. But apart from that, he shares Krister's face and build. What people find most memorable about Helge is his eyes - large and brown with long dark lashes like a girl's. One look from him and people at once take notice. Helge has the same fondness for reading as Krister, and, like Krister, is a bit of a dreamer. He also shows boundless admiration for his elder brother. When Krister is at home, Helge follows him round from the moment he arrives right until he departs. But Helge sees the same weakness in Jørgen as in his elder brother. That weakness has no place in Krister. For while he radiates a confidence and authority which one would not expect to find in a boy who is not yet seventeen, there's also a will and a determination which, when he shows it, causes others to fall silent. Even his father can come under the spell when Krister looks at him. That look is much like hers, Julie's. He noticed this last summer when a disagreement arose as to whether Krister should begin high school or not. *He* was there - his father - opposing both Krister and Julie. It was a fight he was destined to lose, but he stood his ground right up to the time Krister was about to leave. In his view, middle school was enough. Which other farmer's son round here gets this kind of opportunity? And what is the point of more education when he would one day be a farmer in Storvik? When both boys looked at him, he knew what he had known for a long time but had not yet been able to absorb, that it was uncertain whether Krister would take over the farm.

But Jørgen fought on. Krister has to stay at home and help with the running of the farm, there's a need for him here, and it's here he must stay. He said that the next one to go to away to school must be Jostein. Krister had a duty to be generous towards his home and brothers and to stop thinking just about himself. But none of this helped. Krister moved to town and to the high school. Julie pointed out that this didn't mean that the way was closed for Jostein. When the time comes he will begin at the middle school. And with Selma, there is space in both her home and her heart for everyone.

- Oh, so now it looks really bright for getting help on the farm! said Jørgen with deep sarcasm.

It looked to him as though this son had everything, being so clever at school.

The previous summer Julie had met one of the middle school teachers on a trip to town. She proudly revealed what he had said, that Krister had gone through that school like a warm knife through butter. He must at all costs take the *artium,* for such ability must not go to waste. This was one of her strongest arguments when the dispute was at its height.

Otherwise Krister takes part in so many things that people are astonished that he can find any time and space for school and study. He plays the piano well, even though this has recently become more for fun. He now plays mostly without music, popular hits and what they call jazz. This last sounds unpleasant to Jørgen's ears, but there is no doubt it's popular with the young. And right from the time he started school Krister has been appearing on stage, at Christmas festivals, Norway's National Day and other festivities. What he most enjoys doing is reciting poems, and oddly enough has been teased about this by his friends. This may be because he is good at all his other activities. On skis, in free sports, in all this it can seem as though he has grown up so fast that he must soon be ninety! He has always been of an athletic build, and now he is slim, broad-shouldered and muscular. It's almost as if this is too much of a good thing, leading him to become arrogant. But this is not how it is. Every talent he has he seems to take for granted. Maybe it is all so natural for him that he is unaware of it.

What piques Jørgen most is that Krister has a good grasp of all the work required of a farmer. This is very annoying. For when Krister is out there in the fields and Jørgen sees how he handles a pitchfork and all the other equipment, and when he sees those muscles rippling under the suntanned skin of his body, it is then he sees the farmer in Krister.

A memory comes to mind. At a party last year Krister was standing on the stage of the young people's hall and declaiming *Terje Vigen,* all verses from memory. There he was, so grown up and yet so much a child, still dressed in his confirmation clothes, now tight across the shoulders and with the jacket sleeves and trouser legs too short. But his voice was deep and mature. There were some lines in this poem which pained Jørgen and which still torment him in his thoughts.

> Look, *these* were my riches here on earth,
>> this was all I called my own.
> To me it seemed so great a treasure
>> yet for you it weighed so little.

And although these words in the poem were concerned with something other than farming, it was this he thought about. That maybe one day he would come to experience Krister, this farmer's boy from Storvik, casting aside all of his inheritance. If this were to happen, it would be as if a link broke in a chain. There have been Jørgens and Kristoffers on Storvik for generations.

Standing here, what he is aware of in all his anxiety and desperation is something he can barely admit to himself. That Krister actually has a very special place in his life. That he loves this boy deeply. It comes as a reminder of the feeling of ecstatic happiness he experienced when Krister was born. How happy both of them were back then, himself and Julie, the two of them together with the little child. And although he has not been allowed to be for Krister as he would like, this is something on which he has never budged. The sense of estrangement from Julie that he felt then has almost disappeared now. It may flare up at times, but he has accepted that. Krister comes to his mother rather than to his father with important matters requiring a decision. It can build up in him to an inner cry that the child does not understand this. But he can accept all of it, providing that Krister comes home safely.

Jørgen is frozen stiff. Only three men from the neighbourhood apart from himself have remained in place for so long.

- Come on, men, let's follow the others home, he says. We must get something warm inside us. If we're lucky there may still be some coffee in the pot.

They hesitate.

Jørgen does not give up. All of a sudden it has become important for him that they do not reject this invitation, that none of them rejects it.

- Maybe we can talk about it? he suggests.

Yes, say the others, maybe you're right. We can hardly think about sleeping on a night like this. Jørgen breathes a sigh of relief. For he has had the same feeelng that Julie had in the graveyard. It was not enmity exactly, more a vague feeling that the others might be watching him, that they have been looking questioningly at him. It is going to be important for him to have proof that even if his brother has behaved foolishly, he, Jørgen, is trustworthy.

He has been experiencing this inner feeling for some time, but mainly since it all began early in September last year, or after people awoke on April 9th and heard that the Germans had arrived. This was not something that could be overlooked. Julie did not take it seriously when he first mentioned it to her. She said he was making too much of it, and that as long as he behaved respectably people would understand that he was trustworthy. But he is familiar with people round here and knows how they think. They don't need to say something out loud for him to understand it. The way in which they behave and what they hint at says far more than they say directly. He has felt this distancing in his own body. Conversations change when he arrives. There's that little moment of silence before they begin talking about the wind or the weather and other unimportant things.

That Krister, is he still in town? they asked him one day.

- Yes, he is.
- And he's living with Ivar?
- No, he lives with Selma now, says Jørgen.

Standing here, he felt something in his body telling him that he was being interrogated.

- But isn't that the same house? It wouldn't be if we had someone looking after the town. It's too dangerous in so many different ways. You must get him to come home, Jørgen.

He is becoming extremely angry towards his brother who has led him to this impasse. It feels all wrong, for he was one of the first to distance himself from Hitler and all that he stood for. Maybe because he followed what was happening more closely than others in the district, he listened to what refugees were saying, refugees who as early as the 1930s had fled from Hitler's regime to this country. He recalled how frightened he was of Ivar's unshakeable enthusiasm after his trips to Germany, how he described Hitler as Germany's saviour and presented nationalism as the answer for other countries, including Norway. Ivar, who had spent a couple of summers in Berlin and had had violin lessons with a German music teacher There he had met Helene, a young and promising ballet dancer. Her parents live in Dresden, where her father is a music teacher. Helene is their only child.

In Storvik they first accepted Helene with a reserved scepticism, but she soon won them over. With her nature it is easy for people to become fond of her, and she slipped quickly into the local community in a way which amazed those around her. She now speaks fluent Norwegian and has become as Norwegian as anyone, but now it is difficult to avoid the fact that she is German. Whenever Ivar and Jørgen have been discussing the situation in Germany she has left the room. Jørgen had his last serious quarrel with Ivar in autumn, immediately after their father died, and Ivar was here alone on a trip. The two were alone in the kitchen when it took place.

It began with them discussing Hitler's invasion of Poland.

- For God's sake leave the party, Ivar. Remember that you are very exposed now. You are both married to a German and have family in Germany. That can be difficult enough without you being a member of the party as well.

- I have said before and I'll say it again, that I will not give up my membership of anything I believe in. As for politics, that interests neither me nor Helene, nor her parents.

- No, Ivar, you cannot come out with that nonsense any longer. You're say not interested in politics? Man, you're up to your neck in it! Just think about what you're doing.

- It's impossible to have a sensible discussion with you, Jørgen, You're just not open to reason.

- Reason? Jørgen's voice quivered with anger. Reason? That you dare to speak of reason! Do you understand what you are doing to us, to your own family? Has it ever occurred to you that blood might be shed because of your stupid behaviour?

At this point Ivar laughed, whereupon Jørgen exploded in anger.

- Isn't it enough that you took our father's life?

For a moment there was a total silence. Ivar stared at Jørgen, his face pale and his eyes dark with rage.

- Take back what you've just said! he said, his voice quivering, Sooner or later you're going to have to take it back. You can never pretend that what you did to our father was my fault. You are aware that I know nearly everything that went on between the two of you over the years. He then left.

- Satan! Jørgen was seething with a rage which threatened to take his breath away. Satan!

His mother was standing by the door, which she closed behind her.

- What's been going on? Have you two been quarrelling again? I won't have it. You must behave decently!

- Really? Had Ivar been talking to his mother?

- No, he didn't have to. It was his face which worried me after what you'd said to him.

- I said that he took our father's life, said Jørgen, the rage still burning inside him, but he immediately regretted saying it. He should not have said that, and the anger now just drained away, leaving only desperation.

- I'm sorry, Mother, I shouldn't have said that.

She stood in front of him, her face pale. It's your brother you should apologise to. Good heavens, Jørgen, will you never grow up! When will you stop behaving so insanely towards Ivar?

- I've never …. but here he stopped.

- No, Jørgen, listen to me. What you've just said you must never mention again. Never, do you hear me! You must behave like a man and be kind to your brother.

- I don't know if I can promise that, Mother. I can't ignore what I believe to be the truth.

- When I think about all that has happened, how it is now and how it can all turn out, it is unbearable. You must promise me one thing, Jørgen. However, it turns out, that you must never forget that Ivar is your brother.

Her expression made a deep impression on him, with a feeling of grief he could probably never get over. He felt like a child who's just been chastised. He feels shame at allowing his anger to run away with him and speak to her in such a way, for this was something she hadn't deserved. He feels all the more shame when he thinks how little they had understood her grief and pain this past winter and spring. There is this present incident with Ivar, but had they thought about how she lost the man she had lived with all her adult life? About her loneliness?

He had accompanied his father on the ferry on the morning he travelled to town. His father said that his only purpose in going to town was to talk some sense into Ivar.

- If he doesn't listen to me now, it will be a disaster.
Jørgen met his father in the farmyard that evening.
- How did it go?
- It didn't. It was no good at all.
- Where are you going? Jørgen asked as his father made his way over the farmyard towards the barn.
- I'm going to attend to the horses.
- But aren't you going to change first?

The first thing Father did after coming back from his journey was to attend to the horses, but he never went into the stall in his best clothes. Meticulous as he was, this was not his way. He turned to Jørgen and said:

- This would never have happened if Erling had been alive.

These were to be the last words he was to speak.

Jørgen thought it was taking his father a long time to come back out and moved towards the stall. There he was halted by his mother who was standing on the step. He did not know how long she had been waiting there.

- Stop, Jørgen. Maybe your father needs a little time to himself. She then went.

In the end Jørgen could not bear waiting any longer; the scene he then encountered in the stall has burnt its way into his mind. The lantern hanging by a chain from the roof spread a circle of light over the edge of the crib belonging to the old mare, Frøya. His father's head had fallen down towards a bundle of hay which he had held in his hand and had placed in the crib. The young horse Trym stood eating the hay which no doubt he had received from father. But what touched Jørgen most of all was Frøya gently nodding her muzzle towards his father's head and tugging at his coat collar. He let out an angry cry:

- It's too late, Frøya!

For he knew already as he stood there, numb with shock before managing to move towards his father and touch him, the terrible truth that it was too late. Everything was too late. And he still feels it today, as painfully as on the day it happened. How can he ever go back to his brother and beg for forgiveness?

There is movement in the Storvik kitchen. Coal is burning in the stove, and when Jørgen adds a couple of sticks the fire flares up. He puts the coffee pot on to heat, pours in a little water and is bold enough to add a spoonful of coffee which has been ground and made ready for morning. That apart, the coffee pot has become something sacred - a taboo for anyone to touch apart from the women whose job it is. This is how it has been since rationing was introduced last year.

- I expect you, too, are used to drinking coffee made with grounds, says Jørgen as he pours out coffee for the men sitting round the table.

It is dark in the kitchen, with blackouts covering the windows. There is only a weak glow from the oven and from the paraffin lamp at the end of the table.

It is quiet in the house, but now and again the silence is broken by the sound of steps or muffled clicks and thuds from the opening and closing of doors.

- I can hear that people are awake, says one of the men. Well, who can sleep at night these days? Everyone has their own worries, I would think.

- Can you understand why they would want to bomb Kristiansund? What good will that do them?

No, the others cannot understand it either. There are no foreign ships in town so far as they know, and no English or other allies. Nor are there any ground or air defences. Why would they want to destroy this little town in a senseless attack, hitting only civilians? It is true that there are now a few Norwegian soldiers here and there following the orders to mobilise, but no one from this locality is known to be one of these. The battle-ready and those of conscription age have been ordered to Dovre along with a few volunteers. Maybe these were involved in capturing the German paratroops forced to surrender to Norwegian forces at Dombås? The captives were brought to the town where the middle school has become a temporary prison camp for them, 140 in all, Hitler's birds of prey, as *Tidens Krav* called them. According to the newspapers many of the Norwegian soldiers in the town have been given the job of guarding them while at the same time doing their best to protect the town against attack. But an attack from the air, which is what this seems to be, would, for them, be unimaginable. Could the reason be that the Germans wanted to free their own soldiers? But this seems absurd, for then they would be risking killing their own.

- Well, that wouldn't worry me in the least.

- No, that cannot be the answer. If that was their intention, there would be another way of doing it. Haven't they now taken over the biggest towns with their ships? Krisitiansund, lying defenceless and unprotected by islands and rocks in the sea, is no great challenge for German ships. The whole thing is unfathomable.

There have been many warnings recently. The first was on 8th April when the newspapers announced that English naval forces had laid mines in large parts of the Kattegat and the North Sea. That same evening, an English seaplane made a forced landing in the town's harbour. It was towed over to Hjelkrempier on the Goma side of Vågen. There were also rumours of a German seaplane crashing in the Kornstadt fjord. All this shocked people, but not as much as the huge shock they experienced when they heard the first radio announcement on the morning of 9th April: 'During the night German marine forces have invaded several Norwegian towns'. For the rest of the day, there came conflicting reports until the day's newspapers arrived. In the *Romsdalsposten,* the headlines were:

- Tonight, Bergen and Trondheim were taken over by Germans.
- The Oslo fjord has been penetrated by German ships and the city bombed from the air.
- German warships have opened fire on Horten during the night.
- A German force has landed in Valle near Tønsberg and in Narvik.
- Kristiansand was bombed by German troops stationed in Egersund.
- Copenhagen has this morning been occupied by the Germans.

- The most important Swedish ports in the Skagerak have been closed by German mines.

They knew at once what they ought to have known for long enough, that all this could happen. But most people relied on Norway maintaining its neutrality as it had during the last war.

- No, now we've been taken lying down.

This was said so frequently as to have become almost a byword. For even though they should have read the signs, they could not believe that Norway, a little country with few inhabitants, could become involved in anything of this size. This was everyman's view. What those governing the country had thought and understood is something they have never found out.

- It began with Altmark, one of the men says. We should have understood then which way this was all going to go. It was right what the newspapers wrote at the time, that now Hitler could poke his nose in up here.

The men in the kitchen at Storvik are unlikely to be the only ones discussing and bringing up these concerns and asking why. This has been almost the only subject of conversation these last few days. When they meet, people are no longer talking about the wind or the weather, haymaking or their crops. There are so many other things too. Step by step they have crept up, right up to what they have seen today, that terrible fire in the night sky. And even though they are not as closely involved as those unfortunate people in town, it is still terrifyingly close.

There have been several warnings. On Thursday, 25 April, people were perturbed by another alarming newspaper report. Sunndalsøra had been bombed. A whole district with many civilian houses had been bombed into the ground with many wounded. On the same day, there was a reported bomb attack on Rensvik. The aircraft was probably aiming to bomb the Omsund bridge, no doubt with the aim of isolating Kristiansund even more completely. The Germans failed in this, but a high explosive bomb fell very close to the Rena bridge, where it killed a fourteen-year-old boy and wounded many others. The unfortunate boy had just been carrying a sack of wood when the bomb fell. The newspapers wrote that he was killed instantly. Bombs were also released over Angvik, probably with the intention of damaging the ferry there. In both Sunndalsøra and Rensvik, machine gun fire had been directed at the civilian populace.

The newspapers wrote that all this was causing unease in the town. Any hope for a defenceless town like Kristiansund to be treated humanely by the attackers then began to disappear. 'Kristiansund and Nordmøre first experienced yesterday the seriousness of the situation following the German planes' brutal and murderous attack on the civilian population'. 'Totally unmotivated German air attack on Rensvik and Sunndalsøra'. In yesterday's newspaper, they could read about attacks on two of the coastal steamers which serve the district. 'D/S Kværnes was attacked by bombers and machine gun fire at Talgsjøen south of Tunsta on the way into the town'. 'D/S Statsråd Riddervold was attacked in the Freifjord while full of passengers, women and children fleeing into the district'. 'Riddervold', as the boat was popularly known, turned back to the town but was pursued by aircraft. Then something happened which could have ended in the most terrible catastrophe. The ship was struck by a 250-kilogram bomb, but this fell into the ship's hold, where it ended in a barrel where it remained without exploding. The bomb remained on board until the ship berthed in Kristiansund, where it was moved onto land and later buried at sea. This was both a fairy tale and a miracle. Both ships were riddled with holes from machine gun fire. These aircraft circled over the town, where they shot at the populace. Among other targets they shot at the fish market. 'This should indicate to the full the brutality and inhumanity which is obsessing the invaders,' the newspapers write. 'It is nothing less than a miracle that no human lives were lost during this operation'. But they had certainly been warned.

- We've been so stupid as to imagine that war is a battle for the military, between attack and defence. That at least is what I learned when I did my national service, says one of the men.
- Then Hitler sent us a band of murderers. Yes, enough has happened to make people understand that Hitler and his lackeys are not joking. And that is without talking about everything that's happened in the rest of the country.

It is now late, after three in the morning, and the friends want to break off and go home.

- Well, however it is, there's another day tomorrow.

But before they call an end to this unreal day and night, they will call in by the church yard and see what the situation is there. Jørgen accompanies them.

Things have now quietened down in the distance, there is now just a weak reminder of that crazy red glow; now it's black clouds against the sky becoming paler as dawn approaches.

- Goodness! It looks as if the worst is over, says Jørgen.
- Let's just hope that no human lives have been lost and that not everything has fallen apart.

Jørgen undresses quietly so as not to awaken Julie, but she is awake.

- Have we kept you awake? he asks.

- No. It was impossible to sleep. Have you been back? How did it look?

- It looked as if the worst may now be over. Now we can do no more than hope.

- I am so afraid, Jørgen. For Krister, for our children, for all of us. How is it going to be for us all now?

- You mustn't worry about our Krister, he says comforting her - He can look after himself, - I'm not afraid for him. Now, we'll just have to take one day at a time. There's nothing else we can do. Apart from that, I can't help feeling angry with Ivar. Amid all that's going on I still feel that. That he should become mixed up with Germany. And all that talk about Germany being Europe's leading culture!

- But isn't that how it is?

Oh yes! Jørgen raises his voice - Satan's emissaries, vandals, scum, the lot of them!

They continue lying without saying anything more. Pain and anxiety fill their thoughts; Jørgen has a strange feeling of happiness because they can lie down together and be together on this. He remembers all those painful years after she lost her child, that little girl who is never mentioned now. That was the time she thrust their beds apart so that they were next to different walls. She was at the same time pushing him out of her life. He would never cease to be thankful that that time was now past.

- Sleep now, he says and hears that his voice is filled with emotion.

Chapter 2

They awaken to a new day and believe that yesterday's nightmare has passed, but by mid-morning it all starts up again. The same threatening banks of clouds in the west with the drone of aircraft over them. At Storvik, people wander round pale with anxiety and await signs of life that Ivar and Krister are still alive. The mother and her three children who have been evacuated here are also awaiting signs of life from them. But the telephone is silent. Throughout the day, Julie tries ringing. The exchange is always busy. and if she manages to get through the reply is always that they will do their best but that the central board is overwhelmed with people trying to book telephone lines to the nearby town or somewhere else where they have relations who may be affected. In the end she sends Jørgen down to the exchange in the hope that this may help. But he returns with the message that it is impossible to get through to town.

Only the most essential tasks are now being carried out. Farm and other outdoor work has been stood down. Men from farms and the country round about are selling produce down at the harbour or in the shop where people stand round engaging in quiet conversation about what is happening. No boats or ships are expected to visit. An unpleasant silence broods over the whole district and everything is at a standstill. It is only the women who are going about their business as before. There are still animals to be fed, cows to be milked and food prepared. Preparation of food has become something of a headache because of the number of people who have been evacuated here. Numbers have doubled or even quadrupled in many homes. This has been a tough challenge for many of the housewives: if it goes on, how will they manage to feed so many mouths? On farms food reserves are low at this time of the year when supplies are only meant to be sufficient for the farmers and their hired hands. Most people have a fixed notion that visitors are entitled to be treated better than the farmers even on ordinary days. But today even the women are doing no more than they have to. They just want to be together, to find comfort in company and cannot bear being alone.

In the Storvik kitchen people are tripping over each other: Julie and Astrid, Helene and Mrs. Solberg, a stranger who came here with her children along with Helene. Then there is Selma and the two servant girls who wander round with tear-filled eyes, anxious about the family they've left behind in town. Everyone wants to do something to keep themselves busy. Some peel potatoes for lunch, others are washing up, and there is one woman tending to the potted plants by the windows, but everything is happening unsystematically and without proper planning. Selma and Synnøve sit listlessly by their work tables. Usually they keep themselves busy, but not today. Even the three young girls from the town are there in the kitchen; the two tallest are schoolgirls. One is in her first year, the other in her third. They sit quietly by the workbenches together with the two older women, listening to everything that's being said. Only the youngest, a three-year-old, is playing on the floor along with Sven. The two children are more subdued than usual, even though they cannot understand much of what is going on. Nevertheless, they must sense the tension in the room. Everything feels so foreign and strange for the little girl from town, and Sven looks with staring eyes at all the strangers in the room, nonplussed and uncharacteristically shy.

Julie is feeling worn out and disheartened as she moves around with a gnawing sense of unease inside her. What feels so intolerable for people here is not knowing, but this is not something they talk about. At least not much. When the subject does arise, a silence fills the room before the conversation turns to everyday matters. But still the quiet conversations go on inside Julie's head until they build up to an intolerable pain. It is this which is making her restless and impatient. She wants people here, round her, those in the kitchen, these women with their work and everyday chatter which can keep her intrusive thoughts at bay. But she also wants them to be somewhere else. She wants calm. Her feelings are confused and conflicted, and feeling like an insult in the midst of all this is the beautiful warm spring weather streaming in though open doors and windows. This is a time when everything should be a source of joy. Willow trees full of plump catkins, buds bursting, trees full of sap, crocuses, Scylla and beds of snowdrops, all under a sunny blue sky. But today it is a sky darkened by banks of cloud out towards the west.

- Julie scolds the two young girls from the town: Can't you at least take the youngsters out with you instead of having them treading on everyone's toes? She at once regrets speaking so sharply and notices the reproachful look they direct back at her. But they leave the kitchen with a child on each arm. The two little girls scurry after them.
- Be careful, she shouts. Anything can happen.

They understand what she means. It was here that one of those hated German fighter planes came and flew low over the houses. At the time people were more curious than anxious and stood out in the yard watching the plane circling over the farm. The aircraft then turned northwards over the valley, after which they heard an unfamiliar rattling noise.

- The swine are shooting! Jørgen shouted.

They stood there speechless, Julie with Sven on her arm.

- Ooh! Bombers! whimpered the child. He turned two at New Year and cannot yet speak clearly, but in these recent days, he has picked up some strange foreign words.

Jørgen said that the Germans were shooting to frighten people, that the hail of bullets was aimed into the woods, and that this was meant to demoralise people. But next time a plane comes over people must move inside, for another time it can be serious. Then they must not stand out there in the yard like living targets, staring up into the sky like idiots. They have read more than enough in the newspapers in recent days about dangers like these.

- You must stay in the house, Julie shouts after the girls.
- You need to go and rest, Julie, says Astrid. There are enough people here to deal with what's happening. Your face is pale.

Julie takes off her dress and shoes and lies down. The bedclothes feel cool against her body which feels as if it's on fire. She places pillows behind her neck and back, trying to find a position which will allow her body's weight to rest. Her jaws ache after being clenched and tense for hours. She tries to relax, to allow the weight to drain down from her limbs. The tiredness in her forehead is painful, but she remains wide awake.

Flashing specks of light dance behind her aching eyelids, while inside she is caught up in a swirl of thoughts and images. Her child is kicking, directing gentle blows against her ribs like waves. She strokes her distended stomach. Every time the child moves, she feels a tingling in her mind and body. When it is

quiet she listens to somewhere deep within herself. She has
never completely relaxed during this pregnancy, nor did she
relax when she was carrying Sven. What she experienced the
time she lost the stillborn girl has stayed with her, the pain as
strong now as on the day it happened. The accident, the cow
which attacked her, gored and trampled on her, the unpleasant
light in the grey dawn, the ox - all this has become fixed in her
memory, pursuing her in her dreams to this day, even though it
is now eight years since it all happened. She recalls the
following days, the calm within her, the frightful delivery, the
pain when she learned it was a girl. Her grief has lessened over
the years, but she still thinks about the child she never got to see
as her own. She forced herself to ask the priest where her child
was buried. It was in a corner of the cemetery; there was no
grave because the child was stillborn and had not been baptised.
She still goes there in spring when the flowers she planted in the
grass come out and blossom. They flower all summer long, and
she still dreams of that. In her dream she is standing by the
church door and sees the entire graveyard covered with a whole
carpet of flowers. She runs round and cannot find the spot
because there are flowers everywhere.

She never let on to Jørgen that she had found the spot where
the child was buried; this was something she wanted to keep to
herself. She was feeling bitter towards Jørgen without reasonable
grounds, as she later came to understand. Instead of talking, each
of them went their own way. She moved their beds apart next to
different walls as she could no longer bear him touching her.
Every now and again, she was overcome with feelings of guilt
and approached him, but her approaches were always half-
hearted and there was no love there. During the day she would
scrutinise him closely, wondering what it was that had made her

marry this morose and gloomy man, a man whose pain she was unable to detect. Memories of that time make her shudder. Everything was so difficult back then. First the crippling grief over the child - there was a time that she even thought she was losing her mind - then there was their miserable economic situation. Jørgen had many schemes like breeding foxes and similar impossible projects aimed at recovery. Then there was Kristoffer who refused to hand the farm over to Jørgen. There were conflicts between herself and Synnøve when they shared the same kitchen, and she felt that she was nothing more than a servant girl on the farm.

In the end she gathered up her children and went back to her parents. She lived there for some weeks until her father-in-law begged her to come home. She and Jørgen would now be able to take over the farm. Her father-in-law's scheme was to transfer ownership of the farm to herself without telling Jørgen. She thought he would never get over that.

In the weeks and months which followed she tried approaching him, but he would never allow her to come close. In the end she took the decision to show him that spot in the churchyard. Then she would either lose him for good, which would be better than continuing in their present relationship, or maybe it might revive the embers of what had been there in the beginning.

One summer evening she approached him.

- Jørgen, I'd like us to take a walk together.
- Where to?
- To the church.

He walked along quietly beside her; she did not know whether he had any idea of what was in her mind.

They went through the gate, and she walked in front of him to *the place*. Thrusting up through stiff bundles of dry grass from last year and among the flourishing greenery were myriads of flowers, red, pink and white.

She turned towards him, her heart beating against her ribs. She tightened her throat so that she could hardly breathe.

- Here it is, Jørgen, she whispers.

His face is ashen.

- You mean…, you don't mean our child?
- Yes, it's here, somewhere close by.

How long have you known that?

His face changed as he stood in front of her, while she stood looking at him for a moment which felt like an eternity.

- Why didn't you say anything?
- Because…. because I just couldn't do it, not then. Can you ever forgive me, Jørgen?
- Dearest Julie, with all you've had to put up with. He said no more than that but pulled her in towards him and hugged her so tightly that it felt as if he would never let her go.

She then began to weep. She wept as she had never done before. Now, at last, she was able to weep for the child they had lost and for all those painful years.

By some hidden private agreement, they do not refer to the child again, but she is there inside both of them as a pain which has to be worked through, as all such grief must be. The process happens when they are in the church or the churchyard. They go together down to the corner by the cemetery wall. When their

eyes meet, each knows the other's feelings and thoughts. That is
enough, and it is good.

But when she is pregnant again, as she is now, the anxiety
does not altogether go away before the child is delivered and
they have lived through the first weeks and months. That is how
it was with Sven, and that is how it is now. She cannot protect
herself against that.

She did not believe she could have any more children after
having her youngest child. She thought that birth had destroyed
something inside her and felt reconciled to it. It came as a shock
when she finally learned that she was pregnant again. At first she
thought there was something wrong with her. She could not
accept her pregnancy until she felt the first feather-light
movements from the child moving inside her. At that time her
youngest, Helge, was in his tenth year, and for the first time after
the birth of Sven she felt just as clumsy looking after him as she
did when she had had Krister. She remembered how she had lain
with him in her arms for the first time - another boy! - and had
looked down on his tiny face and his wisps of red hair. She
thought how miraculous it was for her to experience all this. And
now it is all happening again. Now, in her fortieth year, she is
about to give birth to another baby - a miracle indeed! But it is
harder to be pregnant now than when she was young. As the
child gradually expands inside her, she feels that years of heavy
toil both at home and on the farm have taken their toll. She sees
this when she looks in the mirror, the wrinkles round the eyes,
the scratches and lines which have left their mark. She sees now
that her youthful firmness of skin is in the process of
disappearing, though her hair is as thick and shiny as ever,
except for a thin white stripe leading from the parting down to
one side of her face. This has been there for many years, neither

increasing nor decreasing. The reason for its being there must be that, at some point, she had received a powerful blow. For her, this is a reminder of how many years have passed. But Jørgen has not yet become grey-haired. His hair is as thick as ever - baldness is not a feature of the men in Storvik - but its colour has faded with the years. There are furrows in his face and his features have become more pronounced. When Julie looks at him she feels a strange sadness. They are no longer young.

The person who helped Julie most through the worst of her apprehensiveness when she was pregnant with Sven was her childhood friend Randi who lived in town. As if by some trick of fate Randi has become pregnant at the same time as Julie. Randi is a couple of years older than her and was a friend of Synna, her sister who died of Spanish flu. After Synna's death Julie and Randi came together forming a friendship which has endured to the present day. The fact that Randi has lived a totally different life from Julie under quite different conditions and in a milieu almost as different from that of the Storvik family as possible, has not shaken their friendship. Randi is married to the socialist and idealist Yngvar Thorsen, who went on to become a journalist for the workers' newspaper, *Tidens Krav*. Nobody has succeeded in destroying the friendship between Julie and Randi, neither those here on the farm nor the Storvik family in town. Nor has Yngvar succeeded in doing this, although his criticism has been more reasoned than that of Julie's family. The two friends have been very close all these years. Randi has been the one person Julie could rely on, no matter what the issue. When they were both pregnant, letters often passed between them, more than before. When Julie gave expression to her worries Randi would write back to reassure her. You'll see that everything will turn out well for us both. We old girls can manage anything.

While Julie's pregnancy came as a shock for her, that between Randi and Yngvar was planned. For them things were looking up. They managed to change their two-roomed flat for one with three rooms, though they were still in the same building, in Fløiavei, the workers' houses in Clausenengen. The three children, one boy and two girls, have been growing up. The youngest was fifteen, the same age as Krister when Julie had her youngest boy, a couple of months before Sven. Randi wrote that suddenly they had plenty of room and that she wanted another child, which is how it turned out.

How is Randi? Has she managed to move away from the hell which it must now be in town? She thinks of Krister who is still there. If anything happens to him, will it be her fault? She was the one who insisted that he should start high school. But it was also something he himself wanted. He thought it was impossible that they would not grant him this privilege, and that he would not get to use his abilities. But she is also aware that Jørgen is only telling the truth when he says that she is ambitious for her children. Not that she is the only one. Without help from Selma, Helene and Ivar this would never have happened. It would just have stopped. They wouldn't have been able to afford to send him away for an education lasting so long. He lives in their big house free of charge, with Selma living alone on the ground floor and Ivar and Helene living upstairs. Selma will not hear of him paying rent, something Julie tries to compensate for by sending him back with some of the farm's produce every time he has been at home. But the thankfulness and joy she feels for all this is overshadowed by the relationship between Jørgen and Ivar which has only become worse as the years have passed. It has become quite hopeless now that Ivar has joined the National Socialists.

- Jørgen rages: My fear is that he may influence Krister with Nazi propaganda.
- No, stop saying that, Julie says despairingly. Krister is just a boy. You should be grateful to your brother that he is helping our son.
- Grateful? I feel my hands tied, knowing that I'm supposed to be eternally grateful to them. It can end with them taking Krister away from us, which is what they did with Ivar.
- No, I don't believe anyone can take Krister away.

For although it is true that Ivar became more of a son for Selma and Erling Storvik than Jørgen was for them, he's of a quite different character from Krister. And while Krister admires his uncle Ivar, Julie has no fear that he won't find out where Ivar stands.

From the kitchen Julie can hear a quiet hum of conversation from the women, cries from the children and a rattling of containers. Sleep slowly overtakes her. When she awakens she finds that it is well past midday. She awakes bathed in sweat after a heavy and dreamless sleep which has left her with a thumping headache. She stands, fills the bowl on the washstand with water from the jug and washes her face and body in the lukewarm liquid. She puts on a complete set of clean clothes, dreading what she may discover when she goes downstairs to meet the others.

Out at sea the sky has become as it was the previous evening, only worse, with the horrendous redness even more intense. People are again assembled in the churchyard, but Julie cannot bear to look. There has been no sign of life from Krister and Ivar. All communication with the town is broken.

Helene keeps to herself for much of the afternoon and evening. At mealtimes she sits quietly, as polite as ever; she says little and speaks only when spoken to. It is only her pale, tense face and dark eyes which betray the emotions she is attempting to conceal. Julie asks how Helene is experiencing all this. First, she must be worried about Ivar, but more than that, she is sitting here knowing that her fellow countrymen are busy destroying the town she has become so fond of and those who live in it. Julie feels that she ought to keep her company, talk to her, and help her so that the frightful burden which has befallen her may lessen a little. But, God forgive her, she cannot succeed in doing so tonight. She has more than enough with her own concerns.

Julie goes to bed early, but finds it impossible to relax. She lies listening for sounds emerging from the gloom. Sounds from those of the house's inhabitants who are still up, voices from passers-by filtering in through the open window. She is aware that the district is living very differently from how it would on a normal weeknight in a busy season. How can things ever get back to normal? she wonders. The only thing that is normal now is the sound of Sven's breathing as he sleeps.

She is still awake when Jørgen comes to lie down beside her.

- How is it looking? she whispers.
- No, it … he says, and she hears the tension in his voice.

They remain lying close together, but neither of them can take any more. He clasps her hand between both of his as they drop off into several hours of exhausting and uneasy sleep.

Early in the morning, before Sven has woken up, Julie awakens to a loud banging on the door downstairs. In a daze she sits up in bed.

- Jørgen, you must wake up. There's someone at the door.

He is already out of bed, standing on the floor and fumbling his way into a pair of trousers.

- Who can it be at this time? he says, still drowsy. He pulls his braces over his shoulders and goes down barefoot and in just a vest without giving himself time to pull on a shirt.

Julie is sitting up in bed; she clasps her hands in front of her breast, her heart thumping inside her.

There must be an accident. Strangers don't knock on their door at this time of day unless something frightening has happened. He does not lock the doors, and if it was someone from the area, they would have come straight in, banged on the kitchen door and identified themselves. But this stranger banged on the outer door. It must be the police or the priest, and the ice-cold thought runs through her that now it has happened, the very worst has happened, the thing which has filled her with anxiety these two days. Krister.

Jørgen opens the door.

- Get up. There are strangers on the farm, he says, adding No, no, it's not dangerous when he sees her pale face.
- Who are they? she whispers. She does not have the voice to say any more.
- You'll see, he says and steps back from her.

She is shaking so much that she can hardly get dressed. She spills water onto the floor and onto the sink as she pours water into the tub, splashing water onto her face.

On the path is a baby carriage full of clothes. She opens the kitchen door and remains standing there, staring in sheer disbelief. It is Randi with her youngest daughter. Both their faces are grim. Their hair is thick and there are specks of dirt, dust and some sea spray on Randi's coat. On her lap a fair-haired boy is sleeping.

- You must see that he is worn out, Randi says, her voice devoid of life.
- Randi! Where have you come from?
- Where have I come from? says Randi and looks at Julie with an expression of incomprehension – Where do you think?

In Julie's presence her face changes and she breaks down into violent sobbing. The little girl clings to her mother and is also crying.

Perplexed and helpless, Julie remains standing. Randi weeps into her breast as she attempts to embrace both of them.

- Oh, Julie, Julie, you have no idea how awful it is.
- There, there, says Julie. trying to comfort her. You are here now. You can be safe here.

She hears herself how feeble these words sound, but how can else she confront such pain?

Then the little boy on Randi's lap wakes up. He looks sleepy and stares around this unfamiliar room. He senses his mother's and sister's tears, and he, too, begins crying.

In the kitchen upstairs, Sven has now woken up and screams angrily at having been left on his own.

This pacifies Randi. She first wipes her nose and then her eyes with the back of her hand. Her face is even dirtier than before but now shows something of her determination.

- No, it's not much help just sitting here and screaming. Try to calm down. Now at last we are safe, she says to Solveig. - It's quite a drama we've put on for you, she says with a pale smile to Julie. We've scared you before the day's even got started, she says, sounding much like the Randi Julie knows so well.

This jerks Julie into being awake. Now she must think about what to do. Even though there are burning questions to be answered she must take her time. She heats up the stove and puts on water.

- You must wash and tidy up, both you and the children. Then they can have some food and go straight to bed. We can leave the talk until later.

- No, first of all we must take off some of our clothes before we melt, says Randi. She and her daughter take off their coats. Underneath is layer upon layer of clothing. Finally, they stand there in skirts and thin blouses.

- Oh, that was good! Randi groans. - But I'm still not feeling quite right. It will be good to wash and tidy up. It looks as if you are sweating, too, she says to the child as she strips away his layers of clothing.

- Would you believe the skipper of the boat we were so lucky as to come here in behaved like a general? He said they were only taking people on board and that the goods could wait. The boy was sleeping in the baby carriage, and because of this, I managed to persuade him that he was still a baby. I had to struggle with the baby carriage, though!

They had to leave their cases on the quay, she explains, but they put on all the clothes they could manage and filled the baby carriage with others. She also succeeded in putting a bag of coffee and a kilo of flour into the carriage.

The boat they were in set them down by Halsanausten. There they were given the offer of lodging on a farm, but when she learned that a lorry was to bring many of those on board out here, she thought at once of Julie. - So here we are, and besides …

- We can talk of 'besides' later, Julie replies.

Julie accompanies Randi and the children up to the bedroom, the one she shares with Jørgen. She apologises for the early morning mess. They will have their own room as soon as one can be made ready.

- Mess? says Randi. - Who notices mess now?

Julie opens the door of the dressing table filled with children's clothing.

- Just take whatever you need.
- This is crazy, says Randi. There must be enough people in the house who need newly washed clothing, but she will accept the offer. The small amount of clothing she brought with her needs to be washed before it can be worn.
- But for now, make yourself at home, Julie says.
Before she goes, she stands with her hand on the door handle and hesitates.
- Randi? she says. - May I ask ….

- I know what you're going to ask, Julie. I've seen it almost
since I came through the door. It's about Krister, isn't it? I saw
him yesterday afternoon. He was completely busy putting out
fires. But Krister is going to get by, you can be sure of that. And
their house is still standing, or was anyway. Ours is, too. I just
pray for it all to be over.

- Thank God, Randi, thank God.

They are sitting round the breakfast table, Julie and Jørgen,
Randi and her children, and Randi is telling how she came to be
there.

After Sunday's scares, it seemed that most fires were under
control by five the following morning. People thought it was
then all over and that they could breathe freely. Randi went
straight to bed, for however it was, she needed to get some sleep.
But she had not yet got out of bed at nine o'clock on Monday
morning when the air raid warning sounded again. Monday
turned out to be the sort of hell she would not wish on anyone.
People were trying to get out of town while the hunters and
warplanes, called the Stukas, sprayed machine gun fire onto the
streets. She cannot bear talking about it now but will try to
describe it for them later. She has not heard from Halvor, who is
studying at the NTH in Trondheim. Kari, her oldest girl, was out
in the streets helping and wanted to stay in town.

After darkness had fallen that evening, Yngvar sent them
away by lorry, but she did not know where it was heading. Then
she had the good fortune to find that fishing boat, which she
believed was heading south to Romsdalen. She intended to go
home to her birthplace and her brother's family. It was only long
after coming on board that she realised that the boat was heading
northwards, the opposite direction from what she had thought.

- To Molde? asked the skipper. - No, I want nothing to do with all the madness going on there. Don't you realise that they are bombing Molde as well`?

Randi notices Julie turning pale. Yes, she says, that is how it is. She learned too that Åndalsnes has been bombed and all that remains of Veblungsnes is a smoking heap of ruins.

Then there are more people to worry about, thinks Julie. Her parents, her sister and all her family back home.

- Don't worry, Julie. Where we live is too small for them to waste bombs on us. But they bombed Ålesund, the devils.
- Bevels, mimics Sven. - Bevels, bevels, he repeats delightedly, drawing laughter from the adults.
- Bevels, says Randi's little boy, attempting the same word and directing a gentle smile towards Sven before shyly hiding his face next to his mother.
- Just listen to that, says Randi. These two are going to be good friends. Maybe you think I've come here to teach the boy naughty words?
- Jørgen smiles: He'll learn them soon enough.

Julie has prepared the room which the two sisters from town have been using. The large movable bed is more than wide enough for two. There is also room left over for the young boy. The two girls can move to the loft in the storehouse now that the weather is good enough. This is where the service personnel live during the summer months.

- I hope they can manage to sleep here, she says.
- It's more than good enough, says Randi - I should have been more than pleased if they just had a sleeping bag on the floor. I could sleep anywhere now.

The young boy on her arm yawns and draws the back of his hand over his eyes.

- Poor kid, you too must be tired with all the trouble you've been through when you are still so little, says Randi.

Now Julie sees how like his father the boy is. He has Yngve's intense blue eyes - she notices this even now when his eyes are dim through tiredness. And he is a good-looking child. Martin is his name. Randi says that he is named after the hero of Yngve's youth, Martin Tranmæl. - A bit of a name to live up to, she adds.

The chaos continues today. Black clouds of smoke shoot up towards the shining blue sky. It is the third day of an Armageddon which seems never to end. In the Storvik kitchen, the women are busy preparing dinner. The household has now been divided into two. Out on the veranda, Synnøve is in charge alongside the maid from town. There are seven of them out there, not counting the maid who is serving food. Now that Julie comes to think about it, she must prepare eleven places at the long table in the kitchen. Here, the servants will be eating alongside the rest of those who live here. There are now only two servants, the maid from town and the farm hand known as Dreng-Anders. She will soon have to employ some new helpers since she has become so plump during her pregnancy that she soon won't be able to manage all the feeding and milking in the cowshed. Later on they will have to hire in some extra seasonal workers. There are already eighteen people to deal with odds and ends in the house. A great deal of food is needed for so many. Today it is potato balls which are on the menu, with an additional piece of leg of lamb cooked together with cabbage. It is nourishing food which Julie knows everyone will enjoy. She knows Randi so well that she has no need to prepare anything extra for her, so she prepares a place for Randi and the children at the kitchen table together with those from the house.

- Don't give it a second thought! says Randi when Julie invites her to sit down. Do you think that I've come here to play the lady-about-town?

But after dinner has been cleared away and the washing up done, she prepares coffee in the living room. She invites also people from round about. Now Randi is going to tell everything that has happened in town during these last terrible days.

It's quiet as a church as Randi begins her account of events.

She awoke early on Sunday morning, she says. Normally they would get up late, but she felt uneasy and could no longer sleep, so she got up straight away. In town there was the usual Sunday calm. The weather was magnificent with spring sunshine in a cloudless blue sky. Later in the morning they heard the sound of an aircraft, and round half past eight heard two violent explosions which appeared to come from Norlandssiden. Immediately afterwards the air-raid siren sounded. They rushed out onto the street, and immediately the inferno was all over them. The Sunday calm was disturbed by explosions from bombs dropping, air raid sirens, the clatter of machine gun fire from fighter aircraft and the infernal scream of the Stukas diving and soaring over the houses and streets. Yngve led them down to the cellar where Randi met the other residents, the elderly, women and children. Men were out in the streets doing what they could. Those in the cellar just sat there as explosions from the incendiary bombs shook the house. They could hear the sound of window panes shattering, but what they were probably most afraid of was houses collapsing on top of them. Every time there seemed to be a pause in the destruction, Randi rushed out onto the street. The sight was one she will never forget. There were fires all along the quay and up on the hill. Columns of flame and thick black smoke rose skywards. Each time she went out she heard their stories from people she met. She learned that the first explosions they heard that morning had come from Dale. Four men had lost their lives there and more had been wounded. One of the first bombs to hit the town dropped onto the street just outside the gasworks. It left there a crater leading to a breach in the town's power supply and a column of water shooting straight up into the air. This made firefighting almost impossible. Apart from that, aircraft were firing directly at those fighting the fires. Some of the bullets punctured and destroyed the hoses, and both the firemen and volunteer helpers were constantly interrupted and forced to seek shelter from the shooting by the planes. In those first hours total chaos reigned.

People attempted to save contents and belongings from the burning buildings and from houses which had not so far been struck. Whenever Yngvar was at home he and Randi helped each other to move contents onto the street.

- God knows how that has gone now, she says.

It was not only high explosive bombs which were falling. The Germans also released incendiary bombs, small sputtering devils which set fire to everything close to where they fell. The newspapers warned people against these and many people had followed their advice to have ready in their house sand and a spade. These bombs could be extinguished by using sand. She herself saw that people were moving bombs from walls and houses out into the streets and then pouring sand over them. Maybe a number of houses were saved in this way, but sometimes the bombs just hailed down over wooden buildings. The onslaught was altogether too strong, and new fires blazed all the time in the town.

- You just can't describe it. You need to be there yourself to believe what you are seeing, Randi says.

At five o'clock in the morning it looked as if things were under control. It had been calm after dark, and most people believed the nightmare was now over. All buildings in the district between Nordmøre Dairy and Tolbod Hill had been turned to ash, as had those along the quayside and up to Hauggate. Virtually all the building work along Torv and Storgaten was now dust and ashes. Any buildings which had not burnt down had been destroyed. The Grand Hotel was burnt, likewise the beautiful and noble Knudtsongård building. This was on Kirkeland, right in the heart of the town. How it was in other areas, on the other islands the town is built over, she could not be sure. For the last few hours she was out in town. It was surreal going round in streets lit up by blazing fires, both surreal and unpleasant. Black smokestacks towered over the ruins of what the day before had been a beautiful and peaceful town.

She herself could not believe it was not over, though most of the fire crews and their assistants had been granted a few hours of sleep. Then, on Monday morning, they awoke to a nightmare even worse than that of the previous day. One bomb load after another was discharged over the town. All of the central part of Kirkeland was in flames. The roof of the Festival House was burning, and the church burned down round midday. As the bells fell, they sounded like some doomsday warning over the town.

- I will never forget that sound, it was just so awful, says
Randi.

Out in town, the heat was so intense that it was impossible
to approach some areas. The other islands were also hit by
incendiary bombs, new fires arising everywhere in an
indescribable inferno.

Of course there was a temptation to panic among those left
in town, but she was surprised by how calm most people were.
They sought shelter in cellars or temporary air raid shelters.
Where else would they find shelter in such an exposed and
vulnerable place? If they ventured out onto the street, they would
be shot at by the planes. Many defied the danger and attempted
to move their belongings from inside the house while fire crews
and their assistants kept order. They sought shelter only when
the machine gun fire became too threatening. As long as there
was daylight, it was impossible to escape from the town since
those fleeing were being shot at by aircraft. These aircraft, Randi
said, shuddering, were diving down from the sky and sweeping
the streets and footpaths with machine gun fire. No one was
killed, so far as she knows, something which cannot be called
anything other than a miracle. But she knows that many, the
elderly, women and children have fled to Karihola, to Keverberg
and other places in the neighbourhood of the town seeking
shelter under cliffs and in caves. Another miracle is that the
weather has been exceptionally fine. If there had been wind and
rain, as there so often is in April, many would have been struck
down by the cold. And how can people look after themselves
when they have to obtain food and other necessities of life?
What about the sick, the newly born and women about to give
birth? Where there is no electricity and no water it does not bear
thinking about. But the worst of all, the thing which will always

remain with her is the memory of planes firing salvo after salvo of bullets at innocent people, civilians, women and children. That is something that can never be forgiven.

- What kind of people do that? No, you can't call Germans people, at least I don't think you can after all I've seen. Animals, that's what they are, just uncivilised swine.

Now Randi catches sight of Helene. She stands and stares at her, her face pale, before leaving the room. Randi's cheeks redden.

- Oh dear, maybe I have used words I shouldn't have. I forgot that *she* was in the room. But maybe she'll get used to it. And I don't regret saying 'swine', because that's what they are. And they went on with it for a third day. How can anyone understand that? Everything must be destroyed by now, there will be nothing left of Kristiansund but a heap of ruins.

Julie goes to the cottage to find Helene. She is sitting on a sofa in the main room, her arms folded over her body, rigid as a statue.

- Does it hurt so? asks Julie quietly.

A long shuddering sob surges through Helene, but she recovers.

- Yes, Julie, but it's more than that. I now know what hell is like.
- But it's not your fault, Helene.
- Fault? Yes, it is. It's my people who are doing this, my own people. Can you ever understand how that feels? Can you understand when I say that this has become my war, more than yours, more than theirs? You can't explain that, you can only feel it. And when I think of the future, my own and Ivar's future,

what will that be like? How will it be living in the town after this? Is it any wonder I'm afraid? If I could just get some sign of life from Ivar.

- Yes, you must be afraid for him too, after all you've heard.

- Of course I am afraid for him, but I think Ivar will be looking after himself during this time. And he will be doing all he can to help. But afterwards, when this is all over, how is that going to be?

Her body, her eyes, and her hands squeezed together in her lap so hard that her knuckles are white, are indications of how upset she is. But her voice is in control, almost a monotone, as she tells how it has been for her this winter.

It all turned serious after 1st September last year. That was the significant date when it all began. The beginnings were tiny. Friends would excuse themselves and turn down invitations when we invited them home. There were friends who did not share Ivar's views, and because Ivar was not all that interested in discussing politics, had still remained close. Then it began to be just *the others* who showed up, members of the NS party. Many of her piano and ballet pupils began missing lessons, and in the end most didn't turn up at all. People she knew, many of whom she reckoned as friends, avoided looking at her and crossed over the street to the pavement opposite when they set eyes on her. Certainly, she had seen the signs. All the same, she thought that if she and Ivar behaved decently this would eventually pass. After all, the only thing wrong was that she was born German, which was something she could never change, and she has long been a Norwegian citizen. But there is also the fact that Ivar is a member of a party which for many is unpopular. Such were her thoughts as she just tried just to be herself and to behave as she had always done with those she met. It's not my fault, she thought, not my fault at all that Hitler is leading the world into a massive new war. But it had been a shock, for she, too, had thought that Hitler would rescue Germany, never imagining that this would end with him conquering other nations. And now, after the destruction of the town? She wants to go back to be with Ivar, though at the same time this worries her. She had never expected to be as worried as she is now.

- But you can stay here as long as you want, says Julie helplessly.
- Here you can be safe.
- The way it has turned out, it's strange that you will even allow me into your house, Helene says and cannot hide the bitterness in her voice.
- No, Julie says, touched. - No, you mustn't say that. You know you are always welcome here.

On yet another evening there is a group of people standing in the churchyard following the tragic events out there in the west. They no longer show disbelief, now it's more a hopeless resignation.

How often have they sat there over the years, Julie and Randi, talking far into the night with a cup of coffee on the kitchen table? The table has usually been Randi's, as it's this arrangement which has functioned best. Randi has never had to come to the village while Julie has had some business in town two or three times a year - shopping, dentist's appointments and necessary errands of that sort. The few times Randi has been here - it never happened before Julie and Jørgen took over the farm and the elderly relatives moved into the cottage - her visits have always been short. Besides, she says she is not the sort of person who pays a visit to the countryside just to play the role of the fine lady from town. However, there is no shortage of the pleasures and sorrows that they have exchanged on late nights by the kitchen table.

Randi is no longer more worried than she would be under normal circumstances about Yngve being unable to protect himself through what is now happening. The person she is worried about is Kari. Kari is so headstrong and reckless, confident that as a young person, she can cope with anything. She hopes Yngve will be able to hold her in check. But what now worries her most is that Yngve does not even know they are here. He believes they have gone to Molde, and when he finds out that it's the same hell there as here, then he will be worried. He won't be able to find out which boat they went on since there are boats everywhere, from small rowing craft to large motor boats. Nor must she forget that people from town, and not least from the surrounding area, were offering their boats to shuttle refugees to the nearby villages.

But there is no point in worrying now, so long as it is useless trying to get through by telephone or telegraph, so long as traffic is held up and there is nothing to be done but wait.

- And you, Julie, just think that you are having another child, says Randi. - That's not bad news, is it? I would have liked another one, but as things are now that doesn't bear thinking about. Then I'll soon be too old.

- Do you think I haven't thought twice about bringing a child into the world at a time like this?

- I can understand how you feel. I've thought quite a lot about that these recent days and about what all he's experienced may have done to Martin. But it's no use thinking about that either, Julie. Children have always been born, no matter how the world looked at the time. It's almost worse for the older ones. Let's hope that this doesn't go on so long that their youth is destroyed.

But it is not just Julie who is ambitious for her children. Randi is no less so. It is true that Yngvar seems more concerned that his children will know which class they belong to and will do their best for the class struggle. Their three eldest are eager socialists, but Yngvar has agreed with Randi that education is no disadvantage, even if you belong to the working class. That is why he offered no protest when Randi supported Hallvor going to high school. Hallvor got a brilliant *artium,* but she was the one who persuaded him to apply to NTH. She was also the one who persuaded Yngve to go surety for a study loan from the bank, even though he complained about it. But Hallvor has shown himself to be very capable and has taken all the extra jobs he can find. But what troubles her now is that it was she who insisted on this. What the boy wanted most after leaving high school was to begin as an apprentice in a building firm. Hallvor was good with both his head and his hands, and what he likes best is to use his hands to do what he calls proper work. But he applied to Trondheim and won a place in building and construction. Randi has received a letter from him since the occupation of Trondheim in which he said that all was well, but now she does not know. Besides, she has the impression that there is now a girl in the picture. If anything should happen to Hallvor in Trondheim, she will feel it was her fault that he went there.

- That's exactly what I've felt about Krister recently, Randi, that I was the one who got him to move into town and to all the misery he's mixed up in now.

- Yes, I've thought about that too, Julie, that even if our lives are about as different as it's possible for them to be, we are so very much alike in many ways. Or is this how we've become? Maybe we've influenced each other?

Both are concerned that their children should get an education. Both of Randi's daughters have attended middle school. Solveig left in spring and now works in a shop. She is bright, Randi says, and saves most of her wages so that she can apply for high school in autumn. Kari has gone on to business school and, in addition, has learned languages by her own effort. She's so interested in languages. And since autumn, she has had a job as a receptionist at the Grand. But that has stopped now since there is no longer a Grand Hotel. Nor is there any newspaper editing for Yngvar to do.

- Yes, I've thought about that, says Julie, - how are you going to manage when this is over?
- I can't bear thinking about that, not now. But if there's one thing I've learned from these days, it's that if you save your life, you've saved everything.
- Did you see anything of Krister before all this happened?
- Yes, he popped in to see us now and again, but he now has so much to do, that young man! And I've seen him with a girl. It looked pretty intense.
- A girl? Julie says, - But he's just a boy.
- There's nothing to be frightened of, Randi laughs. - He's a fine young man, so grown up for his age. You can surely understand him beginning to look at girls. Surely you're not so naïve? We live in a different time now from when we were young.

- What was the girl like? Julie wants to know, but before Randi can answer, Jørgen is at the door. The conversation is at an end.

Wednesday, May 1st begins with the same beautiful weather, but with the same distressing signs that the town is under fire.

At Øra there is to be an event taking place in the People's Building, but no processions are planned. They daren't have processions. These would make too obvious a target for aircraft, which can suddenly appear like lightning out of a clear sky.

Randi is to take the children along. The two sisters from town ask for time off, and Dreng-Anders has dressed up for the occasion, as he always does. That is how it has been in Storvik right from Kristoffer's time, so that even if the farmers don't manage to celebrate the day, the servants will not be working, and no work has ever been seen taking place out of doors. In that way they have always shown respect for what they called 'Labour Day'. This is different from other farmers in the district who have demonstrated by carrying out operations like manure spreading as the 1st May processions went past. 'Labour Day!' they would shout scornfully. Jørgen had never shown his face in Øra on Labour Day, but now he decides to go, despite all the looks this will attract telling him he is not welcome.

He goes together with Randi and, on the way, sees to his surprise that others from the farm have had the same thought as himself. Smartly dressed, they are making their way to the People's Building. This has never happened before.

The hall is full, and the corridors are swarming with people. Jørgen manages to wrestle his way to some standing room just inside the door. In a moment, the thought grabs him that if it

occurred to the Germans to drop a bomb on this spot, there
would then be precious few inhabitants left in the district.

The hall is decorated as on 17th May. Birch leaves decorate
the dais and the stage. A band plays, a choir sings, and poems
are read. This is the first time Jørgen has heard the Norwegian
national anthem, *Ja, vi elsker,* read from a stage. When this
happens a rustle goes through the room. It is most unusual to
hear the fatherland's song on such a day.

A couple of years ago a sawmill resumed work after several
years of inactivity. Now, the owner gives a glowing speech in
which he encourages people to adopt a fighting spirit and to stick
together, not just for their own sakes, but across party and class
divisions. He expresses pleasure that many who maybe don't
feel quite safe at home have still come along. Songs unfamiliar
to Jørgen are now being sung, militant workers' songs, and he is
surprised at the fervour he hears in the singing. When the
assembly finishes with people standing for the *Internationale* to
the accompaniment of brass, he is surprised to find himself
doing something he could never before have imagined doing,
humming along even though he does not know the words.

He returns home with a feeling of having experienced
something significant, the first hint of a solidarity which may
come to bind people in the locality closer together and get them
to forget their irreconcilable class differences. 'Across party
boundaries', today's speaker had said. Yes, certainly across
these. Now all parties must stand together against the invaders.
All of them except one, that is, the Nation Socialists or NS.
There were none of *them* there today. Nor should there have
been, so great has the bitterness people feel towards them
become. A bitterness which grew once Quisling had announced

over the radio on the 9th April that the government had been dismissed and that he had formed a new government with himself as both Prime Minister and Foreign Secretary.

During Thursday they could feel the silence, a sense that something was different. The continual hum of aircraft high overhead had now gone. On the sky towards the west there was now just a thin grey mist, not the towering black clouds of the previous days. Hope is dawning inside them. Could it now be over? That evening, the telephone rings. Julie lifts the receiver. With a heart beating quickly enough to take away her breath, she hears Ivar's voice. He explains that he has found a telephone it is possible to ring from, but does not say where he is.

- Everything is fine with us, both with me and with Krister. I think this is coming to an end now.
Relief, a feeling of thankfulness, sweeps over her.
- When will Krister be coming home?
- That's impossible to say. Everything is still chaotic.
- Is he there now? Can I speak with him?
- I've sent him home to get some sleep.
- So the house is safe, then?

Randi is next to her, making signals.

- How is it on Clausenega? In Fløveien?
- Fine, almost everything has been saved, and Julie nods and smiles towards Randi who continues to wave and make signs until Julie understands what it is she wants.
- Ivar, if you should meet Yngvar Thorsen, can you tell him that Randi and the children are here? You can tell him they are fine and well.

There is a moment's delay before he says:

- I'll see that it gets done.

Helene is also there. Now, it is her turn to pick up the receiver. Standing stiffly and with a serious expression, she listens to what Ivar has to say, tears streaming down her cheeks.

- No, Ivar, I cannot stay here. I want to come home. I want to be with you.

There is an unusual intensity in her voice, which they have not heard in the last few days. She continues standing, listening, but her face crumples before she returns to how she was before, controlled and peaceful.

- Very well, Ivar, she says flatly. Yes, I understand.
- It sounds as if your home has been saved for both of you, says Julie. - That must be something to be thankful for in the midst of all this.
- I'm sorry, Julie, but how can I be happy when I think of all those who have lost their homes or loved ones?

Chapter 3

Randi reads: 'Germany is *not* at war with Norway'. She reads this from a bundle of leaflets lying in a bowl on the floor. These leaflets had been dropped from Germans planes during the first days after 9th April. The boys brought them home. Julie wanted to throw them on the fire once everyone had read them, saying she wanted no nonsense of that sort in her house., but Jørgen prevented her. These must be kept, he said, they will be history one day. So they remained and will be read and commented on.

- Such shit talk from hell! Randi snorts. They are alone in the kitchen where there are no children's ears to overhear them. - Oh, excuse me, Julie. You know I don't usually swear. But there is so much anger inside me that I feel the need to swear all the time. And when I read shit like that …. Just listen to this: 'The major part of the Norwegian army and navy are showing loyalty towards the German forces'. Wherever have they got that from? 'No civilians are to carry weapons. Anyone disobeying this injunction will be subject to martial law'. 'The German defence neither can nor will tolerate any sabotage in its ongoing war with England. If necessary, and in agreement with international law, it will intervene with the utmost force and all military might'. The signature on the pamphlets was: 'The German commandant in Trondheim'.

- What do you think of that? says Randi.

- I have read it so many times that I can almost recite it by heart, but it makes an even stronger impression to hear it read out loud.

- It's strong stuff, says Randi. - Would you like me to read more?

- Yes, just read on.

- 'NORWEGIANS! German and Norwegian troops are working together to protect your country. Do not allow yourselves to be misled by English criminals who want to turn your land into a theatre of war'. Did you hear that, Julie? *'Lay down your weapons! - Resume working. Obey the authorities:* Martial law will be applied against anyone who supports the previous government's orders regarding mobilisation or who spreads false rumours. Anyone seen carrying a weapon will be shot. Anyone destroying equipment enabling traffic movement or hindering the intelligence service will be shot. Anyone using weaponry against the law will be shot. *Norwegians! Those who genuinely love their fatherland are back at work!*

- They'll be shot, they'll be shot! repeats Randi. Have you ever seen such arrogance! Using weaponry against the law. Isn't that just what they were doing when they flattened the town? Swine from hell! Who do they think we are? Do they think we're a lot of illiterate cowards? Do they really think we'll take any notice of such rubbish? So far as I know, they have not won everywhere. And I haven't seen a glimpse of a German either here or in town. They must never think …

There Randi stops, remains seated and stares at the door. Julie turns and sees Helene in the doorway. How long she has been there or how much she has heard, they cannot know. So engrossed were they in their conversation that she arrived unnoticed. She wanders silently and restlessly about the house on her ballet dancer's feet. She may put on outer clothing, walk up to the path, go along it for a few metres and then return home. She does this again and again as if her body is filled with a restless energy, which she suppresses. People have become worried about her, fearing that she could become ill, but her glance is alert; there is just this frightening restlessness.

- Excuse me. I'm disturbing you, she says now and goes out. She closes the door behind her. Then they hear her light, dainty footsteps across the living room before another door is closed.
- Poor girl, says Randi. - However things are, I can't help feeling sorry for her.

Slowly, the district returns to normal. There is a new everyday, but a different everyday. Everyone understands that nothing can be as it was before.

The spring farm work, which has been at a standstill, must now be resumed. What is going to be food for autumn needs planting now. Everyone agrees that life has to go on. There is no point in stopping the world, not even if it's a world whose hinges have fallen off.

Those who have been evacuated from town must decide what to do with their lives in the immediate future. Many have lost their homes and have nothing to move back to. Mothers with children prefer to remain here for a while, until the situation in town allows them to return home. Children of school age will attend school locally. Mrs. Solberg has asked if she may live and send her children to school here since her home, a house in Gomaland, has been reduced to ashes. Her husband has rented a room from Ivar, but he has said that this is just a temporary solution and that there is no possibility for her to move in with her three children.

Randi wants to go home. Yngvar has telephoned and said that he will get in touch as soon as he thinks it is advisable for her to travel. Julie was standing beside her for a moment during the conversation and could not help hearing Yngvar's reply.

- I don't want you there. You must get away from those people and do it quickly!

- What nonsense! Randi answered. - What's so dangerous about that? Then, she became quiet as she listened.

- All right, Randi answered. No, I see what you mean.

She avoided Julie's glance as she replaced the receiver.

- Maybe it's best that I go home, she said. - But I will never forget that you took us in and protected us at this time.

- Oh, no, you can stay here as long as you want, you do know that, don't you? says Julie.

- No, I can't stay here any longer doing nothing. Besides, you have enough people to care for with all those who are living here. It's just a pity your baby didn't arrive earlier so that I could get to see your marvellous new child. But that can come later. We can leave for now the question of exactly how we'll get in touch, she smiles. No, Julie, we'll just have to roll up our sleeves. I'm needed out there and Yngvar needs me. There are lots of people we know. It will all be a bit of a crush, but we'll help as much as we can, we who've been so lucky that our home has been spared. And as I said, Yngvar needs me.

The ferries have just started up again, and early one morning, Julie accompanies Randi and the children down to the pier. She has been to the farm's storeroom and found some food which she leaves with Randi. She is anxious when she sees how the stores have diminished now that there are so many strangers in the house. But it is her own supplies she raids. Synnøve has her own in a separate corner of the storeroom.

- This is all a bit overwhelming, but I cannot do anything but thank you, Randi says. - and I don't doubt everything is going to turn out well.

Julie is dreading the parting. Having Randi with her at this time has been such a great comfort.

- We mustn't lose contact, Randi, Julie says. - And if ever you're in need, you know you're always welcome here.

- That's right, we mustn't lose contact.

- No, for if there really *was* anything that could destroy our friendship, it wouldn't be worth paying that price.

- Yes, our friendship has survived many a bump over the years, so why should we not manage this time round? But we must reckon on seeing each other less frequently than before. You know there have been so many things.

Yes, Julie knows, and has understood it during these days that Randi has with her. As she waves her off, she experiences a sickening feeling inside her. She walks back up the hill slowly, stopping frequently to draw breath. She feels the weight of her child inside her. But it is more than this. There is another weight she cannot put into words.

There has always been some tension between the Storvik and Thorsen families. Certainly between them and Julie's family here, but even more between them and the Storvik family in Kristiansund. Now she understands that this has worsened, making the distance huge. This stood behind everything Randi was saying as she left. She now realises that Jørgen is right. Ivar and all he stands for can destroy relationships more than she dares to admit. That it can take such a toll on her friendship with Randi that she risks losing it. This is not something that bears thinking about. Who will then be left to confide in? It occurs to her that over the years she may perhaps have become too dependent on Randi.

These are the thoughts that are making her irritable when
Helene joins her in the kitchen.

- I can't go on like this, Julie. I need to go home. I just can't
stay here any longer.
- What is so wrong with being here? says Julie brusquely.
Do you never think about all the things you have avoided? You
still have your home; Ivar is fit and well. Maybe you should
think of people who've lost everything, she says and regrets her
words as soon as she sees Helene's face. How long can she
herself go on here caring about everyone and everything? She is
so tired that everything seems to be swirling round her. She
excuses herself with the thought that Helene must learn to
understand that there are others apart from herself who are also
experiencing difficulty. A couple of days after this, Helene
arrives to tell her that she has received a letter from Ivar. He
wants her to come home now. Selma can stay.

On the day Helene departs Julie stands and gives her a hug.
She feels Helen's delicate frame next to her own bulky body,
where her stomach will soon be bigger than ever. Helene barely
reaches up to her chin, and is as thin as a bird. But that she has
strength, and that strong will is something Julie has seen more
than once. Once they have decided that she is going to travel,
that familiar calm which has always characterised her returns.
Helene extends her hand to Julie.

- Thank you, Julie, for all you've done, she says, very much
in control. Thank you for having me here.
- It was the least I could do, says Julie, looking slightly
shamefaced. - You have been so brave, Helene. And you must
go on being brave.

- A wry smile steals over Helene's face before she turns to go.

Julie has received a telegram from her parents. All is well with them and the rest of her family in Romsdal. She has sent a telegram back and has written them a letter. This means she doesn't have to worry about them for the time being. She writes to Krister urging him to come home. Why is he still in town when she understands that all teaching in the town's schools has been suspended? His reply states that he must remain where he is. He explains that there is a need for as many men as possible in cleaning up operations. This infuriates Jørgen. Krister must come home even if that means that Jørgen must himself go to bring him back. What is the lad thinking about? he thunders. Does he think he is so essential that he cannot spare the time to visit his home after all that has happened?

Julie has been infinitely grateful that Krister has come through all this without harm. Rumour has it that one boy perished during firefighting when he was struck by a falling chimney. That could just as easily have happened to Krister. She imagines him, persistent and reckless as ever, and is surprised that he does not feel a need to come home after all he has been through. Might it be the girl Randi spoke about who is keeping him in town?

- It looks as if that son of yours is going to be a real lady killer, she says.

She has herself seen this when there have been arrangements locally, the amorous looks that girls - and not just the young ones - have directed towards him, and that has made her feel proud. But he is just too young to have a fan club, to use the young people's expression.

- Oh, they're just kids, says Randi. - You mustn't be so strict that you don't allow young people their bit of fun. If Krister walks around Vandamman and makes out with a girl, that's hardly a disaster. Remember that you were young once!

- Yes, but in those days, we didn't go carrying on with the boys in public before it turned serious, says Julie indignantly.

- Times change and we just have to get used to it.

What about Julie herself? She was probably no more than seventeen when she and Inge were something of an item. But Inge was three years older than her, a grown-up as she saw it at the time, not a boy who was just turning sixteen, as is now the case with Krister. And there was nothing more between them than holding hands and sharing the odd hug now and then, apart from one terrifying occasion when he almost raped her. This is something she doesn't allow herself to think about, but it occurred after she had broken up with him. She is not proud of this and wants to have a serious word with Krister when he comes home, for up to now he has shared most of his concerns with her.

There are no longer newspapers in Kristiansund. Nor can people rely on broadcasting or other information sources. The few in the locality who subscribe to the *Adresseavisen* in Trondheim have read in the 6th May edition about the bombing of Kristiansund and the other towns in Møre. They read that most of Kristiansund has now been burnt to the ground. German aircraft had bombed the port, which was full of British ships. After this, they read that 'the English had set fire to the town before settling down to enjoy themselves'. It is in the light of this lying description people understand that they cannot rely on newspapers or other public sources of information. This too came from the 'occupants' press service".

All kinds of rumours are in circulation; no one knows who they can rely on. From the town they hear of people's unselfish efforts and the efforts of people from the surrounding district helping in the clearing-up operations both during the bombing and afterwards. Not least have there been stories about boat people taking part in the evacuation of the town. But there were less popular rumours expressing a different slant. These were about people who wanted to avoid publicity, and people exploiting the situation to steal from businesses and private individuals. There were reports of people who had been caught and arrested. There were tales of shop owners who were open for business and asked people to help themselves to their goods as they would all be burned anyway. Decent people were hesitant over what they saw as people defending their own illegal actions, before they gave way and accepted the challenge. So many rumours were flying round that most people learned to take rumours like this with a pinch of salt.

Jørgen was quite serious when he said he would travel to the town to bring Krister home. On Thursday 9th May he left the farm. The fine weather which there had been during the bombing and the following week had now changed. There was a strong wind blowing over Talgsjøen and from the portholes on the boat everything looked grey. There was talk about the laying of mines and of mines floating on the surface. Many of the women were anxious and pale, but most accepted it with a fatalistic resignation.

The sight that confronted Jørgen as he sailed into the town came as a shock. Black chimneys reach up into the sky, and fragments of facades and shaky walls rose from what, at first sight, looked like a stone yard. He knew that what he was about to see here would not be pretty, but never in his wildest dreams could he have thought that it would be like this.

Jørgen's first thought is that today he should be in no hurry to complain. And he realises how incredibly lucky those in his area had been who, in spite of everything, had been able to observe the war from a safe distance.

This is to be Jørgen's first meeting with the 'herrefolk', which people have begun calling the Germans. The pier has been destroyed to an extent which makes it difficult to land, but in the middle of all the destruction are green-clad German guards. Wearing steel helmets, ammunition belts and machine pistols, they keep watch over the landing place and the pier. These Germans belong to the first German battalion, which took over the town on May 7th, an infantry division. Jørgen shudders as he passes them and others of the same type as he makes his way through the barren landscape of what used to be a beautiful town.

The feeling that he is moving through a quarry becomes even more pronounced when he sees the destruction in the streets. It is difficult to know exactly where he is, but when he spots Loennechengård, he knows that this is Kalhakken. In the midst of the ruins stands the old woodyard which in spite of everything has survived as a landmark he can orientate with. In the burnt areas people are working all out to tidy up, and the sight of their indomitable optimism affects him deeply. What fine people these are! Over Allan Meadow a small swastika is waving underneath the Norwegian flag. This is the first time he has seen a swastika with his own eyes.

It feels almost like a relief when he comes further up Langveien, where there are more undamaged areas. The relief soon wears off, for he is dreading his meeting with Ivar and entering that house as he has done in years past. The house, which holds so many good memories, now represents only pain and grief for him. But what else is there to do? He will find Krister and stay overnight; there is nowhere else to go.

He now comes to a house which is hardly recognisable. There is the sound of foreign voices, and in the hallway he must make his way through children playing. At the top of the stairs he sees Helene and greets her. This is a Helene totally different from the timid shadow who a few days previously had been wandering anxiously round Storvik. In a dress with her sleeves rolled up she now has colour back in her face and is energetic. She welcomes him and helps him off with his outer clothes. She apologises for not being able to invite him into the living room as there is a family living there, but the dining room is theirs to use. There is a divan on which he will be able to spend the night. She has prepared coffee. At the entrance to the dining room Jørgen stops and stands and stares. At the table sits a German in full uniform; he is just a boy. He stands politely as Jørgen enters the room and extends a hand towards him. Before Jørgen can pull himself together, he has grasped the German's hand and introduced himself, just as the German has done. More surprised than shocked, he stands and watches as the German leaves. First, he turns at the door and bows before donning his officer's hat and leaving the room. The sound of his boot heels is heard as he departs.

He doesn't have the language to say anything. Helene's cheeks blush with embarrassment.

Ivar and Krister are out, she says. Krister is with the people tidying up, whereas Ivar is in the temporary bank building they are trying to prepare in the Home for Women in Langveien. She is expecting them home for dinner in a couple of hours' time. Maybe Jørgen would like to rest in the meantime?

He rejects the suggestion. He does not feel sufficiently calm to rest.

Helene says that the chief concern of people in town is to help the homeless. She herself is playing host to a family with small children in the living room. When Selma comes back, she will have one of the rooms upstairs. They have already moved her clothes in there and the things which she is most afraid will be destroyed. The home help is living there for the present while Krister has been sleeping on the divan in the dining room. Tonight, she is going to prepare a sleeping bag for him.

- There's not much room, says Jørgen.
- No, but that's no reason to complain.

They then hear someone running up the stairs in long bounds, and suddenly, there is Krister standing at the door. He is wearing a dirty overall, with a check shirt rolled up over his strong brown arms. There are strips of dirt and mud on his face, and his damp black forelock hangs over his forehead. A quick blush crosses his face.

- Oh, Father. You've come!
- Yes. Maybe you thought I wouldn't, eh? says Jørgen and rises to take his son's dirty fist in his. He must control himself not to hug the boy too closely to him.

- You're here already? says Helene. Dinner's not ready yet.
- No, I'm going back. I just became so hungry that I thought I might have a sandwich, he says.

Helen hands him a plate with sandwiches ready. While he is chewing he speaks excitedly.

- More Germans have come to town. Dad, you must come along and see.

On the street outside they can hear quiet singing in the distance.

- Who is that singing? Jørgen asks.

The Germans. They sing as they march. That's their custom. Their prisoners did the same even though they were scared stiff. He tells them about the German prisoners of war who were held in the girls' school. During that first day of the bombing the guards had to use the machine guns they had been issued with to keep their prisoners away from the window where they were standing, looking out and preparing to welcome their friends. On Monday, when the school was set on fire, the terrified prisoners banged on the doors and screamed. That turned out to be the end of their courage! They then were transferred to Allanengen school. That same evening, they were led down to the pier and taken by boat to Varde County School on Bremsnes. This time they were as high as kites. They sang at the tops of their voices as they marched through a town in flames down to the pier.

Jørgen is standing on the street next to Krister and cannot believe his eyes and ears. A hoard of Germans in full uniform and wearing steel helmets is marching through the ruins, singing as if this was a victory parade. He can hardly think of a worse way of showing contempt for the inhabitants. For Jørgen, this is out and out evil. He experiences still more that day, things which awaken feelings in him that he could hardly believe possible. With a bitterness threatening to choke him, he sees that the

Norwegian flag raised above Allenengen school has been replaced with a large German flag displaying the swastika.

- I'll have to go back and help, says Krister.

- No, you don't have to, says Jørgen. We are going back to Ivar's, then you must pack your bags, because you're coming home with me.

- But just look around you, Father, says Krister passionately. Can't you see that I'm needed here?

- You're needed at home. I won't hear otherwise.

- But school isn't over yet.

- I can't see that you're exactly dressed for school. No, Krister, enough is enough. How do you think it's been for your mother these past few days? Don't you even spare her a thought? I suppose you know that she is soon to have a baby?

Defiance shows in Krister's eyes when he meets his father's glance, but Jørgen can see that he has won this first round. He asks Krister to pack everything he can take with him, including his school books. Without saying a word to each other, they go back to the house. Krister may sulk, thinks Jørgen, but it'll be a long time before he's mature. In the meantime, he must get used to the fact that it is his father who is in charge.

Conversation round the dinner table is proceeding slowly. Jørgen no longer engages in discussion with Ivar. He feels unspeakably tired, like someone carrying a great grief. He looks at his brother - the little brother he was once so fond of - and it is like looking at a stranger. He listens half-heartedly to Ivar's description of how their bank securities and money have been saved from the bank vault. They also managed to save machines and other equipment before everything burned. He speaks eagerly of critical points which will soon be functioning normally.

- I understand, then, that you aren't going to be out of work any time soon, says Jørgen drily.

Jørgen is lying on the narrow divan, tossing and turning, with so much disturbance going on inside him that he cannot sleep. He hears all sorts of strange sounds in the house - babies crying, mothers trying to comfort their children and subdued conversations between adults. There is little privacy for those who now live here. But it is probably not this which is worrying them most, for at the present this time the most important consideration has to be the preservation of life and keeping a roof over one's head. He sits up, moves aside the blackout curtain and gazes out over a town plunged in darkness. He sees the contours of chimneys standing out gloomily against the night sky. He seems to glimpse the silhouettes of two German guards patrolling the street outside. He shudders as he returns to bed. He remains lying there, staring out into the dark room while all manner of thoughts swirl around in his head. He has so many good memories of this house, going right back to his childhood. Coming here to Uncle Erling and Aunty Selma here in town used to be something of an adventure. He was most proud of those times when, as a boy, he was judged sufficiently grown up to venture here on his own. Sometimes he was able to stay for a whole week. Those times his uncle always used to come down to the pier to meet him. He would then accompany him up to the bank, and he remembers one occasion when his uncle treated him to a dinner at the Grand. There were just the two of them, himself and his uncle, and he recalls his uncle giving him his first lesson on how to behave in a fine restaurant. Uncle Erling and Jørgen's father, Kristoffer, enjoyed a close friendship. Any time there were challenges, the two families would stand together. Erling Storvik never forgot where he had come from even though he became a significant person in the town. There was a bond between the two families which seemed unbreakable.

With great sadness, he recalls the joy and laughter, the music and the singing in the house. At that time the two daughters were living at home, as indeed they continued to do after Ivar had moved in. He recalls the first opera premiere. Every detail of that evening now comes flooding back, the performance, the celebration afterwards and the dancing. Julie was so beautiful, as was Astrid. And afterwards, when the evening was over, and they realised that it had been a resounding success, they sat celebrating in the living room far into the night. Even now, he seems to hear his uncle's powerful voice and the young women's laughter ringing through the house.

But for him, that evening was like the beginning of the end for the family. Selma had been looking forward to Ivar and Helene having children who would replace the grandchildren she had never had. This did not happen. On the day when Selma and Anne are no more, that will be the end of the line for his uncle's family. He cannot avoid the thought that, at some time, a curse must have fallen on this house, and the thought now stays with him. Then there is all that trouble with Ivar. As his mother used to say, you must never forget that Ivar is your brother.

Julie and Krister are sitting in the kitchen having a quiet conversation. She has made it clear that she wants to be alone with him. Even Jørgen has left after saying to Krister that he shouldn't think he'll be going back soon. This is something they will have to take up in autumn when all this is over.

- Now you're angry with your father, says Julie gently

- Well, is that so strange? says Krister loudly.

- Hush! Quiet! I don't want anyone to hear us.

- Well, first he comes and brings me home as if I was a young kid, then he tells me I can't go back?

- You must give your father a little time, whereupon Krister calms down. You realise that he's worried in case Ivar influences you in some way.

- Uncle Ivar influence me? Dear God, he hasn't a clue what he's become mixed up in. Not yet, anyway. But doesn't that show how little confidence Father has in me? He doesn't believe I'm grown up sufficiently to take care of myself. And anyway, I've thought about moving house.

She stares at him.

- Moving house?

- Yes, with a family I've got to know, he says without daring to return her glance. He blushes, and Julie suspects she knows why.

- This wouldn't be with a girl, you know, would it?

- Yes, but so what? She's just a school friend.

- Krister, have you got yourself a girlfriend?

- Girlfriend? No, I'm not engaged if that's what you're getting at. Goodness, Mother, we're no longer living in the stone age! And it's not good living with Uncle Ivar any more.

- You're not living with your uncle. You're living with Selma.

- But it comes down to the same thing, doesn't it?

- To age, says Julie with a shudder.

They are sitting opposite each other like two gamecocks, mother and son, neither yielding to the other's look, just as they have sat so many times before. They are so alike and understand each other through and through.

- As sure as I'm your mother, I won't let you do it. I won't have you getting mixed up with a girl. That must wait until you're no longer wet behind the ears. Just think about it.

- Mother, listen ….

- No, you listen to me! There is no way that if you go back there you'll live anywhere else than with Selma. You mustn't forget what we owe to her in the middle of all this. You have lived there rent-free all these years, and now you're telling me you want to run away with your tail between your legs as soon as the going gets tough. I thought that with the upbringing we've given you, you would behave properly and not act in this way. It would break Selma's heart if you moved in with someone else, and she's gone through enough already. And who would pay the rent if you moved elsewhere? Just look the facts in the face, Krister. I have to say I agree with your father. You have to stay here.

- Damn! he says and rushes to the door. The noise of the door banging behind him reverberates throughout the room.

Before she settles down, she peeps through the door into the boys' room. She hears all three breathing and can tell which is which. Then she hears the recognisable sound of Krister's breathing. He is fast asleep, making gentle snoring sounds as if he has not had a good night's sleep for a long time. And he is home again, this son of hers. All three are at home.

Jørgen lay dozing that morning and felt good. Most of his spring tasks have now been completed. Yesterday they finished planting the potatoes. 'Just in time', he thought, somewhere between being awake and asleep. The custom here is that potatoes have to be in the ground before the morning of 17th May. It's now the 17th of May and he is wide awake. The reality is that this year's National Day is going to be totally different from any he has ever experienced before. But their best clothes are hanging newly ironed on the wall, all ready for wear. Even though there is a ban on celebrating the day, this does not mean that it is going to be an ordinary one. What people choose to do in their own homes is nobody else's business. Not even Hallgrim's, though Hallgrim has begun walking round and playing the self-appointed policeman. He has posted notices in the post offices and shops: 'All shooting and saluting is forbidden on 17 May'. 'It is strictly forbidden to appear on roads or public places in an intoxicated condition.' What nonsense! Who will manage to celebrate 17 May when the whole country is in mourning. And how dare Hallgrim take this task on himself?

Nordahl Grieg's voice spreads out into the room. In the kitchen at Storvik, it is so quiet that you can hear a pin drop. All of them sit listening to this poem which Greig had entitled '17 May 1940'.

> Among Eidsvoll's green-clad trees
> Today the flagpole's bare,
> But it's just in times like these
> That we grasp what our freedoms are.

The radio they bought last autumn, a brand-new Vidor, makes it possible to receive Bodø radio from where Greig is reading.

> We are so few in the land,
> that those fallen are brothers and friends.

Even the children sit in an awed silence and listen. The adults sit looking at the floor, afraid to betray how they feel.

As the last lines ring out, Jørgen's hand sweeps across his face as he leaves the room. He stands out on the veranda looking out over the countryside, which, despite the beautiful weather, shows no sign of life on what is usually a festive day, the most important spring day of all. Now the whole district is silent, as if in grief. There are no flags waving in the greenery against the blue sky. There are no processions, no celebrations in the Youth Building, and no joyful children's voices. The flags have all been packed up and stored away in the loft or in a shed. When will they come back out? Words buzz round in his head. Today the flagpole is empty, and he shudders as he looks out over a lifeless scene.

- Oh, are you here? says Julie quietly. She has crept up on him unnoticed.
- Yes. Oh, I don't know, this is all too much for me.
- I'm sure all of us feel that.

At Storvik, as in almost every home in the district, it's a feast day. The dinner table is laid in the living room ready there for everyone in the house, big or small. All are dressed in their finery and venison roast is being served with cloudberries as dessert. On Sundays and feast days, the custom on the farm is that they sing before beginning to eat. Today they sing *God bless our dearest fatherland* and the Norwegian anthem, *Ja, vi elsker.* Their voices quiver with suppressed emotions. But, apart from this, it is exceptionally quiet round the table.

None of the boys has left the farm today, but in the evening Krister takes his bicycle and says he is going to visit a friend. He won't be long. Even he seems downhearted and quiet.

- Have you been meeting any girls? Julie asks.

- Yes, he says, some of the young people got together in the Youth Building where they tried to get a dance going with gramophone records. There weren't many people there, he says, and he himself had felt some reluctance. This felt worse when a couple of older people came and said that what the young people were doing was indecent.

- You should think better than to hold a party on a day like this, they had said to the young people. - The seventeenth of May should not be disrespected in this way.

Krister agreed, he said, and came home.

- This has been such a strange day, he said, giving expression to what most people are thinking.

After everything has calmed down Jørgen and Julie are sitting alone in the kitchen.

Jørgen asks Julie if she would like to go for a walk with him, that is if she is not too tired. They step out into the fragrance of the spring night. Hand in hand, they wander along newly planted fields, sweet-smelling and calming. A pure aroma of fresh soil and sprouting grass mixes with odours from the sea. There are snow-capped mountains, and over everything, there reigns a great stillness.

- You know, Julie, this is how it used to be for people, a man and his wife looking over the fields and everything growing in the ground. That was a kind of blessing.

- Yes, I've noticed that you take off your hat when you are sowing, Jørgen. It touches me every time I see it. There is so much respect in that. To *Him* who watches over us.

- Well, maybe that's how it is. But for me, it is all just so natural. My grandfather used to do that, as did my father. I've never thought there was anything special about it.

They sit down on a flat rock in a grove by the sea, a place where they have often sat during summer when they wanted some time to themselves. Jørgen removes his jacket, folds it and places it on the rock so that they can sit there without feeling cold. They remain seated, he with his arm round her shoulder. In one hand he is fumbling with a straw from last year's grass.

- Maybe you think I'm just being sentimental, Julie, but to experience 17th May like this … I may have joked a bit in the past about all the pompous words which have been used on such a day. But today, today I suddenly felt what it means to have a country where you belong, which is yours. And I dare to say it.

He suddenly becomes youthful for Julie. She sees him now, vulnerable and naked, and feels such a tenderness towards him, almost like an ache in both body and mind. Love for him and the warmth from his body flood through her. An old and half-forgotten thought comes to her, that she must never lose Jørgen. It is a long time since they have talked like this. She feels a closeness to him, which reminds her of the days when they were young. It's a moment which lifts them both up over an everyday, which so often threatens to break them down.

Julie lies awake that night long after Jørgen has fallen asleep. She feels a strange unease within herself, but her body is quiet, as is the child inside her. After a while she falls asleep but then awakens to a grey light in the bedroom. She is so wide awake that she sits straight up. She can no longer bear lying in bed and slips a jacket over her nightdress. Her legs are bare as she makes her way out of the room. The fire in the kitchen is still glowing, and she adds a few sticks to cause it to flame. She heats up what coffee remains in the pot, but the pungent taste makes her feel nauseous and she pours herself a glass of milk instead. Shivering slightly, she remains seated in front of the stove, listening to the sounds within her. It is then she feels the first hint of what is about to happen. It comes again. She has experienced this before. But isn't this too early? She had not been expecting her baby until the end of the month. Maybe she has miscalculated. This has also happened previously. Just as new each time is the excitement that now ripples through her. There is a sense of expectation, the fear that something may go wrong, the fear of the pain, but most of all the waiting for it all to be over. Then there is the close connection between herself and the child which will be broken as soon as the umbilical cord is cut. It is this which is the oddest and perhaps the saddest sensation that life has afforded her.

The large guest room over the main living room in which she has previously given birth to her children is now occupied by another family. Fortunately the room that Randi has been using is once more available and the bed is made up with fresh bedding. She will make do with this room. She is already feeling those first familiar throbs in the small of her back and fills a large kettle with water which she puts on the stove. She will make use of the opportunity to wash and prepare herself before the rest of the household wakes up.

She stands naked, facing the hot stove, washes herself all over, drawing the flannel gently over her tight torso. She feels a strange enjoyment, as if she is carrying out a ritual. Just as she is sneaking to the bedroom to find clean clothes, clean underwear and her best nightdress, which she slips over her head, Jørgen wakes up.

- What's going on? he says, are you ill?

- No, not ill exactly. She whispers so as not to awaken little Sven. - But it looks as if there's a new human being coming into the world today. We'd better get hold of the midwife.

Now he springs to life. He leaps out of bed and dresses at breakneck speed.

- There's no need to be in such a rush, she smiles. - It's not a matter of life and death.

Deep inside she feels her first powerful contraction. - But nor is it anything to put off, she adds, recalling how quickly it all went with Sven.

On her way to the birth room, she wakes Astrid.

- There's something going on here, she says. - Can you take care of Sven when he wakes up? And you know what sort of preparations to make. Jørgen is fetching the midwife.

She places a waterproof cloth over the bed, lays a clean sheet over it and says that now the only thing to do is to wait. She smiles as she thinks of Jørgen's terrified expression. He should be used to this by now, but he gets just as agitated every time. Men never get used to births, she reflects. Maybe this is because childbearing is something totally outside their experience. Something which only exists for a woman?

She is surprised that it is about to happen now, before she was expecting it. Can it have been brought on by last night's walk? That time they spent together by the shore remains as a warm sensation inside her.

Suddenly there is no more time for thought. One contraction after another sweeps through her body. She bites her lip till it bleeds in order to avoid screaming or groaning so loudly that she can be heard in a house full of people, including those who do not live here.

- It's going to be quick, she groans in a brief pause between contractions.
- We've gathered that, says Synnøve, comforting her. - But don't be afraid. We'll look after you.

They are sitting on either side of the bed. Synnøve and Astrid have themselves begun the delivery when the midwife appears at the door. At that same moment Julie's waters break and stream out of her in a flood.

- Oh, that was a relief! she groans.
- Now it's time to roll up our sleeves, says the midwife who has hardly taken her coat off and washed her hands before a huge contraction tenses Julie's body in an arch. One contraction after another now threatens to tear her body to pieces.
- You must try to hold back, says the midwife.
- I can't!
- Yes, but you must breathe. The child needs air.

She can do no more than to give way to her body in all this. A long, ugly groan bursts out of her as the child is delivered, and then there is a moment of quiet in the room. Through a red mist, Julie catches sight of the midwife and the other two before the silence is broken by a snip and a weak cry.

- You have a beautiful girl, Julie, but the poor thing is worn out, says the midwife - No surprise after the struggle she's had to come into the world. She grasps the child's legs, pats her on the back and the delicate squeaks give way to vigorous cries.

Everything is swimming before Julie's eyes. Her body is trembling uncontrollably after all that effort.

- What was that you said? she whispers, hardly audibly, - that it's a girl?

- Yes, this girl eventually arrived, smiles the midwife.

It is now all over, and there she lies clean and cared for with the child in her arms, not quite believing it is true. Her only feelings are feelings of relief. Jørgen comes in.

- I want to see my little girl.

He moves to the window, stands there, and stares out. Julie falls silent to give him a moment of peace and is aware of what he is thinking.

He sits down on the edge of the bed and takes her hand.

- We've done it, at last, Julie. Our little girl has arrived.

Tears stream uncontrollably down her cheeks. Jørgen strokes her hair again and again with his hand until eventually the flow stops.

- I'm so stupid, she whimpers as a trembling smile crosses her face.

Jørgen moves aside the blanket which has been covering the child's face.

Aren't you a lovely girl? he says softly. - You are really going to be cared for.

Julie lies and gazes at the child in her arms. She cannot altogether grasp that this is a girl. There is a dense mop of black hair surrounding a tiny face. None of her previous children have had so much hair when they were born. She looks for familiar features in the child's face but cannot yet think of anyone she resembles. She notes a dimple on the chin, which will enhance a smile, and when the child blinks she sees that her eyes are dark, so she understands that they are going to be brown. She places the child on the bed with the intention of encouraging her to cry, but the little child only wants to sleep. Julie pinches her cheeks, at which point she cries a little, a weak, trembling cry before she falls back to sleep. There is nothing wrong with the child, the midwife assures her. It is just the violent delivery which has exhausted her.

- Are you so tired, then, you poor thing?

Julie herself must fight against her urge to sleep. She feels just as exhausted as she would have done after a twenty-four-hour shift on the farm without rest or sleep. The whole process has gone so quickly that she was hardly aware of it before the whole thing was over, but she can never remember having previously been as tired as this after a normal birth.

The midwife comes in to say goodbye. She takes the child from Julie and places her in the crib which has been made ready.

- This little lady will do well. And so will you. If what you experienced today was tough, I'm sure you will get over it. I had to put in the odd extra stitch this time, but you are going to be fine. Just take care of yourself, Julie, and give yourself time to rest. Remember, you are not a little piggy anymore!

That the birth was so difficult was because the child first emerged with one arm, out the midwife tells her. And then the umbilical cord was twisted round her brow. There was never any danger, but it was certainly no laughing matter.

- But you can comfort yourself, Julie, with the thought that soonest done, soonest mended.

The custom which applied when Julie gave birth to her first three children, that women giving birth stayed in bed for fourteen days after the birth, no longer applies. After five or six days, she is back in the kitchen at mealtimes. Also, the custom of women wrapping their children up tightly has also come to an end, though Julie has never done that. It was a young teacher who taught her about looking after children. This upset Synnøve, and although now she rarely involves herself in Julie's affairs, this time, she cannot manage to keep quiet. The child will suffer a hernia and is almost certain to become bow-legged. As for Julie, already out of bed before the child is only a week old, she will undoubtedly pay for this foolishness with back problems and other upsets when she is older.

- Mark my words, Julie, I have a long life behind me and know what I'm talking about.

But such talk from Synnøve no longer upsets Julie. It is more and more rarely that she becomes irritated by her mother-in-law now. Relations between them have become easier over the years but they are never going to be close. Too much happened in Julie's first years here in Storvik for that to be possible. But they respect each other, and for the most part Synnøve allows the children to go their own way. Both Julie and Synnøve are too strong-willed for sparks not to fly occasionally, but Julie is no longer afraid of her mother-in-law's stubbornness. During the winter and spring following Kirstoffer's death, she suffered a lot because of her and also for the trouble with Ivar, but Synnøve now never betrays what she is feeling and thinking deep down.

What now moves Julie is how concerned her mother-in-law is about the little girl. Because the weather is so fine at this time of year, she allows the child to lie in the old cradle in the living room. The older children always had to stay in their bedrooms when they were little. Maybe her excuse is the time of year, or maybe it's because she wants to feel the child close to her that the door between the kitchen and the living room is always ajar. It does not seem as though the child is disturbed by the noises from the kitchen. The signs are that she is going to be a quiet child, and she sleeps most of the time. Several times during the day she sees Synnøve standing over the cradle gazing down at the child, and she is moved by the love she sees in the old woman's face.

- I thought I heard the child cry, and so I just had to see to her, says Synnøve quickly when she realises that Julie is looking at her, and before hurrying back to her own affairs.

The children in the house gather around the cradle so much so that Julie sometimes has to chase them away when they come too close. As for Jørgen, he is worst of all. She has never seen him like this before. When he is at home and hears the slightest squeak from the child, he takes her into his lap or carries her round.

- You can't ever say that I will spoil the child, Julie says.
- But must she just lie there screaming?
- She screamed? Then you manage to hear more than I ever can! Julie laughs.

But it also moves her.

A custom which has not come to an end is that women in the district visit the mothers of the newly born. In the weeks following the birth, apart from feeding and looking after the child, Julie can do little else than welcome her visitors. She need not concern herself with food, for they bring everything that is needed. But there is an expectation that she will put some of her own food on the table. Otherwise she will experience a sense of shame. Some women bring cream porridge, others newly baked waffles, over-rich cream cakes or other condiments. What she values most is that nearly all of them bring with them a container of coffee. Without that, rationing regulations would have made it impossible for there to be such a get-together of coffee-loving women. All of them admire the little girl. As for Julie herself, is she not delighted that the longed-for daughter has at last arrived? As they say, it's never too late. And Jørgen is said to be strutting around as a peacock.

It must be a stroke of luck for there to be a small child in the house at such a time. This gives people something to think about other than all the misery they see all around them. They also know that it was only by a hair's breadth that the child escaped being born on Norway's National Day. For that to have happened would be like having the child born on Christmas Eve. Julie should be happy that this did not happen, for then the little girl would have been cheated of her birthday. But the Seventeenth of May with a birthday the day after, that is fine. And may God grant that they celebrate 17th May next year, they say, crossing themselves. They must hope that all these terrible events will be over by then.

There is one thing Julie realises she does not need to worry about as she sees another deputation of women to the door, and that is conversation. That is something that takes care of itself. She is becoming dizzy with all their talk.

One day she stands looking at the child lying wriggling on the carpet while she unpacks napkins and baby food. It seems that the child is looking at her and right into her soul with that inscrutable gaze seen only in newly born children and the very old. She looks so intense, with a deep furrow between her eyebrows. Is she looking at me? Julie wonders. Then the child smiles, a broad smile, which leads to an excited trembling round that little toothless mouth. Julie knows that this is her imagination, that this was really just a grimace, but she was struck with the clear thought that those dark eyes were smiling.

- You are going to be called Sunniva, she says and has no idea where this name is coming from.
- Sunniva - it is a name at the same time gentle and strong, a hero's name and a saint's name.

She has been dreading having to call her Synnøve. Since she is the only girl among her children, there is an expectation that she will be named after her maternal grandmother, but Julie resists because her sister who died, Synna, was also baptised Synnøve. It has become impossible to imagine that a child round here should be called Synna. There has only ever been one Synna.

Sunniva will, then, be the child's name. She does not know of anyone with that name, but there is no other name by which she can be called.

Chapter 4

People were able to keep more or less up to date on what was happening in the immediate vicinity, at least so long as they managed to sort out the truth from all the rumours. This was not the case with what was happening across the nation. Neither newspapers nor broadcasting could be relied on. The *Romsdalsposten* was the first of the town's newspapers to come back out after the bombing. It came out as a daily newspaper, but printing had taken place in Ålesund on the previous day. Everyone understood very quickly that the content was controlled by the Germans. Most articles began: 'Germans give notice that …' The only thing people could rely on was news coming in from London. It was through this that they were able to learn of the real conditions in the country, and not least of the way the war was developing.

Immediately after 9 April both the British and French governments sent messages to say that they would be coming to Norway's assistance. While waiting for these forces the Germans had to be prevented from establishing connexions to the West Country and to Trondheim. Some believed that there was a possibility that Trondheim could be re-conquered by Norwegian forces, but these lines broke down. Allied troops managed to reach Harstad and Namsos on 14 April and Åndalsnes on the 18th. But the soldiers were untrained and inadequately armed, and the civil air force had been decommissioned. The thought of winning back Trondheim was unrealistic, and the Germans were able to go about bombing Namsos and Steinkjer, Åndalsnes, Molde, Ålesund and Kristiansund without hindrance.

They advanced throughout Romsdal, forcing Norwegian troops under the leadership of General Ruge to retreat. New quarters for the army's high command were set up at Furset on 30 April. There Ruge received notice that the king, the crown prince and the government were on their way to North Norway. He then decided to capitulate to the German supreme power in the south and not to put up resistance in the north. The capitulation documents were finally signed at Rindal on 3 May.

A newspaper announcement which distressed people at the time was that the German airmen who had bombed Kristiansund had been awarded the Iron Cross.

At the end of June, the *Romsdalsposten* also wrote that the town's newspapers had been summoned by the German commandant in order to receive 'details of the Germans' requirements with regard to press activities'. The paper also reported that a number of local issues had been raised, 'such as that German soldiers were singing during their march through the burnt areas'. To this the commandant replied that 'the singing was in no way directed against the Norway or the Norwegian people'. Regarding the question of whether Allanengen school could be made free for teaching in autumn, he replied that 'the assumption is that the war will be over by then'. This last statement weighed down heavily on Jørgen when Krister began talking about travelling back to town.

- You must wait until autumn, was Jørgen's uncompromising reply, and Krister eventually went along with this. But each evening he busies himself with his school books.

Julie wonders how sincere he is being about this. That aside, she is frequently uneasy about the relationship between him and his father. This has become increasingly strained, particularly since Krister began high school. But now he works alongside his father without a word of protest, and she sees few signs of disagreement between them.

Otherwise Krister is unusually quiet and taciturn. In the first days after coming home he spoke openly of things he had experienced in the dramatic days of the bombing. Now he no longer mentions these and backs off when anyone approaches the subject and asks his opinion. But there wouldn't be anything strange in his reaction after those terrifying days in town, and one evening Julie arranges for the two of them to talk face-to-face in the kitchen.

- This is a chance to say what is bothering you, she says. - Is it too painful to think about?

He tries to evade the issue once again this time, but gradually he begins to open up. It was the evacuation of all the sick and elderly and of those from the midwifery unit who are giving him troubling thoughts. But maybe it was not so much what happened as what could have happened that is giving him the worst nightmares.

The health section of the civil air defence has established itself in the cellar of the Festival House, he tells her. On Sunday 28th the elderly and sick were moved in. 20-30 of the elderly were transferred to the home in Clausengate during the course of the evening. Even though a Red Cross flag was flying over the Festival House, this was hit by an incendiary bomb which struck the roof, setting fire to the building. Fire spread everywhere round about and the elderly had to be moved out from the home, many of them on stretchers. Because Krister was a member of the town's Red Cross Youth Wing, it was natural for him to volunteer to help with the rescue work. A friend of his helped with evacuating the maternity home Stella Maris, where there were several women who had recently given birth.

Later came the evacuation of the hospital, work in which Krister also helped. This was the largest and most complex of all the rescue efforts. Although the hospital was marked with a Red Cross on the roof, on the Sunday and Monday the patients were confined to the cellar and ground floor. On Monday it was decided that evacuation would take place if the bombing continued into Tuesday morning, and investigations took place into the possibility of accommodating people in the mission house in Grimstad on the Tingvall peninsula.

The bombardment continued on Tuesday morning and evacuation began straight away. The first things to be moved were equipment, medicines, food stocks, kitchen equipment, bandaging and resources for doctors and carers. Everything was moved down to a small stone pier on Sørsund. This operation became particularly trying since the last part of the journey was through difficult terrain. Boats waited by the pier manned by volunteers. Early in the evening, the first of the boats left the shore along with the first of the fifty-two patients. Half of these had to be carried on stretchers. The boats continued their shuttle traffic throughout the evening and night. Several were shot at but without anyone being injured. Krister got to hear of one of the boats which had been forced to seek shelter and transfer the patients to shore before it was able to continue after several hours.

- They didn't care much about who they were shooting at.
- But wasn't it dangerous just being there?
- Yes, came his quick reply, - But nobody thought about that. They were shooting all the time.

- Were you there day and night? You didn't rest?

- No, who could sleep through all that? There were people sleeping out in the streets, Mother, in the park, under bushes, and just on the grass in Roligheten. I saw them. Others hid themselves in caves or anywhere else they could manage to hide outside the town. Some had moved their furniture out onto the pavement and were sleeping there. The police had to move them on as this was too risky.

One memory from those days has stuck with him, he says. He was present and carried one old woman on a wheelbarrow through the burning town. She was so peaceful, so trusting, as indeed all of them were, but she just wept silently, tears streaming endlessly from her eyes.

- God bless you. You were just boys but so brave, Julie says.

- I have never seen anyone cry like that, Mother. There wasn't a sound, just so many tears. It's as if there was a whole ocean of tears and grief inside her. She's the person I remember best.

- I'm so proud of you, Krister.

- Proud? Anyone else would have done the same. And do you imagine I was brave all of the time? These were planes from hell! I was scared stiff every time we weren't taking part in the action. At other times, when we were up in the middle of it all, there wasn't the time to be scared. Mother, I don't want you talking about this to anybody. That will just sound like boasting, and that isn't my intention at all. It was what's called civic duty. Ivar was there too. He wasn't doing the same as I was, but he rescued some equipment from the bank and took part in the fire fighting. He did his bit, all of the time.

- Are you willing to live back at home this autumn?

- Yes, I can try studying on my own. Besides, it's so difficult to get to town now. You need special permission to live there if you're not on their list of citizens. There is so little room for those who were born there that it can be extra tough for those who weren't. But maybe I'll take a trip there soon.

To visit your girlfriend, Julie thinks. She would have said it out loud if circumstances had been different, but she wisely says nothing.

Julie is lying naked in bed, feeding her little girl. It is early on a Saturday evening, and there is a weekend feeling in the house. In the room where she's lying there's a smell of soap, of the newly scrubbed floor and a slight whiff of salt and the sea emanating from the crisp fresh bedding and from the summer air streaming in through the open window and moving the curtains gently aside with a light breeze. There is also the fresh smell of her newly bathed body and hair. A weekend quiet reigns in the house with the young people playing outdoors in the beautiful summer weather. The only sounds in the room are Sven's light breathing as he sleeps in his cot and the odd satisfied grunt and slap from the child at Julie's breast. Julie has dressed her in a short-sleeved vest and nappy. The child's chubby bare legs rub softly against Julie's own bare skin as her tiny hands stretch out up towards her breasts. The child is sucking in big gulps of air, and a sense of well-being surges through Julie, summed up in a feeling of excitement in her lower abdomen. She meets the child's glance, deep, unfathomable and distant, but at the same time close. She has brown eyes with a darker circle round the iris, something which causes Julie to tremble with excitement. These are her family's eyes. Julie has not herself inherited them, her own are grey with a hint of blue. But Synna, Synnøve, Helge and Krister all have what she calls this animal look, and now it has been passed on to Sunniva. She lies there, noting every expression on the tiny face. The child lets go of her breast, and a huge beaming smile suddenly lights up her face, bringing light to her dark eyes. Julie gasps. The excitement grows and grows within until it bursts out in tears which blind her. That she should have the privilege of experiencing this!

In the first weeks following the birth she hesitated to give in to the powerful feeling of happiness which arose every time she and the child came together and has arisen again in the present moment. She harboured some kind of resentment, a fear that the feeling might go away. Jørgen understood this, too, even if he never mentioned it to her.

- Just look at her; *she* will certainly get by in the world! he remarks.

It is true, and now Julie herself has to believe it. The child seems to possess an unquenchable joy in living and a will of her own. Julie can find no other way of expressing it, even though it seems strange to attribute such qualities to a child barely two months old. In the short time Julie has had her, Sunniva has become a part of the family, so that people feel as if she has always been there. These are exaggerated thoughts which Julie keeps to herself, but everything which little Sunniva does seems to confirm them. What she likes best is the child just lying in their arms when she is awake, when she shows signs of understanding what is happening round her and when she smiles with that inner confidence. Julie cannot remember any of this happening so soon with any of the other children. Sunniva is awake now for many hours in the day and does not cry any more than is normal for a little child. All the same, Julie and Jørgen must take care that they do not always give in to her so that she becomes spoiled.

She thought that problems could arise with Sven, that he would be jealous, but this has gone amazingly well. He spends a great deal of time with his little sister. Now and again, he is somewhat violent in his signs of affection, but he is only two and knows no better. Besides, there are so many people he can go to in the house if his mother is too busy with the little girl. There are his father, his grandmother, Astrid and his three big brothers, so someone is always available. The person he most resembles is Jostein. He has the same red curly hair, the same shiny blue eyes and much of the same temperament, determination and will as his elder brother, although he is not quite as headstrong as Jostein was at the same age. He is a fine little boy, well-balanced and contented.

Sunniva is sleeping at her breast. Carefully, Julie places her on the bed and dresses her in her night clothes. She pulls on a vest and trousers and puts socks on her feet, Sunniva having by now grown out of her baby clothes. Julie walks slowly backwards and forwards over the floor with the child over one shoulder, she rubs her back slowly until the expected belch following a feed emerges. She then places her in the cradle - the family cradle, which is on a stand and is covered in a light flowery fabric adorned with lace ruffles - and folds the quilt over her. Little Sunniva! It is only herself and Jørgen who have used that name up to now, and that is only when there are the two of them together. The local custom is that children's names are not to be used before they are brought to baptism. Julie dreads revealing the name to Synnøve. They have decided that the baptism will take place on the midsummer weekend, a time now fast approaching, and that Synnøve needs to be told in good time in order to avoid unpleasantness on the day itself.

The floor still retains some warmth following the afternoon sunshine. As she walks Julie feels that it is massaging her bare feet. In the evening light she stands facing the dressing table mirror and gazes at herself, at her naked body. She is still slim, her arms and legs are muscular after all her hard work, but there is no hiding that she will shortly be forty and that six births have left their trace. Her stomach will never again be as firm and flat as it once was, and those loose folds of skin left after the birth could be there for ever. These last weeks she has been out in the grounds raking up debris after the ravages and has taken the baby carriage with her. Her legs are tanned up to the knees, her arms almost up to the shoulders, as are her face and a patch down to her chest where her blouse has been open at the neck. All this is in marked contrast to the white skin elsewhere on her body, skin so white that it almost shines by itself when light in the room is dim. But if her body has grown older, in herself she feels almost younger now than she did a few years ago. That was the time she called the painful years. Then she was thin, frail, her face was drawn and her body awkward, just as awkward as she was in herself when she and Jørgen went round tormenting each other. Now her body has become soft and round, and herself more at peace. That she has become a mother again has restored something of her youth.

She leans forward towards the mirror, scrutinising her face. This is rounder even though it bears traces of her life's history. She stretches, strokes her hands over her ample breasts, over her tender stomach and along her hips and experiences the same sense of well-being as she did when feeding her child. This weekend she will be putting on a dress and make-up. She laughs at herself, for isn't she feeling just like a teenager standing here?

She spots Jørgen in the mirror, not having seen him come into the room. He is wearing his work trousers, his legs and the upper part of his body are bare, and his wet hair drips over his sun-tanned shoulders. She remains standing and staring at him, experiencing a moment of shyness that he is seeing her like this, so completely naked.

- Have you been bathing in the sea? she asks, puzzled.
- Dear God, how beautiful you are, Julie.

There is a taste of sea salt and summer from his lips and from his body as water from his hair drips down towards her neck. She hears low guttural sounds coming from him, mixing with her own like an echo from within before her laughter fills the room.

He is lying on his back, shading his eyes with his arms, as his breath comes out in long, heaving sighs.

- What do you think you're doing? she says teasingly.

Carefully, she moves his arm away from his face, supports herself with her elbow and looks down at his face, which at this moment looks as naked as a child's, so open and bewildered is his gaze. For the second time in an evening she is aware of a sensation filling her with such power, such joy and such warmth that her tears blind her.

Julie cannot remember the last time they had such a time together, and the warmth he leaves behind remains within her as a real joy. She hums as she slips into a light, flowery summer dress and tidies her hair. She had once had a perm, but only because this was what others were doing. To begin with, it was a painful and revolting experience sitting there with the hot curlers giving her blisters on the nape of her neck, and the result was a horrible mess. She thought her hair would never get back to how it was before, but now it has grown to medium length and is curled inward in a page-boy style. Usually she wears a parting and fastens it with slides at her temple. When she is dressing up, as she is this evening, she secures her hair at the front with combs in a thick curl over her forehead while the rest hangs freely. This looks so modern! She notes in the mirror that her gaze is still blurred and dark after that exchange with Jørgen.

- You look wonderful! he says, and there is laughter in his voice, laughter mixed with seriousness in her eyes when they meet hers.

There are several people in the kitchen, but she is the only one he sees, following her with his gaze from where he is seated pretending to read a newspaper. He sees her gentle bodily movements as she moves backwards and forwards with food to the table. He sees also how receptive she is, this feminine side of her which he has just encountered, and warms to the thought. He wonders whether she realises just how beautiful she is for him. It seems like a miracle when she comes across to him as she did tonight, yet this is something he will never be able to find words to tell her about.

She is the only one for him. This has always been so and always will be. He knows about other men who play around with different women, but for him this is inconceivable. Certainly he can look at a pretty girl, but more than that is never going to happen. Every time the thought occurs to him he shudders at the memory that there was one time he came close to losing her. That was the time she took the children and went back to her parents. When he learned that she had sent the children away to school he thought he had lost her for ever.

God knows that he needs moments of happiness like the one he has just experienced, something to look forward to on days when his worries seem never-ending, an interminable struggle to make ends meet. While he was growing up in Storvik their financial situation was better than that of most farmers in the district. His father was the bank manager, they owned the post office and had income from these in addition to their profits from the farm. Every time he needed something for his immediate family, he had to approach his father to beg politely for help. And himself a grown man and a father! The memory of that bitter struggle with his father still makes him shudder.

He remembers his desperation, the worst of which was his helplessness when he realised that this was destroying the relationship between himself and Julie. It was such a state of powerlessness. He wanted to be a real man for her, yet he couldn't be and felt himself tied hand and foot. He shuddered at the contempt he saw in her eyes, a contempt mixed with pain and incredulity. Then there was the degrading feeling he experienced every time he received money from his father. Money to travel home or to cover extra expenses for himself or the children. He felt at a cliff's edge.

What now keeps them going is the miraculous feeling that they have found a way back to each other and that he now dares to believe that this will last. There are moments of happiness that he believed he would never again experience.

Following the decline in the late 1920s and the first part of the 1930s the economic situation has begun to look brighter both

here at home and in the wider world. It has settled back slowly.
Unemployment has declined and conditions have improved.

Locally, people have been feeling that times are getting
better. Although the pulp mill was closed down immediately
after the outbreak of the war, there is talk of another business
taking over, and those who worked there have been allotted what
is described as emergency work on the roads and in the woods.
In 1938, the local authority restored the sawmill in Øra which
had been closed down for many years. This will give jobs to
almost twenty men. The Labour Party has been in power in the
local authority since the early 1930s, to the advantage of
working people in Øra. And although many would be hesitant to
admit it, a Labour government under Nygaardsvold has done a
good job in the country as a whole. However, at the present time,
the government must tolerate heavy criticism over its
disarmament policy, 'arming to rebuild the country, not for
military might'. One of those gloating over that policy is
Hallgrim Ås.

- Now they can see where what they have done has led, he
sneers, and begins in a small way to play the role of a petty
monarch. The king and government have run away with their tail
between their legs and are sitting safely in London and leaving
everyone to their own devices. Is that what they believe in? he
says scornfully. What cowardice!

There are a few who dare contradict him, but they are
unsure just what to make of him as he goes about laughing like
one who bears of some dark secret.

One day, Jørgen met him at the shop. He asked how Ivar
was.

- If he comes home, ask him to drop in and see me. - You too, Jørgen. It's a long time since I've seen you on the farm. Maybe there's something we could talk about, he said laughing.

Jørgen stood there looking at him as he went. He was embarrassed at being so taken aback that he hadn't managed to find a stinging reply. No, never! Never again would he set foot in Hallgrim's house. And if Hallgrim goes round imagining that he can get me to change my mind, then he has miscalculated. But then that's just the same as Ivar thinks.

He will never understand Hallgrim. Physically he is short and slippery as an eel. It is odd that there can be so much authority in so small a man. That authoritative voice, that gaze, those facial expressions and the way he uses words to spellbind people; and even though Jørgen is a foot taller than Hallgrim, he often feels he is the lesser of the two. When he thinks back to his youth he remembers that, even then, Hallgrim was always the strongest, the one who succeeded in most of the things he did. But this time Hallgrim must not push his luck. He will understand that Jørgen, too, can be strong when called upon. But Jørgen was left with an uneasy feeling that the last word had not yet passed between them.

Now is my opportunity, Julie thinks as she sees Synnøve leaning over the cradle, gazing enraptured at the child.

- Isn't she lovely?
- Oh yes. She doesn't look much like us, but she is still beautiful. She is just as she should be, and so quiet, Synnøve smiles.
- We'd thought about asking you to carry her to baptism.

Oh no, that's a silly idea, although she cannot conceal her happiness. - I'm getting too old for that, and besides, I was the one to carry Krister and Sven. I don't suppose you'd thought of asking your own mother?

- Mother took Helge because she was asked to.
- And I took Sven because I believe I was asked to.
- Yes, but then I didn't know I was going to have a girl.
- What have you thought of calling the girl?
- Sunniva.
- What was that? queries Synnøve. What sort of name is that?
- Actually it's the same name as yours, just an older form.
- Oh, so Synnøve isn't good enough! I didn't think my name was anything to be ashamed of, says Synnøve, her voice trembling with indignation.
- That's not how it is, says Julie and tells her about the child's sister, that she cannot bear her child having the same name as her own stillborn daughter.
- I just don't understand you, Julie. Wouldn't it be an honour for a daughter to carry her name forward? And haven't you been calling *me* Synnøve all these years? No, you can't make me believe that this is anything other than a mean trick. And don't you think about the child who will be forced to carry a name that nobody else has round here?
- There are lots of Norwegian women called Sunniva. It's even a saint's name - St. Sunniva, have you heard of her? It's your name, Synnøve, just another way of spelling it.
- I hope you will change your mind. Otherwise, people will talk, you mark my words, Julie!
- You haven't answered my question. Will you carry her to baptism?

- I cannot answer that, Julie. There is so much involved. But I can at least say this, that you mustn't take it for granted that I'm going to say yes.

Synnøve turns round at the door, resentment still burning in her eyes.

- If my name isn't good enough, you could always find another one for the child. That would be a way of avoiding all this shame.

Sometime later, Astrid comes in from the cottage.

- Now you've really upset Mother, Julie, but it will blow over when she's had time to think.
- I hope so, because she's not going to force me into changing anything.
- No, of course not, says Astrid and leans over the cradle. - Ah, so you're called Sunniva? Such a lovely name, a saint's name. Then we'll see if you will be a saint and live up to your name.

At this point, the child gives her a smile.

- Oh, you should have seen that, Astrid says, moved.

Julie has received a beautiful letter of congratulation from Randi. She sat down on an impulse to write a reply in which she asked if Randi and Yngvar would be prepared to act as godparents for her daughter. Randi's answer came quite quickly. She thanked Julie for the honour and for her trust in her, but as things are, they do not think they can afford to make the journey. Julie can understand that, but hopes the refusal does not have other grounds. She does not want to entertain that thought, not when it concerns Randi.

Finding godparents for the child now that there have been so many baptisms is not going to be easy. Among the neighbours there is no one she wants to ask, nor will she ask her own parents. Children's godparents have to be young. Then the thought strikes her of inviting Helene and Ivar. That will allow Krister to stand next to Synnøve unless she becomes difficult, and if she does, there's always Astrid they can fall back on.

Her decision to ask Ivar and Helene infuriates Jørgen. She had not expected such a strong reaction, but neither has she thought to give way, and she just lets him rage on.

- You can't think I'll go along with what you're proposing. I can't accept that a man like that can be godfather to my daughter.

- It's your brother you're talking about.

- My brother! he sneers. I would much rather he stayed away from the baptism altogether.

- No, Jørgen, now you are losing your wits.

- It's somebody else who should be using his wits. Here I'm doing everything I can to get people to understand that I disagree with everything Ivar gets mixed up in, and now you expect me to invite him to church as godfather for my youngster? Don't you see where your stubbornness is going to lead?

- Yes, that's exactly what I see. You can never run away from the fact that he's your own brother. Nor should you forget all that he's done for us and our children. You complain often enough that you can never repay him. Well, now you have an opportunity to repay a little of that debt. Not only that, you can also show people round about that you are not distancing yourself from your brother. That you disagree with everything he stands for is another matter altogether. You can demonstrate that by what you do, not by pretending that he doesn't exist. Do you think you will be any better off by denying that he's your brother? Have you seen anyone benefit from gloating over others? No, Jørgen, that sort of thing just diminishes a man, believe me.

- He's behaving like a fool and an idiot, that's what he's doing.

- You can't accuse your brother of being a fool. A dreamer and a fanatic, yes, but he's a good human being who has never done us any harm. And you can hardly deny that he's intelligent.

- I take it, Julie, that you understand that intelligence and wisdom are two very different things. You can be as intelligent as you like but still be a complete fool. And that's what Ivar is.

- Jørgen, listen to me. Ivar has done nothing wrong. He's not a criminal. The only thing is that he is a member of a party that both of us have distanced ourselves from. We cannot judge him for that, that is something for others to do. Besides, what we are talking about now is a child's baptism, a church service. I can't have you bringing politics into that. You should consider, too, that this will be a way of making your mother very happy, of giving her satisfaction, and satisfaction is something we all need. The cost to us is no more than that we live with it.

This last argument has knocked the wind out of Jørgen's sails. Julie can see from his back as he walks out that she has won. Dear God, she thinks he's such a stick-in-the-mud, and there's such stubbornness here in the house every time a child is given a name and brought to baptism, but she feels sure she has done the right thing in insisting that Ivar and Helene should be godparents. She even thinks that the day may come when Jørgen will thank her for this. She knows that deep down, Jørgen is fond of his brother, more than he is prepared to admit either to himself or to her. Julie is convinced that no one can show such furious anger towards another person without having a genuine love for that person. Jørgen has accused her of not using her wits. But she does, and she must do so on those occasions when he neither will nor can. And she knows one person who will come to be very thankful for all this, namely his mother, even though she is still going round obsessing over the name the child is going to have, and even if she has not said yes to being a godmother. Julie knows that Ivar and Helene will be happy. She knows, too, that they need a handshake just at this time. However things may be, they are certainly in need of that.

Julie is standing watching her mother unpacking her suitcase and placing her clothes neatly onto hangers on the wall.

- I'm so pleased that you've been able to come, Julie says, especially now when times are difficult and when you are so afraid of travelling.
- Afraid?

Indeed, had she not written that she was afraid of sea mines and all the things that could happen in the course of a long journey?

- No, I must have forgotten to be afraid. I could hardly be afraid when I saw all those who had lost everything. Molde and Kristiansund were such a terrible sight, Julie. The whole journey was difficult, but we can talk about that later.
- What is that you've got there? Julie says, pointing to a garment her mother has placed back onto her suitcase. - Isn't that your wedding nightdress? And father's nightshirt?

Her mother strokes these delicate garments, the nightdress with its rustling English lace, and her father's nightshirt which she had made for their wedding. Neither garment has been worn since. They have been wrapped in tissue paper with naphthaline balls as a protection against moths. She used to take them out from time to time as a treat to show to her children.

- But what are you doing with them now? Are you afraid that someone's going to steal them while you're away?

- I now take them with me every time I travel. If anything should happen, we'll be laid in our coffins wearing these.

- Whatever are you saying? Julie is speechless and then bursts into laughter. - Now, Mother, give up! You are not yet seventy, and you're as fit as a flea. And Father, he is healthy too. You're not going to say that your life's journey is over now that you've come to a baptism. I just can't accept that.

- You can joke, Julie, but no one knows when their time has come. Maybe you haven't heard that they've now started burying people in paper coffins because of the rationing. - Can you imagine me lying there in a miserable paper nightshirt? Shame on you!

- No, Mother, that's not you! But it's still not nice hearing you talk like this.

- What's not nice about it? Don't we all come to the same end? The only certainties we have are that we are born and that we die. What happens in between is our own responsibility.

- No, this is all getting too serious, Julie shudders. But it doesn't surprise her. She has come to expect many surprises coming from her mother, though this one is going too far. - Now we must eat. Dinner is ready.

- We must try to have a chat this evening, just the two of us, Julie, there's something I need to tell you about.

- Nothing terrible? says Julie nervously.

- No, not a matter of life and death, but it's important all the same.

While Julie is carrying the dinner plates out of the living room following dinner, she sees her mother and Synnøve leaning over the cradle. She cannot avoid hearing what they are talking about.

- What a lovely little girl, says her mother.
- Yes, says Synnøve, and I've been given the honour of carrying her to baptism. I suppose you know that she's to be named after me?
- No, really? That's quite an honour!

Julie feels herself heating up. What's this Synnøve is saying?

- But I thought …. says her mother.

That she was to be called Sunniva? Yes, but this is my name, only spelt the old-fashioned way, as they did in the olden days.

Julie meets her mother's gaze. Synnøve must have told her about the conflict round the name. Relief now sweeps over her, and Synnøve is now so proud that the light shines out of her.

- They say it's a saint's name, says Synnøve.
- Yes, that's right, St. Sunniva. This is going to be a big day for you, Synnøve.
- Yes, it is, says Synnøve as she stands up and meets Julie's gaze. A quick smile flits across the old woman's face.

At this moment, Julie feels that the two of them are alone in the room bearing equal burdens on their shoulders. Both are proud, and neither of them will give way without a fight, but when a conflict arises at least they respect each other. And now Julie experiences a rare feeling of closeness towards her mother-in-law. In spite of all the disagreements there have been between them, there is a sense of belonging, of confidence, and a sense of being a relative, which has built up slowly over the years she has lived here. This is where Synnøve belongs, and now there is room for both of them.

After the household has settled down, Julie and her mother are sitting at the kitchen table. On the table stands a jar filled with an orchid diffusing a heavy, relaxing odour into this room bathed in summer light. She reflects on how often she has sat like this on a late evening by the kitchen table when there has been something important to talk about. This is how it is with Randi, and it is now how it is with her mother. There is a sense of security in all this, the feeling that this is the realm, in some way the women's domain, a place for confidence but also for disagreement. She sits thinking about the huge number of things which have been decided and debated across the kitchen table.

- Come on, Mother, tell me about it.

Very well, her mother says. When she said she was so upset that she forgot to worry, this was because they had an unexpected travelling companion that day. The day before they were due to leave, Inge suddenly appeared at their door.

- Inge? But why was that so strange?
- He said he was on a journey and would grab the opportunity to visit them and at the same time attend to their grandparents' grave.

- So Johanne wasn't there?
- No, poor Johanne… Maybe you don't know that Inge has received a new post, a call to move to Bergen?

No, this is news for Julie. She received a letter from Johanne after the little girl's birth, but she did not mention this.

- It came up quite recently, her mother says. And unless she tells her, she feels that Julie will have no more insight into Johanne than they do. - I feel we have lost Johanne. At least, that's what I think. Even though she has managed to keep the mask in place, she's now nothing but a bag of nerves. Not an hour passes without my becoming worried about her. And it will probably become worse now that Inge has joined the Party.

- Never! Surely, that can't be true!

Yes, it is, and she and Johannes have known about it for a long time. They visited Johanne and Inge a couple of years ago. Even then, Inge was talking with a burning enthusiasm of Hitler's and Quisling's ideas. He was probably a party member even at that stage. And now it has become worse than ever. Johannes has tried to talk sense into him, urging him to pull back before it was too late, but it was all water off a duck's back. He just sat there smiling during all her arguments. It was all very unpleasant. He said that Johannes needed to understand what the war is all about. That it's a necessary war. Yes, it may have been unfortunate for a few innocent victims, but that's just the nature of war. And here in Norway and several other countries a great deal of violence could have been avoided if people had only been willing to accept help from Germany. As things are, Germany is Europe's only hope.

- He really said that! Then he's ten times worse than Ivar.
- Oh yes, Ivar. You, too, have the same sort of nonsense to put up with here.
- But it's impatience in Ivar's case. He's such an enthusiast.
- Well, maybe he is, but he should still have had the good sense to leave the party. That's certainly not going to happen with Inge. He was going to Trondheim and Stikklestad for the midsummer festival along with other supporters.

- With other clergy?

- Yes, that, too. He said that the German church stood together with Hitler in the war and that the Norwegian church would soon come to see that this is the right path,

- Has he lost all sense of reason?

- He said that *Gott mit uns,* God is with us, is written on the buckle of the German soldiers' bandoliers. This is what caused Johannes finally to lose his temper. He forbade him to appear in the house after that. And in the area where we live, Inge would have no reason to appear now that he has no longer has family to visit. Johanne will always be welcome, but not Inge unless he changes his mind.

- What did he say to that?

- He said Johanne doesn't go anywhere without me, and then he smiled. He smiled, Julie, but you should have seen his eyes.

Julie shudders, she can see for herself the arrogant smile, that steely, ice-cold look in his eyes when anything stands in his way.

The next day and during the journey Inge did not mention what had been said but behaved with a studied politeness towards them. They spent the night in Molde with his aunt. Their house had been spared when their fishing business had been burnt down. His uncle has already set up a stall on the pier, from which he's trying to run his business. Fortunately, Inge had nowhere else to stay and had the good sense to avoid talking about the war. In that way he managed to avoid being on tenterhooks about giving himself away, as he did on the rest of the journey.

- I can't bear people finding out about this, Julie. That would be too heavy a burden for both your father and me to bear. I pray to God each day for this to come to an end, that it will end before there's a terrible catastrophe, that there will be an end for all those who've lost everything and suffered, and an end before the shame of it all destroys us.

She was in pieces throughout the journey, her mother says, so afraid to meet people they knew and that Inge would try to provoke discussions with them. She was afraid that he might meet allies and give them away, afraid too when she realised that the Germans on board were unaware of the danger from mines. She did not feel safe until she felt firm ground under her feet on the quayside here. In Kristiansund they had to simply accept the accommodation he found for them. They lodged with a family. She slept on a sofa in the living room and her father on a camp bed. They were friendly people, but she was so flustered that she cannot now remember their names.

- But after I had seen what they had done to Molde, and when I stood next to Inge and saw what was left of Kristiansund, I couldn't hold back any more. What you're looking at now, Inge, do you believe God approves of this?
- And what did he say?
- Say? He pretended that he hadn't heard. But do you know what feels worst in all this, Julie? That it's my fault, that I pushed Johanne into it. I saw it all from the beginning and I closed my eyes to it.
- But they loved each other, Mother, it can't be your fault!
- Johanne, yes, poor girl. But Inge? No, I was so proud that she was going to marry a priest that I didn't want to believe what I was seeing. How he was when you and he had a crush on each

other, that same smile, that same expression, I know more than you think, Julie.

All of a sudden, Julie feels warm and blushes. It cannot be possible that her mother knows what happened that evening when Inge accosted her in their own kitchen. She was alone at home and only just managed to escape him violating her. The scene now flashes vividly before her eyes. She is lying on the floor with her head half under a chair; his hands whip away her clothing; his hard hands explore her body, next there is his distorted face on top of her. Words come, and it was these that saved her: We can't do this here on the floor! It was these words that enabled him to pull himself together. She had broken up with him before this happened, and he knew that her parents and the rest of the family were away on a Christmas visit to Molde just after Synna died. Inge said he had come to show her compassion, and she let him in. Afterwards she cleared away every trace they'd left behind, washed and repaired the clothes he had torn to pieces in order to ensure that her parents would never find out. Was it surprising, then, that she was shocked when she found out that Johanne and Inge had become engaged? At the time she thought it was right that her parents should never find out, and that if they did they might kill her. Inge showed no sign of remorse, no trace of guilt over what he had done. Later, seeing Johanne's unhappiness, the thought occurred to Julie that if she had said something at the time, then the two of them would not have married. At other times she comforts herself with the thought that it would not have made any difference no matter what she had said. It would have been her word against Inge's, and she has no doubt which of them Johanne would have believed. And in that case she would have lost her sister for good. She feels most uncomfortable when the thought occurs to her that Inge took Johanne in revenge for not being able to have her. This is a thought she hardly dare entertain, for surely nobody can be so evil. Least of all priests.

- What was it you saw, Mother?

- I saw all sorts of things. I saw your eyes when I knew you'd been out with him. You were very young then, and I could see that you were sometimes very unhappy. And even if you looked happy, that was not quite in the way it should be; it's almost is if you were drunk and it was wearing you out. Then I remember the engagement party for Johanne and Inge. I remember his eyes and recall thinking that here was a man who could never make another person happy. But I suppressed the thought and even supported the disaster that my daughter was bringing on herself. That was pride, Julie, pride because I thought it showed that I had been right. Today I can admit I was arrogant, and it was an arrogance with a heavy price. Now here you are, you poor thing, dragged down into poverty. Now I see in this house ….

- No, Mother, we won't talk about that now, says Julie quickly. - That's nothing compared with all the other matters. And Jørgen and I are getting on just about as well as anyone can, let me reassure you about that.

Her mother opens her handbag and hands her a hundred kroner banknote.

- Father wants you to have this. You must have had some extra expenses now, what with the baptism and everything.

- I can only say thank you, Mother, even though I would rather not take your money any more. I have received so much from you.

- Don't even think about it. Your father and I try to help you as much as we can. There's not much more we can do. If everything depended on money….

Her mother begs her not to mention to anyone what she has just been told. She may talk to Jørgen, but only after they have left. And they agree that at the baptism they will try to avoid as far as possible any controversial talk about the war.

- Won't Ivar discuss it? Mother wonders.
- No. He never brings it up now.

That night, Julie cannot sleep. Thoughts swirl around in her head, mostly about Johanne. Memories from their childhood arise. She sees Johanne as she was then and later as an adolescent. Chubby and kind, wild and playful, with a temperament which now and then could be scary. She was spoilt, too, by her parents. But what about now, after her marriage to Inge? Now she is cowed and afraid, thin, as if encased in a membrane which could burst open at any time. Julie remembers a time she was at home with the boys when they were young, when, in desperation, Johanne lifted the veil a little and confided in her. This afforded her an insight into Johanne's life which she has never been able to forget. Johanne said she had never been able to live up to Inge's expectations. She was not humble enough and could not succeed in being the good Christian that Inge was. She said she had been unable to have any more children after the first, and that Inge reproached her for this, saying that it was her fault, her *sin*, whenever they slept together. She managed to say all this as Julie listened in shock and disbelief, but then Inge came in and interrupted the conversation. The worst thing was that she was actually apologising for Inge, saying that he was right. It was this which disturbed Julie more than anything else, seeing her sister as a weak-willed and fearful being reproaching herself for Inge's violence. What had become of that strong and vigorous sister she wondered, and still does.

The last time she had been together with her sister and her family was three years ago when she was home on a brief visit. Johanne was then a shadow of her former self. She walked round with a perpetual smile, polite and distant, avoiding all contact. Thin and tense, with her hair in an old-fashioned bun and dressed in good quality though modest clothing, she looked ten years older than Julie even though she was three years younger. She was unapproachable, like someone shrouded in a fog. As for her three children, Julie could have bled for them, shy and cowed as they were, and every bit as colourless as their mother. What is life going to be like for them, now that Inge has a new parish in Bergen? How will Johanne and the children cope with the move after having lived in a country parish in Hardanger ever since they were married? The worst of all is that Johanne will be coming there as the wife of a Nazi priest. Will she have to set up a Sunday school for Nazi children? The only outlet for her expensive education has been as a Sunday school teacher. She had received an education which Julie would love to have had, and for which she envied Johanne. Her mother said that neither Oddmund nor Kristian, both of whom have been to Business College and have good jobs in Bergen, are going to be very enthusiastic about having their sister and niece living so close. Julie can well understand that when she thinks about Jørgen's relations with Ivar. He is quite close enough living in Kristiansund, and she cannot think how it would be to have him living here. But even leaving that aside, there is no point in comparing Ivar with Inge. Ivar is well- disposed and hardly likely to harm anyone. But if Inge shows the same fanaticism in politics as he does in his church ministry and in his view of Christianity, then he can be very dangerous indeed.

Sunniva was born on 18 May and baptised on 28 July, the day before the midsummer festival. Both these days in her life so far are linked to public celebrations and will therefore not be easy to forget. This persuaded Selma to be a godparent, and so Sunniva now has five godparents altogether. This is unusual but it felt right that Selma should be given this honour after all she has done for them.

Sunniva was the last of the children to be carried to the font. There were three boys to be baptised along with her, and she had to wait until last because boys come first. Such is the custom. She, who cries so little, screamed so loudly as they stood there waiting their turn that she threatened to drown both the organ and the priest. The three female godparents all took turns in trying to pacify her. Synnøve blushed red at all the commotion, but during the actual baptism Sunniva became quiet and her baptism became the solemn ceremony it was meant to be.

Julie sat fighting back her tears. This was how it affected her in church. It became a symbol that the family has now come together. She sees that Ivar is moved; he has a seriousness about him, and there is Krister, looking so grown up in the confirmation suit he has grown out of, but which he must put up with having to wear for as long as possible.

The church is full. Maybe this is because it's a special occasion, though people who rarely go to church have begun going again recently. Today, it will have been noticed that Ivar and Helene were acting as godparents for the people of Storvik. Julie feels it is right that people can see this. She feels certain that Jørgen will not be a lesser man in people's eyes after allowing it.

It has been a fine day without any kind of hitch, though it is true that at the dinner table there was a certain tension before everything relaxed and conversation turned to everyday things. There was talk about the former priest whom they are missing today. Throughout all the years he had been a family friend and an obvious guest to invite on such occasions. He retired a couple of years ago, with Sven being one of the last children he baptised. The new priest is young, having had just one curacy before coming here. He is a product of the conservative Church Faculty, which has aroused some people's suspicions. He is certainly more scrupulous than the former priest. The old priest would enjoy a drink and a cigar on festive occasions and always carried a pipe. This was smething that went down well with people here where the pietistic mission-house style has never been popular. Here people support their church and value an easy-going and liberal priest.

- He'll be ok, you'll see, says Jørgen. He's not afraid to say what he thinks, either in company or from the pulpit.

After this observation there is a momentary silence, for all those sitting here know that this priest says exactly what he thinks about the German invaders, both in private and in public. This is maybe one of the reasons Jørgen has not invited him along today. The custom has always been to invite the priest on these occasions, but Jørgen was probably afraid of a confrontation between him and Ivar.

- There is an expression, 'for better and for worse', Jørgen, Julie says after they have retired to bed that night. - That doesn't just apply to relations between married people, but also to those between relatives, don't you think?

Chapter 5

The future now looks bleaker than ever. In the summer of 1940 people came to understand that the Germans' announcements through the radio, newspapers and posters were not to be taken lightly or ignored. During the battles in April some Norwegians had been executed summarily, without trial or justice. And now the brief bulletin announcing that the first official death sentence of a civilian had been pronounced in Trondheim was available to be read. The notification stated that the Norwegian had shot a German soldier because he had 'spoken contemptuously of Norway and Norwegians'. It was then that people realised that all this was serious, that the Germans meant what they said in their proclamation: 'People doing .... will be shot'. They no longer joked about this: capital punishment was back in Norway and could happen to anyone. People felt under pressure now that a seed of public anxiety had been sown. They understood, too, that it was not only the Germans they had to fear but equally - or even more - their Norwegian accomplices, quislings as they were called. Suspicion took over people's minds. Who among their neighbours, friends or family could they trust? People began to think twice before they opened their mouths about things happening both outside and in the home.

On the radio from London it was announced that King Haakon was about to make a speech to the Norwegian people. Both town and country were empty of people during the broadcast. People sat glued to their radios and were shocked to hear the king announce that he had received a letter from the presidency in Storting. In this letter was laid out an agreement they had reached with the German occupying authority. It was clear that this was a recommendation, or more properly a request, for the king to abdicate, 'for him and his house to renounce their constitutional functions'.

Firm as a rock, the king said no to this. This was because, as he put it, it was an exercise of German power and not a free decision of the Norwegian people. He and his government had received Storting's full backing. The Nygaardsvold Labour government had now been supplemented by members of other parties and could therefore be called a government of national unity. He went on to explain that a Storting, which had been deprived of any freedom to negotiate, had no power to dismiss either the king or the government.

There was total quiet in people's homes as the King rounded off his address with these words:

'I cannot see that I would be acting at all in the country's interest if I were to give way to the recommendation passed on to me by the presidency. To do so would be to recognise a form of government which conflicts with the Norwegian constitution and which interests of power are attempting to force on the Norwegian people.

I would thereby be departing from the principle which throughout my reign has guided my actions, namely, to abide strictly by the framework of the constitution.

The Norwegian people's freedom and independence are, for me, the first requirements of the Constitution, and I intend to follow this requirement and protect the Norwegian people's best interests by holding fast to the position and mandate which a free people bestowed on me in 1905'.

The King's firm no to the occupation's forces ignited the first sparks of resistance among people. They had a king who stood up straight when the storm was at its height. Once again, he became a symbol of the future and a free Norway.

During the summer, Terboven negotiated with Storting's presidency to set up a Norwegian government, but with the condition that National Socialism must be included. The presidency negotiated, but without Storting's president, Carl J. Hambro, being present. He had followed the government in its flight to London, and on the radio gave constant warnings against cooperation with the occupying power. Thus the drama leaked gradually out to people.

Following the King's firm No on 8 July, and after the speech and the president's letter to the king had been distributed illegally over the country, negotiations broke down, but they were resumed in September, and this time, the Germans' suggestions were rejected. The president had noted the mood of the Norwegian people, and they weren't going to be cheated again. They could not support a solution which conflicted with the Constitution. Storting had said no.

With this came the end of Terboven's attempt to give the transfer of power any semblance of legality. On the evening of 25 September, he gave a radio talk to the Norwegian nation. Terboven's talk was delivered, naturally enough, in German, and although most people did not understand what he was saying, they still listened intently. Maybe some people were able to understand German, but most had to wait for the speech to be translated and published in the newspapers.

Unlike Hitler, Terboven had a pleasant, cultivated and carefully modulated voice. His speech was given with a quiet authority, which in other contexts might have conveyed a sense of security, but it was not without intensity and a certain appeal, so even those who understood nothing of what was being said gathered that it was not good news that Terboven was bringing to their communities that evening. The speech was a mixture of truth and lies in which he said he would inform the Norwegian people of what had happened in their country since the English had left Norway, exposing the Norwegian army to capitulation and forcing the German armed forces to take the country under their protection.

He lamented that the king and government had moved to London, 'which at the time seemed certain'. He said that the administrative council had approached *him* with a request that he help set up a new political system in the country. Then the Storting presidency came along with a request for negotiations to replace the king and government with a council which would carry out the king's, the government's and Storting's constitutional functions.

People were aware that all these claims were false. The unfortunate truth in the speech was that Storting's presidency, the old party leaders and a majority of Storting's representatives had agreed to the recommendation to dismiss the king and the government. The presidency's famous letter to the king had then been printed illegally and distributed among the people, and its contents could not be explained away. That Storting's representatives had agreed to this was for entirely selfish reasons, Terboven claimed. Now, the Norwegian people would realise what sort of politicians they had elected to govern their country. These had given their assent only on condition that they maintain their mandate, but this request was meaningless when Storting had already relinquished all power. They did this in

order to 'save what was obviously most important for them -
namely their material existence. One can only say: this is a
political assembly corrupt to the hilt, both with respect to
individual personalities and to the assembly as a whole'. 'But',
he added, 'since the Norwegians tried one trick after another, he
had been forced to break off negotiations'. The truth is that the
presidency has finally said no.

His best plan, Terboven said, would have been to refuse
when the Norwegians approached him with a plea for help and a
request for negotiation. He should have referred this to the
National Assembly because this recognised the importance of
cooperation with their German brothers. As it was, he said, the
Norwegian parties had dragged the Norwegian people into an
economic and spiritual dependence on British plutocracy.

He now declared that the old political parties had been
dissolved. From now on only the National Assembly under
Quisling's leadership would be permitted as a political party in
Norway. He was, he said, still willing to work together, but 'one
thing the Norwegian people must finally be clear about: for a
Norwegian resolution of the present situation, i.e. for a solution
aimed at winning back a far-reaching freedom, there is only one
way. It will now be the Norwegian people's internal business to
decide.

On the same day, Terboven set up the commissariat, or
active ministry, as it was called. This ministry consisted of
thirteen men, nine of whom were members of the National
Socialist Party and one who joined later. The Ministry for
Foreign Affairs and the Ministry of Defence were both stood
down since there was no need for either in an occupied Norway.
Officially, Quisling was not a member of the new ministry, but

he had meetings with its NS members every Friday in their building on Victoria Terrace, although this gave him no special powers. Quisling's power arose from his definition as leader of the National Assembly, but in reality the ministers ran their departments at Terboven's behest.

Terboven's speech, all his diatribes against king and country, his scornful jeering at elected politicians and treatment of them as traitors, his blatant lies about Norwegians coming to him and agreeing to negotiate and his appeal to a national Norwegian spirit; all these could have had more dangerous consequences than they did because people were informed of the truth via information coming in from London. Terboven's speeches now had the opposite effect from that intended and generated a great deal of hostility. The effect of what he said was what mattered. This was that all genuine political activity in Norway was being suppressed by force, that the person governing Norway was a German with the name of Josef Terboven and that he was doing this through a puppet government of NS supporters.

In a way this was a relief because people now realised what it was they had to deal with. The pieces of the jigsaw were now coming together. Power ended with Terboven, the commissariat, the National Socialists and Quisling. The king and Norway's constitutional government were in London, and the representatives' hope was that one day Norway would again become free and self-governing. Until this came about, it was up to every single Norwegian to decide where they stood in relation to this new administration, but there were very few who believed that Quisling's call for 'freedom through the NS' was going to win support from the average Norwegian.

Gradually, as attempts were made to put into effect Terboven's plans, both those possible and those impossible, people came to feel in their hearts what the change of power was going to mean for them.

One of these plans, which was to come into effect immediately, was for the surrender of weapons. Jørgen was not the only person who cursed when the message came through that all weapons must be handed in at the merchant's building on the pier. He owned a shotgun used to hunt grouse and other small game and a Krag-Jørgensen which he had used when hunting deer. This had given him some hard-earned kroner with which to ease his economic situation. He was furious that this was now going to be confiscated. If he was going to continue hunting game, he must now change his method to the time-consuming business of setting snares. In the corridor outside their drawing room hung two guns, muskets with shiny sabres. These were treasures which had hung on the wall for as long as he could remember, museum pieces which could not be used for anything whatever. He now took them off the wall.

- Complete nonsense, said Julie. Who can understand the Germans bothering to collect old scrap metal which is of no use to anyone but us?
- Yes, but with people like that you can expect anything.

There followed a great deal of discussion round the guns as to where they should be hidden. In the end, Jørgen decided that Jostein and Helge would take them up to his summer farm. The boys took this as seriously as if they were going to war. One evening, they set out with the guns and bayonets packed safely away in cardboard. If they met anyone, they would say that they were spending the night up there and would be rounding up sheep the following morning. Julie thought that this was a risky mission to give to the boys. If they should happen to meet someone of a certain way of thinking who found out what they were doing, the consequences could be a great deal worse than having a couple of old guns hanging on the wall as decoration.

Towards the end of the following day the boys came back home. Of course they had spent the night up there, and had pretended that their purpose was to round up sheep. They spoke excitedly across each other as they described their experiences. Yes, they had met people, and these weren't just any old people but Hallgrim Ås's two eldest sons. These two are grown up now, approaching twenty, and are among those that people have learned to beware of. For a long time, they have gone round swaggering and boasting about Quisling's activities. There may be an element of youthful exuberance in all this, but these two are more like their mother than their father. They say that Gunnhild Ås is overbearing while Hallgrim is more placid. He knows the area well and how to behave.

It was these two that the boys had met up there in the evening light. However, they were well prepared and had their strategy ready. Helge was in front with their food pack and was to warn Jostein, who was following a good way behind with the crucial goods. If he met anyone, he was to pretend that Jostein had stopped for a breather and would shout to him to hurry up. But he nevertheless received a shock when he realised who it was he had met.

Are you ready yet? he shouted back as soon as he saw them. The whole episode came as such a shock, and his heart was pounding so loudly that he thought these two might be able to hear it. He was very thankful that the darkness hid his face, for otherwise he would probably have given himself away, so taken aback had he been when they showed up out of the darkness. But Jostein had the time he needed to bury the guns by the side of the road.

The Ås boys wanted to know what they were up to so late in the evening. Jostein and Helge said that they were looking for an ewe and two lambs which had gone missing. They would stay overnight at their farm in order to have the following day free to carry out a search. The Ås boys said this had also been their concern, that they too had been looking for a couple of animals which had gone missing, but that there was no trace of them anywhere on the hillside. This being so, Jostein and Helge might just as well turn round and go back with them to the village. Apart from that, they assumed that all was well at Storvik.

Satan! said Jørgen, - how did you answer that?

Hallgrim is a member of the Ministry of Supply, and Jørgen knows that he is kept up to date on the number of animals roaming free and of those housed on farms. Jørgen himself had stupidly said to Hallgrim that he had been to Ås and had picked up a couple of his own animals which had somehow gone there along with Hallgrim's flock. These were the last of his own flock, and he had now accounted for all of them apart from two lambs taken by a fox when the flock had been put out to graze. Jørgen had found both their remains when he was looking for his flock. He had almost certainly told Hallgrim about this, as it has always been normal among farmers to talk about such matters. But, such has the world become, nothing is normal now.

- You didn't meet anyone else? Jørgen asked.

No, but they had waited a long time before daring to go back and look for the guns. These are now stored safely, hidden between wooden planks and rubbish up at the summer farm. Today they say they have been searching up there for animals which they know perfectly well are here. They say this as if they are boasting of some great deed.

A couple of days after this a police officer appears on the farm accompanied by Hallgrim. These move from house to house, taking an inventory of all weapons stored on the farm. The police officer, who only has a year or two left before reaching retirement age, has always been a respected man in the district. Everyone knows that he distances himself from NS and has been a close friend of people in Storvik. He gives the impression of not being entirely happy with the task he has been given. He keeps quiet, allowing Hallgrim to do all the talking, which Hallgrim does with his usual self-confident authority.

Rumours had been circulating in advance of the visit, so Jørgen was quite prepared when the two of them arrived. Both guns lay on the kitchen table, ready for the inspection.

Are these all you have in the house, Jørgen? Hallgrim asks. I thought you at Storvik were better supplied with hunting weapons.

- If you are accusing me of playing tricks and lying, you are quite free to search all the buildings, says Jørgen, his anger boiling up inside him. I take it, Hallgrim, that your right to search is backed up by the highest authority.

- I'm just doing my duty and seeing that everything is done properly. And I thought you had more weapons here in the house.

- It sounds as if you know more about what I have here than I do. Yes, my father left behind him a shotgun and a gun for hunting. But Ivar has taken these. You can ring him if you don't believe me. No doubt the two of you have plenty to talk about these days.

Hallgrim laughs, but Jørgen catches a warning glance from the policeman.

- Just to make sure everything is correct, let us go over to Synnøve's so that she can confirm everything you've said and then get it all down on paper.

Burning with humiliation and anger, Jørgen leads them over to his mother's house. As they are standing outside and are about to leave, Hallgrim points to the wall and laughs.

You can just hang up your decorations again, Jørgen, he chuckles. - You know, that useless scrap metal. But what if it hasn't ended up with Ivar?

Jørgen stands there, speechless, feeling like a child caught red-handed. He manages to pull himself together and then shouts after Hallgrim.

- It's hardly dangerous for you to come here, Hallgrim. I'm sure your overlords have seen to it that you can hang onto your weapons.

At this, Hallgrim turns, comes towards him, and confronts him closely eye-to-eye.

- Now, Jørgen, stop behaving like a fool.

The threat in Hallgrim's voice is no longer hidden, nor is the warning in the policeman's eye. Jørgen curses as they move away. Satan! People are now going round terrified of their neighbours.

On the day the weapons are to be handed in at the shop, the men in the district assemble. The police officer and Hallgrim check the lists and cross off names to ensure that the weapons handed in correspond to the inventory that has been submitted. As Ås's two eldest sons help pack the weapons away into boxes, people can see the police officer's embarrassment, but Hallgrim and his two sons appear entirely unaffected by any insinuations or taunting looks.

The men assemble in groups in front of the shop and outside on the pier. They are unwilling to set out for home before having given vent to their outrage. All are furious at the treatment they have received, feeling both humiliated and harassed. Their anger is directed chiefly towards Hallgrim. They feel sympathy for the police officer, as he seems only to be Hallgrim's lackey. For them, it's hard to have to hand in weapons which are used only to obtain food or at the gun club, and never for shooting people. Equally hard is having to stand in front of that good-for-nothing Hallgrim and be treated like criminals. If it had been Germans who stood there and took their weapons from them, they could more or less have accepted that, but to have to experience it from one of their own? This is too much, but they now understand that they can expect anything from Hallgrim. And one thing they can say with certainty is that, as of today, people from Storvik will not open their doors to the Ås family. Gunhild may now drink her coffee in peace. If anyone should be invited to a coffee party at Christmas, as is the custom, the room there is going to be empty. This they decide here and now. And if it feels dangerous to say to people upfront what they think, there are many ways of demonstrating their revulsion just so long as they stick together.

- After all, he can't arrest a whole village.

If people in Ås are keeping an eye on the village, the same applies the other way round. In Âs, as elsewhere, there are people employed there who babble and let drop information, not least when there are amusing incidents to report. People in service there say that Gunnhild has become so overbearing that there's no room for anyone else in the house. She shouts and makes threats about the most trivial things. It's said that people working there try to get out as quickly as they can so that Gunnhild can be free to employ people of her own kind, but that there are not too many of these about.

One day when Julie is doing a quick shop, Gunnhild sweeps in through the door, dressed to the nines as if she was about to have a relaxed day in town or go to a party. She's wearing her best coat, hat, silk stockings and high-heeled shoes, and to crown it all, a fox fur round her neck. Julie is standing there in rubber boots with a cardigan over her work dress as Gunnhild addresses her obsequiously.

- So good to see you, Julie, she says taking Julie's measure in a single condescending glance. It's such a long time since we met.

For a moment Julie feels like some down-and-out in her working clothes, so different from Gunnhild's finery. But then she recovers quickly.

- Are you off to town, Gunnhild, seeing that you are all dressed up? she says, smirking every bit as much as Gunnhild.
- No, but I like to dress well when I'm going to be seen out of doors.
- Such a nice fox fur you're wearing!
- Yes. I don't suppose you will have one like this, Julie. I hear it hasn't gone too well with Jørgen and his foxhunting.

- On the contrary, says Julie, with the sweetest of smiles, - I have two furs like that, but I don't feel the need to wear them every day.

Ridiculous! laughed Jørgen when Julie described the meeting later. But it's good that they can laugh at those people from Ås. Things are serious enough apart from that.

The time for sheep slaughtering is drawing near, a concern of the Ministry of Supply. They require a count of sheep and information about how many are to be slaughtered. The decision is that at least half of those slaughtered must be delivered to traders for selling on. This applies not only to sheep but to all farm products: potatoes, vegetables, corn, milk and animals. People will be permitted to retain a quota determined by the number of people in the household, but the rest they will be required to sell. This annoys the farmers, for they have always sold their farms' produce, but never before under compulsion. Now, in matters both great and small, the power of decision-making has been taken from them, though many are becoming quite adept at circumventing the regulations imposed, something most of them achieve without any qualms of conscience.

Rumours are circulating in anticipation of the Ministry's visit. This sets Jørgen thinking about the two lambs which the boys had supposedly been searching for and which - equally supposedly - had not been found. They could do with three extra killings, and Jørgen decides not to mention these animals until the Ministry arrives on the farm.

An old mill house stands down by the river, unused and overgrown, but could come in very handy for housing three sheep for a couple of days. Jørgen informs Julie and the boys of what he intends to do, and unexpectedly, Julie raises no

objection. Jostein and Helge are to help him move the sheep
down to this mill house. Dreng-Anders must not find out about
this since it's not certain he can keep his mouth shut.

One dark night they set out on an expedition which is
significantly more dangerous than their previous trip to the hills.
They are now dealing with living animals which could emit
sounds. However, everything goes off trouble-free. Their next
task is to see to it that the animals are sufficiently well looked
after to prevent them from making a noise. Jørgen does not dare
to think about what might happen if the sheep were to start
bleating, and the noise was understood to be coming from the
mill house. However, the sheep's behaviour is exemplary, so
much so that Jørgen said afterwards that they deserved a better
fate than to be sent to the slaughterhouse.

Jørgen feels no trace of bad conscience about what he has
done, and he will see to it that others reap some benefit. Many
people come and go asking to buy meat and it gives him no
pleasure having to say no every time. It's mainly people from
Øra who come, but some come on bicycles from further afield,
not infrequently from the town itself, to buy meat, butter or eggs.
Although these small-scale transactions take place out of sight,
there is never any question of overcharging. Jørgen refuses to
have anything to do with the black market, though he is not
averse to having a couple of extra points added to his tobacco
ration. He is more than satisfied that he has managed to pull off
the trick with the sheep, so satisfied indeed that he gives the
boys five kroner to share between them. This is something that
does not happen every day.

- Pay for my two brave warriors, he smiles.

On Christmas Eve, the family stands outside on the veranda just as it has always done and listens as the church bells ring in Christmas. The two smallest children are quiet as Jørgen lifts them up high in his arms. A light fall of snow covers the ground where icy conditions have existed for the last few days. The snow bestows a glimmer of evening light over an otherwise dark village. Not so much as a flicker escape from the blacked-out windows. A great calm reigns, broken only by the sound of the bells, and even this seems muffled by the snow. People talk about it later, the remarkable feeling of sadness there was in the bells that Christmas, a mixture of solemnity and sadness in what should have been a time of joy.

In the last few years the boys have taken turns with the reading of the Christmas gospel, which forms part of the Christmas dinner ritual. This year it is Krister's turn and he reads it beautifully. But there is something about this gospel which makes it new every time it is read. For Julie, it has never been more beautiful or more powerful than it is this Christmas when Krister reads it. There is no writing at all more beautiful than this, nothing which awakens more beautiful pictures inside her; it is pure poetry. The solemn language carries words which transform everyday concerns into something beyond. A poor stable becomes a temple, a newly born boy the Son of God, a poor woman is elevated to his mother who 'wrapped him in swaddling clothes and laid him in a manger, for there was no room for them at the inn'. With voices trembling with the solemnity of it all, they sing the most beautiful of all the Christmas hymns:

My heart is always joyful at news of Jesus' birth,
My thoughts now come together as nowhere else on earth.
My longings all are answered

Now Jesus Christ is born,
Forget him can I never
This wondrous Christmas morn.

Christmas dinner is a meal which lasts a long time, for it is interrupted by the singing of the old Christmas hymns. Even the two youngest children are affected by the atmosphere round the table. Sven has been told that he's a big boy now and must remain seated until everyone has finished their meal, while little Sunniva is sleeping on Jørgen's lap. She is dressed in her first-ever real dress; which Julie has made out of a piece of red velvet she found lying around. Onto this she has crocheted a white collar and cuffs, a task which has given her enormous pleasure, as now, at last, she has a girl she can dress up! Sunniva's hair is already thick, unusually so for a child of barely seven months, and this evening is adorned with a red ribbon which she keeps pulling off. Julie has also knitted her some white socks with an elaborate pattern of holes. She is filled with a feeling of great tenderness as she looks at her child sleeping on Jørgen's lap. The child's cheeks glow red as she lies there with her thumb in her mouth, her ribbon having fallen off, and her hair sticking to her forehead.

A feeling of grateful thanks sweeps through Julie as she sits feeding her child later that evening. There has been so much violence this year, but it's a year which has also given them the miracle that is this child. She can never be thankful enough for that.

There are three churches in the parish. This Christmas the Christmas Day service is to take place here. Services in the other churches will be on Boxing Day or the day after, according to the rota.

The church is packed. Everyone from Storvik is here, with the exception of Astrid who is at home looking after the two little ones, something she has kindly offered to do. As time goes by, Astrid is seen less frequently out in public, and on a day like this, when the whole village gets together, she says she is quite happy not to be seen. The residents of Ås are also present, Hallgrim and Gunnhild surrounded by their six children whose ages range from three or four right up to twenty. Hallgrim has clearly been quite productive in that department! Jørgen remarks. On a day like this in a crowded church, people are not over concerned about sitting on the men's or women's side of the church. The people from Ås occupy almost an entire row in one of the front pews. Some people say that they're sitting there just to show off how important they are. There are two vacant places on the pew, but both are empty. People would prefer to squeeze into a place on a full pew rather than sit next to this family.

People know the order of service so well that they pay little attention to the words, but they will notice at once if something goes wrong. This year, the priest breaks off in the middle of a prayer, at the point where the wording is normally 'May God preserve the King and all the royal family, his ministers and all his servants'. The pause is a long one and the words are not spoken, but they hang in the air and have more effect than they have ever had when read aloud. The silence in the church is so profound that it feels like a physical wave passing through the church, echoing those unspoken words. It creates a deep impression on those experiencing this for the first time, though it is later to become an integral part of the service. People sitting from where they can see Hallgrim report later that his face was lobster red and his jaws white, looking as he always does when he is angry.

Following the service, the priest was invited back to coffee at Storvik. There he told Jørgen that the primate, Bishop Eyvind Berggrav, had sent out a recommendation to all clergy to pause the liturgy at the point where the king, the government and Storting were normally mentioned. Thought is free, he had said, and the congregation could themselves fill in the missing words in their minds. He added that Berggrav had had his recommendation distributed *before* his eminence the Reichskommissar managed to ban it. People were very happy about this. They were also happy that the priest had managed to shake Hallgrim out of his composure to such an extent that he could no longer succeed in concealing his anger. These were perhaps small consolations, but they were significant at the time.

It has always been the custom in the district for neighbours to meet for coffee or supper in the aftermath of Christmas. This has proceeded on a rota basis, for the Christmas period is not so extended as to allow this to take place in every house. This year, the Ås household is the one whose turn it is to invite their neighbours round.

On the day that they were due to hand in their weapons to Hallgrim, the men in Jørgen's household had sworn that they would never again set foot in his house, not even at Christmas. But as time went on they came to change their minds. When they met each other on the pier, in the post office or in a shop, they decided that maybe it was important to accept Hallgrim's invitation, which they knew would be coming. It might make sense to see something of his life and find out what he was up to. As they remarked, there could be quite a lot. One of the things which has concerned people this autumn is how the local authority should be run and there is speculation that Hallgrim has his eye on the role of Mayor.

On the district council, the roles of chairman and mayor have, up to now, functioned quite informally, but now people have had to submit to new regulations which came into place during autumn. There should actually have been a local election in autumn, but the events of spring made people realise that the election could be postponed indefinitely. Then, when Terboven declared that all parties other than NS had been stood down, the understanding was that there could not be an election at all. Had everything been normal and an election had taken place, the district would have had a new council and administration as from January 1, 1941. This would not have meant much for the political situation locally, for the Labour Party has for years been the largest party here, with a majority on the council and the mayor a member of that party. There has been the same mayor since the party came to power, and he would have continued undisputed after the election.

Now, everything is uncertain, and people await the changes they know are bound to follow. From radio and the press, they know that councils and many of the mayors in local authorities throughout the country have been dismissed. To replace them, a new mayor has been appointed, followed by a deputy mayor and a pair of so-called chairmen. These, along with everyone in a public position of leadership or trust, must be approved by those at county level, and these make their recommendations with the agreement of the National Assembly. In the final instance it is Terboven and the constituted statesmen in the Department for the Interior who approve any recommendations. As early as October, Terboven came out with this announcement: 'From now on, the constituted cabinet members have a legal right to dismiss or transfer any public servants who cannot be assumed to be totally in favour of the new system'.

This means that local authorities will lose their autonomy and will now be controlled by the state and NS. Democracy has been dissolved; local authorities will now be governed by a self-appointed NS mayor who can come to have unlimited power apart from being subject to the state as the final authority.

What people now ask is whether there are sufficient NS supporters to occupy these posts. Here it seems the 'herrefolk' are going to have big problems. The number of NS supporters can be counted on the fingers of one hand. Hallgrim, self-evidently is one, as is the shoemaker. People are now speaking as if this is someone they may have misjudged. He is an immigrant from Sunnmøre, as are so many people in Øra. It is not that local people are suspicious of anyone from outside the area, but that Sunnmøre people are reckoned to belong to a class of their own. Teetotalers, fanatics for Nynorsk[1], religious zealots and misers are the uncomplimentary terms most frequently heard about them. If you come here as a Sunnmøring, you have to be in possession of rather special qualities to be accepted. The shoemaker has not shown that he has anything to boast about. He is taciturn, quiet when out in public, and, like most people from Sunnmøre, he carries out his work very conscientiously. But some people say that if he is provoked, he can come up with some sharp replies, that he can be sly, and that his bright, piercing eyes contrast markedly with his quiet demeanour. From living a quiet working life, he has suddenly rocketed to

---

[1] The minority Norwegian language

becoming a very visible person locally, someone people can no longer overlook.

Apart from these they don't know of any others of that way of thinking. Of course, here, as anywhere else in the country, there will be a handful of people who, if not exactly sympathisers of the NS position, are nevertheless not entirely hostile. There are people who wait to see how situations develop before committing themselves. These, like others, are wary of speaking out loud about the most important issues of the time. People recognise that it is not going to be easy for the new rulers to set up a council to manage the village's affairs, and this is why they accept Ås's invitation to come along to his festivities on the fifth day after Christmas. If they manage to offer him a dram or two of Christmas brandy, they may even be able to get him to give something away - who knows? And he is not the man to turn down such offers.

Julie hesitates to agree to this. Her sense of decency will not allow her to approve such behaviour.

- I'm not much in favour of mixing celebrations and politics, she says.

But Jørgen manages to talk her round. If the neighbours have accepted the invitation, why should he and Julie stick out and reject it? Besides, he says, Hallgrim was once one of his best friends.

Julie is working busily to prepare for the party at Ås. She is happy because she has now made the effort to alter one of her old dresses. As a result of rationing it has become virtually impossible to get hold of new materials for clothes, and manufacturers are using whatever material they can acquire mainly to make children's outfits. Julie has had a dress hanging up, which, up to now, she has been hesitating to alter. This is one of the finest garments she has ever owned. Of a cream-coloured thin woollen fabric with sequin embroidery at the waist, the dress has only ever been worn on special occasions and still looks as fresh as it did when she first had it made for Johanne's engagement party. But now it is hopelessly old-fashioned with a waist lying far too low on the hips. Because of this she has cut it off at the waist and made a smooth bodice to fit over the pleated skirt. Into the wide belt she has inserted a recess at waist level. To make the dress a better fit over the shoulders, she has inserted a border made from a piece of old velvet which she happened to have lying in her leftovers basket. She now has enough of this remaining to add some edging round the neck and sleeves and to make a broad belt. With large shoulder pads the dress now accords totally with today's fashion. Julie has become an expert in creating new out of old, and the neighbours are always coming along and asking her for help both to make new clothes and to alter old ones. She feels very pleased with herself now that she is ready for the party. She has also been busy with her hair, having heated the curling iron, curled her hair at the ends, and pinned it over her forehead in the fashionable way while leaving the rest hanging in locks at the back of her neck. When Julie dresses up for a party, Jørgen says, it's sheer magic. Despite her hesitations, she feels excited as they make their way along to Ås that evening. It's now a very rare event for them to dress up and go to a party.

In the aftermath of Christmas at Ås, it's usually only people from the five nearest farms who meet on an evening. This time, the neighbours are very surprised by the number of guests filling the main hall. More surprising still is the identity of the guests they are mingling with. The shoemaker and his wife are here, as are the manager of the sawmill and his wife, all of whom are people rarely seen out in the village, and certainly not at parties. That the shoemaker has been deemed worthy of an invitation is not too difficult to understand, nor is it hard to understand the invitation to the manager of the sawmill. Hallgrim and Gunnhild may be no better than others, but they are very keen to be seen in the company of those who have a high status locally on account of their jobs. The sawmill manager, Sigurd Myhre by name, is a likeable man and popular for someone from the east of Norway. He arrived here when the sawmill started up again, and in the two years or so since then, he has come to know most people in the area and is not afraid to get into conversation with people, no matter what their status. He is a committed and capable businessman, punctilious and careful in his dealings both with his employees and with the farmers who deliver wood to his business. Though an 'immigrant', he has been received with open arms. An unusual thing about him is that he may drop in on people without warning. He has been doing this just as the locals do and, as is the custom, shares with them a coffee at the kitchen table. This has not made him any less popular. In parties like the present one he quickly becomes the centre of attention. He's a good conversationalist and behaves like a real gentleman when it comes to complimenting the ladies. Sigurd Myhre has style.

Gunnhild is loving her role as the busy hostess. She is wearing a blue silk dress with a gold necklace and earrings. The women present note that these are recently acquired items: it would seem that Hallgrim has been quite generous with his Christmas presents this year. Gunnhild may be described as a large lady, filling out her dress at the chest and hips and at the rear. As the years have passed, Hallgrim looks puny when compared with his well-endowed wife. What is most attractive about Gunnhild is her pale blue eyes and light blonde hair with its natural curls. Her hairstyle is the same as Julie's but pulled back from the ears so as to expose her jewellery to full view. Malignant voices whisper that she bleaches her hair to make it look so light, but Julie can never recall having seen it any other colour. One of Gunnhild's daughters, of Helge's age, has inherited her mother's eyes and hair. Solveig is her name, and she looks like a true 'child of the sun' with light curly hair and blue eyes. But Helge says she is a troll, sharp-witted and given to creating intrigue among her friends. But, leaving that aside, she is one of the brightest of their children. She certainly seems bold as she and an elder sister give their mother a helping hand with the serving. All the Ås children are bright and have been brought up to work, and for that, Hallgrim and Gunnhild deserve praise.

Apart from the blackout curtains on the windows there is little to indicate that this is the first wartime Christmas. No expense has been spared. Platters are laden with Christmas food, smoked salmon sandwiches and scrambled eggs, ham, rolls and pickles, cold ribs and hamburgers. Along with the savoury food, home-brewed beer and spirits are served, with aquavit for those who want and can tolerate it. Afterwards there is coffee served with cloudberries in cream and a good supply of traditional Christmas cakes. In this house there has certainly been no shortage of eggs, white sugar or fine white flour. Gunnhild, like everyone else, has had to rely on artificial coffee, but her guests can taste that this is mixed with a fair amount of the genuine article. Finally, the ladies are offered a liqueur and the men a glass of fine brandy.

When guests drop the hint that there is little in this party that brings to mind rationing, Gunnhild answers that this is all

because of thrift on weekdays and leaving over a little extra for
weekends. Nor does she hesitate in saying that she and Hallgrim
have been far-sighted in putting a little aside before rationing
became too strict. That this was a wise move is now self-evident,
she adds, as it has ensured that all the coffee, sugar and flour
they have had has been acquired honestly. This has enabled them
to avoid bartering and black market deals, unlike so many other
of their neighbours. She knows that some people have gone to a
fisherman on Øra and have carried out an exchange for quality
white flour from a stock that this fisherman had somehow
acquired. Did people really think he'd acquired it by honest
means? She can inform them otherwise. Both the flour and other
items he had loaded onto his boat during the fire in town. Did
people believe he could afford to pay for all this? Hallgrim
knows that he only escaped arrest by a hairsbreadth, he and
others with him doing similar business out there while the chaos
reigned. They 'rescued' goods, furniture and other household
items for people. There's also a question about whether people
who have done business with this man in advance of Christmas
know that their Christmas cake is baked with stolen goods. It is
unacceptable that those responsible escape without punishment
for their lying and cheating, and it was only the chaos in town
during those days that has saved them from this.

Julie is not the only person who feels hurt and upset after
this diatribe from Gunnhild. She knows that most people present
have used a similar opportunity to obtain a little extra for
Christmas. Late one evening, she had sent the boys to the
fisherman with a bucket of wholemeal bread flour which they
exchanged for a couple of kilos of fine white flour and one of
white sugar. In that way she had been able to bake the usual
small cakes, even if these were smaller than in the past. Should

these cakes now leave a bad taste in people's mouths? Stolen property? Gunnhild had no need to come out with her salvo. And everyone here has been left with the same question. How is it that Hallgrim knows everything going on in the area? The thought is not a consoling one for those who are present this evening.

Once the food has been cleared away drinks appear. Home-made wine for the women, coffee, brandy or toddy for the men. Nor does it escape the women's attention that a bowl laid down for the men is full of white sugar.

There are two large rooms downstairs in the Ås household. Now, as is customary, the women are in one, the men in the other. Everyone will now chat about their own affairs and interests. However, on this evening the women are not so absorbed in their own conversation that they fail to hear the men's.

Up to now, Hallgrim has avoided politics and controversial matters, and he has been careful not to drink too much. The war, which is what most people are concerned with, is mentioned only when it touches on everyday things which everyone has to contend with. But as the drinks begin to take effect, people become more daring and the discussion becomes louder. Julie becomes aware of Jørgen's voice, penetrating as it always is when he has had too much to drink.

- No, that blighter Hitler should be locked up before he turns the whole of Europe into a battlefield.
    Julie stiffens as she listens.
- Don't be such a damn fool, Jørgen, says Hallgrim warmly.

- Me, a fool? says Jørgen angrily. - If there anyone who's a fool round here, it has to be you, Hallgrim. If you don't soon come to your senses.

Hallgrim's voice is brusque as he answers.

- You had better watch out!

The silence which now fills the room is broken by Sigurd Myhre, who interrupts:

- As you all know, there are two subjects which should never be discussed in polite company, religion and politics. - And there is one thing we've forgotten, gentlemen, he says, sounding cheerful - we've forgotten to take care of our ladies!

He now suggests that the tables and chairs be moved to bring the whole party together. This takes the sting out of the gloomy mood which is beginning to settle over the whole assembly, and he succeeds in getting a light conversation going. But the men now refuse any more drinks, and when one of them blames sickness in his barn and wants to break up, the other neighbours take up the hint. When they stand at the entrance saying goodbye neither Hallgrim nor Gunnhild gives any sign that this has been anything other than a highly successful evening. Only some angry red spots on Gunnhild's cheeks and throat show that the episode has had an effect on her.

The immediate neighbours leave together, while the rest of the party, all of whom live on Øra, wait for lifts home.

If people were full of speculation before they went to Ås that evening, they are no less so when they leave. As they walk along in groups they review their hosts. The women consider in detail how Gunnhild has presented herself. Was she not arrayed in a new silk dress as if she was going to a ball? And what about the jewellery she was wearing? Did they notice that new necklace? One of them recognised it for what it was: The Sun Cross, Quisling's badge in gold. And that she made such a fool of herself in front of neighbours! Everything is talked about, the serving, the food and the drinks. And what was Sigurd Myrhe doing there? The men have outright praise for Jørgen who dared to say what he thought to Hallgrim. This was more than any of them dared do. Now they have final proof of where Jørgen stands. Maybe he knows they have been a little wary of him on account of Ivar? Jørgen swaggers and says that it is about time that they recognise him and give him their confidence. Julie is the only one who does not say anything. She has never before been to a party where the hosts have been subject to such searching criticism. She almost regrets going and that she gave in to Jørgen.

Midnight is approaching as they arrive home. It is still warm in the kitchen. Helge is sitting along under the lamp with a book and has kept the stove warmed up.

- Why are you sitting here on your own so late? Are Krister and Jostein in bed?
- No, they've gone out.
- Out? At this time of night. Would you happen to know where they've gone?
- They'll be dancing down at the youth club.
- Dancing, you say? Surely not Jostein?
- I know nothing about that. Anyway, they went together.

Do you hear that, Jørgen? Jostein may have gone dancing, so you will have to go and bring him home. He isn't even confirmed yet, Julie snorts indignantly.

- That's nothing to worry about, Jørgen says. It's all just innocent fun.

- Innocent! snorts Julie. Maybe, for all we know, they'll be getting him drunk.

There has been a local tradition to arrange a dance in the Youth Building on the fifth day of Christmas. All that has now been put a stop to, but Krister has been talking about getting the young people together for a dance to gramophone records. There are not many youths present, and no one can deny them their right to enjoy an innocent get-together just after Christmas. That is all very well, but Krister should have known better than to take along his unconfirmed brother.

- If you won't go, then I will, scolds Julie, but before she can put her coat on the boys arrive home.

Both are happy and excited, but their mother's face brings them sharply down to earth.

- Where have you been?

- To the youth club. You know that, says Krister cheerfully, just a little too cheerfully in Julie's view. It's not that he looks drunk, but he has probably had a taste of that awful black beer, a home brew made with molasses instead of sugar.

- And you thought it was all right to take your brother to the dance, did you? You know what people round here are going to say about that?

- Oh, come on, Mother, that was no party! Jostein and a couple of his friends sat in all innocence and watched while the rest of us danced. What harm was there in that?

- What others do is none of my business, but none of my children will show their face at a dance before they've been confirmed. What are people going to say in the village? And what will you say, Jostein, if your teacher or the vicar hears about it?

- You're just talking rubbish, Mother, says Jostein sullenly. - Why do we always have to be the same as everybody else?

- Now calm down, says Jørgen, - Let's keep quiet and have a bite to eat. Maybe Mother will find something good for us to eat if we behave ourselves. But Jostein, you can't yet just do as you like.

- No, and you will know about it if this happens again! Julie scolds.

But she makes a sandwich and takes out a plateful of Christmas cakes. It is moments like these that most appeal to her, she and Jørgen sitting together with their growing sons. The boys have now grown sufficiently to be able to take part in adult conversations. This evening, as on most others, it is the war which they talk about.

- You see this and that, Krister, living in a town full of Germans, Jørgen says - But do people want to have anything to do with them? I'm not talking now about my brother, but are there many others who mix with them?

- Oh, yes, says Krister - especially women.

- Women! says Julie, incredulous. - You don't mean that….?

He knows of many such, women behaving as if they have never seen a man before.

- You know that there are plenty of them, of Germans, that is. And quite a lot of them are good-looking. I know of a couple of girls who swoon when they see a good-looking German.

She stares at him, speechless.

- What was that you said?

- But, Mother, it's true! he insists, laughing.

Helge stares fixedly down at the table. Jostein giggles hysterically, his face blood red.

She stands in front of him, white with anger.

- How dare you speak like that in your own home and so that your brothers can hear you? Where did you learn such talk, and how much experience do you have, I ask myself? she says, her voice trembling with anger.

- Go to bed, you two! she says to Jostein and Helge, who then crash out of the room.

Krister sits there and looks up at her face.

- How dare you behave like this? she says in a whisper.

- Mother, stop being such a prude! What I'm saying is what everybody knows, he says with an expression of tolerant amusement.

She does not let up before slapping Krister's face and leaving a red mark. He stands up, and the two face each other, his dark eyes confronting hers.

Slap away, Mother, he says. - But just listen to what we say about you, Jostein and I. You sometimes behave as if you were God himself, and you expect the two of us to behave like angels. But that's not what we are. We're just the same as other young people. But somehow that's not good enough for you. We wonder sometimes what you're trying to prove when you carry on like this.

In shock she stares at her son. What is he saying to her as he stands there?

- You're not going out again?

- Yes, I am. I think I'm old enough to make up my own mind.

- Krister! Jørgen shouts threateningly, but all he hears is the outer door being banged behind Krister as he leaves.

- Did you hear what he said, Jørgen? Why didn't you say something? Why didn't you help me? It's strange how tolerant you've suddenly become with Krister.

- That's an argument you need to sort out between the two of you. But Krister is right about this, that he'll soon be old enough both to say and do as he likes. It's no good now being furious with him, as you were a moment ago.

- Furious? Yes, I was furious. I've always done my best for my children. But now they go talking behind my back as if I was some sort of despot.

- You must let them grow up and find out about life themselves.

Julie lies staring out into the dark room.

- What have we done, Jørgen? she says. - Is it the times we're living through, the war, that makes us lose all sense of decency?

- No, and now you must stop taking everything so seriously, Julie. You know you think too much!

- But can't you see how everything is changing? The boys are behaving like grown-ups at too young an age; even Helge does. You can see that they're still young. And did you see the defiance in Jostein's eyes tonight? Did you hear Krister's language when he described us as an awful couple? And all those things he is too young to know about?

- Times are no longer what they were when we were young.

- But it's not just that, it's not just young people it's about. I think about you. You, who almost never used to swear or use strong words in the house, now swear like the worst of them. And how did we behave on the way home from Ås tonight? We criticised our hosts in the most awful way imaginable, we turned upside down everything they had done in preparing a party for us, the food they served and the clothes they wore. We behaved like the most awful gossips when all they'd done was invite us to a party and offer us their best Christmas food. We can say what we like about the people from Ås, but tonight all they did was treat us well.

- Are you defending everything Hallgrim and Gunnhild did?

- No, but then both we and our neighbours should have had the decency to turn down their invitation. What we did was unacceptable.

- Sometimes, Julie, you are so moral that no one can live up to your expectations!

- Well, maybe. With Krister I suppose you think I'm being straight-laced and pernickety.

- No, not exactly straight-laced, but maybe a bit over-sensitive. And you mustn't be so pernickety, Julie. That young people grow up so quickly is hardly surprising with the way things have been. You should remember that they have seen more shocking things just recently than we have ever experienced in our lifetime.

- But what about the way they talk to us? It's just not acceptable!

- When it comes to the use of bad language, I don't think they are letting us down. Nor is it powerlessness or desperation; it's more a way of expressing these. It is clear that we are changing because everything around us is changing, and it's the times we're living in that are abnormal, not us. We have to try to tackle our everyday challenges as best we can. Then, I think we can experience something positive in the middle of all the misery. If people are going to help each other out and a sense of community is to increase, we have to put up with using some strong words here and there.

You mentioned decency, Julie. That's an important word to relate to in these times. And I'm not just talking about harmless tittle-tattle about our neighbours. No, what decency is about is taking a standpoint and standing up for it so that we will all be able to look each other in the eye when all this is over. I think the most important thing now is that we stand together.

- I do hope you're right, Jørgen, but maybe you can understand that I'm worried?
- Who isn't? But you needn't lie here worrying about Krister. He came home in fine form. He'll get by in life. I have no worries about him.

Gossip about everything that's happening at Ås is a source of entertainment in the whole area, and those who work there are more than willing to bring it to public knowledge. This is how people came to know that two German officers from Kristiansund graced the farm at Ås with their presence the following day. It was still something of a sensation to see Germans in the district, so their car was observed the moment it crossed into the village. But what were the Germans doing at Ås? Those who worked there couldn't explain it, but another girl was able to report that they had been received with food and service on a grand scale, while their chauffeur was served food in the kitchen. What most surprised people was that Gunnhild, Hallgrim and the oldest children conversed with the Germans in their own language, which meant that they had been teaching themselves German. This is incredible. And the Germans gallantly kissed Gunnhild's hand both when they arrived and went. *Meine liebe Frau,* they said as they kissed the blushing Gunnhild's hand. People can hardly be blamed for then using this as an excuse for referring to Gunnhild by a nickname. From then on, she was the *Liebfrau.*

The bombshell drops at New Year. The district council, along with the mayor and councillors, have been dismissed with immediate effect. As a long-standing trusted member of NS, Sigurd Myrhe has now been appointed as the new mayor. This news is first received with stunned astonishment. To begin with, people don't believe that it is true, it's so scary. That nice, good-humoured man who has been so readily accepted, who has dropped in on friendly visits to rich and poor alike and who has charmed people and ingratiated himself with them and their relatives. People begin to reflect on what they might have said to him during these visits and quickly remember that they have spoken to him about things they ought never to have mentioned. But how could they believe something like this about such a man? Afterwards they understand that he has a cunning way of getting people to open up to him, and, when they come to think about it, this has something to do with his eyes. They recall now that he never said anything derogatory about Nazism, even though they may have done, and they now realise how dangerous this could be. Who knows what is hidden behind that smooth exterior? Hallgrim has been appointed deputy mayor, and, apart from Hallgrim and Myrhe, two others who are not members of the NS have also been appointed. Those who understand these things say that this is to give the arrangement an illusion of fairness. These two further so-called officials could not refuse to accept their appointment, which came from a high authority, even though they felt ill at ease about it. What people now know is that Sigurd Myrhe is the man most to be feared in the district. Compared to Myrhe, Hallgrim is very small fry. When all is said and done, Hallgrim is one of *their* number, someone they know and from whom they know what to expect. But Sigurd Myrhe? They can never forgive themselves for confiding in him and for having allowed themselves to be deceived by such a charlatan. He was a Judas living among them and they had not understood it. Anger is also directed towards Hallgrim, who must have known about this all the time Myrhe has been here. That explains why he has been walking around with that contemptuous smile these recent days. People have been caught sleeping and so thoroughly deceived that this can never be forgotten.

Chapter 6

Food rationing has changed dramatically since the war broke out. To begin with it was only coffee, sugar and flour which were rationed, but this quickly increased to embrace most foodstuffs. There is now rationing on all imported foods as well as those to be found most frequently in any home: coffee, coffee substitutes, sugar and syrup, four, bread and lard. During the course of this year, the second year of the war, rationing has also been applied to all kinds of animal products including eggs, milk and dairy items. Peerhaps it is just a matter of time before vegetables and potatoes will be on ration.

Housewives are desperate. Amounts of rationed goods are small, and shopkeepers dare not cut out the dates on people's ration cards for fear of interference from the Ministry of Supply and other controlling authorities. In any case, this would only delay matters and make things worse for customers. But it is not just limited rations which are causing worry. The quality of goods has become significantly worse, and items which were formerly to be found everywhere are now disappearing from the shelves. Good quality white flour is now just a dream. The flour available for baking is crude and of poor quality, and ordinary yeast is becoming hard to obtain. Some people try making sourdough to get their bread to rise, as was the custom in earlier times, others are using saltpetre, but this just makes their bread green and heavy. This poor-quality baking flour affects the bread itself, making for heavy, soggy loaves which it is impossible to bake right through. The bread on sale at the baker's is even worse. It is virtually inedible, though people are becoming used to it. They can become used to anything, but daily life is now a huge burden for people. Looking after an ordinary household has almost turned into a paperwork exercise. It is no longer just a matter of asking your child to pop out to the shop if there's something you need. It is now ration cards which decide, those hated cards which are now more precious than money. It doesn't help having all the money in the world if it's shopping you need. And that is how people's everyday lives have become.

Julie knows that she should have no cause to complain about shortage of food. After all, she is living on a farm with free access to nature. Her life cannot be compared to that of town dwellers or people living on Øra. All the same, she is tired of hearing comments both from locals and from those on Øra when they arrive either to exchange or buy items. They seem to believe that those living on farms are gorging themselves. She has given up long ago trying to explain the reality, and in a sense there is a modicum of truth in what these people are saying. On the farm they have potatoes and vegetables, meat stored in the shed which will last out the winter if they are careful, flour for baking and barley flour, but all this is far from being an abundance. They are obliged to stick to fixed amounts on the farm - a certain number of bags of bread, flour, wool and meat. Milk they sell in agreed amounts to established customers from Øra. Any milk left over they separate out to make into butter.

Aside from the timber trade and woodcutting, it is the cowshed which is the best source of income, but principally in the summer and autumn months when most of the cows can benefit from grazing outside on the meadows. There is payment for timber each spring, and the money earned goes as a rule to buying fertiliser, seeds and necessary equipment as well as to the paying off of debts.

The most difficult time is when the spring shortage sets in, and there is little left in barns and cellars or in the storehouse. This spring, Jørgen has had to buy in hay, which he mixes with straw. In addition to this they have been feeding the cows with cellulose soaked in water to which they add molasses. This is filling rather than nourishing for the animals and contributes little to the milk output. They have watered down every drop from the calf-bearing cows, but in the end, milk has become so scarce that Julie has not been able to fulfil the quotas for her customers. She has tried as hard as she could to distribute the milk so that families with small children are given the most. In times like these it can take weeks before they can collect enough cream to make a knob of butter. Good quality butter is now only served on special occasions. They are pleased to have margarine while it is still on sale. When their quota is used up they must manage as best they can until the next quota. Topping on bread is sour jam or a soft cheese made with skimmed milk or buttermilk. An appetite for sweet food has to be satisfied with black syrup, and it is this which has become the standard sweetener. For drinking they resort to skimmed milk or buttermilk when that is available. Julie will not allow complaints about food. We should be happy that we can eat our fill, she says.

To have ready cash available is a problem now, as it was before. They are not able to live off what the farm provides. There are some essentials which have to be bought at the shop, and any help they receive also has to be paid for. Unforeseen expenses are also both an ongoing and a recurring problem. Most of the butter Julie produces goes to the local shopkeeper, but she also tries to sell some to private customers. Private customers pay better, for Julie and Jørgen receive nothing for what they supply to the shopkeeper. This all disappears because of the accounting; it is only the private sales which yield cash in hand. Julie earns a few hard-earned kroner from the sale of milk, butter and eggs, but for these she still has to provide accounts. Her dairy customers must have a so-called milk-book in which every last litre they buy has to be noted. If there are families with many children, Julie frequently increases their quota when there is enough milk available in the dairy.

The system is turning people into petty crooks. A couple of women in the district have been caught red-handed by the shopkeeper delivering butter mixed with margarine. Since then he has been inspecting all deliveries of butter. Now, while those who deliver the butter are still watching, he slices their delivery in half. The quality of the margarine has become very poor. It contains, among other things, added water and because of this cannot be mixed with ordinary butter without causing white clumps. Julie has not been tempted to take part in this sort of crookery, nor has she been tempted to travel to town to sell on the black market as many have. She knows, too, that some people are selling to the Germans, and that incredible prices can be obtained for a pat of butter, a piece of bacon or a bag of eggs. The most incredible stories circulate about these business deals and Julie is not so moral as to condemn it all out of hand. She and Jørgen have even talked about this possibility of earning extra income, but they have never made any serious attempt to give it a try. They have promised that they will be able to look each other in the eye when this is all over. When it comes down to it, neither is prepared to benefit from other people's losses. And to do business with the Germans is totally off-limits.

A source of constant irritation is men's constant whingeing about tobacco. Here, the word decency goes out of the window.

Jørgen would willingly give the last piece of meat in his storehouse for a pinch of pipe tobacco or a couple of packets of snuff. When there is no tobacco available, which often happens now, he becomes unbearable to live with. He flares up at the slightest provocation, shouting at Julie and the children, while Dreng-Anders goes round as if he's expecting the end of the world to come and Jørgen goes round sucking on a cold and empty pipe.

This spring, Jørgen and Anders have been sowing tobacco plants on a sheltered patch close to the wall of the barn. They attend to these plants as if they were living beings. It is a matter for both laughter and tears when grown men lose their senses for a pipe of tobacco.

Krister, too, has begun with the habit. Julie caught him red-handed in the henhouse, stuffing his pockets with eggs. Shamefully he had to admit that this was in order to swap the eggs for tobacco. She was so furious that it was only by a whisker that she avoided slapping her son's face.

Keeping a family going with food and clothing has always been a mother's concern. It is now the biggest problem of all, overshadowing all others and demanding both time and energy. As time goes on, mothers become ever more adept at creating something out of nothing. They make 'crisis cream' and 'surrogate filling' for cakes; potatoes replace almonds, herbs are heated and added to coffee substitute and dresses are made out of bedding and discarded curtains. Newspapers and magazines are now becoming full of advice about such matters. Even those who are well off have to rely on measures like these, as there is not much point in owning money if there's nothing for it to buy.

Krister is at home and is being a great help this summer, just as he has always been. Jostein and Helge are also working hard, which means that there is no need to hire extra help to load hay. Jørgen says that having had three sons who have grown significantly is now beginning to pay off, and he is cheerful as he works with his sons around him.

Krister will have just one year of high school left when he begins in autumn, and Jørgen has become reconciled to him living with Ivar. He has come to trust that Krister is not going to be affected by Ivar's relationship with NS. Krister reports that Ivar has been offered a post as district mayor but that he rejected the offer straight away on the grounds that he was not suited to political work. He continues to live as he has always lived, going to work at the bank and enjoying music and painting in his spare time. At any rate, that is how it seems to Jørgen, but the two brothers do not talk much when they meet. Whenever Ivar visits, he keeps to the cottage with his mother, which is best for everyone.

That the family members in town mix with Germans is only to be expected, since Ivar is still a faithful member of NS and Helene herself is German. The family which was lodging in their house after the bombing has now moved out, apparently at their own request. Krister believes that they were probably afraid of being seen as supporters of Ivar. There are now four German officers living in Selma's flat. The Germans have now taken to requisitioning housing according to their needs, whether or not the owners are Nazis. The officers taking over Selma's flat are polite and rarely seen out in public. It might be thought that their presence would cause unpleasantness in the house, but in fact that is not so. Quite the opposite, in fact; there is often a party atmosphere and a great deal of music. Ivar has found many

musical friends among the Germans living in town. Small-scale
domestic concerts are arranged, and as time goes on, people with
nothing to do with NS come to these.

Jørgen is uneasy about all this, but it does not seem to affect
Krister. He says that he either sticks to his room with school
work or goes out with friends. He is not particularly enjoying the
situation he has found himself in but keeps well clear of youths
who have anything to do with NS. He knows that his friends
trust him and says that if they didn't he could not go on living as
he does. Jørgen can be quite certain that Ivar will do nothing
which will influence him in any way.

Julie is much relieved by this, for she realises how easily
influenced young people can be at Krister's age, and this has
been worrying her. Having Ivar and Inge on the wrong side is
more than enough already; that any of her children should
become involved is unthinkable.

A few Germans have arrived in the area as leaders of a
project to build an anti-aircraft battery out in the fjord. The work
itself is being carried out by locals. Some criticise the workers
because they are working for Germans, but most people accept
this and understand that people without work are grateful for
every krone they can earn. The Germans are said to pay well,
and, leaving that aside, the work is something people have been
ordered to do. As these workers say, it's easy for other people to
criticise when they are secure and have a job to go to every day.

People do not see much of the Germans. They have taken
over a couple of farms, and people there report that they keep
very much to themselves. They prepare their own food and in
the main are polite towards those they have to deal with. True,

people would rather not have them under their roof, but there is no point in refusing when the 'herrefolk' are involved.

People sometimes meet them in the shop, or at weekends when they can be seen strolling along the roads. They visit people at Ås, Sigurd Myrhe, obviously, and the few other local sympathisers. Once people have become used to the sight, it is no longer particularly scary, apart from the uniforms which can provoke a shudder. After all, if something happens in the village people like to have something to talk about, and it is even better if they can laugh about it.

One Saturday evening, a couple of Germans came to visit Hallgrim. There was no shortage of alcohol that evening, and laughter and shouting were heard far into the small hours. In the morning, Hallgrim was scheduled to row the Germans back over the fjord in his boat but was still so tipsy that he did not think it was a good idea for him to be doing the rowing. One of his farm workers was given the job while Hallgrim remained in the boat to see that his guests arrived home safely. One German had had so much to drink that he became hot-headed and quarrelsome. Matters only became worse as the journey proceeded, and his companion could not manage to hold him in check. As they approached the other side this German stood up in the boat and started waving his revolver in the air, at which point Hallgrim snatched the revolver away from him. In the scuffle which ensued the boat capsized and everyone was left flailing in the sea. Many people saw Hallgrim that morning struggling up the hill back towards Ås with the farm worker at his heels. Both were soaking wet and furiously angry.

The farm worker thought his last hour had come when the bullets whistled over his head. It took a long time for him to recover from the shock, but he was nevertheless willing and eager to describe the trip in the smallest detail to anyone who was prepared to listen. He also quoted what Hallgrim had said as he emerged breathless and panting from the cold sea: - We should be thankful it was a summer's day! This was to become a standard expression locally.

People love the story, but it also aroused a certain amount of respect for Hallgrim. He could certainly have been shot, and he has been out on winter days before, so what he said was true. The farm worker says that Hallgrim was frothing with rage for the next few days. He heard him say to Gunnhild that he should have reported the German to his superiors, but because Hallgrim was so intoxicated he thought it best not to. The German has been to Ås many times since, so the episode is largely forgotten, and everything has been straightened out between those involved. But the district still remembers the story and enjoys it for its entertainment value. But nor is it entirely free of people jealous of Hallgrim's ability to afford expensive drinks, while if they want to binge they have to be content with dark beer, which is not pleasant to drink and can also make you sick. There is much to be outraged about, but also much to be thankful for.

As time goes on there are many rules and regulations which people might laugh about, though they no longer dare to do so in public unless they are sure about those around them. In late summer, there comes an announcement that wipes the smile off everyone's face. Radios are to be handed in. This requirement is met with disbelief and an indignation which goes over all bounds. There was indignation enough when weapons had to be handed in, but that was, in a way, understandable and did not affect everyone in the way that this requirement does.

The news from London has been the only reliable source of objective information about how the war is proceeding. Now that this source is to be taken away the result will be total isolation from all objective sources anywhere in the country. People's indignation is in no way diminished when they learn that members of the NS are exempted from this rule, but this was only to be expected.

All came to a halt in the district when this news came through. Men gather in groups on the pier or in the shop to give loud expression to their anger and indignation. In the shop conversation drops away as Hallgrim comes through the door. He greets everyone with a smile as if this were an ordinary day.

- Isn't it getting hard to shop in these conditions? he says.

No one answers. A wall of clouded, miserable faces turns towards him. The shopkeeper fumbles nervously as he wraps up Hallgrim's shopping while Hallgrim stands there in the stunned silence with a smug grin on his face. As he is about to leave, one of those present can no longer restrain himself.

- I hear you can hold on to your radio, Hallgrim. It certainly seems that some people are different .

Hallgrim turns in the doorway, and he is no longer grinning.

- You could too; anyone can if they are sensible.

The requirement to hand in radios was announced in the newspapers on 1 August. Locally, the handing-in was to take place on the 7th.

- I'll be damned if I'm going to hand in the Vidor.

Fortunately, Jørgen has not yet thrown away his old set. The boys have been using it as a toy to tinker and experiment with. If what he has in mind proves possible, it may once again become useful. But for this he is going to need a helper, who will have to be the shopkeeper, since radio sets are to be delivered at the shop which is where they are to be held until further notice. Even though the situation is such that soon no one can trust anyone else, he will need to take a risk with the shopkeeper, not that he has seen anything to suggest that he is untrustworthy. One evening at closing time he goes down to the shop and waits until there are only the two of them.

- Now I need you to help me, Jorgen says. - I'll come straight to the point. I want to hang on to my Vidor radio and to hand in the old one instead.

- No, don't even think about it, says the shopkeeper. All the boxes will be opened and searched, and everyone locally knows about the fine new radio Jørgen has bought.

- You can't risk being punished, Jørgen!

No, so now they must begin to make other plans. In the end, they agree that the shopkeeper will ensure that the box containing Jørgen's radio will be easily accessible, and they will find a solution later.

- But just remember this, Jørgen, this is your responsibility. I don't want to be mixed up in anything. What you are proposing to do is a criminal offence.

- I know, and you mustn't worry about that. You haven't heard a word of what I've just said, and don't mention it to a living soul. The responsibility is mine.

- But how are you going to hide it?

- It will be fine, but that's my business. I, too, feel it's a big responsibility, but that there has to be some way for people round here to find out what's going on in the world.

- It's a huge risk you're taking, Jørgen.
- I know. But it's something I have to do.

Up to now he has not disclosed his plans to Julie, but he has told the boys what his intentions are. He has been in some doubt about involving Helge who is only thirteen and therefore very young to have all this thrust upon him, but it would be very difficult to hide it, so he must just take a chance on this. One day, when they are out in the fields he gathers the boys around him for a brief rest.

Wide-eyed, they listen to what their father has to say. He will try to find an opportunity to come to the store after the delivery date and replace the Vidor with the old radio set. What the boys need to do is to assemble the old set so that it looks more or less in working order. Later on, he may have a further use for them, but says he will return to that later.

- Now I have real respect for you, says Krister.
- And why should you not respect your father? Jørgen smiles.
- But one thing they need to remember is that this is not child's play they are engaged in. Not a word must be said to anyone, not even to your mother, at any rate until we see if everything is going according to plan. Not a word even to your best friends. And you, Helge, I'm now treating you as a grown-up. You're not to say a word to anyone, no matter what the temptation. Will you give me your hand on this?

Solemnly, and slightly embarrassed by the formality of the situation, all three take their father's hand.

- Can I rely on you to understand what a handshake means between grown men?
- We promise, Father. Word of honour,

On the day that the radios are to be handed in, people stream along with their expensive equipment. Some have made a special effort by packing them in wooden crates to ensure that they will not be damaged. This proved to be a waste of time. Every set was removed from its packaging and placed in a brand-new wooden crate, which was then nailed down and locked. People say afterwards that this is one of the strangest schemes the Germans have come up with, for here their priority cannot be money and expense. But Jørgen freezes at the thought of what might have happened if he had turned up with his old radio.

It is the police officer who is responsible for this operation, just as he was when the weapons were handed in, and as on that occasion, Hallgrim and his two sons are helping out. The police officer no longer shows the concern that he did then.

When Jørgen arrives at the counter for his turn he makes no attempt to conceal the anger he feels.

- It's infuriating having to hand in a brand-new set.
- You'll get it back as good as new, says Hallgrim. - Here we keep records and do everything properly.
- I'll need to see that before I believe it. Buying that radio was probably money down the drain.
- You are such a pessimist, Jørgen! says Hallgrim and sounds so cheerful that a murmur arises among those present, but it stops the moment Hallgrim turns to look at them.
- Now that you've delivered, you may as well go home, he says curtly.

None of them has a mind to go. They will stay there until all this is over. And as long as the police officer is the one giving instructions they have no intention of taking any from Hallgrim, no matter how much he may appear to be in charge. If they cannot do anything else, they can at least make him feel his neighbours' objections and indignation on this darkest of days. They have to do as they are told now, but they say darkly to one another that Halgrim must be made to pay for all this when the time is ripe. They then head homeward, having yet again been compelled to give way to force.

Everything has been carefully planned, but Jørgen still feels his pulse beating faster than normal as he makes his way down to the shop with a cart laden with sacks of new potatoes to deliver to the shopkeeper. In one of the sacks, camouflaged by potatoes both above and below, lies his old radio. The boys trudge along beside the cart.

The timing of the operation has been carefully chosen. It is the middle of the day, a time when there are few customers in the shop. Jørgen's first thought had been to do this at night, but he decided that this was too risky as then there are always eyes to see and ears to hear. The middle of the day, and what appears to be a completely ordinary task, is the safest and best option.

He was right. In the shop there are none of the usual busybodies who like to poke their noses into whatever is happening - they will all be enjoying their lunchtime nap. The only customers present are two or three women taking a break in the middle of a quick round of shopping, but Jørgen is shocked when he sees that one of these is Gunnhild Ås. She is dressed up as usual and stands imperiously at the counter turning and inspecting carefully everything the shopkeeper places in front of her. It takes quite a while to serve Gunnhild, but for the others present this is an entertainment which they prefer not to miss.

Maybe it's a good thing that Gunnhild is here, for then Jørgen can do what he has to do without being disturbed.

- I've come with the potatoes, Jørgen says.
- Oh good, good! says the shopkeeper. - Can you put them in the storeroom yourself? You can see that I'm busy.

Jørgen hopes that he is the only one to notice that the shopkeeper is looking nervous.

- That will be fine; I have the boys to help me, and they want to take the sacks back home
- If it's not too much trouble, you can empty the potatoes into the bin. But won't you pick up the sacks later?
- No, I'll take everything now, then that's everything done.

It is easy to find the crate with Jørgen's name and registration number. The shopkeeper has done just as he promised, both making the crate easily accessible and loosening the nails. While the boys bring the sacks of potatoes into the store room and drop the potatoes into the bin, Jørgen quickly swaps round the two radio sets, places the Vidor into a jute bag, and goes out with what looks like a bundle of empty sacks so long as no one decides to inspect them closely. The empty sacks now lie in a heap on the cart with the Vidor at the bottom.

- Very well done, boys! Jørgen shouts in everyone's hearing, though he directs a warning look at Krister, whose face is one broad grin.

He then sends the boys home with the horse and cart.

- Take care of the horse! he shouts after them.
- You can rely on us! Krister replies.
- Would you like a receipt, Jørgen? asks the shopkeeper.

- No, just finish off what you're doing. Our midday nap is ruined anyway.

- There were quite a few of you today, Gunnhild remarks. She still hasn't gone.

- Oh yes, the boys need to learn about work.

- That's good, Jørgen. The country now needs young people who know what's right.

- How very true, Gunnhild, Jørgen says and feels the irony as he says it. - That's exactly what the country needs.

Gunnhild is not so stupid that she misses his undertone, but she contents herself with a toss of the head as she sweeps out of the shop.

- Rotten old hag! says Jørgen, much to the satisfaction of the other women still waiting to be served.

- That one can easily spend the whole day shopping and doesn't care about people who have to go to work, they grumble.

- She can get away with that for now. But believe me, the time will come for those at Ås when it'll be others who are laughing.

Jørgen takes the receipt for the delivery of three hundred kilos of potatoes. The money for this is entered into the business register, but today this means nothing. Today he is feeling good, better than he has for a long time.

- I hope everything is all right now, the shopkeeper says as he goes.

- Oh yes, you can depend on it, says Jørgen.

He is very happy and whistles as he makes his way back up the hill. That Gunnhild was there added spice to the whole affair. If only she'd known what was going on right before her eyes, that nosey old cow from Ås. It's no surprise that Jørgen is whistling and enjoying himself as he walks along. Just so long as it's possible to deceive scum like that, there is something to be thankful for. And this is no small matter the way things have turned out.

In the kitchen the table is laid out for coffee. Today it's waffles with syrup and the usual dishwater which passes off as coffee, but today actually tastes acceptable. Whatever is on the table would taste acceptable to Jørgen at this moment. He can see by the expressions on the boys' faces that they are ready to talk about what they have just experienced, but the glance he sends in their direction is a sufficient warning for them to behave so as not to arouse suspicion. As he sits there with Julie in the middle and the others round the table, a shudder runs through him. The excitement he has been living through in these recent days now breaks out, and he is trembling so much that the coffee in the cup he has been holding spills out over the bowl and onto the floor. He sits staring at a brown spot oozing out over the tablecloth.

- What's happening, Jørgen? Julie laughs - have you suddenly turned old and wobbly?
- No, it's just …. I've been lifting some heavy weights.
- Lifting? And what have you been lifting that makes you tremble?
- You saw me moving all those potatoes.
- Yes, but is that anything to get excited about and tremble for? she asks, puzzled.

After sending the others out to work Jørgen asks Julie to help him to sharpen the scythe.

The sound of the scythe on the grindstone ensures that anything they say will not be heard.

- I've been to pick up the Vidor.

Julie stops grinding and stares at him.

- What was that you said? What have you done?

- You heard what I said. Now get on grinding.

- This can't be true, Jørgen. Do you realise what danger you're in?

Yes, he has thought it all through and she must just trust him. He knows that it will turn out well just so long as unreliable people don't find out about it. And it is up to them to see that they don't.

But what about the boys, she wonders, and the others? Does he imagine that he can manage to conceal the fact that there's a radio in the house?

No. People in the house, with the exception of a few helpers from outside who come in occasionally, need to know about it. From them he must have their word of honour and be able to rely on it.

But does he really think that he can impose this on the boys, and what about Anders? Is he reliable?

He has every confidence in Anders on such a serious matter, and the boys have already given their word of honour.

- Have you got the boys involved in all this? Do you realise what you're doing? It's not just you that can be punished; both Jostein and Krister are old enough to be sent to gaol, people say for at least two years, and some people end up in Germany. What you have done, Jørgen, is what is known as a criminal offence. Are you quite clear about that?

No, Jørgen does not feel in any way a criminal for having brought back his own radio, which the rabble had stolen from him. A radio which he has paid for and of which he is the legal owner. Then again, someone has to take responsibility and dare to do this. It is insufferable to live cut off from all the news about what is going on in the world. So, for once, Julie must trust that he is grown up and responsible for his actions.

She says she is indignant because he has kept this from her, and because he could not involve her in his dangerous plans.

- I know you well enough to know that you would not have allowed me to go ahead with this.
- Yes, that's right. You should know too, Jørgen, that whatever happens, this does not have my consent.
- Then the best thing for me is to ask for your word of honour to keep quiet about it from now on.
- It's something very unpleasant you have brought upon our home today, Jørgen, she says, trembling with indignation as she departs.

The radio has been placed in one of the guest rooms upstairs. The only person who has been living there this year is Selma, and that was only for a few days in early summer. The radio has been safe throughout all this time. However, it has been something of a struggle to set it up without arousing suspicion. To receive foreign broadcasts properly the medium wave is needed, and this requires an aerial long enough to take in all frequencies to be found on that wave. For this reason, an aerial has been installed extending from the barn roof to the main building. Too visible, Jørgen thinks as he looks upwards and hopes he is the only one who notices it. Without this aerial they may as well forget about tuning in to London, so it's all or nothing. If anyone mentions it he will have to find a plausible excuse for the aerial being there. A further problem has been to connect that aerial with the room. He has been up on the roof pretending to be fastening loose slates and has stood on a ladder hammering on a slate which had worked its way loose. He covered the cable with cladding before carefully feeding it in through the window. All this he has done in full view of everyone, making it look like ordinary repair work. He is happy that the connection into the room is invisible.

The radio stands on a table covered with a cloth reaching down to the floor. When not in use it will be hidden under the table. This applies also to the battery. Maybe this isn't the best possible hiding place, but so long as the room is unused it will have to do. The battery has recently been charged and should last for some weeks. How he will succeed in getting this to and from the workshop which charges it up for him without being observed will be a problem for him to solve when it arises. That part of the aerial inside the room is hidden behind a wall tapestry hanging behind the table and extending from floor to ceiling.

When everything is in place, and with the radio and battery hidden under the table, Jørgen stands in the doorway contemplating a neat and tidy room. No one looking in would see anything to arouse suspicion.

So far everything has gone smoothly. There remains the task of calming Julie. This is going to be fun! Ever since the day he informed her of the project she has gone round as if all the world's troubles had landed on her shoulders. But it has touched Jørgen to see how Anders reacted to the situation.

- Thank you, Jørgen, for trusting me. I won't ever forget that.

Astrid received the news with composure.

- I hope you know what you're doing, was all she said.

Jørgen was in some doubt about whether to inform his mother, but came to realise that this was something he had to do. So long as the radio is here, it cannot be hidden from people living in the house. She is shaken, which is to be expected, and cannot refrain from warning him.

- Mother, you must mention this to nobody. Promise me that.
- You said nobody, so you mean nobody at all.
- Not even Ivar. Especially not Ivar. I expect you understand why?

A shadow crossed her face as he said this.

- You should not have said that, Jørgen. I am very well aware of what word of honour means. But I also know right from wrong. And I have to say this, that I don't like you treating your mother like a traitor. Nor Ivar, for that matter, though there's no point in my saying that. But you can rest assured. He will hear nothing about this. At least not from me, but you must permit me to say that what you are doing is dangerous.

It is as if it's a festive occasion when they sit round in the room listening to the familiar signal coming in from London. Although it is not so very long ago that they last heard it, it feels as if it has been an eternity. The feeling tonight is that their whole environment is changing and that they can breathe more freely. With an unfamiliar feeling of well-being Jørgen is sure that what he has done is right.

It is only Anders and Krister who are with him on this first evening. Jostein and Helge were upset because they were not allowed to be present, but on this matter Jørgen is firm. If there should be an unexpected visitor there has to be someone in the kitchen. There will be changes, and they will be able to listen along with him later when their own turn comes. Everyone must accept and learn to live within the rules.

They sit listening intensely. Krister writes down the most important points. He began doing this when he came home for the summer holiday. What he then did for fun has now become serious. There are a few selected and, in Jørgen's eyes, totally reliable people in the area to whom he will pass on the news. It is important to have it written down to ensure accuracy. When Krister leaves, Jostein and Helge will take over the task. The boys have maps on which to chart the troop movements. These are pinned to a board and the battlefronts marked with flags. They hide the board under the bed and the radio and accumulator under the table once the broadcast is over. It is totally forbidden to listen to the radio other than during broadcasts from London, but this is something the boys accept without complaint.

Julie feels a little easier now that she has seen the room and the care Jørgen has taken over everything. She says she will see to it that the room always looks uninhabited, which is what it normally is.

- But I still wish you hadn't imposed this burden on us, she tells him.

- I had no alternative, Julie. And you can trust me that this will all work out.

The school year is about to begin, and Julie decides to accompany Krister when he returns to town. Little Sunniva is now weaned and runs around both indoors and out. People here are willing to look after her and Sven, so Julie does not have to worry about them while she is away for a couple of days. She has a number of things to do in town, but the most important is to see with her own eyes the conditions under which Krister is living. Apart from that, she has not been in town since the bombing and wants to see how everything is now after the destruction. She could also do with a good chat with Randi. She has hardly heard from her during the past year. That is how it is now. Everyone has their own troubles and cannot deal with much else.

German soldiers and others belonging to the new administration are given priority on ferries and buses. If a civilian wishes to travel, they have to plan a good while in advance. Permission must be applied for, the purpose of the journey declared and valid identification shown. This is one more burden for people to bear. They are living through a situation where everything has become a mountain of paperwork, of regulations and restrictions, of applications which have to be sent in for anything they might want to do, all of them things to which previously they would not have given a second thought. This robs people of both time and energy. Julie has now spent almost a whole working day waiting for pointless conversations which will allow her permission to travel, and says that people will soon have to apply for permission to satisfy their basic bodily needs. Like everyone else, she is in despair about all that is making life unbearable.

It is a mild morning, but the air feels clear and sharp, with just a hint of autumn. Julie stands in a queue, looking up towards the village. It looks beautiful in these late August days. Not bright green as it was in midsummer, for now the landscape is more like a multi-coloured carpet of green, gold and brown. The sky is clear, as only a late August sky can be, and the sea transparent and bright. Every stone at the bottom, every blade of seaweed stands out in the water as clearly as if it were a sculpture. Julie always feels a twinge at this time of year. It has always been like this, a feeling of restless expectation mixed with sadness. These are feelings which others associate with spring, but ever since she was a child autumn has been the season Julie loves the most.

When the weather is as it is now, Julie prefers to be out on deck. Most of the passengers are German soldiers, one of whom offers her a place on the bench where he is sitting. These soldiers are beginning to get a reputation for being very polite towards ordinary civilians, though many say this is just a ploy carried out by order to cover up all the terrible things they are doing otherwise. She sits looking at them, and it strikes her how young they are. Many of them are not much older than Krister, and she thinks about what it must be like to be sent to a foreign country to fight in a meaningless war. Do these young men think about this, or do they feel such a sense of victory that it blots out everything else? Nor can she let go of the thought that these young people have mothers and fathers back home worrying about them. Or is it a pride they feel about their son who has gone to war?

In the last few days Julie had brooded a great deal over the nature of war. This is the second large-scale war she has been through. Even if Norway had no direct involvement in the previous war, she remembers the problems it created for people, the feeling of desolation it brought with it, the news which caused anxiety and horror but also evoked sympathy, the lists in the newspapers of fallen Norwegian sailors and the chilling news of suffering and death. She was so young then, and concerned with herself in the way that young people usually are. But what will always remain in her memory as a symbol of that frightful war was the loss of her sister Synna from Spanish flu. Synna died just after the end of the war, during the time when that frightful plague which took so many lives was coming to an end. For her family, this tragic event cast a shadow over the peace process and the reassurance given by the nations that *never again* was this going to happen. It seemed so improbable that it would ever happen again. A new war, one whose consequences no one dares to think about and which has already caused so much damage that it can never be atoned for, was certainly not going to happen again in their time. A war which has already had consequences for their own family which cannot be repaired, and where the prophecy of scripture that brother will stand against brother has become horribly true.

As Julie looks at the laughing and chatting soldiers, a word springs to mind: cannon-fodder. She imagines all the mothers who have carried them at their breasts and given birth to them. Can a mother who has brought a son into the world bring herself to feel pride when he goes out to kill? Can she ever accept that he has become cannon-fodder? This is an altogether impossible thought. When she looks at these young, not yet quite mature, faces, it seems unthinkable that these youths are able to arouse such desperation round them, yet that is how it is.

She catches sight of Krister, who is caught up in an eager conversation with two of the soldiers. She gives a loud shout then unpacks their picnic.

- I don't want you going round talking to them.
- But does it really matter?
- Yes. People we know will see you. Haven't people enough to talk about without this?

- Mother, you worry too much. Surely it can't be dangerous just talking to them? They are just people. And I find it's quite fun trying out my German.

- As I said, I won't have it. And it seems to me that where you live, enough German is spoken without you trying out yours whenever you feel like it.

Krister has always been interested in languages, and Julie is well aware that he speaks German almost like a native, having shared a house with Ivar and Helene. Now that there are other Germans living there he can get as much practice as he likes.

But she makes it clear that she doesn't want him to start conversing with foreigners when local people can see.

- I can't accept you publicly bringing shame on us, she says indignantly. - You mustn't forget that we in Storvik need to be a bit more careful than others because of your uncle.

- I never thought you were one of those who hated Ivar, he said heatedly. - Wasn't it you who stuck out for Helene and Ivar to be godparents for our Sunniva? I seem to remember that Father was against it. No worries then about people talking! And you weren't against staying with Helene and Ivar that time you went to town. You don't say no to them allowing me to live here rent-free. There's a big difference between what you say and what you do. For you the thing that bothers you most is what people say. For you nothing is more important than that.

- Hush, Krister, don't talk like that.

- On no, just think that people might hear us, he says with derision in his voice. - Forgive me, Mother, but sometimes there's a need to speak out.

- Krister, she whispers, please, not now!

- Just remember one thing, Mother. There's such a thing as double morality, he says as he departs.

She sits there feeling miserable. Krister's words have hit home more than she dares to admit, giving her an insight into a self she does not recognise. Up to now, she has been trying hard to find extenuating circumstances for what Ivar has done. She has claimed to see a difference between Ivar the man and the party he represents, while Jørgen has not budged in his views. She has thought of Jørgen as intransigent, too harsh in his judgement of his brother. But now it could be that Krister is the most honest of them all, while her own judgement has been driven by selfish motives. For her, the most important thing has been her children's schooling, giving them a proper education and a future. But whatever the truth, Krister's salvo has left a bitter taste in her mouth, leaving her with something to think about which she has so far suppressed because such thoughts were too unpleasant for her to admit.

As they are about to leave the boat Krister picks up her heavy bag and gives her an embarrassed smile, a clear sign that he is feeling a certain regret for the level of intolerance he has just displayed towards her. But he need feel no shame for this. She will come to see that this has been a correction that did her good, no matter how unpleasant it may have felt at the time.

It is high tide, and gangways lead steeply down from the boat to the pier. When one of the young soldiers extends his arm to help Julie down she is so taken aback that she does not manage to protest. On the pier she gets her first terrifying sight of how the Germans can look. The landing place is crammed with armed sentries. In steel helmets and with automatic pistols and heavy cartridge belts, they control the passengers as they land. The thought of the bag of food she is carrying makes her shudder, but she sees that Krister has already passed the barrier and come clear of the sentries. He tells her later that he knew one of them. There are often Germans in Ivar's house, and this is one of the musicians Ivar has most respect for. Now and again it is good to have contacts, Krister says, and once again Julie hears in his voice something of the same reproach she heard they were speaking on board the boat.

Julie had expected her encounter with the town to be a shock, but that the destruction should be so widespread was something she could never in her wildest dreams have imagined. Most of the centre looks like a building site. Along the pier and as far up as she can see there are barracks lying close together among the ruins. She can now see with her own eyes what she has been told but has not so far been able to picture. The beautiful town is no more, destroyed for ever. Indignation sweeps through her as she watches her fellow passengers from the boat and the young soldiers marching through the streets singing cheerfully away. The ruins in the background offer a striking contrast to the singing and reinforce the madness of the destruction of the original town.

Even now Julie cannot enter the Storvik house without a sensation of respect. This has remained with her ever since Jørgen brought her here for the very first time. Nor can she forget the joy which used to be present. The music, Erling Storvik's powerful voice, she is struck by the stillness. Everything is so different now. Even the smells seem foreign.

Helene welcomes her at the foot of the stairs. Helene too has changed, her face is thinner, and she seems tense. But her smile is warm, showing that her pleasure at seeing her sister-in-law is genuine.

- So good that you've finally found time to visit us, she says, stroking Julie's arm.

- There are some things you should know before we go up. Peter is here.

Both Julie and Krister look at her in surprise.

- Peter? says Julie. - Is Anne with him?

- No, he's here on his own.

- Has something happened to Anne? Julie whispers as a feeling of foreboding ripples through her.

- No, nothing has happened other than Peter having been ordered here.

- But Peter isn't a soldier. Besides, he's too old for that.

- He's not here as a soldier, but has been ordered to come here as a welfare officer for the German troops in town. He is not living in this house but has visited as often as he could in the time he has been here.

- I must just warn you before you meet him. He… he is not looking well.

After her previous meetings with Peter Julie has always had the feeling of having met a highly refined human being, someone surrounded with an aura of culture. In spite of this he gave off at the same time an air of authority and security which are the hallmarks of someone who has found his proper place in life, a place he fills with his music and his partner Anne. Rarely has Julie seen a couple so well suited to each other, so secure in each other's love, as these two. That they are childless seems to have brought them even closer together in an unbreakable mutual dependence. One of Peter's hallmarks has been his joy in living, his capacity for spreading happiness around him. This is why today's meeting has been a total shock for Julie. She was glad that Helene had warned her, for otherwise she would not have been able to accept that Peter was now nothing more than a shadow of the person he had been.

His officer's uniform seemed totally out of place on him. This uniform, which is so much a symbol of power and authority and which disseminates fear, has the opposite effect when worn by Peter. He looks pathetic and thinner than ever when in uniform. Of course he is older now, and it is a number of years since they last met, but his eyes can hardly meet Julie's and the troubled look on his face makes him appear a stranger.

Their time round the coffee table feels strange. Krister makes an excuse that he has an appointment about the re-opening of school and leaves as quickly as he can without appearing rude. Helene tries as hard as she can to keep the conversation going. Selma makes no attempt to join in but just sits there with a fixed and distant look in her eyes, while the other three, Peter, Helene and Julie, converse almost as if they didn't know each other. Peter makes polite enquiries about the family and Julie's life with Jørgen and the children, but their eyes do not meet, and it seems clear that he simply wants to be out of this situation. It feels like a relief when he says he must go.

He grasps Julie's hand before he leaves. For a brief moment their eyes meet and she is aware of desperation, a grief and powerlessness which hits her like a blow to the stomach.

I think so often about Storvik, Julie. It brings back so many good memories. It is so beautiful there where you live, such a lovely village, and such good and friendly people. I will always remember them.

His voice trembles, but it is still so strange and lifeless that Julie feels at a loss and unable to speak.

- Farewell, Julie.
- Farewell, Peter.

At the door he turns, clicks his heels together in a military salute, dons his uniform cap and leaves.

The silence remaining in the room feels like a lament after he goes.

Krister is having an evening out with friends. Helene and Ivar have withdrawn early, leaving Julie alone with Selma, who clearly feels a need to talk to her.

I'm so pleased you've come. Helene and Ivar are good people, but there are some things it's difficult for me to talk to them about. I believe I can talk to you because, with the way things are going, I don't think I can go on much longer. I love Ivar and Helene as if they were my own children, but it's Anne living down there in Germany that I need to talk about. And now there is this with Peter. It will soon be all too much.

Selma recounts that she had was shocked the day Peter came to the door in his full officer's uniform. He was just so happy to be here, and it was this which made it feel so terrible. He had asked to be sent to Norway, and his wish was granted because of his familiarity with the town and the language. Peter speaks fluent Norwegian. Like so many Germans, he had been told that it was the English who had bombed and devastated the town, and like them, he believed he was coming here as a helper and rescuer. She had to tell him the truth, and it was such a dreadful shock for him when he found out that it was his own people who were responsible for all the destruction. When he found out that he is an enemy here, he broke down in desperation, and in the short time he has been here has changed and become the man Julie saw earlier today. He cannot live with knowing that whenever he goes out onto the streets, here in a town which, because of his relationship with Anne, he has become so fond of, he is looked on as an enemy. He had been so happy when he was granted his wish to come here as a welfare officer. He had been looking forward to partaking in what he remembered as the town's rich musical life, and what he had come to was a ruin caused by his own people.

- Poor man! says Julie, moved by what she has heard. - Peter is an artist. I can't understand him having anything to do with the military. And I certainly don't understand what sort of fairy stories they're feeding people in Germany.

- No, says Selma, - and it's even harder to understand that people there believe the fairy stories.

Selma reports that Peter had become involved in a violent discussion with the Germans living downstairs in her flat. Since then he has become depressed, hardly uttering a word to anyone. She says now that he can no longer bear living in the town. He wants to be transferred to somewhere nobody knows him or who he is, and this wish is now to be granted. He is due to move in the next few days to Trondheim or somewhere further north in the country. Selma has heard rumours in the town that the German officers now want rid of him. They haven't much use for weaklings or penitent sinners.

Selma has written to Anne, begging her to come home. She cannot bear the thought of Anne on her own back there in

Germany while Peter is in this country. But Anne is unshakeable. She says she will come home only when it's all over. As things are now she must stay where she is and take care of her house and home. Selma does not dare to report anything about the situation here at home because she is afraid that the post may be opened, making things difficult for Anne.

- But she, too, will believe in the fairy stories, she remarks bitterly.

As she sits listening to Selma, a picture comes into Julie's mind. She has seen Selma like this once before, just after the time that her youngest daughter, Sigrid, died. Selma sat then as she does now, fighting hard to pull herself together as her hands fumbled with her handkerchief or flew restlessly over the table, betraying the disturbance raging inside her. But the present Selma is older, too old and tired to hold the mask in place as well as she did then.

- Then there is the worry about Helene and Ivar, she says.
- You know how much I wish that Ivar hadn't become mixed up in all this. I have tried to make excuses for him as I must if I'm to live with it. But you know that for me, as for most Norwegians, Germany is the enemy. I have to tell that to somebody. As I think about this terrible war, the destruction, the murders, this is now part of our reality. But what it's doing to us as people, the way it's splitting families, the way that friendships are ending and brothers are taking sides and becoming bitter enemies, at the end of the day all this is very hard to bear.

Selma weeps into her handkerchief, an old, worn-out woman sitting here and looking into the ruins of a life.

- I miss Erling terribly. If he had lived, everything would have been so different. If nothing else, I would at least have had someone to share my worries with. The only thing I ask of life now is to get to see Anne again. That is the only thing that keeps me going. There are no words of comfort for a time like this.

- Oh, Julie! Randi says and looks so taken aback that Julie has to laugh.

- What's the matter? You look as if you've seen a ghost! Have I come at a bad time? Maybe I should have called you before I came, but it's so difficult with the telephones where I live now, and…. Oh yes, I have brought some little trifles for you, says Julie, regretting slightly that she had not told Randi about her visit. But they know each other so well that they have never been too concerned with formalities. However, she does not feel as welcome this time as she usually does.

- No, it's no trouble, Julie, says Randi who by now has pulled herself together. - Come on in and take us as you find us.

A woman Julie does not know is sitting at the kitchen table. She introduces herself and then goes. Randi explains that this woman and her family are renting a bedroom and sharing the kitchen.

- But isn't that a bit of a nuisance in the long run? Julie wonders.

- Oh no, it's all right. We must just be glad we can help people the way things are now. In spite of everything we're lucky not to have lost our house and home.

- But isn't there a loss of privacy?

- Yes, says Randi quietly, but you get used to that.

Julie places on the table the food she has brought for Randi, a little meat, some butter, eggs and a bag of flour.

- I'm sorry there's not more, she says, - but there's not much left in the storehouse at this time of year, and there is so much control nowadays that you are afraid to carry too much baggage.

- Bless you, Julie. This is so good, but we have had more than enough from you already. You are embarrassing me, Randi says and looks surprisingly shamefaced.

She appears tense and feverish as she prepares the coffee table.

I don't want to cause you any trouble, Julie says, somewhat ill at ease. - I have had breakfast, so you mustn't….

- No, no, you must have coffee, if you can call this stuff coffee. And I can offer you a bit of food today, fresh potato cakes and cream cheese. How about that?

- Randi, is there something the matter?

- No, what might that be?

- You can't fool me.

- Don't sit there imagining things! says Randi, irritated.

- Well, if that's how you feel…, says Julie, surprised that her friend has suddenly become so distant towards her.

The conversation proceeds hesitantly. Randi is restless and somehow elsewhere. They speak only of everyday matters, of house and home and how the children are doing. Julie sits there with a nagging feeling that the trust between them has vanished.

As Julie is about to go, Randi says that she will come with her since she has a couple of errands to carry out.

- The weather is so fine we can sit for a while in the park. That is if you have time, says Randi.

- Here is somewhere we can talk in peace, Randi says when they have found a bench they can have to themselves.

- Is the reason why you were so uneasy that you can't trust everyone in your house?

- Yes, the person you met is certainly all right, as is the rest of her family. But apart from that, as things are now you cannot trust anybody. And Yngve thinks ….

- Yes?

- No, it was nothing.

What's the matter, Randi? Are you in trouble? Is Yngve out of work? Because of course there haven't been newspapers for some time.

No, there are no problems of that sort. Yngve is once again working full-time at Storvik as a mechanic. And the newspaper is something he's proud of. The editorial board was of one mind about stopping after everything was burnt during the bombing and after the Nazis and Germans took control. They refused to publish a newspaper which was controlled and censured by the occupants and their lackeys. No, economically, everything is fine.

- Well, what is it then? Tell me now, Randi, you know you can trust me.

- Julie, you don't know how difficult it is for me here. I don't know quite how to say this, but… Yngve will not be very happy hearing about you coming to see me today.

- What are you trying to say? says Julie, taken aback. Do you mean that …

- Listen to me, Julie, says Randi, placing her hand over Julie's and looking her straight in the eye. This is not about our friendship; nothing is going to change that. It's just that we need to be very careful now. You know your family here in town, your brother-in-law and all those Germans going in and out, that can be dangerous for us here. And already I've said more than I should.

- Dangerous? But how do I fit in? Don't you trust me, Randi?

- Yes, you know I do, but I cannot altogether trust those around you. I know it's brutal, Julie, but Yngve has forbidden me to have anything to do with you until all this is over.

- Yngve has never liked me, says Julie bitterly. - And here's the final proof. What I don't understand is that you accept that. I always thought our friendship was firm as a rock, but maybe you are right. You cannot rely on anyone but yourself.

- I can well understand your bitterness, Julie, but in this case I have to listen to Yngve. But please understand that this has nothing to do with our friendship. We are all living a nightmare now, but one day it will all be over, and everything will be fine once again.

- Do you really think so? Have you never heard of things which get smashed to smithereens and are beyond repair?

- Think about it. Think about what I've said, then maybe you will understand.

- Will I understand you, of all people, sitting here treating me as an informer and a traitor?

- I've never said that. That was a horrible thing to say.

- Well, excuse me, but that is how I feel right now.

- No, I can't take any more, says Randi and get up to go. Goodbye Julie, and …

Looking at her even from behind, Julie can see that she is crying. She is downhearted as she sits staring after her. She cannot believe what has just happened. She remains seated, shivering in the frost, a frost bleaker than the shadows which surround the bench on which she's sitting. Selma's words from the night before are swirling round in her head. Families split, friendships destroyed, and closest friends becoming enemies, but she had never imagined that anything of this sort would happen between herself and Randi.

Despite all the destruction she knew she was going to see, Julie had been looking forward to her trip to town, and the thing she had most been looking forward to was seeing Randi. Then it turned out like this. She is still too upset and angry to feel grief for what has happened, but she knows that this will come. Randi has been as close to her as anyone outside her family can be. She feels that this is going to be an irreparable loss.

The meeting with Peter and the conversation with Selma both remain within her as a deep pain, and when a group of soldiers walk past the bench where she is sitting she feels in herself something like hatred. She had never before thought that such a feeling could be good, and yet here she is sitting and hating. But deep down in herself a voice is murmuring. Now, the voice is saying, now, Julie Storvik, you are capable of hating, because it's about you. Maybe this is Krister's double morality?

Jørgen listens to the news from London every evening and is kept up to date on everything happening on the war front. Also on what is happening in Norway, which otherwise they can only know through distorted German propaganda. So far, this has gone without a hitch, and he is convinced that what he has done was right. Even the 'theft' of the radio - some would call it theft - which was carried out in anger and indignation, he has never for a moment regretted.

The greatest problem Jørgen has had so far has been the charging of the accumulator battery. This needs doing at intervals of every four to five weeks. He has to inform the owner of the workshop when this is to be done. However, the owner is totally reliable and this gives no cause for concern. A bigger problem now is moving the accumulator backwards and forwards. He has an agreement with the owner about delivering it and bringing it back home, and it is Helge who has the great responsibility of carrying outh these expeditions. This is because Jørgen thinks it quite unlikely that anyone will be bothered about what a young person has in his bag. Helge is always despatched in daylight to arouse the least suspicion, and every trip is disguised as a trip to the shop at Øra. An additional advantage to this arrangement is that the workshop owner's wife has a knitting machine, and Julie has always used her to make the socks and stockings needed by people at home when she herself cannot manage to knit them by hand. This means that the accumulator can always be covered by skeins of wool or completed clothes. Up to now, Julie has only done this twice a year, but they must now find an excuse in case anyone becomes concerned about it.

The boy faithfully sets out on these perilous journeys with a bag hanging from his cycle's luggage rack or bound securely to the shopping sleigh in winter. He is still young enough to feel excitement about this and to feel he is playing a significant role. But he also understands its seriousness. Sometimes he comes home pale and frightened after meeting Germans or Nazis along the road. One time he arrived home and burst out crying.

- Whatever has happened, Jørgen asked, afraid.

He had run into Halgrim, accompanied by a German, on the way home. Hallgrim had stopped to talk.

- What's going on?

He did not say much. He asked why Storvik people had begun shopping in Øra. Helge had been so terrified that he could barely remember anything else that had been said.

- Do you think he was suspicious?
- I don't know. I don't think so. He was pleasant enough and asked how things were going at school, things of that sort.
- I imagine he was showing off to the German, showing how in touch he was and how he cared about the locality. I've heard that this is what he does when he's with a German and has met other people.
- Father, you've no idea how scared I was, though I don't think I let it show.
- You're a brave soldier, Helge, says Jørgen hoarsely. The day may come when you will understand what a great thing it is you're doing for me, and for all of us, yes, for ….

His voice breaks off as he hands Helge a krone and strokes his hair.

- Today, my infantryman must have his pay.

But Julie is furious.

- How can you expose the boy to this? Have you no sense of responsibility?
- He'll get by, our Helge. It even helps him grow up, as I expect you've noticed.
- When he's so afraid that he cries? What if they caught him one day? Have you thought about that? Aren't you playing games and using your own son as bait?
- They can't punish a boy. So either he does this, or I do, then I'd be the one to be caught. - You must admit I would have a problem if I said I was taking the knitting to Anna in the

middle of my working day. No, Julie, you have to leave this to
me. I know what I'm doing.

Jørgen has allowed himself plenty of time to think about
which of his acquaintances and neighbours he can trust
sufficiently to inform them about the radio in his house. The
shopkeeper and the workshop owner know already, and he now
tells a handful of neighbours. These soon set up a system in
which they take turns coming to Storvik to listen to the news. All
these have sworn to Jørgen that they will not tell a living soul.
Not even their wives. Especially not their wives, for everyone
knows what gossips women can be, Jørgen says.

While they are listening to the news in the room upstairs,
there is always one of the boys on watch down below. So many
people visit the farm. Neighbours pop in for a chat, milk
customers, both adults and children, come in from Øra, and the
adults never leave without chatting. Not all of these are equally
welcome or trustworthy, and it is the boys' responsibility to
report each time who has been in the house so that Jørgen can
keep track. It has occasionally happened that he has had to
smuggle one of the guest listeners out of the house while he
pretends to have just arrived home. At this time of year,
everything takes place under cover of darkness; it will be more
difficult when the seasons become lighter. The biggest danger is
that rumours may spread about extra people coming to Storvik in
the evening. It could then happen that someone might put two
and two together.

The two boys take turns taking notes from the news as
Krister has taught them.

Both quickly become expert and seasoned reporters. Even
Helge, young as he is, has become a wizard at extracting the

essence of the most important news items. These reports become vital for those who may not have actually been listeners, for people are extremely wary about talking to each other aloud about the news.

In the loft at Storvik, the news is fresh and properly summarised before it reaches others in the village. In this way those concerned have learned that Japan has attacked the Americans at Pearl Harbour on Hawaii and in the Philippines. Later in the same month Germany declares war on the U.S.A. In June of that year Hitler's troops attack the Soviet Union. Things have now expanded into a war threatening the entire world, and the chat reaches new highs when the men meet. Even though the Germans are spitting out their usual propaganda about 'German victories on all fronts', people are beginning to see some grounds for hope. There is no doubt that Germany's war machine is gigantic and frightening, but people wonder how there can ever be enough troops to carry out everything they are hearing about. People are saying that Hitler will soon have gone in over his head, and the hope of seeing an end to the tragedy arises within them; at Christmas this year, the hope is that this will be their last wartime Christmas.

Helene and Ivar visit Julie in the period just after Christmas. When Jørgen learned that they were about to come, he hid the radio and all the other equipment along with the maps and notes in the barn. He dared not take any risks with Ivar in the house.

Ivar sticks to the cottage with his mother and does not show himself either in the kitchen or living room, though Helene comes in to talk to Julie. Helene is fascinated by the two young children, especially with little Sunniva who is now mouthing her first words. She immediately wins Sunniva's confidence, and

Sunniva follows her wherever she goes, whether inside the house or in the cottage.

- What a beautiful child! - Do you realise how lucky you are, Julie?

A wall of ice divides the two brothers. They do not speak unless they have to, though Julie scores by arranging for Ivar and Helene to join them for dinner one day soon, even though it will be a meal where everyone breathes a sigh of relief when it is over and the guests can return to the cottage.

- You might try to pull yourself together and at least show some common decency, Julie scolds.
- Can you give me one good reason why I should do that? Jørgen answers tartly.

One day he meets Ivar in the farmyard.

- Have you been out for a walk? Jørgen asks.
- Yes, I've just been to see Hallgrim.
- And I take it he was well? Jørgen says sharply. I'm sure you two have had plenty to talk about.
- Yes, it was good. They asked me to give you their best wishes, he says. A surge of rage sweeps through Jørgen, though he manages to refrain from coming out with the sarcastic reply he has on the tip of his tongue. They have exchanged enough words, or at least Jørgen has. Words uttered in anger, in desperation or in indignation, wasted words which only trouble him in their aftermath. Futile words, which is what his mother always says. But he finds it hard to accept Ivar's tone of voice, a tone which for Jørgen seems full of scorn and contempt and which drives him crazy.

Before Ivar leaves, he points to the radio aerial having
between two roofs.

- You should take care to remove that, he says.
- That's none of your business! Jørgen says angrily. - That I
haven't yet managed to get all my clearing up done, isn't that my
own affair? I'm the one living here, and I surely have the right to
carry out the work at my own pace. You have no right coming
here and ordering what I must do or not do in my own home.
- No, no, I just mentioned it. It can be dangerous having
things like that now. And I can't see what there is for you to get
angry about.
- Hell! says Jørgen as he stands there watching his brother
move away.

He should have left most of that exchange unsaid, but there
is nobody who can provoke him as much as Ivar can. And that
day, he has received a blow. Can it be that someone has
mentioned the radio over there at Ås? Maybe Hallgrim is
suspicious?

- May the devil take the lot of them.

Chapter 7

It is the height of summer, a Sunday afternoon and one of those rare occasions when Julie can allow herself some free time. Sunday is not just a free day, it is also a day which allows time for thought and peace of mind. All work except that which is absolutely necessary has been put on hold. Even the jobs which women usually resort to in their free time have been set aside for today.

Julie is sitting on a bench in the garden. She has pulled the skirt of her sleeveless summer dress up over her knees and feels the sun's heat warming her bare arms and legs. The air around her is filled with the scents of summer as the flowers bloom in their beds, columbines, peonies and poppies. Along the short wall of the house next to the lawn where she is sitting, gladioli bloom in all colours of the rainbow. These are her great delight and she tends to them like little children. Maiden's Blush roses send waves of scented air towards her. She can hear the buzzing of insects and a silence broken only by the happy cries of her two youngest children, who tumble around half-naked as they play on the lawn. Then there are the voices of her three oldest children jumping over the hurdles they have set up. These, too, she hears as cries of joy. But their voices are no longer children's voices. Even Helge, who was confirmed this summer, has now left the change of voice behind.

As Helge walks over the lawn towards her, she is struck by how grown up he now is. All this has come about during spring and summer, and he will soon be as tall as his two older brothers. He has now turned fifteen and has acquired an adult body early, as, indeed, the other two did before him. Although she thinks of the others as fine boys and has always thought of

Krister as the best-looking, she now thinks Helge is more than merely good-looking and would even go so far as to call him beautiful. He has outgrown his awkward boyish movements and looks as if he will soon be in total harmony with his body as he walks towards her, bare-legged and clad only in a pair of shorts. He is still slim though broad-shouldered and narrow-hipped, and his muscles are becoming visible following his work in the fields. He is also keen on all forms of sport, for even though public sporting events are no longer allowed unless organised by NS, young people locally can always find an opportunity to play sport in their leisure time. They meet to play football in back yards or out in the fields, they run races, they run cross-country, and in winter they go skiing and skating.

Helge sits down next to Julie on the bench, his long suntanned legs stretched out in front of him. There is a sense of sea and summer about him. His skin is a light copper colour and his arms and legs are covered with a golden down, also visible in his face. Julie must be careful not to touch him or stroke his warm summer skin as she knows this would cause him embarrassment. The shock of light hair hanging down heavily over his forehead is pale because of the long summer sun. Then there are his eyes, brown and surrounded by dense dark eyelashes. They are Synnøve's eyes, she reflects, which have also been inherited by Krister and Sunniva but which, in Helge's case, form such an odd contrast to his blonde hair, a contrast even more emphasised by the tanned glow of his skin.

- You can probably get what you're looking at, she says.
- What was that? he says, a blush appearing all over his face.

- Oh, I was just thinking out loud, she says as she ruffles his hair. - Now he'll have finished his midday rest. Today, with the weather as it is, I think we'll have our coffee out of doors.

Julie and Jørgen have every reason to be proud of their children. Jostein and Sven are the most alike in both appearance and temperament. Both have an excitable nature and the same hasty manner. These, too, are now affected by the sun but look somewhat reddish, as red-haired people so often do, with a rash of freckles covering their face and arms. Both have bright blue eyes with thick golden eyelashes. Jostein has grown to be a powerful man with a workman's powerful fists. Krister and Helge have the same eyes and look alike in both face and body, but Helge has a weightiness about him which Krister lacks, an air of authority of which she is also aware in Jørgen but even more in Ivar. Sunniva has Krister's colour but Jostein and Svenn's excitable temperament. She feels strange looking at them as she does now. One thing they all have in common is that they all have beautiful eyes.

If only it could always be just like it is now, for there has certainly been no excess of tolerance this year. There have been the usual confrontations between herself and Jørgen over the children's future schooling, but most of it is because of Krister and his clashes with his father. She has slowly come to realise that Krister and Jørgen are never going to be able to work together. That they hardly speak the same language and will almost certainly never be reconciled.

Krister has been at home helping out since leaving high school. This has been the agreement between him and his father. Even though Krister has shown that he is unhappy about it, he has not complained, carrying out all the work his father has asked him to do. But more recently he has shown that he wants to move away, to make use of the things he learned at school. This infuriates Jørgen. Krister must stay where he is. Isn't he going to be taking over one day? Expressions like these are sufficient for Krister to distance himself from his father because of anger. How often has Julie seen that Krister has thrown down tools and walked away from work to avoid huge confrontations after Jørgen has given him a dressing down? And once Krister has taken his leave of the battleground, Jørgen vents his anger on her.

- Now you can see what all this has led to: you are insisting that he should go to high school. Do you see now what ideas you've put into his head?

In these situations, Julie chooses to remain silent.

But Krister comes to her with his concerns.

- I can't take any more of my father's unfair treatment. I never hear him criticising Jostein, while I'm the one who gets blamed for everything that goes wrong, not just for what I do but also for what I don't do.

This pains Julie because she knows that these two, father and son, love each other deeply, but both are so stubborn that they won't admit it. There is nothing she would like more than for the relationship between them to improve. This applies equally to the relationship between Krister and Jostein. Even though there is no actual hostility between them, she cannot avoid seeing that there is tension there and how easy it is for them to come into conflict with each other. She used to think that this was down to jealousy, as there has always been jealousy between them ever since they were small children. But she has now come to see that there is more to it than mere childhood jealousy. The two brothers are just so different in their thoughts and attitudes, and everyone can see that Jostein is a natural farmer, much more so than Krister. Jørgen does not want to hear of this and refuses to see it, which worries Julie when she thinks of the future and wonders how things will turn out.

Jostein has always been a father's boy, more so than the others. Right from when he was small, he has always been at Jørgen's heels, imitating him, and as time has gone on, has learned most of what a farmer has to do. And everything that Jørgen has done is right in Jostein's eyes. He has turned seventeen now, but seems older and has become quite an experienced worker. It often happens that Jostein and his father sit discussing the running of the farm and its workings just like equals. There is rarely any disagreement between them, though it can occasionally happen that Jostein, with his short temper, can drown out his father. One day, Julie overheard a heated exchange of words between them. Jostein was complaining about a job Krister had been supposed to carry out but had not done.

- I am just so fed up! Here is Krister thinking he can leave all the rubbish jobs to me while he swanks around. He should just remember that he's the one who's going to be taking over here and that all the work I do on the farm will one day benefit him.

If Krister had spoken like this to Jørgen, a row would have broken out immediately. But Jørgen is very easy-going towards Jostein. She thinks that he should have more respect for him and should treat Jostein as more than just a seventeen-year-old.

Jostein can be stubborn, and once he has come to a decision it is rare for him to change his mind. He is quite as capable of academic work as Krister, and once Krister had left high school Julie wanted to send him to middle school in town. Jostein flatly refused and the reason he gave was absolutely clear. He was not going to live with Nazis and Germans. In this, he is in total agreement with his father. One day he came and announced that he had enrolled in the Norwegian Correspondence School. He will study towards the middle school examination on his own at home. In the evenings and in his free time he pores over his books, and Julie can only admire his strong will and persistence. She feels sure that Jostein will get on in the world, whether he will or will not.

A battle that Julie has managed to win is that Helge will begin middle school in town in autumn. This decision has not been achieved without tough negotiations between herself and Jørgen. Helge is an exceptionally quiet and well-behaved child, the best-behaved of them all. He has never been entirely comfortable around wrangling and noise and wants to be friends with everyone. He says he can study at home, just like Jostein. If Jostein can do that, why shouldn't he? Couldn't they even help each other out? But Julie does not give way, mainly because she is aware that Helge does not have Jostein's strong will and persistence. He is too disorganised to carry out the demands which studying at home would involve and needs the firm structure which regular attendance at school and homework would give. Then again, Helene has become important by way of support. Helge has shown himself to be a competent pianist, and Astrid, who has taught him up to now, says she has taken him as far as she can. So Helene, who also teaches piano, can take him further and perhaps explore new possibilities for him. We can't turn down an offer like this, Julie insists when she is arguing with Jørgen. Jørgen finally gives in, this time without the same display as when Krister was moving to town.

- You never give up, Julie, until you get your own way.
- Yes, I can be firm, but when it comes to the children, nothing matters more than that they should have a future. People can say whatever they like.
- You were wrapped up in your thoughts, Mother, Krister says with a smile.
- Oh, was I?

Out on the road three young girls are strutting by, arm in arm. One of these is Solveig, one of the girls from Ås who, for the past year, has been attending middle school in town and is now enjoying a visit from two of her school friends. All three are in uniform, a blue skirt and blazer with a badge on the left breast showing the sun cross in gold against a red background. Under their blazer, they wear a white blouse and blue tie, and on their heads are naval-style caps.

- That's quite a way to dress for a walk in the heat! says Julie, and I can't see why Solveig would want to go round showing off that schoolgirl uniform to the whole village.

The three take their time to pass by, giggling and joking as girls will, and it is clear that they are paying considerable attention to the boys in the Storvik garden.

- It looks as if you'd like to try your chances with those three girls who've just passed.
- No, Mother, they don't attract me. I wouldn't touch them with a bargepole, Jostein says, even though his face is bright red,
- Now, now, Jostein, Krister says with a grin. Don't use strong words like that, you who are always so honest and upright. You don't exactly dislike Solveig, now do you?

Jostein jumps up, he throws himself onto Krister and they roll around on the lawn, their arms entwined. First one has the advantage, then the other.

That was all a bit over the top! Jørgen says with a laugh, and I really can't believe how much the poor lad was blushing. You have to be quite grown before you stop blushing when it's all about girls. Just look at them, Julie, they're not so grown up as to stop carrying on like puppies.

Julie, too, smiles. How many times has she seen them wrestling, though more in play than actually fighting? She is not sure whether it is herself or Jørgen who says that things have now gone far enough, and who realises that there is more to this than just a brotherly tussle. She sees this reflected in their faces, particularly Jostein's, which displays an anger the like of which she has never seen in him before. She sees that he is now on top of Krister and is sitting astride his chest with his fist raised. Jørgen springs at once to his feet and seizes Jostein's fist so that it just touches Krister. But he still delivers a blow to the mouth hard enough to draw blood from Krister's nose and upper lip.

- What on earth do you think you're doing? Jørgen hisses as he drags Jostein away from Krister.
- Have you gone mad? croaks Krister, wiping his nose and mouth and staring in disbelief at his own bloodstained hand.

Jostein tries to shake himself free from his father's grasp.

Jørgen stands in front of him and looks Jostein straight in the eye.

- No, you're not going to get away with this. Sit down, and you too, Krister. The pair of you must learn to behave like adults. Can't you see that you've got an audience? Are you determined to bring shame on yourselves in full sight of everybody?

The three girls have now stopped walking and have been watching everything.

- You see what I mean, says Jørgen. - And now I want to know what is going on here.
- It was Krister provoking me, grumbles Jostein.
- And you think you should shame your brother for that?
- No, that's all complete rubbish, says Krister. Don't make such a fuss about it. We were just playing.
- Playing so much that blood flowed? snaps Jørgen angrily.
- That was an accident, says Krister and goes off to deal with his bleeding nose.

Jostein also goes out bent forward, but Julie sees even from behind that anger is still raging inside him. Helge has disappeared, and the two little ones sitting on Julie's lap are frightened by all the fuss.

- Can you make sense of this? Jørgen says, looking at Julie in desperation.
- I've been waiting a long time for it to happen, Julie says and shudders.

Although it is outside Norway that the main events of the war are now taking place, this does not mean that Norwegians have given up fighting the occupants. The resistance movement has grown enormously, and there are now many Norwegians who risk their lives carrying out heroic actions in secret. Acts of sabotage, actions requiring a dangerous level of courage, the passing round of illegal newspapers, and people afraid of being arrested are smuggled out of the way to England and Sweden. Couriers work at great risk to their lives.

People learn about this. The occupying force reports everything in the press, naturally from their own viewpoint. This applies particularly in the case of the lists of people who have received the death sentence. These are followed by the list of executions. These lists are extremely detailed in order to terrify, to warn and to spread fear among the people. They achieve their aims. It is silent round people's homes when news of this kind appears. But something else is happening that the occupants and their helpers have not reckoned with, namely people's determination to resist.

After a while it is not the ordinary German soldier who gives rise to the greatest anxiety. What people have come to fear most of all is the Norwegian Nazis, who, with their crafty infiltration into the community can betray loyal Norwegians and send them directly into the clutches of the Gestapo. This is people's greatest fear, for it means that people always have to be on their guard. They can no longer discuss matters freely except with people in whom they have one hundred per cent confidence, and even then they must be careful.

Here in the village they look back with horror on the shock they received when Sigurd Myrhe came out as an NS member and became mayor. They now see Hallgrim more as the mayor's lackey, even though he still struts around boasting and clearly has a very high opinion of himself. Apart from being deputy mayor, he has also taken on the appointment as the district's police officer. Once in the past, Ås was where the police station stood, and Hallgrim says he thinks it only right and proper that this honour has once again been conferred on the hamlet where he lives. The former police officer has now been dismissed, and Hallgrim has been awarded the post because Sigurd Myhre turned it down. Even though people think they know Hallgrim, how he thinks and is likely to behave on most issues, it still means that he has achieved an unnerving level of power. But he is well known as boastful and his motives are easy to read. The mayor, Sigurd Myrhe, on the other hand, is the one who really frightens people. He is every bit as jovial and talkative as ever, always smiling and accessible, but people now see his joviality as cunning, and recognise that the man behind the smile is as hard as steel. They see that his smile never extends to his eyes, which can appear icily cold, and they never know how to react when Sigurd comes to chat with them.

Apart from these, there is no more than a handful of Nazis locally. People have always been aware of the shoemaker and a couple who turned out to be members when the radios were collected. They were allowed to keep theirs, which was how this came to light. Otherwise there are a few people described as 'stripies'. These seek to curry favour with NS people and Germans in order to gain advantages. This only awakens contempt, because by now people's will to resist has become firm, and they begin talking about decency.

One group which has become more and more visible as time goes on is the Horde, Vidkun Quisling's soldiers as they style themselves. They have become more visible here in the village even though there are not many of them here. This spring the shoemaker, his oldest children, the older Ås children and - as was discovered later - Gunnhild had all been off on a course organised by the Horde. At a church service early in the summer the Ås contingent shocked the village by turning up in full Horde uniform. Gunnhild was dressed in the organisation's women's outfit, a brown belt with the sun cross on a blue background over her left pocket. Round her neck and over her white blouse she wore a brown scarf and on her head a simple hat. Her older sons were wearing a blue uniform with what looked like a skiing cap. The younger children were wearing the Horde children's uniform, blue for the girls and brown for the boys. Hallgrim was the only one of them in civilian clothes. People remarked afterwards that he had more sense than to challenge people overtly. But it was still frightening to see the Ås family all showing off in the oppressors' uniform that Sunday. They completely filled a pew, though it felt more like the whole church. This was the day when people fully grasped that the Ås family was on the opposite side. It was a frightening experience for people and created a revulsion and contempt which they could not hide in the looks they directed towards the Ås family. They could see, too, from Hallgrim's cold expression and the angry colour of his face that he understood.   But, as they remarked later, thought is free. Gunnhild did not seem to notice people's contempt as she showed off her new costume, a brand-new gala dress. 'Silly old goose', people said, but such expressions leave behind a taste, for in times like these even this sort of silliness can be quite dangerous.

The shoemaker also appears in full Quisling uniform. He has now become a group leader and makes a fool of himself by marching along the road in uniform with his service weapons fully on display. Goodness knows if there is anything more to this than stupidity, but people are aware that such stupidity can have dangerous consequences.

People have never believed that the Horde were much of a threat locally, but they know that this is not the case in the cities and larger towns. In particular, they have heard that members of the Horde's youth organisation can be extremely zealous when it comes to spying on and betraying loyal Norwegians. This reminds people of the notorious *Kristallnacht* before the war when Hitler's rabble launched their outrageous attacks on the Jews. Now they have their own rabble here in the village, young whippersnappers who go round in a uniform which gives them a sense of power, a power more dangerous than people are ready to admit.

At Ås they now have their own farm workers, people they can rely on and of their own way of thinking. They had doubtless heard rumours spread by their earlier workers regarding life on the farm, and therefore Hallgrim set out his requirements. They have recently obtained a new workman in Ås who came as something of a surprise. This lad is from a neighbouring village, where his family has a reputation for being honest and trustworthy, people with an unblemished record and a reputation for being genuine patriots. But this young man stands out from them. Like the Ås boys he is a keen sportsman, and through sport has become friends with Hallgrim's two eldest sons and has enlisted in both NS and the Horde. These three youths have taken part in a number of big competitions. In April this year they took part in the Horde's skiing competition at Skeilkampen and in May there was the Horde's relay race which attracted a thousand competitors. They did well in all these events, returning home with both prizes and certificates. People locally heard about this, and those at Ås now go around boasting of their young people and their sporting achievements. Gunnhild was not one to allow modesty to hold her back from launching into a lecture at the local shop in which she eulogised her own children and expressed contempt towards all the others. She referred to them as worthless good-for-nothings, as lazy and showing a lack of enterprise. They should learn from her children, making full use of their young bodies instead of destroying both body and mind in meaningless activity in their free time. Those hearing her tirade had some difficulty in keeping quiet, but had learned that the best plan was to remain silent and pretend that they hadn't heard what it was she said. But those who have the courage to speak about it say that they are thankful to their creator that their children do not parade around in the Horde uniform or partake in their sporting events. Later, they come to understand that this attitude is somewhat naïve. Young people are impressionable and easily led. Nothing is obvious any more, and even in the best of families there can be black sheep.

It is said that the Ås farm worker's family are in despair about what is happening and has tried to get him away but without success, while the young people of the village say that he is even more fanatical than any of Hallgrim's children.

Last winter and spring, when the nights were still dark, he would frighten people by sniffing round their houses and farmyards. He could suddenly bang on a kitchen door without anyone having heard him come in at the main entrance. Some people had come across him in a cowshed or byre, while others had seen his face staring at them through a window or had seen the shadow of a man round the farm buildings and knew that the shadow must be his. If he is caught red-handed he always has a plausible excuse for his visit, an errand for Hallgrim or a visit to the young people of the house. This frightens people. They feel they are being spied on and are under threat, and many now begin locking the door as darkness falls. This has never happened before in the village where people are used to sleeping without locking up. They feel a little safer in summer, but he still sometimes shows up. Larris is the nickname the village people have bestowed on him. Larris is a sly, impossible trouble maker who makes life unbearable, Larris who sneaks around carrying out all sorts of shameful deeds under cover of darkness.

One evening, Julie is sitting in the cowshed milking. Suddenly, she sees Larris standing on the floor, staring at her. She receives such a shock that she almost knocks over the milk pail.

- What are you doing here?
- Oh, I just wondered whether Jostein or Krister was around.
- What would they be doing in the cowshed? she says sharply. - Just go through to the kitchen, they'll be in there.
- The kitchen was empty, he says and gives her what seems to be a look of pure innocence.
- They were talking of going down to the pier. You will certainly find them there.

When they have gone, she goes out into the yard and peers through the doorway to make sure he has gone. She remains standing until she sees him disappear down the hill. The way he moves, those quick turns of the head and the way he seems to be observing everything around him are indicative of a person who is not all he is giving himself out to be. The fear she feels makes her feel sick, and her heart is beating fast. The radio, she thinks, dear God, the radio, can he have sniffed that out?

In spring this year, both the youth club and the People's Building are to be used as a secure holding place for the convict workers for the Todt organisation. This has led to the village being invaded by Germans acting as guards for these convicts. They walk along the roads in their grubby yellow-brown uniforms with red armbands displaying swastikas. This has made people more cautious than ever about what they say or do. For Jørgen the radio has become a danger he must now take very seriously, and he has come up with what he thinks is the perfect solution. This spring he laid a new floor in the part of the hayloft built over the manure store. This floor is roughly a metre higher than the rest of the floor of the barn. On the end of this he built a secret room with a hatch for the boys to creep through. When the hatch is closed it is virtually impossible to discover from outside. When the news from London is on the air the boys cluster round the radio set; the one taking notes uses a shaded pocket torch with a beam so weak that it cannot be detected from outside. Nevertheless, there is always one of the boys outside keeping watch.

Since the Germans arrived Jørgen has become even more restrictive about who may visit. Now never more than one person from outside comes to listen. Sometimes he allows these to come no further than the kitchen, where he will sit and talk while the boys do the listening in the loft. It has sometimes happened recently that he has received visits both from people from Ås and others he would prefer not to see on his farm. Otherwise, just as before, there is always one of the boys keeping watch in the kitchen so that unexpected guests can be kept talking until Julie or Astrid has been informed. Up to now this has functioned well, though sometimes only by a hairsbreadth. Several times Jørgen has heard hints that Sigurd Myrhe or Hallgrim has wondered how people in the village come to be so up-to-date about news from the front. They could not have obtained it from the newspapers. He knows, too, that they have wondered whether there are illegal newspapers in circulation which people may be picking up in Kristiansund. It has sometimes happened that people returning home from a trip to the town have had their luggage turned inside out or have even been strip-searched but without anything being found.

After events of this sort Jørgen has lain low, even allowing the radio to be silent until things have calmed down. What frightens Julie more than the radio is the notes the boys have been taking during the broadcasts. She asks for these to be hidden in a place far away from the radio, somewhere so secure that no one can find them. She herself does not even wish to know where this hiding place is, for she is all too well aware of how it can be for people who distribute illegal material.

That evening it is Helge's turn to keep watch in the kitchen. Julie's head is spinning with fear when she thinks of Jørgen sitting with the boys, listening to the news while the farm worker from Ås is in the cowshed. She sits motionless, listening for sounds from the loft while she struggles to get the rest of the milk from a cow which has also become restless in this new situation, but she does not hear a sound from the loft.

Jørgan is standing in front of her, his face white with anger.

- What was that lump of slush doing here? he asks.
- He was asking about the boy, she whispers.
- Wasn't Helge on duty?
- Yes, I don't know what happened. The kitchen was empty, she says.
- Hell! says Jørgen, heading towards the door.

She hopes that he can control his anger so as not to be careless. No one knows for certain that Lariss will not come back. When Jostein and Krister come crawling down from the loft they, too, look pale and fearful.

- Get down to the quay at once, she says. I said that's where he would be. See to it that fake German does not come back here tonight.

Back in the kitchen there sits a furious Jørgen holding a newspaper.

- Have you found Helge? she asks anxiously.

- Yes, he'd forgotten it was his turn to keep watch. He was lying in bed reading. You can be sure this will be the last time he does that!

- I hope you weren't too hard on him. Remember, he's just a boy.

- A boy? He said he was old enough to take responsibility. And I suppose you realise the danger he's landed us in? It was lucky that Jostein was so wide awake when he was watching at the barn window and saw that sneak come into the yard, so that we managed to turn off the radio. He should have had a good hiding for that.

- I've said all along, Jørgen, that your idea of having a radio in the house will be trouble one day. It's not just yourself you are putting in danger. If it all goes wrong the boy is involved as well.

That night Jørgen lies tossing and turning in bed, unable to sleep. He had thought he was protected because he has a brother who is a party member, someone who can pop in without warning at any time, a brother who also has contact with both Hallgrim and Sigurd Myrhe. He has felt confident that this placed him beyond suspicion for one reason and another. When talking to Hallgrim he has experienced that same feeling. But now maybe this dreadful low life of a farm worker is going to mess it all up. He hopes that it's just the shock he has received tonight which makes him feel like this, but he must now have even tighter rules. Bloody hell! he hisses.

- What did you say? says Julie, only half awake beside him.

- Bloody hell, he repeats angrily.

- You shouldn't swear like that, Jørgen,

- No, but just now I think I've got good reason. I think I may be forgiven this time.

The rumour spread like wildfire over the village. A farmer, one of their fellow villagers, has been arrested for illegally possessing a weapon. It was Hallgrim and his eldest son who were responsible for the arrest. Hallgrim, who usually goes round in civilian clothes, turned up that day in full police uniform and his son in that much-hated Horde uniform. This young farmer, still in his thirties, has been sent to Trondheim escorted by Hallgrim's son and a German military guard. When people hear that he has been sent there, a silence descends over the farms, and unease sneaks into every house and home. Trondheim, they think, that means Gestapo and, even worse, if this poor man should fall into the hands of the extremist Rinnan group. The whole village feels overcome with unease and misery. This farmer is the first person from here to be arrested, leaving behind his wife anxious and shocked and faced with the task of looking after the farm and four very young children. It's fortunate that the people on the farm are still fit and energetic. This poor wife needs all the help she can get, and so three of her nearest neighbours arrange support in case things should become really difficult. But it is worst of all for the man who was arrested. He is a peace-loving and thoughtful man, respected local for his honesty, and not known to take risks. No one can believe that he concealed weapons on his farm.

Once his wife has recovered from her terrible shock, she can tell what had occurred.

Just before the war began in Norway, Torstein had bought a great new hunting rifle. He did this mainly because he was a keen member of the district hunting club. Like many others, he had scrimped and saved for a long time in order to be able to afford such an expensive weapon, and when the weapons were handed in he could not bear to part with it. Instead of the new gun, he handed in an old one of his father's which he believed was unregistered. He cleaned it up, so no questions were raised. He had hidden the new gun in the loft and had more or less forgotten it was there, but when the Germans arrived in the village he realised that he had better find a better hiding place. On the farm there was an old broken-down grain store which was never used. One summer night, when it was darkest though not completely dark, he sneaked out to the grain store with the gun hidden in a sack. While doing this he neither met nor saw anyone, so he retired to bed, secure in the conviction that the expensive weapon could remain there until the war was over. He had said to his wife who had been waiting anxiously that the misery had to come to an end sooner or later. Two days later Hallgrim and his son stood at the door. The farmer and his wife were seated at the kitchen table enjoying an after-dinner coffee, and he knew at once what Hallgrim's purpose was and that something had gone wrong.

Hallgrim was as jovial as ever. He greeted them warmly and behaved as if this was a social visit. The farmer was equally polite when he offered his visitors a place at the table while his wife brought cups and served coffee.

As is normal in the village Hallgrim began by talking informally about this and that, but the farmer's wife was shaking so much that she dared not even touch her coffee cup.

- There's something I need to talk to you about, Hallgrim
said. - I suggest we take a trip to your grain store.

- Yes, very well.

Outside on the steps were two German guards.

- I see there's a few of you here today, said Torstein.

- Well, we sometimes need extras, Hallgrim replied.

His wife heard no more of the conversation between them.
One of the Germans remained standing on the step while the
other joined the others in walking over the fields to the grain
store. What happened there, she does not know. She had had
enough with her own anxiety and her attempts to calm down
those of her children who were old enough to understand.

She stood at the window watching them return. Hallgrim's
son now had her husband's gun over his shoulder, and she felt
the world collapsing round her.

The three came into the kitchen, and it was now quite clear
who was in charge. It was Hallgrim who ordered Torstein to sit
down at his own table while he and his two sons sat opposite.
His wife felt so estranged from her body that she handed over
the children to their grandparents. Afterwards she could not
understand how she was able to be so calm about this. Maybe
she hoped that it could still end well? And she still could not
believe that Hallgrim would send one of his own away to a
terrible fate.

- This is looking sad, said Hallgrim. - What have you to say
for yourself?

- First, I want to ask how you found out about this.

- Well, said Hallgrim, - let us just say that you were
observed during the night.

- Dare I ask who observed me?

- No, said Hallgrim warmly and still smiling, though his eyes were cold. But now it's my turn to ask the questions and to hear your answers. Have you had the weapon in the house since the confiscation?

- Yes.

- Now tell the truth.

- Yes. That is my honest answer.

- And you know that it's forbidden to have weapons in your house?

- Yes, for us ordinary people, that seems to be how it is.

- Don't try to be funny! says Hallgrim, and now there is ice in his voice. You'll soon realise that it pays to cooperate. Why did you hang onto the weapon? Do you realise how stupid that was?

- Yes, it was stupid, but the gun was new and ….

- Was that really the reason? Weren't there others involved apart from you? Maybe there are other hidden weapons here in the village?

- Other weapons? What do you mean?

- I don't think you're telling me the truth. I think you are hiding things. The wise thing would be for you to tell me now, then you would not have to give a truthful account later on to others than me.

- What the hell do you mean by that? Who are these others you are talking about?

- If that's the way you want it you should prepare to say what happened when you get to Trondheim.

The farmer turned pale. Trondheim? he whispered.

- You cannot mean that, Hallgrim.

Hallgrim has now stood up and with an icy calm in his voice says: - Torstein Sand, you are under arrest for the illegal possession of weapons. You will now be escorted to Trondheim. You can prepare for the journey, change into travelling clothes and take any clothing and toilet articles you think you may need. Kari, can you pack up some food for your husband?

As Torstein went up to his bedroom to prepare and get dressed, Hallgrim asked his son to go with him.

- In case Torstein needs help, he said.

Torstein had that to put up with, says Kari. The humiliation of having that nosey whippersnapper guarding him while he washed and dressed. She was choking with rage.

- Shame on you! Kari says. - That you can behave like that towards a neighbour. That you dare to treat my husband like a despicable criminal.
- But, my dear Kari, wasn't he the one who broke the law?

She then broke down completely, begging Hallgrim to show mercy.

- You can't do this to us, Hallgrim, she wept.
- Torstein has done nothing so bad as to deserve this. Don't you think about me and the children? How will it be with us if you take Torstein away?
- Torstein should have thought about that before he landed you in this situation. Yes, it's sad, Kari, but I have to carry out the job my position requires. It has always been the case in this country that if you break the law you have to be prepared to take the punishment.

She will never forget this, she says. Hallgrim's icy stare and that fake warm voice, the sheer falsity of the smile which shows nothing but contempt for them and their situation.

What they went through that day with Torstein taught her the meaning of hatred. She now understood that hatred could drive people to kill. But worst of all was the thought that Torstein had been arrested by one of their own people. It would have been easier to accept if the action had been carried out by the Germans; that she could have understood. But now she is going to be worrying day and night about what has happened to her husband.

After learning what had happened that day to the Sand family, people understood that now they must exercise more care than ever. They have stopped joking about Hallgrim. He is a Judas among them who has now shown his true nature as a man mad for power. After hearing that he had said there could be weapons hidden in the village people's unease increased. That they can expect their houses to be searched starts off as a rumour, but it causes unease both among those who have something to hide and those who do not.

Anything in the house which could lead to reprisals was now hidden somewhere safe. Housewives with expensive food items took care to move them elsewhere, and at Storvik, Jørgen's only concern was the radio. This must never be discovered after everything has gone well for so long. But in these troublesome times the radio is no longer in use, and those who come visiting come no further than to the kitchen where they sit and talk quietly about what has been going on. In the barn the hay containers are full now that the harvest is over. Only a tiny portion of the barn floor lies empty. There will be straw down there after the harvest. But Jørgen has taken care to spread hay in such a way as to conceal the difference between the two floor levels. This is all he can do. There is no safer place for the radio.

The rumours turned out to be true, and house searches began. Or at least a sort of house search, for it was quite unpredictable where Hallgrim and his companions would turn up. But the task must be impossible if it's weapons they're looking for. For example, they would have to turn upside down every steel container in every one of the barns. That would be an impossibility, even if they had a whole battalion of helpers. They are surprised that this did not occur to Torstein before he hid his weapon, but he probably thought that it was safe enough in the ramshackle grain store for as long as the war lasted. It could have been safe there if he had not been observed moving it there. People remembered Hallgrim's expression, that Torstein had been *observed*. Not much imagination was required to know who it was who lay behind the observation. Larris, the Ås farm worker, for if Hallgrim is a Judas, this worker is his chief accomplice.

One day Hallgrim turns up at Storvik along with his eldest son and a German soldier. All are wearing uniform.

- We just wondered if we might take a little look round, says Hallgrim.
- Be my guest, do whatever you like, says Jørgen and looks pleased that Hallgrim has picked up the sarcasm in his words.
- You can come with us, snaps Hallgrim.
- Oh, thank you so much, that's very kind of you.
- Be careful, Jørgen.

- No, Hallgrim, what I must say is this, that you should not
have stooped so low. Have you forgotten that you used to be one
of us?

- Used to be? Hallgrim says.

- That's what I said, used to be, Jørgen says and does not
turn away from his former school friend's glance. He follows the
delegation up to the loft and watches as Hallgrim's son opens
cupboards and drawers and peers into cubby holes. He feels
uneasy as they go into the room where the radio used to be
before it was moved, but the bit of the aerial covered by the
tapestry remains undiscovered.

Back in the cottage Synnøve is sitting alone in the kitchen.
Her eyes widen as she stands to meet the delegation.

- I'd never have believed, Hallgrim, that you could have
made such a fool of yourself in front of the village.

This is the last straw for Hallgrim.

- What in heaven's name do you people in Storvik think you
are doing? Do you think I've come along here just to be
insulted? What I want to see is some respect for the law. Or do
you think you can do what you like just because Ivar has had the
good sense to go along with us? Don't fool yourselves for a
moment, either you, Jørgen or you, Synnøve, no matter how old
you are!

- Synnøve is by now trembling with indignation. - Don't
ever think you can scare me. I wiped your nose too often when
you were just a kid and other parts of you as well for me to be
scared of you now. If you think you can come here and scare an
old woman, you're making a big mistake.

Hallgrim is now flushed with rage and turns on his heels to
go. The German who has been watching everything says

something to Jørgen in German which he doesn't understand. He seems agitated, but Jørgen doesn't answer and just brushes him off with an irritated wave of his arm.

- Barn and hayloft, says Hallgrim as he leads the delegation across the yard.

- I can see you've had a good harvest of hay this year, he says and has calmed down as they stand inside the entrance to the barn looking up at the huge steel containers filling the space from floor to ceiling.

- I can't complain this year, Jørgen answers calmly, though he can feel his pulse racing throughout his body.

- And the new floor, that has been fine?

- Yes, fortunately that worked out well; if it hadn't, we'd have been covered in dirt.

Out in the yard, Hallgrim points to the radio aerial hanging between the house and the barn.

- I've said before that you need to get rid of that.

- I know, but things get put off and never done.

- You should be sufficiently organised to see that it does get done.

- How did it go? Julie asks anxiously as he returns to the kitchen now that that delegation his left the farm.

- Very well. I feel absolutely sure that he suspected nothing. He just grumbled about the aerial as he always does when he comes. I've never felt so relieved.

- Heavens, Jørgen, what times these are!

The big search, as people call it sarcastically, is a source of entertainment, giving them something to talk about and sometimes even to laugh at. A village woman was looking after a piglet when the Supply Board visited the farm. While Hallgrim

was waiting she hid the pig, which was by this time almost ready
for slaughter, in the toilet. But the pig started squealing and
caused such a fuss that of course Hallgrim found out everything.
But it was then that he showed that he had maintained something
of his old sense of humour. He laughed a great deal about
finding a pig in the toilet.

- I didn't think a good person like you would be cruel to
animals, he said, teasing the bewildered woman. Releasing the
pig from the toilet, he gave it a whack over the back, which sent
it squealing across the fields, giving the inhabitants a great deal
of difficulty in recapturing it.

- I don't suppose the pig is a registered citizen. Ought we
report it to the Ministry of Supply?

People watching said that the woman was so frightened that
she lost her voice and was unable to speak, but Hallgrim was just
one big grin as he left the farm.

Stories like this come as something of a relief for the
village, they are stories they can twist and turn around. For they
are not exactly spoiled for entertainment the way things have
become.

Regarding Hallgrim's visits, which he called at the time
routine searches, people now see them in retrospect as attempts
to scare people. One thing is certain, that by going to arrest one
of his own neighbours Hallgrim has placed a serious distance
between himself and the villagers. He has betrayed every rule of
community living, faithfulness and loyalty. Nor can he say later
that he was just doing his job, exercising his responsibility as a
police officer. Had he wished, Germans could have carried out
the arrest, which would have allowed him to play a more
anonymous role. People know this and avoid him as much as

possible. They reply in monosyllables whenever he tries to start a conversation and make no attempt to conceal their contempt when they look at him. They cannot be arrested for things they have not said, and people's contempt will ensure that Hallgrim is never going to forget what he has done to one of the village people, and so to them.

The farm worker from Ås is also an object of hatred. It seems unbelievable that he dares to appear in public after all has happened, yet he does. He turns up in places where young people gather and appears entirely unaffected by the hateful looks directed against him. People call him an emissary of Satan. The young people of the village talk of beating the life out of him, but when it comes to it they dare not. He has become too dangerous for all of them. Such is the power a young man they formerly thought of as a naïve and innocent farmer's boy currently has over their village.

The village was soon to have more to talk about. They find out that the next oldest of the Ås boys, who is the same age as Krister, and the farmer's boy have enrolled as active volunteers in the German army. Both have been away on a training course, but no one can find out where. It was Hallgrim himself who revealed this as he mingled with a few men waiting for the post. He boasted that these two young boys were showing their responsibility as good citizens, a responsibility which he said more than they should have shown in this out-of-the-way village. His eldest son would also have enlisted, but with all the work his job entails Hallgrim cannot dispense with both his sons. The eldest one now has the responsibility of running the farm.

- You've lost a useful worker there, haven't you? Jørgen says, unable to resist this dig at Hallgrim.

- Yes, you could say that. But maybe you could recommend someone who's reliable?

- No, no, you'll soon find somebody who's just as reliable as the one you've lost.

The things this man says! these men remark after Hallgrim has moved on. Here he was boasting that his son would be fighting along with the Germans. But *where* will they be fighting? If they end up on the eastern front these two will most likely be wounded if they're even lucky enough to escape alive. Kept up to date with the real news as these men now are, they know that things are going badly for the Germans. They cannot understand Hallgrim standing out there boasting when he is most likely sending out his own son as cannon-fodder. But at least the villagers know just how deeply Hallgrim believes in his dream, the dream of the German Reich. He must have taken leave of his senses, they say, shaking their heads.

A good emerging out of all this is that the village will now be rid of the traitor, that fawning farm hand whom they've come to feel has been such a danger to everyone. But before leaving for the training camp he still succeeded in bringing about some more misery. In the final days before he left he went home to be with his parents. While he was there, he heard a rumour that one of their neighbours had a radio. A couple of days after the boys left this man was arrested. It was again Hallgrim who was responsible for this arrest since his responsibility as a police officer also covers the neighbouring village. People knew it was the farm hand who stood behind the arrest. The unfortunate victim probably believed that he had hidden his radio as safely as Jørgen had hidden his, but was probably insufficiently attentive to the danger this oaf represented. Jørgen froze when he heard the news.

- We've been luckier than we deserved, Julie said.

The farmhand's parents are reported to be crushed by everything that has happened. When his mother heard that her son had enlisted, she took to her bed, so people said. In any case, she no longer dared to show herself in public. His father cursed Hallgrim and the people of Ås who had dragged their son down into all this wretchedness. It is not that people do not feel sorry for these poor parents. These are decent people who have never hurt anyone and deserve a better fate. But now, here in the village, people are breathing more easily. They are at least rid of a quasi-German who has cast a dark shadow over their lives.

A strange feeling comes over Jørgen as he enters the post office one evening. Men who have already received their post and have been hanging around for a chat suddenly become quiet as he appears in the doorway. He has the impression that they have been having a lively conversation which they have broken off as he came into the room. They stare at him, causing him and look down to see if there is something wrong with his clothing or if there is some other reason why he's the focus of their attention. He cannot see that there is anything unusual, so he pulls himself together and greets them. They answer, but their voices sound strange. He receives his own post, but the businessman's wife, whose duty it is to hand it to him, avoids his gaze. It is only when he has the post in his hand that he understands everything, and it feels as if all the blood in his body is rushing up to his head. At the top of the bundle there is a letter for Krister; the letter has been re-addressed from Ivar's address in town, and at the bottom of the envelope is the NS's stamp.

Jørgen stands staring at the letter without fully grasping the situation, though he understands that this dreadful gossip of a postmistress has told the men standing here about the letter. Words fail him, either for explaining or explaining away the situation. He later recalls saying goodbye as he lurched out and made his way back up the hill, swearing as he had never sworn before. Satan! The anger! As he opens the kitchen door back home he feels an ice-cold rage which threatens to take all his breath away.

Julie is sitting having supper with the three eldest boys. The smallest are already in bed.

- Whatever has happened, Jørgen? Julie says, you look as if you've seen a ghost.

He throws down the letter in front of Krister.

- Tell me what this is about! he says, his voice hoarse and unrecognisable.

Krister looks in surprise, first at his father then at the letter.

- How should I know?
- Open the letter.
- But father, isn't it my letter? Shouldn't I be the one to decide whether to open it or not?
- Open the damn letter! I say.
- I really don't understand you making such a fuss, says Krister, but he opens the letter and glances quickly at its contents.
- No, it's just some rubbish, he says and begins replacing it in the envelope.
- Hand me the letter! Jorgen says.
- What do you mean? Who has given you permission to read my private letters? says Krister, himself now flushed with anger.

- It's not private. It concerns every one of us. And just so long as you are under age and live in my house, I can do anything. Anything, do you hear?

- Jørgen? Julie interrupts.

- Be quiet! I am boss in my own house.

Jostein and Helge are sitting with their eyes firmly focused on the table. Julie remains silent. She has learned that when Jørgen is as he is now it is best to be silent. When Jørgen is in a bad mood, he can rant and rave at the top of his voice about the least bagatelle. This frightens nobody. But when he is as he is now, his voice quiet and his manner ice-cold, then those around him know to keep quiet. Julie cannot remember the last time she saw so much anger in him.

Krister shrugs his shoulders and hands the letter to his father.

- There you are. Just read, he says with a feigned indifference.

Jørgen's face turns white as he reads.

- Serving as a volunteer in the German army? What is this you've become mixed up in?

- I haven't become mixed up in anything. It's just rubbish.

- Rubbish? Now you're bringing shame on all of us. Wasn't Ivar doing that enough?

Krister has now risen to his feet. His eyes flash in defiance of his father.

- Shame on us all, he says, and his voice is now every bit as cold as his father's. - I am just so fed up with hearing that!

You'd think that this was the most important thing in the world. Oh, you mustn't bring shame on the village, he mimics.

I am so tired of hearing that this damn village should control our lives. And now, Father, you must listen to me. Ah, but maybe I don't have the right to explain because I'm not legally an adult?

- Now you're being insolent!

Krister slams his fist on the table so hard that the vessels on it jump.

- Sit down, I said, and listen.

Julie looks at the two of them. They have taken possession of the whole room; she and the two others are no more than witnesses, having no effect on what happens. Two strong wills sit facing each other as Jørgen sits down opposite Krister.

Coming into contact with both Nazis and Germans was unavoidable during the years Krister had been lodging with Ivar in town. Even though most people look upon them as enemies many of these are perfectly agreeable people. He had gained a great deal from conversations with many of the German visitors to Ivar's house. Most of these were polite and friendly without ever seeking to dominate, and many had artistic interests. It was hardly surprising that many NS members in town thought that Krister was playing along with Ivar, given that he was a member of the family living there. It was inevitable, too, that some ordinary people in the town would be suspicious of him.

- Are you listening, Julie, to what I've said? And you want to send Helge to that same rats' nest?

- I've said that I don't have to go there, Helge says nervously.

Krister hears this. He explains that he did not care about what other people thought, just as long as he felt he was doing the right thing. Nor did he go round in town boasting that he got along with everybody, even though there might be good grounds for thinking that this was true. He was sensitively aware that he was living on Ivar and Selma's generosity. But he had neither said nor done anything which could so much as hint that he sympathised with NS. He was totally neutral. He had not done anything to even remotely imply that he was interested in volunteering or in any way serving NS's interests; if his father looked further into the letter he would see that it was all just part of a recruiting campaign and that the whole dispute was a misunderstanding based on nothing more than the fact that he had received a letter.

- It doesn't matter what you said, Jørgen says, the damage has been done, and he goes on to speak of the reaction he had received at the post office.

- They knew about the letter. That damned postmistress had seen to that.

- That damned postmistress has no right to show people's private mail in public, says Krister.

- But that's what she did, and now it's all round the village. What people are saying now is that in Storvik there are others apart from Ivar who are in cahoots with NS.

Krister now stands up, his face as white as Jørgen's. At the door he turns round and looks at his father.

- You've never trusted me, Father. And now that's enough. I'm going to move away. But before I do, I'll see to it that the village finds out the truth about this letter. I'll show them that my heart is in the right place even though you are saying it isn't. You won't have to put up with being shamed in the village because of me, he says, slamming the door behind him.

- Now just leave the boy in peace, Julie says, her voice trembling with emotion.

Jostein and Helge go out, leaving Jørgen and Julie by themselves.

Jørgen, you have to stop this. You're overreacting. Neither Ivar nor Krister can be blamed for the letter arriving in the house. But apart from that, I agree with Krister that I'm tired of this damn village controlling our lives.

- You're swearing, Julie.

Yes, and for once I'll allow myself to swear. I can no longer bear the blame for what your brother has done. That is what it all comes down to, isn't it? Ever since he joined the party our lives have been damaged. I can't take it anymore; do you hear?

Jørgen's anger drains away. He remains seated at the table with his head in his hands. Julie stretches out a hand towards him to stroke his back but then withdraws it.

- Hell!
- No, that's enough, Jørgen. You need to apologise to your son. You and Krister need to talk before it's too late, and before everything between you is ruined.

She stands looking at Jørgen's back as he leaves. It looks like the back of some poor old man. Whatever are they doing with their lives?

Days followed in which not a word was exchanged between Jørgen and Krister. Each avoided being alone with the other. This can go on for ever. One day they are out in the fields dismantling the empty haystacks after mowing. There is the same silence between them as has gone on since the upset over that fatal letter. They are so familiar with this kind of work that they can do it without speaking. Jørgen loosens the strings from the drying racks while Krister loads them onto the spool. Jørgen is feeling miserable after what has happened and is finding the silence between them intolerable.

- Let's take a break, Krister, he says. - Come over here to where we can sit down.

Krister's unwillingness shows as he sits down next to his father.

They sit side by side on the warm ground. In front of them are the houses in Storvik with the gentle fields and meadow further back, out towards the fjord. Jørgen spreads his arms wide as if to embrace the scene.

- Everything that you see here, Krister, will one day be yours. And you won't have to wait very long before you can take over. I took that decision when things were at their most difficult between my father and me. I decided that my son would not have to go through everything that your mother and I had to endure.

For the first time he tells Krister about all that happened, right up to the point when Julie and himself obtained the title deeds to the farm. He does not want Krister to go through all of that - he will be able to take over while he still has his youth and energy intact. Krister is about to turn twenty. If they look forward ten years, it seems reasonable to assume that in that time Krister will have his own family and that Jørgen will still be young enough to help out on the farm. Also, he will be able to hire help from outside so that he won't have the burden of caring for himself and his mother.

Krister says nothing while Jørgen is speaking. He sucks on a straw while looking straight ahead of him.

- I think it's time that we had a little chat about your future. Maybe you should begin to prepare for what's coming. How about beginning at an agricultural college?
- No, Father.
- No? Do you think it's too early for that?
- No, says Krister, now looking troubled. - We now need to stop lying to each other. You know that I'm never going to go to an agricultural college and that I'm never going to take over here. I'm just not cut out for farming in the way that Jostein is.
- Are you sitting here giving away your inheritance? Jørgen can hardly get the words out. This is something which has been inside him, gnawing away at him and upsetting him, but which he has suppressed and has refused to look at. Now the words have been said and he feels within himself an infinite weariness and a dismay which threatens to smother him.
- And what will you do with your life now? Jørgen asks, his voice devoid of expression.
- I want to study.
- In Oslo, by any chance?
- In Oslo.
- How have you thought of financing it? Because you don't think that we …? The words he is saying sound as if they were being uttered by someone else.
- Well, it won't be this autumn. It's too late for that now, Krister says eagerly, clearly relieved that his father is so composed. - It's easy to get a job now. I can start as soon as the heavy farm work is out of the way. Besides, I imagine it will be easy enough to get a job in Oslo in addition to studying.

A feeling that all this is unreal seizes Jørgen, and his indignation spills over.

- Oh, he says sharply, - so that's what you've been thinking. I dare say you'll get a job with the Germans?

- With the Germans? Be careful what you're saying. You are not exactly beyond criticism yourself, are you?

- What do you mean? Have I ever worked for the Germans? What is you are daring to say?

- I don't suppose it was work for the Germans when you and others from every farm round about drove sand for Nordag, that time they were building the dam and the power station?

- That was work which benefited the village.

- Oh yes, you can make that excuse. But there's no getting away from the fact that it was work organised by Germans. Nor should you believe they saw that as only benefiting the village. It was all part of a bigger plan they have for our country and their future activity here. I seem to recall, too, that the work was rather well paid.

- You don't know what you're talking about. Besides, the money was of benefit to you.

- I can no longer bear hearing you talking to me about morals, Father. Anyway, I have been promised a job at the seafood factory.

- Oh, you've thought of working for them, have you? You've had your plans in place for a long time, I can see. Very well, do what you want, but you must know that there is no longer any place for you on the farm.

Krister stands up. He remains standing and stares at his father.

- Do you mean that you are throwing me out?

- Nobody's throwing you out. It's you who have chosen to leave us. And now go away, please. I just want some peace.

- Father, please ….

- Just go! Or is that asking too much?

Jørgen watches his son leave after yet another quarrel. He can scarcely recall ever feeling so miserable. Will he never be able to reach his son? Is he going to become more and more of a stranger to him? When Krister was sitting there and turned down his inheritance, this was like receiving a punch in the stomach. From somewhere deep inside him there arise memories of his own father. Up to now he has suppressed the memories of all their confrontations and his own secret dreams of being able to escape from Storvik. But he knew where his duty lay and that it was this family duty which weighed more than anything. He knew that he had the right to inherit and that to do so was his duty. Now Krister is breaking that tradition, and it feels like another link in a chain breaking. A feeling of desolation seizes him, as if this is a warning of disaster threatening the entire family, and he freezes as he sits here on this warm summer's day.

He also feels miserable over the way in which he has tackled this and that once again Krister has caused him to lose his temper. He sits here feeling like a loser in comparison to his own son. How can he atone for that? What has he done to deserve this?

He can see from the unflinching look on Julie's face that Krister has told her what has happened.

- Where's the boy now? he asks. He can hear the desperation in his own voice.

- He's gone to the summer farm. He said he was going up there with Astrid for the weekend. What have you been thinking, Jørgen? When are you going to learn that setting hard against hard just doesn't work with Krister?

She stands in front of him like a pillar of strength. There is no point in attacking her either when she is like this.

- You should have supported me instead of always standing up to me, he says bitterly as he goes out. He cannot do with any more reprisals from her now. He has had enough.

It is not always easy to keep a clear course through life. Especially working life. For however paradoxical it might seem, the war has given people work. Here in the village, the organisation Nordische Aluminium Gesellschaft, or Nordag as it is referred to in everyday speech, has brought many jobs. This engineering firm is administered by Germans, but the work itself is led by Norwegian engineers and experts. The firm's main aim is to carry out a comprehensive watercourse development to contribute to the German aluminium industry in Norway. People are aware of this, but they have still undertaken work for the firm, some because they were ordered to, but many on a free-will basis. It is well-paid work, and even if people say it stinks of German money, the work they do benefits the district.

Nordag has constructed dams up on the lake by the summer farm and installed a pipeline and power station in Øra. From what they have been told, this will all contribute to the gigantic development of the Aura plant at Sunndalsøra.

Among other things, the road leading up to the summer farms has been improved to allow the movement of materials. A pier has been built so that cement and materials can be loaded onto cattle boats and carried to where the dam is situated at the narrowest part of the lake. In winter, once the ice has settled, farmers used to bring sand for the same purpose. At Storvik, they had two horses, and both Jørgen and Dreng-Anders took part. This arrangement created sought-after jobs. Jørgen can still remember the exhilarating feeling they experienced at the first pay out. Five hundred kroner for some. A thousand kroner for Jørgen. The feeling was like a high point in the year. People stood in line to receive their pay, which was handed out in brand new hundred kroner notes. Jørgen can still remember the rustle of these banknotes. Many people had probably never held so much money before. Then, it certainly never occurred to anyone that this money might smell.

German work or not, the village acquires a new power station, and those who live on the edges or do not have electricity can look forward to having it soon. They will be able to speculate later as to whether or not this is morally justifiable. But one thing they agree on is that the engineers and experts responsible for the installation are very able people and highly efficient. The new power station will soon be complete and will supply more than enough electricity both to households in the village and to the industries out on Øra. Thus, people believe that both building the power station and working there are defensible. Their story is quite different for those who work directly for Germans. People locally hesitate to do that, and here in the village, there is little such activity. At the outset of the war, a coastal defence station was built out in the fjord with people from the village taking part in its construction. A consolation for these is that they were acting under orders, and there has been no further talk about this locally. But again this was well-paid work, and some villagers fell prey to the temptation. In Ørland in Trøndelag and in Kristiansund, the

Germans are building enormous fortifications, and those who have allowed themselves to be tempted by the promise of easy money are not always looked on kindly. This also applies to those who deal directly with the Germans, even though this is easier to understand. In the case of goods which are in short supply the temptation to deal directly can be too strong, and the most tempting currency is cigarettes and tobacco. Both butter and eggs, which are the main items in the smuggling trade, disappear from housewives' shelves and are exchanged by a husband in a good mood because he has once again been able to light his pipe. Even Jørgen, no matter how upright he may claim to be, cannot claim to be entirely free of this temptation. Such temptations have now increased because more Germans have arrived in the village in connection with the Todt camps.

Even though people dislike all Germans coming to the village, this can have a stimulating effect, however improbable it may sound. It means at least that something is happening in an otherwise grey and miserable wartime existence. People are intrigued by these convict workers and are uncertain as to what exactly their status is. They are certainly not being treated as free citizens, but nor are they treated as prisoners so far as people can see, and it seems that they are sometimes allowed to move about freely. Those living in the Youth Building sleep on straw mattresses laid out over the floor in the main hall. This is hardly a holiday camp existence, but they do not appear to be suffering from any lack. Rumour has it that quite different conditions apply further north, but this would seem to depend on nationality. Here in the village, the majority are Frenchmen, with some Belgians and a few Dutch and in the Youth Building one Spaniard.

What people have found out about the Todt organisation, or OT as it is known, is that it is a semi-military organisation founded in Germany by a man called Franz Todt. OT's activity in Norway is associated with the construction of fortifications along the coast in what is called *Festnung Norwegen.* However, OT also plays a part in road works and other civil projects.

Those stationed in these camps are people expelled from German-occupied countries, but can also include volunteers and even a few Norwegians, though there are none of these in the village's camp.

Here, the convict workers' task is to dig out sand from a gravel pit and load it onto large sand barges, which then carry it away for the production of cement and for the development of fortifications in and round Kristiansund. The camps and work scenarios are kept under close scrutiny by German guards dressed in the characteristic Todt uniform. Some of the guards are very young and are keen to display a brusque approach. This, Julie says, arises from anxiety and insecurity since it cannot be pleasant coming to work in a foreign country in which you feel both unwanted and unwelcome.

Helge experienced a nasty shock one day when he went to the workshop to pick up the accumulator after it had been charged. He had placed it in a bag on the cycle's luggage rack, well hidden under some ordinary shopping. Just past the gravel pit, which is right next to the road, there is a slight incline. Helge stopped to rest and stood looking at the work on going on the gravel pit. At this point, one of the guards began waving his arms at him, roaring and shouting.

- *Achtung!* the German shouted and stormed over to him. In a mixture of Norwegian and German, he shrieked that stopping here was forbidden as it interrupted the work. What was Helge doing here, and what was in his bag?

- Frightened out of his wits, Helge managed to stammer that he had been to the shop to buy food. He opened his bag to show some loaves at the top of other items.

- *Nein! Nein!* Shrieked the German. Don't stop here! Go! *Schnell!*

When he arrived home he had calmed down sufficiently to joke about the incident.

- But what if he'd asked you to empty the bag? Julie says.

- Oh, he was so stupid he wouldn't have known what an accumulator was, says Helge confidently, though his face is still pale after the experience.

- I've told you, Julie insists, this is all going to end terribly.

A few days into a very busy mowing season, the convicts have been ordered to help out on the local farms. They have worked like heroes and have been a great help, but people say that this is just part of the Germans' plan. They want to show how positive and friendly they are. People are also surprised that some of these foreigners go along the coastline picking up shells, which they then boil in seawater in tin cans. This they appear to eat with gusto. When people ask if they do this because food is scarce in the camp, they answer that no, no, it is a delicacy. This is how they learn that the French here on the land eat fishing bait for food! This seems very odd. As time moves on the foreigners pick up some words of Norwegian, though normally communication between themselves and the villagers is by signs and pointing.

In Storvik, they often receive visits from the Spaniard from the young people's house - his name is José, though people locally call him Hosse. He has told Krister, who is good at languages, that he fled to France following the Civil War. He was then caught by the Germans and sent here to work for Todt. He appears in Storvik whenever the opportunity arises, and people quickly grasp the reason for these frequent visits. There is a farm girl from one of the islands, a bright and good-natured little girl. The Spaniard looks into her eyes and is so taken with her that it is painful to see.

- The poor lad is in love, Jørgen jests. - Which is not so strange when they are so starved of female company.

The girl is teased and feels uncomfortable with the attention, so the lad's warm feelings are unlikely to be reciprocated. She has also attracted the attention of a local boy, so the chances of any amorous adventure are not looking good for the unfortunate foreigners. They are guarded too scrupulously, and when the reveille is sounded in the early evening all must be indoors.

- Amore, sad, Jørgen teases and assumes a sad expression.
- Yes, yes, amore sad, José blushes and sighs.

But there are consolations.

The commandant for Todt in the village is called Schnitler. A small fop of a man with the temperament of a lemming. Nobody has heard him speak with a normal voice, and he shouts and screams and behaves as if he were the Führer himself. It does not take long for the villagers to have had enough of this caricature of a man. Then something happens which sets the village alight.

One Saturday evening Krister and Jostein are sitting together with three or four friends. They sip some strong beer, indeed don't only sip but consume a substantial amount of the foaming liquid. Jostein, who is the least experienced in dealing with this brew, becomes sick and disappears home to bed without his parents suspecting anything. The others become quite cocky but are bored. They have not had sight of a girl all evening; everything is dull, and they need to find some outlet for all that energy buzzing away inside their young bodies. Krister is the first to come up with the fatal idea.

- Let's go to Øra and get Schnitler!
- Are you joking? He's a madman! He'll shoot us!
- Nonsense! He has no right to lift a weapon against innocent civilians. We'll just tell him not to go round a respectable village behaving as he does.

The boys egg each other on as they make their way along the road. In the end, they feel invincible and capable of doing anything. When they come to the house in which Schnitler has requisitioned lodging, they knock on the door, which is opened by the lady of the house.

- Is Schnitler still awake?
- Yes, says the woman, frightened. - He has visitors.
- Tell him we'd like a word with him
- But they cannot ....

But she isn't able to finish speaking before Schnitler himself appears on the step. Speechless, he stares at the young boys in front of him. Krister begins the speech they've prepared in his fluent German but does not get many words out before Schnitler explodes in a blind rage.

- Assault! Murder! he screams and withdraws his service pistol from the holster he always wears. He fires a couple of shots into the air before bringing the pistol down and pointing it at Krister. Behind him, the lady of the house is standing rooted to the ground in fear.

It just so happens that the person visiting Schnitler is Hallgrim, and he is the one who prevents the evening from ending in tragedy. He manages to calm Schnitler down and explains to the enraged officer that this is just the behaviour of a few drunken boys.

He bundles the boys into his car.

- I should actually have arrested you here and now, he says.
- But you can expect a visit when you have slept off your drunken state. And don't leave the village, is that understood?

The boys, deathly white with shock, simply nod.

Hallgrim doesn't say another word on the journey back. He hands them over in turn to their parents, whom he informs briefly of what has happened. Krister is last. He sits in the front seat next to Hallgrim and detects a faint scent of brandy from Hallgrim's breath, though he appears to be quite sober.

Julie and Jørgen have retired to bed but are woken up by Hallgrim calling from down below. Jørgen stands there only in his underpants listening to Hallgrim recounting what has happened.

- I'm relying on you to keep the boy on the farm until I've investigated this, he says briskly as he leaves.

Jørgen was lost for words while Hallgrim was present. Now, his fear causes his anger to flood over.

- What in heaven's name have you been up to?

Krister looks down at the floor.

- Was this what you meant when you said you'd show the village that you're a responsible adult? He wheezes and shakes Krister so violently that he staggers and almost falls.

- No, Jørgen, stop! says Julie, who by now has arrived on the scene. - No more for now.

She is trembling so much that she can scarcely stand upright.

- I'm going to bed, says Krister in a voice which is barely audible.

- Yes, do that. We can talk tomorrow, Julie says.

- You can write that down, that we'll talk, Jørgen shouts back at them.

- Dear God, what if the boy is punished? says Julie.

- We now have to be prepared for anything, says Jørgen.

There is a delay of almost a week before Hallgrim appears, a week during which four boys have been living through a nightmare of anxiety and have hardly eaten or slept. He arrives at Storvik in his full police officer's uniform and asks Krister and Jørgen to come with him into the lounge. For as long as Krister is under the age of responsibility, Jørgen ought perhaps to be present.

He says he hopes Krister understands the seriousness of what he has done. A breach of law and order, as well as threats against a higher officer - these are serious charges and people have been punished for less. However, to avoid the incident growing out of proportion, and particularly for the sake of the parents, Hallgrim has fought for the boys to be let off with a warning and a fine of a hundred kroner each. But Krister must understand that the matter has now been reported to the appropriate authorities. Any further escapades could land him in the danger zone.

- Maybe you thought I'd waited a long time before coming? Hallgrim says – but I thought they could benefit from a gentle approach and think about what they have done. If it wasn't for me, they could have wound up somewhere where they would have had a great deal of time to think about this.
- I hope this will be a lesson for you, Krister, he says.
- Otherwise, let us be thankful you have not had to face punishment.
- I'll pay you back the money for the fine, Father.
- Now go away, I need some peace.

Jørgen is left with a feeling of resentment that after this, he will spend the rest of his life owing a debt of thanks to Hallgrim for saving his son from the clutches of the Gestapo.

The village boils over with gossip after what has happened, and once the initial fear has died down, the funny side emerges. For weeks and months, the unfortunate boys are sworn at and teased for their audacity, which came to such a miserable conclusion.

Summer is waning. It is already late August. Julie is busy getting Helge ready for his new school year in town. One day, a long-distance telephone call arrives from home. As always, when she receives such a call, she fears there may be something wrong. And as always, she is reassured when she hears her father's steady voice, He speaks first of this and that and wants to know how things are with her and hers.

- Is everything fine with you? Julie then asks.
- I'm afraid it's not particularly fine just at the moment, he answers.

- Is it something serious? she asks anxiously.

- He says he does not know exactly how to reply. Her mother has had a stroke and is paralysed down her left side, but she can speak quite well and, in her waking hours, seems clear.

- But she is asking about you and Johanne, but mostly you. She's saying that Julie must come and help her now. Would it be possible for you to come, do you think?

- Yes, of course, I'll come. I'll be there just as soon as I can get my travel permit.

- Don't put it off too long, he says, and Julie's heart sinks, for now she understands that this is serious. - Do you have enough money for the journey?

- Yes, yes, don't think about that now.

It is inconceivable that Julie's strong and energetic mother is ill. She can scarcely remember that she has been ill and in bed at any time apart from when she was giving birth to her siblings. And as she is not yet seventy, is she not too young to have a stroke?

Chapter 8

Jørgen wants Krister to accompany Julie on the journey. Things are so unsafe both on land and at sea that he does not want her travelling alone. Fortunately, this is a peaceful time between farming seasons, but even so he thinks it would be unwise for him to go with her and that it would be inadvisable for both of them to leave everything behind. The autumn harvest needs to be prepared, and then there are the children, Sven and Sunniva. Both are so young that it would be difficult if both parents were to leave them.

Leaving is going to be hectic for Julie. She rings Halgrim and asks if it might be possible for Krister to come to pick up their travel permits for both of them, but it turns out that both are required to meet up in person at the police station which Hallgrim has set up at Ås. Julie feels frustrated. She must wear make-up and dress respectably for a meeting like this, and feeling generally uneasy as she does, she is frustrated at having to waste so much time on unnecessary details.

Hallgrim is welcoming and cooperative. He says that in the present situation, they will receive their travel permits on the same day. He also shows an understanding that Krister is to go with her, though he cannot resist the temptation to give Krister a little reminder of the last time they met.

- You should not have come here and sounded off. With your education, you could find better things to do than to go round playing stupid pranks.

Krister doesn't answer, though his face darkens. As they make their way home, he lets drop a few mild curses and kicks some pebbles down the road.

- It's no use being angry, Julie says. - What you did was your own fault. Nor can you escape the fact that it was Hallgrim who saved not only your skin but also that of those you lured into your prank.

She must now get together clothes for herself and Krister and see to it that Helge has everything he needs for beginning his new school year in town. He will almost certainly have moved away by the time she returns. Finding clothing for the boys has become what she terms an unsurmountable problem. For Krister, she has altered a pair of Kristoffer's old trousers which he uses for everyday wear. These have been turned inside out and are already worn down at the knees and behind. She has also altered the jacket from Krister's confirmation outfit and the remains of its now worn-out trousers. On the jacket she has extended the sleeves and the lower hem and has inserted a shoulder pad. Once it has been ironed this will suffice for his travelling clothes. She herself will be wearing a light summer dress. Finding suitable clothing is so easy in summer. In addition, she has a light, three-quarter-length summer coat dating from long before the war, which she has altered several times since in order to keep up with the fashion. Julie is adept with a sewing machine and has become quite an expert at making much out of little. That she learned dressmaking when she was young has proved an invaluable asset over time. But she is now thoroughly tired of all the twists and turns this involves, of turning up sleeves and snipping away at skirts and bringing new out of old. Sometimes she dreams of working with beautiful new material and of creating something really special.

For Krister's high school leaving ceremony, he needs a new suit, dark blue with pinstripes. The suit is made out of a miserable crisis material called cellulite. This looks fine when newly ironed, but after a couple of hours' wear any effects of the ironing will have disappeared. It cannot tolerate moisture and after a downpour looks more like a flannel, but this is going to be the same for everyone. When it comes to shoes and clothing, people have become used to not having too high expectations. Krister has managed to exchange something in town for a pair of brand-new shoes, solid and black leather throughout. Wearing such shoes these days feels like being a millionaire, and he keeps them for special occasions. Julie has a pair of pumps, also dating from before the war, which she too treats as special. These are quite worn but in good condition, as things bought in the time before the war were quality items. For the journey she has sandals with wooden soles and leather straps. Krister will be wearing white training shoes which suffice as summertime wear. Julie whitens these with bleach so that they look almost new.

Aside from all the practical preparations, there are the two small children clinging to her skirts and whingeing that they want to go too. She had promised to take them instead to the summer farm. She always spends a couple of weeks up there between the main farming seasons. These have always been the best days of the year for her and her form for a holiday. To be up there with the children, possibly sharing a few days with Jørgen, has been a way of recharging her batteries, of reassembling her forces for the long winter. Up there, with no other commitments than the care of the livestock, milking morning and evening and attending to the milk feeds, she has been able to enjoy the freedom and silence of the mountains. Sunniva is still quite small and won't remember much from last year, but Sven is sulking because he is being deprived of his fun.

She says in desperation: Come on, you're a big boy now. You know I have to go away because granny is ill, but next year we'll all be able to go there again.

- Is Granny going to die?
- You mustn't say that!
- But she's old, you know. He says this sounding like a small adult, something which shocks her.

If they go on sulking like this when she's away this is going to wear everybody out, she complains to Jørgen. She asks why they cannot send them up to the summer farm with Astrid. This turns out to be the solution. She engages a newly confirmed girl from the village to cope with the children's tantrums, while Synnøve will no doubt be pleased to tend to the farm.

In the past two days, Julie has telephoned home several times. Her father reports that there has been no change in her mother's condition. Julie should not be too concerned, even though her mother is always asking about her, but it's good that she's coming.

On the evening before they are to leave, she sees Helge and Krister sitting together on a grassy slope outside. They are holding a lively conversation while sitting so close to each other that Krister has his arm over Helge's shoulder. It warms her to see them like this. No doubt Krister has some good advice with which to send Helge off at the beginning of his school year. These two have no problem understanding one another. She has a suspicion that Jørgen is sending Krister with her because he does not want to be alone with him without her being available to come between them and protect them both. Apart from this, he is not worried about her. He knows that she can look after herself.

Julie is standing on deck and watching her home town coming closer. This is a sight she treasures and always thinks of as home when she dreams of it at Storvik. However, its reality becomes more foreign for her each time she returns. The village, the mountains, the familiar farms and homes are all so close and yet so distant. As she stands here she remembers one time she came, summoned that time as now. Then it concerned Synna, her sister and the closest friend she has ever known. When she met her father on the pier that time she could see from his face that the worst had already happened. She was then just eighteen but can still recall every detail. The silence as they made their way homeward on that freezing starry night. Her father's words were out of range for the people on the pier to hear.

- Yes, Julie, I'm sure you understand. We have lost Synna.

Even today, a pain remains within her at the memory. The death is as impossible to understand now as it was back then.

With this memory inside her, she goes on land and sees her father on the pier waiting to meet them. They shake hands and greet each other as they always do, and relief sweeps across her as she sees his face. She knows she has come in time.

- It's so good you've been able to come, Julie.
- How is she?
- It's not looking altogether without hope, though it's difficult to know when someone has been affected in the way that she has.
- But you haven't changed, Father. You're never going to look really old, are you?
- Oh, you know, I feel my years. But I can't complain yet when I'm as healthy as I am now.

It is now three years since they came to Sunniva's baptism and Julie has not met them since. Nor has she been home to her birthplace since before Sven was born. She was not able to come to Ingrid's wedding just after Christmas in '39 as Sven was then too little either to leave behind or to take on a long winter journey. Since then, the war has put a stop to all unnecessary travel. However, she has maintained contact by letter or by telephone if she yearns to hear her father's voice.

Her father is keeping well. He has not changed much over the years. Certainly, he looks tired, and his face is grey and drawn, but that is only to be expected after the pressures of the past few days. She still feels that familiar sense of security from being close to him as well as that odd feeling of being a child coming home. His face lights up as he greets Krister.

- My, what a fine man you've become! Your mother must be very pleased that you've come with her.

They will drive home by horse and buggy, as has always been the case. Julie's father has bought a van but does not drive himself - this task falls to Asle, Ingrid's husband. The van is used mainly for driving to and fro from the factory. Getting it started is something of a miracle, a cumbersome business involving the firing up of a generator and all manner of inconveniences. Quite apart from that, it is not suitable for carrying fine ladies, her father says, smiling at Julie. For this, the buggy and their old horse Herta are best.

Every time Julie comes here, she sees changes. Stretches of road resurfaced, and new houses were built where none had been before. The road leading through the area has now been widened with the most difficult bends straightened out. When she remarks on this, her father smiles.

- Maybe you think everything here should be put on hold and be as it was when you lived here? Don't you want a future for us, Julie? Anyway, the new roads are something we have to thank the Germans for. They have at least done us some good.

If Julie has seen big changes as they drive through the district, she is speechless when they drive onto the grounds of their house. She knew that the house had been extended, but she had no idea that it had become so huge. The new part is larger than the old. What she now sees is a real mansion, extended and whitewashed. This is no longer the home of her childhood. The buildings are all painted and well-maintained. She thinks of the shabby houses back in Storvik, how people there try to fix everything but can never afford to. But there is also the point that her father cannot abide things crumbling around him; he has always been a tidy person.

Ingrid meets them outside. She stands there with a six-month-old baby girl on her arm. From behind her skirt, Julie spots a small boy peeping out. He is the same age as Sunniva. Julie embraces both Ingrid and the baby.

- My, how *you* have changed!
- Well, is that so strange? Ingrid says smiling, though Julie detects a caution in her eyes and gives a shudder even on this hot summer's day.

Julie hesitates at the door to her mother's kitchen, overwhelmed as she is by the feeling of being home. This is so strong that she bursts into tears. She has been suppressing her fears of what might have confronted her when she arrived.

The door to her mother's bedroom is open, and her mother calls out:

- Julie? Is that you, Julie?

Julie does not know what she had been expecting to see. There have been some fearsome possibilities she has refused to face: her mother paralysed, mutilated, disfigured, and her face distorted. She is lying propped up on white pillows, her grey hair in a thick plait covering her ears and forehead, yet her face seems so tiny, like a child's. Julie just stands there, rooted to the spot.

- But …won't you…. say hello, Julie, her mother says, extending her arms towards her.

Her voice was so mild, so infinitely weary, at the same time so familiar and yet so different. Julie stumbles across the floor, blinded by her tears and sits down at the bedside. She leans her head in towards her mother and weeps, weeps uncontrollably.

Her mother strokes her hair.

- There, there, she says, there, there.

This strange mildness in her mother's voice leads to even more tears and more weeping from Julie.

- No, but … Julie. Are you going to cry … every time … you come home?
- Yes, I suppose I will, says Julie, standing up and attempting a smile. - But when you frighten us like this?
- It has been … like this, says her mother, the tiredness showing. And now Julie is aware of the fear in her mother's eyes. She sees, too, that her mother's face is very slightly distorted on the left, especially round her mouth. The corner hangs down slightly, and her smile is uneven. Her right arm lies lifeless on the duvet with her hand clenched and turned towards her body.

- I am so tired …

- Well then, you must sleep, Mother.

- Yes, … I can sleep … now that … you've … come.

Julie has not yet taken off her coat.

In this old part of the house, everything is just as it used to be. The same blue walls in the kitchen, the stove with its shiny brass rod at the front, the embroidered hand towels on the shelf above the washbasin, the washbasin itself with its jug, the embroidered cloths on the long table and work surfaces, and the rugs on the floor.

- You've preserved this so well, Father, Julie says, showing how touched she is.

There's not much to thank him for, he says. There is now nobody but himself to disturb things. Ingrid keeps him supplied with midday meals, while other meals he takes care of himself. The biggest problem is feeding Helga. She is having difficulty swallowing. The only thing she manages to get down is some thick porridge. They have tried feeding her milk and coffee, but these just make her choke. Even water is having this effect. They spoon-feed her but are concerned about how little they can get her to eat, and she herself becomes angry that she is so helpless. There is a nurse who comes in to care for her, but she is busy with so many other sick people who need her services. However, the family members have learned how to proceed and hope to be able to manage on their own now that Julie is with them. Things have been particularly difficult for Ingrid who also has her two small children to cope with.

- What does the doctor say?

There is nothing he can do. Helga needs rest. Complications may arise, maybe another stroke or inflammation of the lungs, or she may recover, but they must reckon with her spending the rest of her life restricted to her bed or in a chair.

- How is mother going to cope with living like this? She has never managed to sit still for a moment without something to do with her hands.

- I've thought about that, Julie, but she's very strong, your mother. I think she'll manage.

- I saw fear in her eyes, Father.

- I know. But it's not herself she is thinking about. It's Johanne. In recent years it's all been about Johanne. She becomes desperate with worry, and this is not just because Johanne hasn't come this time.

- But have they not rung and told her how she is? That her mother is asking about her and that she's at risk of coming too late?

- They have called time after time, begging and beseeching her. But Johanne is now hardly one of the family. Her voice is so distant when her father speaks to her; it's as if she is a total stranger. She says that of course she'll come when reason demands, but Inge has told her that this is not a suitable time.

- Not a suitable time? says Julie, upset - when her mother could be on her deathbed?

It's not Johanne who's to blame, her father says wearily. She's his daughter. He knows her so well and has heard the fear and desperation in her voice. Johanne is no longer altogether well. She's a shadow of who she once was and completely subjected to Inge's despotic will.

- I can never forgive myself that I failed to put a stop to that relationship.

- What could we have done? She was so much in love.

She wasn't in love. She was blinded. But if Inge prevents her from coming now, that will be one step too far. Oddmund and Kristian are due to arrive very soon, and he has asked Oddmund to bring Johanne with him. Not only Johanne but also the children because he doesn't want to leave them alone with their father. He sincerely hopes that this will go according to plan, for in a strange way, he feels that Inge has respect for Oddmund.

A weak flush crosses Julie's face, for it was right here in this kitchen that Inge had attempted to rape her. She decided at the time never to speak of this terrifying experience to anyone. Then, last year, she received a surprise visit from Oddmund taking a stop-over on his way to Trondheim. Since years passed between the times these two siblings met, there was so much to talk about that they stayed up talking nearly all night. They discussed Johanne and her miserable life with Inge. Then, disturbed by everything Oddmund was able to tell her about Inge's tyrannical behaviour towards Johanne and the children, Julie poured out her own story. Pale and incredulous, Oddmund listened to what she had to say about their brother-in-law, the Nazi priest.

- What a swine! And yet you didn't put a stop to the relationship?
- How could I? she said in desperation, - It would have destroyed Johanne. She was just so happy.

She instantly regretted having told Oddmund something she believed to be hidden deep inside her. Now, it had all come to the surface again.

- You must promise me that you won't tell anyone what I've said. Not a living soul.

- I promise not to tell anyone else, Oddmund replied, but if the day comes when I have to set hard against hard, I may have to take it up with Inge.

Is this what Oddmund is doing now, setting hard against hard?

- I feel sure that Johanne will come, Father.
- Yes, for all our sakes, let's hope she does.

Through the window, they see Krister walking the grounds, no doubt to become reacquainted with the area. She is moved by the adult feelings he has displayed, as has Ingrid for allowing Julie to be alone with her mother in those first difficult moments. Her father says he will take Krister down to the factory, and Julie is thankful to have a moment by herself in which to deal with her own painful thoughts.

She opens the door to their best room. Here, too, everything is just as it used to be. Plush furniture, crocheted tablecloths and cushions, and white crocheted curtains in front of the windows. The years that have passed now drop away. She recognises the coolness in the room - even on the hottest summer days, there is a strange coolness here. She recognises the smells; the room is dust-free and clean, with a characteristic smell of soap and of rooms not lived in. All of a sudden, she seems to detect a pungent scent of flowers, of white lilies, kala and carnations, chrysanthemums, and the sight of Synna's dead body lying on straw. She shudders before closing the door behind her.

But in the midst of all this pain, there is joy at seeing that Ingrid is so happy and content with the life she has chosen.

- It seems you have got everything you wanted, Julie says to her. - I will marry and have lots of children, you said. Do you remember saying that?

- Is that what I said? Yes, but it's true. I ask nothing more out of life. Is there any better in life for a woman, Julie?

- Oh, you know there can be some who want a bit more than that, Julie smiles.

- Do you mean education and things of that sort? Not for me. That has never been part of my thinking.

- But do you have the ability for it?

- What you mean is, do I have any need for it as a mother?

The upstairs bedrooms look just the same as ever. A room, known as the weaver's room has been made ready for her. The loom remains standing there, as well as the two beds. Julie peeps into her old room and is at once assailed by memories - the three beds are still in their old places. Each of the girls had their own bed: Synna, Johanne and herself. She recalls whispered conversations late into the evening, with Johanne indignant because she did not share her elder sisters' secrets. She feels as if she can still hear their voices and laughter, young girls' dreams and expectations. Julie is pleased that she will not be sleeping here, so she will not have to suffer those good and bad memories. Her mother's illness has now brought everything so very close.

With great reluctance she hangs up Krister's suit - a simple black creation with a white collar. She was equally reluctant when packing these items into her suitcase, but she dared not risk doing otherwise. If the worst should happen, both she and

Krister must be decently dressed. With a shudder she remembers the time she came home to what she believed, and wished to believe, would be Synna's sickbed. She came without a proper dress and recalls her desperation when her mother forced her to wear Synna's dress for the funeral. This appalled her: Synna's face in the white coffin and herself wearing Synna's dress! It was a nightmare then, and it would be an unthinkable nightmare now. She imagines herself going to her mother's funeral in one of her mother's dresses. A host of bad memories which had been suppressed and which she thought she had forgotten, now revive the pain so that everything now feels as uncomfortable as when it first happened.

She lies down on the bed, burying her head in the pillow as she seeks to escape the memories assailing her, and against which she can find no protection: upsetting and acrimonious conversations with her mother, her mother's hostility towards Jørgen, the way in which she saw failings in him which she pointed out to Julie, how dragon-like she was in her behaviour throughout those dreadful years she and Jørgen had to live through. Then there was Julie's endless struggle to please her mother, how she always felt she had to be that strong, clever girl who must overcome everything in order to earn her mother's love. These are feelings Julie has suppressed and worked on during long separations. The thought now arises that she must speak for herself and try to wrestle back power from her mother.

Jørgen has told her that she must take care to leave no unfinished business between herself and her parents. He can never get over the fact that he was never able to talk to his father.

Julie is sitting at the bedside, holding her mother's hand.

- I am so pleased … you've brought … Krister. I would …
so like to have seen … you know … the little ones.

- Yes, but you know that would have been difficult, Mother.
Jørgen needs help, and it's too risky to take children on a long
journey at a time like this.

- Yes, but I … would … so much like …

Her mother now seems relatively well after several hours'
sleep, and her eyes are clear and wide awake.

- You haven't asked about Jørgen? Julie begins.

- Have I not? Oh, no …

- You have never liked Jørgen, have you?

- Yes, but I … can't … No … not now. You … you
shouldn't…

- Forget it, Mother. I shouldn't bother you with that, says
Julie, identifying her own egoism in this. - You must now get
well, Mother

- Well? I was expecting … more of the … false words.
When … not you … understand … - Oh, Julie, her mother says
with tears pouring down her cheeks. - It has been so … painful.
There are so … many who … need me. There's Johanne …

She drifts off again, falling asleep. Julie sits there quietly
and waits a while before carefully trying to release her mother's
grip. Suddenly, her mother seizes her hand and holds onto it
tightly as in a claw and with a strength which sends a sudden
shock through Julie.

- Has Johanne come yet?

- Soon. She'll be here soon, Julie whispers, trembling under
her mother's gaze.

- Yes, because now … I've been … hanging on … in bed
waiting… waiting for Johanne.

- What are you saying, Mother? says Julie, the fear rising icily within her.

- What? says her mother, staring at her in terror. - No, I must have … was talking … nonsense.

Julie prepares her mother for the night. She helps her to move around and bathes her. Seeing her mother naked makes Julie feel shy and awkward; that naked body is white and surprisingly smooth, and her genitals are also almost bare, like a little girl's. This is all so unbearably painful.

Her mother is lying with her healthy arm covering her eyes.

- Don't go there! she cries in an agonised shout - the shame…

- You mustn't be ashamed, Julie says, trying to be cheerful. Think of all the times you've done this for me.

But her mother's pain, her helplessness, her sense of shame and despair – all these are affecting Julie, and combining with her own pain and helplessness.

Helga has had a peaceful night, her father says. Maybe there's hope? But during the morning, she slips away and sleeps most of the time. Julie is seated at her bedside.

- Is that you, Johanne? Her mother says in a clear voice, though her eyes remain closed.

- No, it's me, Julie.

- It was good … that you've come now, Julie. You must stay … here and … help me when, you know, Synna…. It's frightful… that she's … gone from us now. You must help me… look after your little sisters. There's Johanne… And that poor little … Ingrid.

- Yes, Mother, don't worry.

- You have time … ahead of you … you know. I believe you'll …. be like a … be like a princess … But first … you're needed … here.

- Yes, Mother, Julie weeps.

Her mother slips away again, making a strange gurgling noise when she breathes. Julie runs out of the kitchen.

- You'll have to come, Father. I think she's become worse. She's been rambling and …

- Ring the doctor, Julie.

It's not looking good, the doctor says. It seems that she may have had another stroke. He thinks he still has some contact with her. She is not unconscious but is in the borderland between unconsciousness and being awake. He will ask the nurse to come this evening. In the present situation, she will be able to do more than the family can.

Her father is sitting at the table, his head buried in his hands.

- Dear God, that it should all end like this, he says, his voice betraying his agony. - That they couldn't get here while she was still able to see them. The boys may be able to deal with it, but what about Johanne?

Julie runs her hand down her father's back. There are no words to comfort his pain.

The following morning, her condition remains the same. Now and again, their mother opens her eyes, but they don't know whether she can see them. Her gaze is blurred and distant as if she is able to see right through them. Occasionally, she mumbles disconnected phrases, but they cannot grasp what she is saying. From time to time, she becomes restless, tries to sit up and wants to get out of bed, but for the most part, she sleeps.

They feel that the only contact they have with her is when she grasps their hands tightly or when they try to leave her and hand over to the next person to sit with her. They do this by taking turns, Julie, her father, Krister and Ingrid. Yes, even Asle sits there for short periods. This is how they want it to be, and the nurse is always there to tend to the patient's needs. The nurse is an outstanding person who gives them the security of knowing that everything that can be done will be done and that it will be done by someone who knows her job.

During the afternoon, Oddmund rings. He, Kristian, Johanne and the three children have now arrived in Molde. They can be expected on the ferry that same evening. At this point, Julie experiences something she could never believe would happen. Her father, that strong rock of a man who has represented security for them all, begins weeping uncontrollably.

Dumfounded, she stands staring at this helpless figure slumped over the table before her father rises to leave the room. She has always seen him as a figurehead, standing erect through every crisis which has beset the family. Shaken after what she has just seen; she now understands the huge demands that have been placed on his shoulders. He has been a rock they could rely on whenever the unexpected happened and the person to smooth out or make light of any disagreements. It has always been obvious that he would be there for them. Always. But have they understood what this has cost him? Have they ever before seen him grieve?

He comes back into the room and sits down at the table. Julie pours out coffee for them both. His face is furrowed and grey from sitting up at night grieving.

- You must forgive me, Julie. I'm ashamed that you've seen me being so weak. But suddenly, this has all become too much for me. There has never been anyone else for me but Helga your mother, and I just don't know what I'm going to do without her.

His voice breaks, and he passes his hand over his eyes, a movement so helpless that on seeing it, the pain shoots through Julie.

- Then there's Johanne. It would be unbearable if she were not to arrive on time.
- You should rest now, Father.
- No, no, it's over now. I have looked the worst in the eye, and nothing can change that. We must be strong and make the last journey as easy as possible for the person lying there. No, Julie, don't cry. - We'll get by. With God's help, we'll get by.

He is calm once more; that calm she knows so well now streams out over her, giving her the power to deal with her grief.

- I think that now we're alone we should use this opportunity to have a chat about Krister.

She looks at him in surprise. Why should they want to talk about Krister now?

Her father says, he has spoken to Krister over the past few days and has understood that relations between him and Jørgen are not at their best. Krister has also said that he is going to apply in autumn for a job at the fish food factory and save money towards his further education. It now seems that he and Asle have grown quite friendly with each other. Krister has been helping people in Asle's factory recently and has evidently enjoyed working there. Could a solution not be that he should remain here to work in the factory? There will be plenty of work for him as they can hardly keep up with their orders for chests and barrels. If he understood Krister correctly, Jørgen was not over-enthusiastic about Krister working in a factory back in his home village.

- Has Krister been asking you for a job, Father?

- No, but I mentioned the possibility, and he seemed to like the offer. You know, Julie, this could be a good solution. And for Krister it would be a chance to get away for a while to think things over.

- I think you're right, Father, if Jørgen can be persuaded to change his mind. But how do you manage to think of this now?

- However things are, life has to go on, Julie. And it could benefit me having the boy here. It would be less lonely.

Julie scarcely recognises her sister. All she can think of at this first meeting is to take her frail form into her arms and hug her without letting go. But Joanne just extends a cool hand, marking the distance between them as if she were a stranger.

- Good evening, Julie. It's so good to see you again, she says, her voice as lifeless as her appearance.

Julie cannot find the words to reply. She looks into Johanne's eyes, and the cold she sees in them creeps through her. She later recalls the three children standing round their mother, all with serious expressions. The eldest will be fourteen at this time, she is tall and slim, with Inge's features and colouring, that same narrow pale face and blue eyes. The other girl, a thirteen-year-old, looks as Joanne did as a child, chubby but with livelier blue eyes than her sister's. Both are fair with long, old-fashioned pigtails. The boy, aged eleven, looks like the family here. Dark, with brown eyes, like Julie and Helene's father when he was young. Common to all of them is a serious demeanour which you would not expect to find in children of their age. But Julie's brothers are the same as ever. Both have visited her with their wives and children a couple of times in recent years, and Oddmund came on his own last year. Both of them embrace her, which is good. It normalises the situation.

- May I go in to see Mother by myself? asks Johanne.

- Yes, by all means, says her father. - She has been expecting you, expecting all of you.

Julie helps the children to hang up their coats. She chats to them and gets them to take their place on the bench by the kitchen table before pouring them all some juice.

It's good to have something to drink when it's so hot. She is pleased that there are more people than her in the kitchen. She is quite used to having children around but doesn't know what to say to those who are sitting there so politely, like miniature adults and answering only in monosyllables.

Johanne stays with her mother for some time. When she emerges from the sick room, she is still wearing her coat and has vivid red spots on her cheeks, but it is clear that she has not been crying.

- She knew I was there, she says, her voice thin and high-pitched and like a child's. - She heard what I said and grasped my hand.

- I understand, Johanne. Mother knew you were there. She knew that you wanted to be with her.

- Come along, children, and say hello to Grandma, she says.

Julie sees that the children have not been crying, but notes fear on their faces.

She then accompanies her brothers to her mother. With tear-filled eyes, she sees them sitting on either side of their mother's bed. She watches them stroking their mother's hair and talking to her, and she sees that both are crying. She does not know whether she is imagining it, but she has the impression that her mother's face looks more at peace now than before they arrived. She remembers, too, her mother's words that she had been hanging on in bed, waiting for Johanne to come. Might this mean that the waiting time is now over for her mother?

That evening, the children are seated round the table, shy, polite, and with their eyes focused on the food in front of them. There, too, sits Johanne, so tiny and even thinner than she was when they met. There's that dreadful hairstyle, the ribbon round her head and that unfashionable ugly dress. All of these conspire to make her look older than she is. There are only the small childlike curls on her forehead and round her ears, both of which she has inherited from her mother, which do something to soften her angular appearance. But it is her eyes which dominate. She tries to avoid their gaze, but it occasionally happens that Julie's eyes meet hers, allowing her to see the fear before Johanne turns away. Julie sees that her expression is distant and dead, a veil covering a deep anxiety smouldering underneath.

Later the same evening, the nurse says that she thinks their mother's condition has deteriorated. She seems to have sunk into a deep coma, and they send at once for the doctor, but he is in the neighbouring village. They sit round the table waiting, everyone except the children who have gone to bed. They take turns to sit by their mother's bed. The kitchen is quiet, so quiet that they can hear the clock ticking on the wall. They sit anxiously, each of them sunk deep in their own thoughts.

Occasionally, they look upon hearing sounds from the sickroom, Mother coughing or moaning quietly. Then, the nurse emerges.

- You had better come now, all of you. The end is near for your mother.

Their father is seated and the bedside, holding mother's hand. All five children, together with Asle and Krister, are round the bed. Mother's breath comes in short gasps before; finally, she draws in a long, gurgling breath, which escapes with a hiss. Then it is quiet, as quiet as if time itself had stopped.

- Now you're at peace, says their father so quietly that they can barely hear him.
- I would like Mother to have a hymn for her journey, he says. Singing from half-broken voices fills the room.

> Take my hand in yours and lead me on,
> 'Tis you the one to lead me to my heavenly home.
> I cannot go without you; the way's not clear,
> but now, with you to lead me
> I have no fear.

Through these feeble tones, Ingrid's weeping can be heard.

- I would like to be alone with Mother now, Father says quietly.

They all file quietly out of the room, closing the door behind them. Each of them feels a silence taking over the house.

One after one, they leave the kitchen; Ingrid and Asle go into another room, Asle with his arm round Ingrid's shoulder. The brothers go out into the murky summer evening; Johanne goes upstairs to the big bedroom where she is to sleep with her children. Now, only Julie and the nurse are left in the kitchen.

Julie would prefer to be somewhere else. She wants to be out, just as when she was young, to take her feelings and find once again some quiet place by the sea, but she is needed here.

- It was good that your mother left us now without having to suffer, the nurse says, but it always hurts to lose someone. Especially when it's your mother, she adds quietly.

The doctor now appears at the door.

- Is it over? he asks.
- Yes, just now, says the nurse. - Her husband is with her.
- Then I can wait, the doctor says as he sits down at the kitchen table.

Julie pours him a coffee mechanically, feeling somehow outside herself. But she knows herself sufficiently well to be aware that everything she feels can seem as if it is taking place outside of her.

Their father now comes out to them. Julie can see that there is a great sense of calm about him now. For the doctor, all that remains is for him to write the death certificate. Once he has left, Father also goes out. Julie stands by the window and sees him walking towards the sea. She stays watching until he disappears into the night.

- Do you think you can bear to lay your mother out? The nurse asks. - Or shall I call a neighbour?
- I'll help.

Once again, she stands looking down at her mother's naked body and once again feels helpless in the face of her mother's nakedness. But she feels too that there is a strange solemnity taking part in this, as if this is her final farewell to her mother.

- She's to be wearing her wedding dress.
- Good. Can you go and find it?
- There! How good she looks, says the nurse.

Yes, she does look good. There's a calm on her face now. But Julie sees signs of worry and grief that even death has not erased.

The last thing they do is to place a bandage round their mother's face, something which suddenly makes her look different.

- In the past, they used to place a bible under the dead person's chin, Julie says. - And coins in their eyes.
- I know. It was a good custom which perhaps we should have kept.

Julie is alone in the kitchen tidying up and preparing for the next day when her father comes back. He sits down heavily at the table.

- Where are you going to sleep tonight, Father? You can hardly …
- Oh, I can always find a bed to sleep in.
- There is a spare bed in my room.
- Well, maybe, he says in a distant voice.

She strokes his cheek before she goes.

- Don't leave it too late, Father. You need rest.

The first rays of the morning sun are creating bright shafts of dust in the room as Julie wakes to see her father lying in the spare bed. She understands that he has been sitting with her mother through all the intervening hours and that he is keeping as still as possible, unaware that she's awake. She hears him draw a deep sigh before this turns to rhythmic breathing and light snores. As she looks down at him in the morning light, she knows that one day she is also going to lose him.

The coffin is lying propped on two trestles in the main hall, covered by a white sheet. Her mother is lying in an open coffin, as is the custom. In her hands is a bunch of roses from their garden. Even though the windows are open, the air in the room is heavy and somewhat sweet. This scent becomes stronger as the room fills up with wreaths and bouquets in urns and vases. White flowers Julie always associates with death.

These days, preparing for the funeral is busy and made all the more difficult because of rationing and the food shortage. But now, as always, the neighbours are eager to help with gifts. Small bags of coffee substitute, sugar, a pat of butter, wraps and flatbread. On the day itself women will bring a cream cake, supposedly so that Julie will not have the trouble of making one.

Again, Julie experiences the sense of community which exists between neighbours on occasions like these. Neighbours may disagree, they can criticise each other and talk behind each other's backs, but when it comes to it, they stand together, showing that they care for one another, and they demonstrate this when the situation arises. For Julie, this will be a chance to meet neighbours and friends she has not seen for many years. In this way, her childhood home comes closer.

Her father is concerned that the funeral will be carried out according to local custom and as Helga would have wished. A four-year-old calf will be slaughtered, and most of the meat will be made into mince, no matter what the Utilities Board may have to say. The funeral meal will be, as local tradition dictates, meat cakes in brown sauce, with mushy peas and potatoes. In the garden, plum trees are bulging with fruit so that a porridge made with fresh plums can replace a prune porridge by way of a dessert.

Johanne, who always disliked housework and tried to avoid such duties when she was young, has, much to Julie's surprise, shown herself very capable. She carries out her jobs quickly and efficiently when she gives Julie a helping hand. The same is true of the little girls, they set the table for meals and both clear away and wash up afterwards without having to be asked.

- You've brought them up well, says Julie.

- They are old enough to know what to do. They are now so good that they can take care of everything that needs doing in the house when I'm unwell.

- Are you unwell, Johanne?

- No, no, says Johanne emphatically. - But aren't you sometimes ill, Julie? Surely, anyone can have a headache, a cold, or the flu.

- Yes, that's true, says Julie and gives her sister a searching look. - But these youngsters are almost too capable. Isn't it normal for them to play and do the same sort of things that other children do at their age?

Johanne looks at Julie with a look that makes her shudder.

- Normal? What do you mean by that? she says hastily. Are you implying that my children aren't normal?

- No, no, that's not what I meant at all. I just expressed myself clumsily. But you yourself, how are you actually?

- Why should I not be all right? Don't worry, I live a good life.

- I'm not sure I can believe that.

- Stop interfering in my life, Julie! Johanne says, her eye flashing towards her. You have always harassed me, interfering with things that have nothing to do with you. Your own success makes me sick. And now it's my children there's something wrong with. But I think I know what you're thinking. You think I came here too late? But I did come, didn't I? I came! I can't stand you anymore. I just want a bit of peace.

- But, dear Johanne …

- *Dear!* Oh, dear this, dear that! she shouts, mimicking Julie's words. It's my life, it's my life, do you hear?

Thoroughly taken aback, Julie stands staring as the door slams behind Johanne. Her sister was so upset that she even slipped back into her old dialect. But it was good to see some life in her and to see that she was still capable of becoming upset and angry. Going round with her these past few days has been a pain. It has been impossible to get a conversation going on any but the most everyday subjects, and all they have done is to exchange empty phrases like complete strangers. Johanne speaks with received pronunciation, and this, too, creates a sense of distance. Here, she has been going round with that same protection round herself that she had last time Julie met her, only worse than it was then. This must break down some time. The shell her sister has built round herself is so fragile that one day, the forces inside her will have to break out. She has caught glimpses of desperation in Johanne and seen how she uses her forces to hold the mask in place. Her thin face becomes so clenched that there are visible nodules at her jaws. One day, as she put her arm around her, she felt Johanne's body was as tense as a wound-up spring. It was like touching hardwood.

The last time they met, it burst. A small crack appeared in the shell around her. Out of her mouth poured frightful details of her life with Inge. Julie will never forget what she found out that day. But then Inge turned up and interrupted the conversation. Johanne retreated back into herself, and the shell was back in place once more. Afterwards she looked at Julie with something like hatred in her eyes. Julie still shudders at the memory. But how is it going to be this time? She has not seen Johanne cry on any of the recent days. How is she going to cope tomorrow with the funeral?

Before she settles down for the evening, once the cooks have prepared the next day's meal and have been sent home and she has tidied up the house, Julie peers through the door in the main hall, knowing that her father is sitting there, she sees his silhouette in the darkened room where two lit candles are standing on a table in front of the coffin.

- Is that you, Julie? He says, sitting there with his back to her.
- You should go to bed now, Father. Tomorrow is going to be a busy day.

She has experienced this once before. But this time, it is her mother in the coffin. It is not Synna.

Julie is standing outside on the steps together with her father. At this early morning hour, the air is cool before the sun has taken full effect, but the day is wonderfully clear, full of summer scents from grass and trees and flowers.

- Helga's got a good day for her journey, says her father quietly.
- Will you cope today, Father?
- Oh yes, I'll cope. The worst is over now. I am just deeply grateful that she went so quickly. So glad I had that day with her, both before she died and afterwards.

- She puts her arm round him, leans her head in towards him, and he holds her tightly. She feels his embrace again, awkward and slightly embarrassed, and is overwhelmed by the same feelings she experiences every time they embrace. It happens so rarely. A warmth builds up within her, filling her until it overflows in tears streaming down her cheeks. She looks up at him and sees that his eyes, too, are tearful, as a single tear rolls down his cheek.

- I love you so much, Father, she whispers.

- I know. And it was good for us to cry, Julie. That way, we'll get through today together.

In brilliant August sunshine, Helga's coffin was taken to the cemetery on a cart covered in black cloth. This was drawn by their horse Herta, whose back was also draped in black. In front of every house and every farm, birch twigs are strewn along the road, as has always been the custom. But what Julie will come to remember from this journey will be the empty flagpoles throughout the village, a reminder that they are living in a time when nothing is normal. But it is not the war which has been upmost in her thoughts in recent days.

She is missing Jørgen, who was unable to get away, but is pleased to have Krister for support. At the graveside, her father is quiet and dignified while the relatives weep quietly, all except Johanne. She is standing by Julie's side with her children near to her. Julie places her arm round her and feels the frail body trembling as if in a cramp.

Her eyes follow her for the rest of the day. She notes how her hands tremble when she is using cutlery or lifting a coffee cup and how her face is bloated round her eyes and mouth. Heavens, if only she could cry! She has seen this before, the disturbing sight of suppressed shut-in weeping. It is also painful to see the fear in the children's eyes.

That evening, when all the guests have left the farm after feasting on breakfast, lunch, dinner, coffee cakes and supper too for those with the longest journeys and everything has been tidied away after a long day, Julie and her father are seated at the kitchen table. Otherwise, the house is quiet.

- Do you think it went well, Father?
- Yes, Helga had a worthy funeral. I have you to thank for that, Julie, that you were here and took charge of everything. That's how she would have wanted it.
- It was very strange, as if Mother was beside me throughout the day saying, this is what you need to do, Julie. Things like that.
- Yes, her father smiles; that is how she was. Everything had to be done properly. But if she had seen us today, she would have been pleased.

Something happened to her in her youth that she ought to have dealt with. Something which had been forgotten by everybody but her, but which never let go of her. Nobody should have anything to blame either her or her family for.

- Yes, I agree.
- You young people noticed it, too. Life can be tough when you're carrying that sort of burden. Sometimes she could be quite bitchy towards me and towards you all.

He had been able to live with that because he knew her so well. Right from his youth, he had been obsessed with Helga and still sees her as that frail little girl, light on her feet and quick-witted. It was his big moment when she finally agreed to marry him. They came to love each other more and more as the years passed. But there had been someone else. This was Jacob, whose parents owned a farm on Lì which he was destined to inherit. Helga was in service on the farm, and she and Jacob came to have a relationship, which her mother put a stop to and with Helga being dismissed. She never forgot this and never overcame her bitterness towards the people on Lì, and especially towards Jacob, who was so cowardly as to give way to his mother's will. But even though Johannes knew from the outset that he was a replacement for Jacob, he was still a happy man. And even though she was drawing on her bitterness and that this was driving her, he envied her for it. In the end, he understood that it was he who had become the person she chose. She demonstrated this in so many ways, even though she was too proud to put it into words. This was why he envied her dream of Jacob and the power it gave her.

- It's good to be able to talk about these important things. If you have been attached to a person all your life, there is nothing more important than that love, Julie. Nothing can deprive you of that.

- I knew about Jacob, Father.

- What! You knew about it? Did you hear about it in the village?

- No, it came out once when Mother was angry with me.

It was after Synna died that she used to go out and meet Hans Lì. Frequently. Finally, her mother found out about this and was furious. She said she would never permit any daughter of hers to move in with the Lìs and then told Julie the whole story.

- I have never seen Mother so furious.

- I can well believe it. So she destroyed your relationship? Maybe that was the reason Hans moved to America, leaving behind his inheritance and everything else.

- No, that was because of Synna.

- What's this you're saying? Synna?

- Yes, Synna. They were secretly engaged. She used to help them to meet. She provided cover for them among the other young people and helped Synna sneak out to a secret rendezvous after her parents had gone to bed. Strangely enough, they managed to keep all this hidden from the village. They refused to say anything about their relationship either here or in Lì before they had rings on their fingers, for they knew of the disagreements between their two families. But it never got as far as the rings. Synna died, and she had never seen such grief as she witnessed in Hans on that day. This is why she met him as often as she could, for she was afraid he might harm himself. Because everything had been kept secret, there was no one else to talk to apart from her. That is why he could no longer bear living here.

- Did your mother know about this?

- No, I thought it best that she didn't find out. Their secret was so private. Hans took it with him when he moved, and Synna took it to her grave.

- How amazing is this life we are given, Julie? Do you ever hear from Hans?

- He was at agricultural college with Jørgen. We exchanged letters every Christmas for the first few years. But so far as I know, he is well, and he is probably married over there.

- Do you remember, Julie, just how beautiful Synna was? That is how she will always be remembered, as radiant and beautiful.

- Yes, she was beautiful, and good. I still grieve for her.

They remain seated, both sunken in their own thoughts, until her father stands up.

- It's been a long, hard day, Julie. We have had a great deal to think about, and it's best that we now get some rest.
- But just one thing before you go. What shall we do about Johanne?
- Yes, Johanne, Julie says, leaning hard against the table.
- I don't know what to think. Things look worse for her every time we see her. There has been so much to think about, but something needs to be done. I don't quite know what, but I can no longer stand watching my daughter falling apart.

Even though his grandmother's death has affected Krister, it is good to see that he is flourishing. The tension and restlessness which has been surrounding him recently seems now to have vanished. Julie has never said anything to Jørgen about Krister remaining here and thinks it best to leave this until they meet face-to-face. Johanne's children also seem less anxious after their grandmother's funeral. The two little girls are busying themselves with Ingrid's children, looking after them and playing with them, having trips along the road with the youngest in a baby carriage. The boy follows his grandfather around or plays with a neighbour's boy he's got to know. This, too, is good to see.

In the evening, before she returns home, Julie sits with her father and sisters. The living room table is set with coffee and cakes. This is what their father wanted: for everyone to get together before they all went their separate ways. There are just himself and the five siblings. The children are in bed. Krister is next to Asle.

- It has been good to have you all here, even though the occasion has been a sad one. It's good to feel once again that we're a family, their father says solemnly. Good, but with one exception, and that is my concern for you, Johanne. He looks at her, compelling her to return his glance.

- You're concerned about me? whispers Johanne.

- Yes, says her father gently - I can no longer bear to see you suffering like this.

Johanne looks back at him wide-eyed before collapsing onto him, sobbing loudly. He embraces her and strokes her back.

- Just cry, he says. Cry as much as you need to. It's high time. And then you can tell us how you are really feeling.

Everything she has had to put up with now pours out of Johanne. In a flat monotone she tells them of her life with Inge. It has all become much worse since he joined the party and has become a Nazi priest. He has forced the children to join the Horde's youth wing and dresses them up in its uniform. Johanne has fought against this, having seen how the children have been bullied at school and how their friends have dropped away, but all this just runs off Jørgen. He is a strong believer, both in God and in Nazism. He has tried forcing her to join the party, and so far, she has been able to resist him and has refused to sign up. But she does not know if she can go on defying him. Then again, she has never managed to be a true believer. When she has been disobedient, he forces her to sit at the back of the church while he is preaching, and the children sit in the front pew. Another time, he punishes the children in the same way. He was against her coming here even though she begged and cried and protested that her mother might die. He said this was God's punishment, and if Oddmund had not intervened, she would not have been here now.

They listen to her in shock, including Julie, who has heard much of this before. Ingrid's face is white. Suddenly, it seems that Johanne senses this and looks up at them in confusion.

- What are you getting me to say? It is dreadful to speak like this of the person you're married to. Inge wouldn't have punished me if I'd done nothing wrong.

Julie gives a shudder. She recalls Johanne telling her that Inge punished her once when they had lain together, maintaining that Johanne had led him into sin.

Her father puts an arm round her, his face ashen.

- You are not the bad person here, Johanne. It's not you who deserve to be punished. But we are going to help you. You won't be alone any more. You can stay here, both you and the children, until you're better.
- Oh no! says Johanne terrified. - Inge will never allow it.
- Yes, he will. I'll ring now and order a phone call, and then you can tell him straight away.
- He'll be so angry, I daren't!
- You dare. We are with you, and Inge is too far away to harm you.

They sit in silence, waiting for the telephone to ring. All give a start when it rings.

- Inge, I'm not well. My father … father wants me to stay here until I recover.
- What? What did you say? Yes. Yes. No, I'm not confined to bed.

Johanne now stands listening. The others see how she collapses into herself, how her voice changes, becoming quiet and submissive.

- Yes, Inge, of course. That was stupid of me.

Her father then seizes the telephone from her.

- Johanne is ill. She will not be coming home until she has recovered. The children's schooling? We have good schools in the village here. No, Inge, you don't need to come. You needn't worry about that. We'll take care of Johanne and the children.

Everyone hears the warning tone in her father's voice, no doubt including Inge himself. They just hope that the people in the telephone exchange won't notice. They are notorious for reporting everything to the whole district. But this is the least of their concerns now.

- He was so angry, wails Johanne. - I'm sure he's going to come and take us away.
- Then we'll have to use force, Father says. - And Inge will not be the one to win.
- No, I'll see to that, says Oddmund; I'll see to it that he stays where he is.
- That we can promise you, Johanne, says Kristian, holding in his anger.

Julie lies awake that evening. More has happened in the last week than normally happens in a whole year. She reflects on Johanne and her mother's death, and she never thought that losing her mother would be so harrowingly painful, most of all because of all that had remained unsaid between them. But then she would come to understand that this did not matter. She had come to understand that there was nothing more for them to talk about because they had always been speaking different languages. More than anything, conversations with her father have helped her to see this. She no longer has any doubt that her mother loved her, but now understands that she had herself demanded more love than her mother was able to give. She grieves, but with more sorrow than pain, and so it continues. Now, she dares to admit that she loves her father more than her mother, and maybe her mother understood that. There are so many threads in life's tapestry.

Suddenly, Johanne appears at the door, dressed in a long white nightdress, though Julie can barely make her out because of the twilight in the room.

- Julie, may I sleep with you? Johanne asks in a voice like that of a weak young girl.
- Yes, of course, come on in.

Johanne snuggles up close to her and cries like a child.

- It's all going to be fine. Father is going to look after you now.

It's strange how everything repeats itself. Long ago, when Synna died, Johanne came into her bed just as she does now. Now as then, she holds her sister's childlike body while Joanne cries herself to sleep.

Julie arrives home on a Saturday evening after sleeping overnight in the Storvik villa and making sure that Helge is there and ready to start school.

Jørgen is standing on the quayside with a group of men all in their weekend clothes as the boat approaches the quay. As always, when Julie has been away on a journey, he is there to meet her. Catching sight of her, his eyes light up with pleasure. This touches her, and she realises that she must take care not to give him a hug. To do that would be unheard of if seen by those who have come to inspect the boat and welcome the passengers onto land, an entertainment they rarely miss. Jørgen holds out his hand.

- Condolences, he says somewhat stiffly and solemnly - and welcome home.

He looks all around him.

- Have you come alone?
- Yes, Krister wanted to stay with Father for a while.
- Ah, so that's how it was.

They begin walking silently up the hill towards the farm, Jørgen carrying her suitcase. Sometimes, he directs a look at her but then turns his eyes away when his eyes meet hers, and she understands what she is thinking.

- All it means is that it may do him good to be away from Storvik for a while.
- Oh, but … No, we won't talk about that now. I would rather hear how it was for you to be there.
- You know it was hard.
- Yes, it was sad that it went as it did. She was still too young to go like that. Was it painful for her?
- Well, you know … But she had a good and worthy death.
- You know how much I wanted to be there for you?
No, it … don't think about it. How has it been with the children?
- They've had a whale of a time up there on the farm with Astrid, he says. The teenage girl looking after them has become

their great heroine. They certainly hadn't missed either him or their mother. Astrid has spoilt the life out of them these past few days. He went today to collect them but they pleaded with him to let them stay, after which he didn't have the heart to bring them home.

- Even though you knew I was going to be there this evening? she says and feels a childish sense of disappointment.

- Yes, even though they knew that, he smiles. We can go together tomorrow to bring them home.

That night, they stay up late. There is so much that Julie wants to tell him, but she feels that Jørgen is inattentive and distant.

- It's Krister you're thinking about, isn't it?

- How can I not think about him?

- Oh, come on, Jørgen, Krister is a grown-up now. We can no longer take over his life. If he wants to study, it's not up to us to stop him. And what if he wants to work for my father rather than get a job in the fish food factory here? Have you no respect for the fact that he wants to earn money and get by on his own?

- Respect? Wasn't I the one to suggest that he should help you out on your journey? He's used that to run away from everything. I think he probably had his plans all worked out before he left.

- That's not true, Julie says. That was my father's suggestion.

- Oh, yes, your father. He took over, just as he's always done, he says bitterly. When is he going to stop interfering in our lives?

- Don't you dare speak like that of my father! Julie says, her voice trembling with rage. You have so much to thank him for.

- Do you have to remind me of that? Will you ever let me forget it? He says, making his way towards the door.

- No, don't just walk away. How would it have been here if it wasn't for father?

- This is not about your father, he says, sitting down again. It's about Krister. Have you ever supported me? Have you ever tried to understand how it feels that he is wrecking everything here? Can't you understand that I have lost my son?

Julie stands leaning over the table and looks him straight in the eye, her anger aflame.

- You should be ashamed of yourself, Jørgen. I've just come home after losing my mother, and I'm sick with worry about my sister's unhappiness. Nor is that all. There are thousands of young men dying every day on battlefields all over the world while others are rotting in prison camps. And here you are talking about losing a son! And not just a son, but a son who is both fit and healthy and who only wants to live his own life. Besides, how do you think Jostein feels when you go round sulking about Krister? Jostein does far more on the farm than should be expected of a boy, and that's just to please you.

- Are you trying to get round me with words yet again?

- Oh, shame on you. Grow up!

- There was no need to say all that. I've heard it all a bit too often, he says, and this time there's no stopping him. Julie just stands there in desperation, watching as the door slams behind him.

Anger pours out of her, and she experiences a deep tiredness as she sits absorbed in her thoughts. It has happened again, another of these battles over Krister and the other children, over his family and her family. They have both tried discussing these matters calmly in good times. They have said to each other that life is too short to quarrel over who is right. She has tried to get to the bottom of his bitterness, but every time, they end up quarrelling as they have just done now. She sits back, amazed at how deeply the bitterness is buried in him.

She may not be the easiest person to live with, but nor is he easy to live with. A stubborn mule if ever there was one.

She is lying awake when he comes to bed.

- We should stop quarrelling like this, he says.
- I know. I'm ashamed that I let my anger run away with me tonight. Especially now when life is hard for you.

It ends with them becoming reconciled this time, too. They see warmth and comfort in what cannot be taken from them, the trust they have in each other. A trust which carries them through all the pain.

The following morning, they go up to the summer farm to bring their children back home. The two rush to embrace their mother, throwing themselves into her arms, and she then realises how much they have missed her. But after that first display of delight, they go back to their games. The girl looking after them has helped them to construct a model farm using stones and shells as animals, with little houses made of twigs and a fence round it. They quickly become so preoccupied with this that they forget all about their parents. Julie sits watching them. They are all changing so quickly. Even in the short time she has been away, she seems to see that five-year-old Sven has grown out of his chubby toddler body. With those long, thin legs, he will soon be looking like a little man. Sunniva, now three, has a tight, chubby body bursting with energy. Her dark hair is thick and shoulder-length and tied up with a ribbon hanging at an angle.

The children look golden in the sunlight. Both are dressed in tops and shorts. Sunniva's skin is brown and even, while Sven's is reddish brown with freckles.

- That young lady won't go far wrong in the world, says Jørgen as they watch the girl take charge of the elder brother. - Now I wonder who she takes after, he says teasingly.

To get the children to leave willingly Julie needs to tempt them by promising that she has presents waiting for them down on the farm, brand new colouring books and crayons. As they make their way back down the road with the two children scurrying around, Julie grasps Jørgen's hand.

- We mustn't complain, Jørgen, when we have such great children.

Julie cannot stop thinking about Johanne and all that's happening to her. She has rung her father but they dare not speak about personal matters on the telephone. All he says is that Johanne is feeling better and improving each day. The children, too, are doing well at school and thriving.

- Oh, by the way, I can tell you that some people you know maybe separating.
- Separating? Julie says, shaken. Then, it dawns on her what he means.
- Really, so that's what's happening, she says quietly, even though her heart is thumping against her ribs. - Well, maybe it's all for the best.
- Yes, I take it you understand.

Are Johanne and Inge going to separate? How will that affect Johanne? Will she be able to tolerate the village gossip and the shame a divorce will bring? So far as she knows, no one else where they live is divorced. She is worried but still relieved at the thought that Johanne will escape from the hell she has been living through. Deep down, Johanne is strong, for otherwise, she could not have survived for all these years. With the family around her for support, there is every hope that she will come through this. But Julie is still nauseated after finding out everything that has gone on.

Finally, the letter they've been waiting for arrives. 'Registered contents, 100 kroner' it says on the envelope. As she opens the envelope, she thinks of the number of similar letters she has received from her father over the years. Money to help them through all sorts of crises and difficulties. Also the odd surprise letter telling her to buy something new for herself or the children. But she cannot understand why he is sending her money this time.

Inside the envelope, there is a letter to her from Krister, a long letter from her father and a separate envelope marked: To Father.

- This is for you, she says handing the envelope to Jørgen.

He opens it, and there are the hundred kroner. He reads the few words Krister has written to him.

Scarlet in the face, he hands her back the envelope together with the money and the letter.

Here, you can take these, he says and goes.

Julie quickly reads the few words Krister has addressed to his father:

'Dear Father, I am sending you the hundred kroner you had to pay that time I was fined, and I thank you for that. I am enjoying my job in the workshop here and hope that the autumn harvest won't be too much of a strain for you now that neither Helge nor I will be there any longer. With best wishes from Krister'.

She lays this aside and does not wish to think about it now, although she understands that Jørgen will be feeling hurt by it.

The letter from Krister to herself she also reads quickly and she decides to keep the letter from her father until last. Krister tells her that he is enjoying himself even more than he had hoped, both at work and in the village. He becomes more and more fond of Asle as he gets to know him, and already has made many friends among the youth of the village, and the parcel of clothing she has sent has arrived.

As she perhaps knows, a great deal has happened since she left, mainly with respect to Johanne. Inge had been furious and had wanted to come and take her and the children back by force. Her father had blocked this, saying to Inge that Johanne would not be leaving before she was strong enough. He had also written to Inge setting out plainly what he thought. The result was a furious letter back from Inge in which he made all manner of threats. These, Julie should know, were not trifling. But then Julie knows Inge. Inge cannot scare him. But Johanne scared him when Inge wrote to say that if she did not return home now, then she need not come at all; moreover, she should not reckon on ever seeing her children again as he was coming for them.

Then Oddmund took over. And strangely enough this was the point at which Inge changed course. They received a highly formal letter from him and his solicitor in which he said he was filing for a divorce settlement. This was because his wife was *irresponsible.*

Johanne has agreed to this. In her condition she would agree to anything just so long as she and the children escaped. She was upset at first, but her present position is that while she must escape from Inge, they will not tolerate any reference in the divorce papers to mental illness. The hope is that it will be all over before Christmas. If things are difficult now, it is wonderful to think that she will soon be free of the yoke she has been carrying and which has all but broken her.

Her father will see to it that Johanne has a medical certificate so that she will not have to appear in court. Oddmund has said that he is willing to represent her there.

Johanne is accepting all this more calmly than had been anticipated. Of course, there are bad days, days in which she sinks back into gloom and regret. Then her concern is what effect all this is going to have on the children. But it always ends with her saying that she dares not go back there. Not after all this has this happened. She now hopes never to see Inge again.

There is the odd bright spot in all this, he adds. The children have settled down almost miraculously well. The eldest has begun at senior school and the other two in ordinary schools. They have all found friends and are even picking up the local dialect. He himself is being spoiled by Johanne, who is looking after him. Above all, the house has become livelier with so much happening that he, old as he is, feels blessed by it all. Krister is a pure joy to him. So strange the way in which life can change! All this mitigates his sense of Helga's loss, though this is still with him every hour of the day. It is a loss which will accompany him every day of his life, he writes.

- You can read all this yourself, she says to Jørgen, who has returned by now. She herself feels empty, drained of energy. - It's like reading a novel.

Jørgen sits engrossed in her father's letter and then shakes his head.

- There's a lot to think about there.
- Yes. What else can I say?

In autumn, the Todt camps are to be emptied. The convict workers will be sent to Kristiansund to work on the fortifications. As they left, so did the Germans, and the village became quiet. It has also been quite entertaining having these remarkable Todt camps here.

After a while, the village discovers what happened to Torstein after his arrest. His wife has received a letter from him, a censured letter from Grini which is where he has ended up. But what he did not write about, and could not write about, his wife has discovered from other sources.

When he came to Trondheim he was lodged first in the Mission hotel. Even to hear the name mentioned makes people shudder. The Gestapo, Rinnan, people dare not even think about what he must have gone through there. Because of course the poor fellow had nothing from the village to report, no matter what those swine did to him. He apparently came out of it without being completely broken, but his wife has found that it took a long time for him to get back on his feet. From the Mission hotel, he was then transferred to Vollan prison, where he remained until he could be sent on to Gini. He says he is keeping well there, but his wife cannot find out more. Now, she is worried that he may be sent to Germany. The village feels sorry for her, and people do what they can to help. But Hallgrim is going to have a lot to answer for.

There are other subjects of conversation. Hallgrim's son, who volunteered for the Nazis, has been sent home from the training camp on grounds of illness. People have been told that he has tuberculosis, or consumption as they call it. This is a terrifying disease which afflicts so many people, and particularly so many of the young. This village in which nothing can be hidden hears that the doctor has visited and that the boy has been sent to Reknes Sanatorium in Molde.

The neighbours are closely following everything happening at Ås at this time. All the rooms in the house are being disinfected with smoke, all clothing which can be boiled is then hung out to dry and all bedding items and mattresses are aired. Some things are burned.

- Hallgrim could always try something else, some are saying. - Like keeping Germans away from Ås.

The Germans have heard about Hallgrim's son and are terrified of any sort of infection.

In October, the farm boy from Ås, Larris as the villagers call him, is sent to the eastern front. It is Hallgrim who reveals this to men waiting at the post office one evening. Even though he has been quieter of late and is clearly affected by his son's illness, he still cannot refrain from bragging about his son.

- The boy has a real sense of purpose, he boasts.
- But it's not going too well over there, some bold spirit says. - Maybe your son has been lucky to get away and come home?

- Lucky? says Hallgrim, flushing red with anger. - My son is no coward, not like so many young people here in the village. He thinks it's a pity he can't be there to fight for what he believes in, to fight against the devil of Bolshevism. There are many who would regret it if they came here and took over.

The fourth Christmas of the war is now approaching. Italy and Mussolini have capitulated and the Germans are facing strong resistance on all fronts. Yet people are still feeling discouraged. They can see no end to the war and don't even dare to think of its coming to an end. This autumn and the time leading up to Christmas have been drab. People are worn down by the war, by rationing, by food shortages and by the secrecy. It feels as if a leaden lid has been placed over the land and its people. The very young know nothing other than war, and at Storvik they will be celebrating their first Christmas without Krister.

Chapter 9

After Christmas 1944 the winter is bitterly cold. Jørgen works in the timber yard along with Jostein and Dreng-Anders. Both horses and men are out in the cold in snow metres high. Anders is wearing his old home-made trousers and a shirt which is still wearable even though it has been patched and repaired until it looks more like a rag rug. On his feet Anders is wearing hand-made boots which he has inherited from Kristoffer. Jostein is also wearing boots and a windproof ski anorak on top of a woollen sweater, but, like Jørgen, he has to wear an overall. This does not keep out the cold even if the wearer has on wool underwear. The worst dressed is Jørgen. On top of his woollen sweater he is wearing an old suit jacket. His boots are worn out. The last time they were repaired he attached wooden soles, but when the uppers are in tatters there is now nothing more that can be done. Even though he is wearing woollen stockings and socks tucked into his boots, he is frozen stiff. His boots fill up with snow even before work begins, his legs are soaking, and both he and Jostein are wet right up to their waists. They hardly dare to sit round the bonfire when it is time to take a coffee break. The one performing best is Anders; his heavy-duty trousers keep out the cold and the worst of the moisture. Buying new clothes is impossible now even if you have the money. New warm shoes are a utopian dream. It's a dog's life, but they cannot live without the work in the timber yard. It is the money from this which will be used to pay the merchant's bills and all the expenses involved in running the farm. Other expenses have to be paid out of profits from the cowshed. At the present time, this is less than nothing, with only a few drops of milk being yielded by the stall's calf-bearing cows. They cannot let the cold stop them. Timber is needed for building even under winter conditions.

In the evenings Jørgen sits in front of the fire rubbing his cold feet until they ache. One evening he cannot get warm at all. He sits close up to the hot stove which still remains cold despite its being continually fed with fuel.

- Are you feeling unwell? asks Julie.
- No, I don't have time to be unwell. It's just that I feel so cold, but that's hardly surprising when it's as cold as it is now.

He is just as cold when he goes to bed, even though the stove is turned up in the bedroom and he is covered by both a duvet and a woollen blanket. The following morning, he wakes up hot and with a high fever. His throat is sore, his chest hurts when he coughs and he gurgles and squeaks when he breathes.

- I think we'd better call the doctor, Julie says.

She lights the stove in one of the guest rooms and prepares it for Jørgen. It is late evening by the time the local doctor arrives, though people here are used to waiting for a doctor who serves a large area with a number of hamlets. People wonder about how he can find time to rest and sleep. After being served snacks here and there round about, he will often fall asleep in a chair, taking what he calls a catnap. People find this funny. They say they cannot understand how he ever managed to have children with a wife who rarely sees him in bed at home. He has been here a long time and is now beginning to show his age, though people know and trust him, even if they hesitate to call him out unnecessarily. He is very well known in Storvik and was a close friend of Kristoffer's.

After examining Jørgen he confirms that he is not suffering from inflammation of the lungs, but of a heavy cold and bronchitis. He says he will call in the next day to see if the cold has developed into anything more. Jørgen is not to worry even if it should be inflammation of the lungs, as there are now new medicines available to deal with this. He is given fever reducing medicine and a strong cough mixture and is told to remain in bed until the bronchitis is in retreat. The doctor adds that he should avoid the hardest jobs once he is back on his feet.

He tells Julie that Jørgen must now slow down a little and leave the heaviest jobs to others. As she knows, he has quite a number of things to deal with.

- Do you mean that there's something wrong with his heart? Julie asks alarmed.

No, the doctor says, but she knows how it is with Storvik men, and it's best to be sensible and not to challenge fate. Jørgen's situation is not made any better by the fact that he had rheumatic fever when he was young, a disease which can weaken the heart.

- He has never told me that.
- No, he won't tell you everything. A remarkable thing about local villages is that people living there often look on illness as something to be ashamed of. It's as if it diminishes them in others' eyes.

This is true, she thinks. Jørgen is ashamed to admit that he had a hernia as a child and had to go round for some time wearing a bandage. To this day he is ashamed when he meets strangers who wonder about the finger he cut off when young and which meant that he could no longer play the fiddle properly. She recognises this as having arisen back home and how she reacted over the missing finger when they first got together. Now she no longer notices this defect in him.

- Have you mentioned all this to Jørgen?

- No, the doctor replies, - I don't see the point. I don't want to frighten him. But just take care of him a little, try to get him to apply the brakes when he's driving himself too hard.

- That's not going to be easy. You know how stubborn he is.

- I do, but it does no harm to keep this in your thoughts when he's going flat out. You don't need to show him you're worried.

Not to show she's worried when she's so afraid that her breast is seizing up inside her?

It is not inflammation of the lungs, but Jørgen is ordered to stay in bed and not to be tempted to get up too early even if the fever leaves him.

Jørgen worries about his timber business, but when Julie offers to send a message to Krister he won't allow it. Don't even mention it, he says. And she realises that he is too proud to give way. Instead she sends Jostein to find someone locally to take over. Even though this costs money which they could well have another use for, this is what Jørgen decides to do. The work cannot be delayed, the timber yard must go on.

Jørgen has a great deal of time for reflection during these days in bed. His thoughts mainly revolve round Krister. He tries to think back to when their relationship began to change. He sees him as a child holding a book in his hands every free moment. He has already understood that. But what then misled him was Krister's ability in all kinds of farm work. He has never ceased to be proud of Krister, but neither has anyone hurt him so badly as Krister did with the hundred kroner he sent recently. This came as a slap in the face. Then there is Krister's ability to nonplus him just as Julie does. This causes him to lose his temper when he clashes with the boy in discussions and arguments.

He cannot bear having any more arguments with Julie about their son. It's bad enough as it is without this creating division between him and Julie. He realises that the battle is lost and that Krister is lost as far as Storvik is concerned, even though it may take a long time for him to accept this. So it is to be hoped that relations between the two of them may improve, that time will work towards that end.

He must talk to Jostein and ask him to take over one day. He is not afraid that Jostein will say no, for it may well be that this is what the boy has always wanted. Julie is right when she says that Jostein is a born farmer and that he deserves to know that everything here will one day be his. Jostein is very capable and has given him a great deal of pleasure for as far back as he can remember. Now he only comes to his father after each working day in the wood to say what has happened and to ask his father for advice. This touches Jørgen. It strengthens him in his decision that Jostein should know that he will one day own the Storvik farm.

He mentions this to his son, and Jostein turns red with a mixture of joy and embarrassment.

- Thank you, Father, he whispers.
- Have you perhaps been waiting for this? says Jørgen mildly.
- Yes, I suppose I have. Hoped for it at least.
- Then I think we should shake hands on what we've decided.

They do this, both embarrassed by the feeling of formality in the room.

Once Jostein has left, he is not too much of a man to give way to tears. No one sees him, no one hears him. This is his own private matter.

Afterwards he feels a great sense of relief but also of emptiness. It has now been decided. Change, but there is a link missing. Kristoffer and Jørgen. For him these are more than just names.

- You're looking strange. Has something happened? Julie asks anxiously.

- Only that I've said to Jostein that he'll be taking over one day.

She sits on his bed and takes his hands in hers.

- Thank you, Jørgen. Now I have real respect for you.

She places her cheek next to his.

- Now I think it's all going to work out. What you've just done is something I'm sure you won't ever regret. But I know too what it has cost you.

That same evening, she writes a letter to Krister in which she tells him what Jørgen has done. You are free now, she writes, free to plan your own life. And you should know that whatever you choose, I wish you the very best.

After she has finished writing, she falls asleep with exhaustion after this toughest of working days.

Jørgen remains in bed for a fortnight. A week after that he is back to full-time work. Julie keeps reminding him to be careful. She must stop doing this, he says: can't she see that he is well again? Maybe she thinks he's no longer well enough to work? Or a real man in the prime of life? She has never interfered with his work before. Yet he is not upset that she is suddenly showing concern for him. Women are a strange breed. This will all stop when she realises that he is as fit as he was before. This is something of which he has no doubt.

At this time the news comes through that the farm hand from Ås has been killed in Russia. Those who follow the news coming into Storvik know how conditions are in that country. The Germans are fleeing westward. It is not that they have been defeated by the Russian army, but what is beating the German forces is the extreme Russian winter. They say Hitler must be mad to be sending wave on wave of young soldiers to a certain death. So far as they know Hitler does not have a son of his own. Is this the reason he is sending others to their death without a second thought?

It is reported that Larris's parents are crushed. His mother has taken to her bed and refuses to meet people. His father is furious and has publicly called Hallgrim a murderer. If it weren't for Hallgrim and his son, their own son would never have become involved.

Hallgrim avoids both the post office and the shop just after this has happened. But people talk. Some say that his son on Ås was lucky to get away with consumption. If they had a choice between this illness, terrible as it is, and a mass grave on the Russian front they know which they would choose.

- Yes, the devil helps his own, some say maliciously.

But after a while they understand that it is Sigmund Myrhe who is behind most of Hallgrim's actions. It seems inconceivable that Hallgrim has become so power hungry that he does not understand this. He is a total lackey for the mayor who is now the most hated man in the village. Myhre is totally unscrupulous. He has a terrified shadow of a wife who almost never goes out unless she is forced to. Rumours are circulating that Myrhe beats her into obedience, and it amazes people that these rumours have a semblance of truth. Other rumours suggest that he has connections in Trondheim, with Rinnan and his lackeys.

They have also found out that the training camp the boys attended was in Germany and not in Norway. They find it odd that Hallgrim did not add that to his list of boasts.

People feel sorry for the farmhand's parents, and even though he was a pest and a plague for them all while he was living in the village, they also feel sorry for him. The probability is that he was easily led and could not bear responsibility. He was just a young boy whose life came to a meaningless end. He came from a good family, and even if he behaved like an idiot and a clown, people have seen more than once that when they mature boys like that can turn out well. This was a disaster, both for the boy and those around him. But one thing is certain. Once the war is over, and that day cannot be so far away now, both Sigurd Myrhe and Hallgrim Ås will have a high price to pay for what they have done. They could not have lived with a neighbour's son's life on their conscience. But in Hallgrim's s case he had become so hardened that he tried to present the boy as a hero. Maybe he needed to do this, both to quieten his own conscience and to legitimise what he had done. It is said that he went to visit the boy's parents in the neighbouring village but had not been allowed over the threshold. The boy's father drove him out giving a clear message that he must never show his face there again.

Back at Storvik, they were to receive another message, which shook the family. This was a letter from Helene reporting that Peter has been killed, again on the eastern front. They have additionally received a letter from Anne in which she wrote that the two emissaries reporting his death were both friendly and cooperative. They took time to talk to her and to praise Peter. They said that he had died a heroic death. She was awarded the Iron Cross on his behalf.

Helene reports that Anne's letter was short as if it had required a lot of courage to write. Life is getting lonely now, she wrote. She did not write much more, but behind the words lies her grief.

Selma has written to Anne, begging her to come home.

In the years Peter has been stationed in the north of the country, Selma has remained in contact with him by letter, and he stayed with her once while he was on leave. But in autumn last year, the flow of letters stopped. The letters Selma sent were returned marked 'address unknown'. It was also obvious that they had been opened. It was then they suspected trouble. Selma tried to comfort herself with the thought that Peter had been moved to somewhere else in North Norway and blamed the return of the letters on the postal system. Now Selma herself is devastated by grief. All she asks now is that Anne should come home.

Julie and Jørgen sit sharing the letter, lost for words at the tragic situation. Anne is sitting alone in Berlin, a war widow a very long way from her loved ones. And they think of Selma. How will she be coping?

- There's a great deal going on all at once, says Jørgen.

- Can you understand Peter being sent there? He was too old
to be sent out as an ordinary soldier.

- Yes, but he had an officer's rank.

- A welfare officer, yes. But can you see Peter as a fighter?
Can you see him murdering someone?

- No, I can't. But it looks as if Hitler is panicking now.
Sending everyone he can scrape together over there. It's sending
sheep to the slaughter.

- Don't talk like that, Julie shudders. What can we do to
help them? Shall we pay them a visit? Maybe we could comfort
them?

- We'll wait and see how it all turns out. - Aunt Anne needs
rest now. I'll go and tell Mother that I'm sorry about what's
happened. Everything's pressurising us now, Julie.

Julie cannot get Peter out of her thoughts. She remembers
their last meeting during the first year of the war when he sat
there with Helene. His face was pale with shock at the sight of
the bombed-out town, and it was then that he said he could not
stay. She recalls the sight of him as he departed, a foreign figure
in his officer's uniform. With a shudder she recalls that this was
the last time she'd seen Peter.

In March the village is invaded by some uninvited guests.
The vanguard consists of two Germans who go round with
Sigurd Myhre requisitioning rooms. It is pointless either denying
them these or trying to make excuses. When they arrive at
Storvik, Synnøve is the person to protest loudest. Here on the
farm they need the space for their own purposes. Besides, they
have never had a need for boarding accommodation on Storvik
she adds indignantly, but she then falls silent as one of the
German reaches for his service pistol. Myrhe smiles and says
that so far as he knows there has always been more than enough

room in Storvik. Besides, those who are coming are nice people and will pay well for their lodgings. They requisition the large guest room which will house two Germans, and the smaller room, known as the 'radio room', where there will be room for one. Julie freezes inside as she shows them this room, but it all goes well on this occasion. No sooner are they out of the yard than Jørgen dismantles the aerial and removes every trace which might reveal what the room has been used for. What he is most worried about is how they are going to listen to the news with Germans in the house.

These Germans who are coming to the village turn out to be surveyors. They are here to draw new maps of the area. People say that once again it looks as if they will be here for ever. People dislike being compelled to have Germans living with them, though they have to admit these are less trouble than they had anticipated. The rooms they hire are kept in military order. Some ask for the room to be cleaned once a week, but many carry out the work themselves. Most are middle-aged, and the work they do is civilian work even though they wear uniforms. There are many Austrians among them, though they are all called Germans in the village.

At Storvik, there are two Austrians and a German. All have a low officer status. One of the Austrians, the sharpest in manner, is in command over the other two. He has the bearing which everyone associates with a German officer. The others are more jovial; they speak to the children and give them sweets, which they tempt them into taking, even though this is forbidden. Sven and Sunniva learn quickly that these objects, which are so nice and which they have never tasted before, are called bonbons. They learn, too, how they can ingratiate themselves to have them given. The people living with them are quiet and keep themselves to themselves. But after they have been on the farm for a while one of the Austrians, the 'nice' one as the children call him, begins paying brief visits to the kitchen. He clearly needs company, Jørgen says, but is not sure he likes having this German mingling with them. However, having been brought up to be welcoming, neither Julie nor he can bring themselves to say that these visits are unwelcome. Nor can they deny that Mayer, which is what this man is called, is good company. He talks about the place he comes from and shows them pictures of his family, his wife and three children. He says he does not know how these are kept and has received no news of them for months. Julie sees that his eyes moisten as he looks at her two young ones.

She tells Jørgen that she cannot help feeling sorry for him. There is pain in his eyes, which affects her. It must be dreadful being in a foreign country, away from your family and knowing that you may never even see them again, especially when you are as unenthusiastic as Mayer appears to be.

- Don't forget that he's the enemy, says Jørgen.
- Oh, I know that, but somehow I cannot look upon Mayer as an enemy.

But she does fear the other two. They only show themselves when necessary and then are formally polite. It has occasionally happened that the boss, as they call him, has knocked on the kitchen door without Julie hearing his approaching footsteps. She later feels uneasy about this, afraid that she and Jørgen may have been talking about controversial things.

She warns the children not to talk to the Germans and says that they must on no account report what grown-ups have been talking about. The men living with them speak fluent

Norwegian, and it is never easy to know what the young people hear and pick up. Even the four-year-old Sunniva seems to understand Julie's meaning when she speaks with a serious expression. It is as if the time they are living through has given children more understanding than you would expect them to have at their age. Both nod in assent when Julie says that it can be dangerous if they tell the Germans something which they should not know.

- Does that mean that the Germans can take Father and put him in prison? Sven asks with a serious expression.
- Yes, it could mean that, she says, even though she is reluctant to frighten them unnecessarily.
- Is that why go round saying, Hush?
- Is that what I do?
- Yes, since the Germans came, you've been saying Hush all the time.
- All the time, Sunniva repeats.

The young do not know anything but war, and Julie wonders what this may have done to them. They have not experienced bombing or shooting, nothing as dramatic as that, but they cannot avoid feeling the drabness and general unpleasantness. Is this going to stay with them into the future?

One day, when Sven and Sunniva are sitting at the kitchen table with their colouring books, Julie overhears a conversation between them.

- What is war? Sunniva asks.
- War is the Germans coming and taking our country, Sven answers.
- Oh, go on! It can't be possible to take a whole country, I know that much!

- Can't it? You ask Father. The Germans came bombing and shooting at us, and that was war. But we'll soon shoot back at them, bang, bang, crash, Sven says, waving his arms.

- But what if they shoot us?

- They won't be able to. We'll have taken away all their cannons and guns - everything. Then we'll shoot them and chase them home, and there'll be peace.

- That's not what Grandma says. She says that peace is when we can have oranges and bananas and chocolate and all sorts of nice things.

- That, too, stupid.

- Hush! says Julie.

- There you go again! says Sven.

The problem with the radio was not as Jørgen first thought it would be. The Germans leave the house in the morning and after work dine in the People's Building where the commandant is stationed. Consequently, they do not return until eight or nine in the evening, by which time the news from London is over. However, Jørgen has had to set up strict rules. He and Jostein take turns listening, and the listener also takes notes. No one from outside comes in to listen now, and people on the farm keep watch, something that has not become any easier since Helge and Krister left. He entrusts the news to one of the initiated entrusted with passing it on, but they must always do this by mouth. He never shares his written notes with anyone. He has no wish to know what those he shares the news with do with it, that is their business, but he gradually finds out that many more people than he expected are kept well up to date with the news. But then he relies on those he has chosen as accomplices to know what they are doing. All the same, he is still not entirely comfortable when he hears the voices from London and bears in mind who his lodgers are.

One day in May, Ivar rings to report that Selma has died. They found her in bed that morning, he says. She must have died in her sleep.

Synnøve turns ashen as they receive the news. She sits down in a chair and looks as if she cannot move.

- I've been waiting for this to happen, she says. - Poor Selma, she just couldn't go on. The news about Peter and Anne being so far away proved all too much for her.

Synnøve goes to bed asking to be left alone. All of a sudden she looks old, and they are concerned that this may also be too much for her.

Selma has been an important family member. She has come to stay with them every summer, and in recent years either Ivar or Helene has accompanied her back and forth on the journey. Each time they saw her she looked smaller, until in the end she looked like a porcelain doll. But they have never ceased admiring the strength housed in this small body and the way in which she has remained upright through all the blows life has dealt her. For the children, she has been like a spare grandmother. She will be missed by all.

Synnøve gets back on her feet, and even though they can see her mourning the loss of her sister-in-law she exhibits a strength which brings to mind the Synnøve they knew when she was fully herself. Once again she takes command. She will go to the funeral and wants Julie to accompany her. Jørgen cannot afford to travel on account of his spring farm duties, she says.

- Wouldn't it be better if Astrid went with you? Julie suggests.

- No, she must look after everything here. I want you to come along and represent the household here at Storvik. Helge can represent the men.

Neither Jørgen nor Astrid objects to this decision. Their mother still has the power to make decisions for them. This applies particularly to Astrid. She has just turned forty-five. Julie cannot think about her without feeling a sense of guilt. But what could she have done? Astrid arrived here with a sorrow that came close to breaking her. She refused to mix with other young people and, to begin with, ate to comfort herself until her whole body grew bloated and fat. She erected a shield round herself and was not greatly concerned about how she dressed. This phase passed, and now she is as slim as she was when she was young and quite meticulous about how she looks after herself, even if she is still somewhat withdrawn. She has reddish-blond curly hair gathered into a tall bun at the top of her head, and she dresses in an outdated fashion. Julie frequently steps in and asks her about this, thinking how attractive she could still be if she really wanted to. Astrid, who could be so rough round the edges, has now become mild, though just occasionally bitter wrinkles can be seen on her face. She has lived on the farm as a free helper all these years, so self-sacrificing and self-denying as to be almost invisible. But what would people have done without her? For the children she has been a second mother to whom they can go as readily as they do to Julie. Then there is her music. Her sharp features soften when she sits down at the piano, and an air of youthful dreaminess comes over her. She has been patient as a teacher of the children, and it will soon be Sunniva's turn to try playing, though Sven is like Jostein and is not sufficiently patient to succeed. It sometimes happens that Ivar brings his violin when he visits, and the two siblings can then give them an experience that turns the clock back, with vivid memories of a time that has now passed. At times like these Julie can see something of Astrid's unfulfilled potential.

- You shouldn't be here, Julie says.

- Do you want me to leave, Julie? Astrid asks with a smile. - No, Julie, I belong here.

This is going to be how she thinks now. All her youthful years have been spent here in caring for them all. So, indeed, it is what her life has become.

In the boat heading towards town Synnøve and Julie are seated together in the almost empty saloon. Even though it is a mild day in May Synnøve is afraid to sit out on deck.

- I'm going to miss Selma, Synnøve says. But it just has to be accepted. All of us will be taking that journey sooner or later. But there are other things which make all this so hard to bear.

It is inconceivable that this whole branch of the Storvik family is gone. Yes, for she also regards Anne as lost. She thinks of the position the family once held in town, the respect they were accorded in all areas, from politics to culture. Does Julie remember all the festivities in this house? All that is gone now that Selma is no more. Not one grandchild is left. And when she thinks of everything that Selma has borne with that unshakeable bravery! Now all that remains is the house, which she hopes Ivar and Helene will look after and manage. But many will feel that Ivar has brought shame on an honourable house, and that is a thought which is hard to bear.

- No, it cannot have been easy for you, Mother-in-law, Julie says. This is the first time Synnøve has brought up the subject of Ivar.

- Easy? says Synnøve bitterly. It has been a nightmare ever since Ivar got mixed up in all this. Both Kristoffer and herself tried to talk sense into him, but Ivar was simply fascinated by Germany and all things German. He was fascinated, too, by Hitler, though she now knows that this fascination has passed. Kristoffer once said to Ivar, who by his own admission was not interested in politics, that he should never join a political party. But he said he wanted to show what he stood for. Besides, he committed no crime. NS was perfectly legal when he joined, just like the other political parties. The irony is that it is now the only legal party.

After the war began, Synnøve begged him to leave, but again he said he must stand by his choice. And later it was too late to step back.

- Do you think that was cowardly of him, Julie?
- In a way I can understand that it could have serious consequences for him. But it's not for me to judge.

No, it has not been easy for Ivar, Synnøve says. Later on, he distanced himself from all that Hitler set in motion. He was deeply hurt when the Jews in the town were taken, some of whom he considered to be his good friends. But what could he do, a mere nobody in that context? He has always asserted that he has never done anything to harm his compatriots. Quite the opposite. On the quiet he has helped many who have got into difficulties. He has also been to Ås to visit Hallgrim, telling him to behave reasonably towards his neighbours. It is this which has borne her through all that has happened. That he has opened his house to Germans was for Helene's sake. She knows, too, that there are many Germans who are unhappy. Young boys thrust out into something whose consequences they cannot see, boys whom Helene has taken in and tried to give something resembling a home. Bless her. The only thing she has done wrong is to be German. She never even joined the party. But now the disgrace is something she must have the strength to bear. The disgrace, and what is perhaps the most painful thing of all, the relationship between Ivar and Jørgen.

- I am old, Julie. I'll soon be going the same way as Selma. I'm now begging you to do all you can to bring my two sons together when all this is over. I could not bear going to my grave, knowing that they would be lifelong enemies. I only have two sons.

- I promise you that I'll do everything in my power, says Julie, touched by the confidence Synnøve has placed in her. She has never before allowed Julie to come so close.

When the boat draws into the pier it is Krister who greets them.

- What, are you here? Says Julie, surprised and delighted to see her son again.

- Yes, I must accompany Selma to her grave.

To give Synnøve an opportunity to spend time alone with Ivar and Helene, Julie takes a trip into town along with Krister. He has a couple of errands to do, and she wishes to spend some time alone with him in order to hear news from home which is not intended for others' ears. He has become a real adult in the course of the short year in which he has been away from home and seems more self-assured. Following his father's decision that Jostein will take over the farm, a burden has been lifted from his shoulders. Still, his first question to Julie is how his father is reacting to this.

Your father will need time before he can fully accept what has happened, she replies. But she believes the day is approaching when he will realise that this decision was right. Maybe he realises this already, but his pride won't let him admit it. When the day comes that he dares to admit it, the relations between himself and Krister will once again be good.

- What are your thoughts about the future, Krister?

He says he has so many plans. There are some plans he does not want to talk to anyone about until he knows whether they are realistic. But he has decided to move to Oslo the following autumn.

- Oh dear, I'm not too happy about you moving away.
- If you worry about everything, you might as well stop living!

She then wants to know how everything is back home. How are things working out with Johanne? Both she and her father send short letters as though they're afraid these will be opened.

Johanne is as well as can be expected, he says. She was miserable just after the divorce. Inge made a huge spectacle out of the process, coming out with all manner of threats. Oddmund had to show real muscle before Inge withdrew his claim for Johanne's personal property, things she had been given by her parents and personal gifts. The rest of the estate she had no interest in as this would have reminded her of her life with Inge.

Immediately following the divorce Inge threatened to come and take away the children, but this calmed down. In letters, he started appealing to the children's sympathy, saying he missed

them and that the loneliness was making him unwell. When this
didn't succeed he resorted to sarcasm. They had let him down by
choosing to live with their mentally ill mother instead of their
father who could have given them such a good life. This affected
the children, but it hit Johanne even harder. Strangely enough it
was Oddmund who also put a stop to this. It seems that Inge has
total respect for Oddmund. Inge now writes to the children less
frequently, and his letters are brief and uninformative.

- How has Johanne coped with the gossip? Julie asks.

This has gone better than expected. It seems that rumours
about Inge and his connection with NS had reached their village,
with the consequence that Johanne experienced more sympathy
than condemnation. Former friends have begun visiting her
again, and grandfather remarks she has become livelier and is
beginning to look like her old self. As of autumn, there are going
to be three schools in the village rather than two as previously.
Johanne has been invited to apply to be a teacher for the
reception class.

- My goodness, it's wonderful to have some good news for
once, says Julie.
- Yes, and you should just see the children. You wouldn't
recognise them. Even the boy has thawed out and is beginning to
develop into a happy and fearless young scallywag.

They are so absorbed in their conversation that Julie fails to
notice Randi before she stands right in front of her on the
pavement. Both are equally surprised at a meeting like this. Julie
suddenly feels a warmth surge through her body. It is now years
since they last met, their only contact having been cards each
Christmas. Randi is the first one to act. Somewhat stiffly, she
politely shakes hands with Julie.

- Good afternoon, Julie. It's so nice to see you, and it has been such a long time. But she does not look Julie straight in the eye.

After exchanging a couple of conventional sentences, Randi says she is busy, that unfortunately she must go, but that she hopes they can meet again soon.

- You look upset, Mother?
- Randi was my best friend, and you've seen how she is now?
- Isn't that how friendships are? They go well for a time and are worse at other times. You'll see it all turn out well between you and Randi one day.
- No, I don't really think it will.

Helge is becoming more grown up every time Julie sees him. He has a new gravity about him, but each time she sees him, she wonders how he will get on in life. However, she is happy that he is enjoying school and doing well in all his subjects.

That evening she sits with Helene after the others have gone to bed. She never ceases to admire Helene. If Selma was strong, Helene is not any less so. She looks as if a breath of wind might blow her over, yet there is undoubtedly a strength in her which has become clear in recent years. Her body is almost as it was when she was young, and she continues to teach dancing. She moves in the way that dancers do, creating the impression that she is gliding round the room as her toes reach out towards the floor. Her face is more mature and although her skin is still smooth, small wrinkles are beginning to appear along her cheeks and round her eyes, especially when she smiles. Her hair is just as shiny as ever, in the same style, with a heavy bun at the nape of the neck. But in Helene this does not look unfashionable as it is the classic ballerina hairstyle. It emphasises the pure features of her face and her expressive eyes. Julie believes that Helene has become more beautiful as the years have passed. But her narrow pale hands have become a housewife's hands, displaying signs of hard work.

Helene describes Selma's last days. She had written to Anne begging her to come home. It was so distressing seeing her sitting there every day waiting for the post to come. This was her only remaining hope of seeing Anne. Finally, a letter arrived and Selma read it again and again until, at last, she just sat there, apathetic, with the latter in her lap.

- It was a heartrending sight, says Helene. - In the end, she asked me to read the letter. I have it here, but I didn't have the heart to let Synnøve read it, although I would like you to read it, Julie.

The first part of the letter is about everyday things. Anne is keeping well, all things considered. She is beginning to accept Peter's death. 'Dear Mother', she writes 'You are asking me to come home. Home to Kristiansund? Home for me is here; it is where I belong. And as you know such a journey at this time would be impossible. Mother, you are old, and maybe we shall never see each other again in this life. But you must know that I love you and that you are in my thoughts every minute of the day. I miss you so much that it hurts. You will always be in my thoughts, my dear, brave, beloved mother. So be brave at this time, I beg you, be brave'.

They remain seated in silence after Julie has read the letter, both fighting back tears.

- That is just so upsetting, says Julie.

- Yes, Helene says, - and the most distressing thing is what Anne is trying to say between the lines, what she must have been feeling as she wrote. She knew that the letter would be opened, for that is how it is now with all the post coming from my homeland. There will be much to answer for one day.

Selma went to bed after Helene had read the letter.

- She looked at me with that special look. You remember how she could do that, Julie? She looked at me and there was a calm about her. I can't take any more, Helene, she said. Now I have lost everything. Now it's up to you and Ivar to take care of things here. All that has been and all that there still is.

Helen wiped her eyes with the back of her hand.

- It was as if she was already saying goodbye to me. And it turned out to be true. She really couldn't take any more.

She refused to get out of bed and refused all food. She just sank deeper and deeper into herself as each day passed until one morning she was found dead in bed.

- It'll empty here without her, Julie. She will be hugely missed. She has been like a mother to me from the very first moment I entered the house, and the opposition in recent years has only drawn us closer together. To me, it feels unbearable that she will no longer be here.
- I can understand that, Julie says.
- That was all very serious, Helene smiles, - but there are things to be happy about. It's good having Helge in the house at this time. I don't think you can fully realise what it has meant for us to have your children here with us. We've even enjoyed our music together.
- Yes, how is Helge getting on with his playing?

- He has talent, there's no doubt about that. - But he's not too strong on things like patience and persistence. Like Krister, he wants to play jazz and light music. And maybe that's just as well. To be a classical pianist requires an iron will, something she unfortunately finds Helge unwilling to acquire. He cannot be forced, but the most important thing is for him to find pleasure in music.

A large procession accompanies Selma to her grave. Not quite `so many as at Erling Storvik's funeral, but most of the town's most distinguished families are there. Not only these, but also people who have worked for them, either at the bank or in the home, and also family and friends. It is noted that there are Germans present. Those who have been lodged in the house and have come to know Selma. Surely Ivar and the shame he has brought on the family will come to be mentioned in future, but now people are seeking to pay their last respects to Selma. Not only that, they are meeting up to show respect to a family which has meant a great deal for the town. A family which, with Selma's passing, is either inactive or no more.

Synnøve walks between Ivar and Helene behind the coffin as it is carried to the cemetery. Behind them are Krister and Julie. A mild spring rain falls on Selma's bier.

The ceremony ends at the graveside, and after the mourners have passed reverently expressing their condolences, the family returns home to dinner. It is not as it was when Erling Storvik was buried. That time there was a reception with food served at the Grand.

For Synnøve, it is this part of the funeral which she finds hardest to accept. Selma deserved more than just a poor get-together. But for those from the village, a huge reception would be unthinkable. And this was Selma's wish, so it must be accepted.

- She at least had a worthy funeral, our Selma, she says when it is over. - It was good to see that the family wasn't forgotten. I hope that the family will be able to make a comeback some day.

One evening, Julie sends Jostein up to the Germans with a bunch of handkerchiefs she has washed for them. They always pay for these small services. When there is a delay, and he does not return straight away, Jørgen becomes uneasy.

- Do you really think he should be talking to them?
- Take it easy. He just wants to try out his German.
- I won't have him mixing with them, says Jørgen indignantly.
- Their boss went to Kristiansund today and will be there for a couple of days. That will be why Jostein is just seizing this chance.

After half an hour has passed, Jørgen goes off to find his son. He is not going to tolerate this kind of behaviour, he says.

When he doesn't come back, Julie becomes so uneasy that she sends Anders up to see what is happening. When he, too, fails to return, she begins to feel that something must be wrong. In the end she cannot bear waiting any longer and herself goes to check out what has happened.

Even outside the room, she can hear loud talking and laughter. Synnøve looks towards the door as Julie goes upstairs.

What's going on? Are they having a party up there? she asks.

Julie bangs on the door for a long time before they hear her through gales of laughter. Mayer, who opens the door for her, has red round his eyes and the shamefaced look of a boy who has just been told off.

Julie cannot believe her eyes. Here are three males, all sitting with reddish eyes and a cigarette and spirit glass in their hands. All three have a cigarette pushed behind both their ears. They look up at her sheepishly.

- You'd better drink up, she says, for now, the party's over.

Obediently, they drink what is left in their glasses, put out their cigarettes and pop the precious stub into a shirt pocket. The German looks every bit as ashamed as Julie's family. As she follows them downstairs there is a deathly silence in the room they have just left.

- Now I've seen everything! she says angrily once she has them seated on benches in the kitchen. - I never thought I'd see you sitting and drinking with a German. Aren't you ashamed of yourselves?

- Don't take it like that, Julie, Jørgen says. - Those two were just taking their chance while their boss was away. They don't have a lot of fun.

- Taking their chance? And what about you? You were the ones taking your chance. But that's the way it is with you men. When it comes to cigarettes and spirits, all principles go out of the window.

Looking ashamed, Jostein and Anders leave the room.

- Yes, you're right to be ashamed of yourselves, Julie shouts as they go.

She sits looking at Jørgen, whose face is still flushed from the drink, and he, too, is looking ashamed, like a beaten dog. Suddenly, laughter bubbles up inside Julie. She laughs and laughs, unable to stop herself.

- Do you think this is a laughing matter? Jørgen asks sharply.

- Oh, it's so good to laugh again, she blurts out. - You should have seen yourself, Jørgen, there you were, caught red-handed, and the Germans were just as embarrassed as you. I do believe I managed to scare them.

- Was it so strange they were scared when you were standing there like some sort of ancient fury? They are surely just as scared by furious women as we are. They must have people back home who yell at them.

- But what if people in the village find out about this, Jørgen? Do you think people would laugh about it then?

- Oh no, says Jørgen, we mustn't let that happen.

- But that I managed to scare the Germans?

- Well, if there were more like you in our country, we would have won the war long ago.

The Germans' crushing defeat at El Alamein in North Africa and the dreadful battle over Stalingrad two years ago had ignited people's hope. They believed that this would be the beginning of the end for Hitler. But no one thought that it would drag out for so long, and a sense of despondency once again sinks over people. Soon they will be into yet another year of the war. People have become worn down by this war and in many ways feel worse than ever. For some time in spring there were rumours of an allied invasion, though no one knows where. This ignites hope, but time passes and nothing happens. Then, one day comes the good news they had been waiting for. Jostein was alone with his radio when the news reported that the Allies had landed in Normandy. This was on June 6th, 1944.

In the kitchen in Storvik that evening they have difficulty controlling the joy they feel. Jørgen has already shared the good news with one of his accomplices, so there is probably joy in more than one home by now. But they must still be careful to speak as quietly as ever when sharing the good news of what has happened. It must mean that the end is not far away. British, Americans, Canadians - it will be impossible for Hitler to stand up to all these.

The Germans who are living with them do not come back before midnight that evening. Synnøve, who was lying awake when they returned, said she could hear that they were unsteady on their feet as they staggered upstairs. At this early stage, they keep more to the background than they did previously and come home late in the evening. Even Mayer's visits to Julie in the kitchen have all but ceased. But this is as well because Jørgen is so passionate that he forgets all caution as he sits glued to his radio and listens to the news. Difficult French place names stream across the ether, Jostein scribbles notes for dear life, and pins keep being moved around on the map. Julie and Astrid are posted to keep watch.

The radio urges the Norwegian people to keep calm. The war is not over yet, and no one should imagine that Hitler is going to capitulate until the very end. Besides, Norway is geographically distant from the theatre of war in the south. The Germans remain in power here, and there are still many of them in the country.

This gives rise to a growing anxiety among people. Everyone knows that Norway, with its west-facing ports, has been a fortress that Hitler is going to hold on to at any price. Can it be that Norway, too, will become a theatre of war? People ask whether there is a possibility that allied and German troops might clash in their country.

In July, the surveyors leave. People feel that it's good to be rid of them even though they have given people little to complain about apart from their being German. But it is liberating once again to be a master in your own home and to be able to talk freely under your own roof.

The evening before they leave Mayer pays a final visit. Julie is alone in the kitchen.

- Where will you be going now? she asks.

He says he is not sure where they are going, but he knows they have been ordered further north.

- Is that also for surveying?
- Oh no, it's not surveying that this is about, he says, and she hears the bitterness in his voice. - We will be going to the far North.
- Why north? I thought it was in the south that things are happening now, she says boldly. She dares to say this to him.

Mayer shrugs his shoulders and reverently extends his hand towards her.

Goodbye, he says, and she sees to her surprise that his eyes are moist with tears. She can hear his voice trembling with emotion. - I'll never forget the times you've welcomed me into your kitchen. Here, for a moment, I dared to hope that the world could become normal again. I value it even more highly because I think I know what it must have cost you. He presses his hand down on hers before he leaves.

This felt afterwards like a hand gesture between friends who trust each other. And this is how it was. Both have said more than they should say in such times. Yet on paper they are enemies.

Out in the yard the following day, Julie can see nothing in his eyes or face which might give away anything about their conversation the previous evening. Along with the other two, he formally shakes Julie's and Jørgen's hands before he clicks his heels in a military salute. Not one of the three turns to look back as their jeep drives out of the yard.

Once these have left there are few Germans left in the village. Those that are live privately on Øra. What they are doing there no one knows.

- They'll no longer be sitting here as watchmen seeing that we dance to their tune, people say.

That summer, Russian allies bomb East Finnmark. People first refuse to believe this, dismissing it as rumour. But once they realise that it is true, it seems inconceivable. Can it be possible that their own allies are wanting to cause ruin in Norway?

Since the invasion into France Hallgrim has lain low. He is rarely to be seen in public and has hardly ever been to the shop or the post, preferring to send his children on expeditions of that sort. He has gradually realised that people are now bold enough to show their opposition and coolness towards him, which is also how the other Nazis in the village are experiencing things. People are tired of showing good manners; they have done that for long enough. They dare not go so far as to show contempt as yet, but they can express coolness, and they do this by keeping their distance and refusing to engage in conversation.

Those who are keenest in their condemnation of Nazis are the 'stripies' in the village. These are those who have not joined the party but who have ingratiated themselves with both Myrhe and Hallgirm. They may have visited them in their home and exploited them for their own advantage. They are what people call 'false friends', people who use the war to their benefit. It is these who are now screaming loudest of all, and they can get their passports signed.

- Go home and get your act together, people say to them without making any effort to hide their contempt.

After the bombing in the north, Hallgrim once again enters the limelight. With a gloomy face but oozing with authority, he turns up again among the men who meet in the post office each evening.

- Now you can see what idiots you've been, he says. How do you think it will be if the Bolsheviks take over the country and the Red Army invades us? That would be something else! It's beyond my understanding that you people can't come to your senses and join the Germans in putting a stop to all this. There are enough brave German soldiers here, as well as Norwegians who know what they are fighting for.

The worst of all this is that people are so dumfounded by what has happened that they can't find words to stop Hallgrim's blustering. They don't know enough to be able to give him answers.

In Finnmark, Germans pile over the border from Finland in full flight from the Russians. This German retreat leaves Finnmark and North Trøms in ruins. The civil population is driven out of their homes as the Germans set fire to everything behind them. Houses, means of communication, commercial buildings, fishing boats, everything is left in smoking ruins.

A stream of refugees now moves southwards. The Nazi newspapers first maintained that these were free evacuees and that it was Russians, the Bolsheviks, who were forcing people to flee and who were terrorising, raping, murdering and carrying out a scorched earth policy.

This is the truth, according to the newspapers, and Hallgrim uses all of it to demonstrate that people are stupid.

But then refugee families arrive who have relatives in the village. The Germans try at first to put in place a ban on receiving refugees, but this proves impossible to enforce. When Myrhe turns up at the homes of people who have taken in refugees, the hosts enquire whether it is no longer legal to welcome family members on holiday visits. But Myrhe soon has more to think about than a few homeless people. From the refugees, people learn the truth of what has really happened.

They tell how people have been ordered out of their homes without being allowed to take with them anything more than a few absolute necessities, how they were loaded onto boats or vans with no idea where they were heading. The Germans made the excuse that they were rescuing men and women, the sick, the old and infirm and children from the Bolsheviks. With no opportunity to protest, all have been sent south towards an unknown fate. Behind them their homes were burning. This action has been carried out with inhuman cruelty and brutality. Even the most dilapidated homes in the most out-of-the-way places have fallen victim to the flames. Some residents managed to escape in time and hid in caves and other inaccessible places, but even these had to watch their homes being burned.

People are horrified when they hear these descriptions. It's said that there are several hundred thousand German soldiers in Norway, most of them in the north. Are they going to continue carrying out this raid toward the south? Are their homes going to be destroyed in the same way? Where can they go for help? To the Russians? The other allies seem to have enough going on with the inferno further south in Europe, but there is also bombing in south Norway. In Bergen, many civilians have died recently after bomb attacks by allied aircraft. People are becoming disorientated, vacillating between hope and despair.

Early on the morning of 12 December, Kristiansund is hit by a tragedy which shakes the town and the whole district roundabout. A British bomber released a load which must have been meant for German ships berthed at Storvik Mechanical Dockyard. But it missed, and the bombs fell in Dalegaten, in which four houses were hit and totally destroyed. A fifth was burned to the ground, and many others were damaged with splinters. Twelve civilians died, some of them children, and nineteen people were seriously injured. Once again, civilians had been exposed to an allied bomb attack, which it was impossible to believe had happened. This supplies Hallgrim with new ammunition for his attack.

- Now, do you see? he says scornfully. - Did you seriously believe that the English were friendly?

People have never felt as ground down as they do now. The hope they had after the invasion that this year they would celebrate their first free Christmas has been shattered. Now they are moving towards a Christmas which looks more miserable than the last. They know that this cannot go on forever, but what people are now asking themselves is how much more will be destroyed before it is all over.

The resistance movement has greatly increased in strength this year. But this has the consequence that innocent civilian lives are being lost. They remember the last conclusive action in the battle over heavy water in February when the 'Hydro' ferry was sunk on Tinnsjø at Vemork. 14 Norwegians and 53 innocent passengers were drowned when the heavy water sank to the bottom of the lake. Persecution of those betraying NS people held to be dangerous has also increased. The NS refers to this as cowardly sneak-killing and puts in place frightful reprisals from the Germans and NS.

Germans and Nazis are impatient and aggressive, the civilian population is increasingly becoming terrorised, and innocent people are being tortured and executed. Fear spreads among people, even as they desperately hope for peace. Just before Christmas, the village discovers that Torsetein Sand has been deported to Germany and has ended up in the concentration camp at Sachsenhausen.

There is little to rejoice over. Shortages are worse than they have ever been, and in the towns, there is real need.

Rumours abound, both true and untrue. As before those in the village are concerned about their what their neighbours are doing and thinking - they say that this will soon be the only entertainment people have left. More than ever, they are concerned with what the people on Ås are doing. Gunnhild has become milder since her son became ill. She is not often seen in public now. Her son has returned home from Reknes Sanatorium. Once a month he travels to town for treatment of his damaged lung. None of the others on Ås is reported to be infected, but there are reports that Gunnhild collects all the linen her son uses and boils it up in a large pan. This must mean that her son is still infectious.

Their eldest daughter has now returned home. She is the same age as Jostein, nineteen. For the last two years, she has been a housemaid for a prominent merchant in Trondheim, a well-known Nazi. He is said to be a close friend of Myrhe and is known to have visited Ås. The girl is reported to have come home on account of disappointment in love. Rumour has it that she was as good as engaged to a young German officer, but then it was revealed that the man was married and had a wife back in Germany. True or not, that is the rumour.

In August Krister had been home, which enabled Julie to get together clothing and the other items he needed for his new life in the capital. He was disappointed that the University was now closed, but he would be able to study on his own until everything returned to normal. This has not precluded the journey to Oslo, which he has worked and saved towards for so long. He has obtained textbooks both for the introductory course and for the first-level course in French; apart from that, he has been so fortunate as to obtain a job as a bank clerk.

During this time, he has been busy writing. He tells Julie that he has now mastered most of what he has been studying. He is very happy in Oslo, even if it is a strange experience seeing such a big city in darkness, and that it is next to impossible to get hold of even the smallest thing. He writes, too, about girls. This is a subject Jostein never mentions to her, but Krister has always been more open. So open that it may occasionally occur to her that it goes a little too far. She has been worried that Krister is continually falling in love, a love which is intense for as long as it lasts, which is until the next love comes along. She has lost count of all the girls he has fallen for but has later grown tired of.

- You might at least think of the poor girl before you get involved, she complains.
- Oh, Mother, you take everything so seriously, is his usual smiling reply.

In his Christmas letter, he writes of yet another great love, and as always, this abounds with superlatives about his choice. She is beautiful, pleasant, intelligent and intent on becoming an actress. Through her, he has come into contact with a group of young actors who get together in each other's homes to read plays together. They hold auditions and perform scenes in which Krister is allowed to take part. At present, they are working on Ibsen's *Brand*. Now, perhaps she understands that he is having a wonderful time.

His letter oozes with a breathless enthusiasm, but when Jørgen reads it, he shakes his head.

- On an amateur basis, that's fine. But I really hope he doesn't choose that as a way of life.
- But don't you see that he wants to go on studying?
- When it comes to Krister, nothing is going to surprise me.

He makes no further comments.

It appears that people have become less resistant to illness than they were previously. The young are hit by tuberculosis, and diphtheria has claimed the lives of two children in the village. After New Year, it is Jørgen who is struck. This time, it is inflammation of the lungs, and after the worst is over, he must reckon with a lengthy period of treatment followed by convalescence. Jostein is a student at Germundnes Agricultural College this winter. With both Jostein and Jørgen unavailable, the running of the timber business is going to present a real problem. Without asking Jørgen, Julie sends a telegram to Krister.

She receives a telephone call back from him and can hear that he is afraid.

- What's all this about Father? Is it serious?
- Not anymore, but it may be months before he will again be ready for work. You'll have to come home. Anders cannot look after everything.
- You surely cannot mean that, Mother?
- Yes, Krister, I do mean it. Right now, I think you need to act responsibly. I think you owe that much to your father. You have the time available. You surely can't be serious about Jostein interrupting his college course?

There follows a long silence. Then she hears that Krister's voice takes on his devil-may-care tone.

- I'll come, but only on one condition: that you have herring balls ready for me when I arrive home.

On May 2nd, the newspapers proclaimed that Hitler died in Berlin on April 31st. The newspaper Free People wrote: 'The Führer died a hero's death in his fight against bolshevism'.

A Norwegian woman wrote in *Aftenposten* May 3rd an obituary for Hitler: 'The people of Europe do not yet know what they have lost. It is natural that Hitler's real enemies - international Jewry, international capitalism, bolshevism and freemasonry - are all triumphing. What is much worse is that millions of others, in their insane blindness, are triumphing over this historic tragedy. (…)

The martyr crucified in Golgotha could also have saved himself but refused to do so. And, just as Christ triumphed through his sacrificial death, Hitler will do likewise. (…) Adolf Hitler may be dead, but Adolf Hitler's cause will live on.

On May 7th, the ageing poet and Nobel prizewinner Knut Hamsun's obituary to Hitler is published in *Aftenposten:*

'I am not worthy to speak out about Adolf Hitler, whose life and work are not subjects for sentimental reflection.

He was a warrior, a warrior for humanity and a missionary for the Gospel and for the rights of nations. He was a reformer of the highest rank, whose historic fate was to be active at a time of the most deplorable brutality, which in the end killed him.'

The Western European dares to see Adolf Hitler's death thus: 'And we, his close associates, bow our heads at his death'.

People shake their heads as they read these words written by their own countrymen.

Jørgen has moved the radio from its secret hideout in the barn to the 'radio room'. Some of the inhabitants of the house listen continually throughout these days. They tune in to the news from London and to both Norwegian and Swedish radio.

On the morning of May 7th Swedish radio announced the German capitulation. Jørgen carried the radio down to the living room and set everything up. At 15.50 the German broadcast from Oslo announced that Germany had unconditionally surrendered to the whole of Europe. At that time the living room at Storvik was full of men waiting for the message and eager to hear it with their own ears. They sat there solemnly listening to the German words, knowing what they meant.

Then jubilation broke out. Grown men could not manage to hide their tears when they went home to their families. But then they came back. Men again filled the living room. They sat there until the message was repeated from Oslo at 17.30 and confirmed later from London at 18.30.

Then Jørgen found the flag. The whole family, and a couple of neighbours who could not bear to leave, all stood round him. Some tried to sing the national anthem but didn't have the voice for it.

As they stood there, D/S 'Driva' entered the fjord. From the bridge, the captain must have spotted the flag raised above Storvik for he now sounded the ship's siren. This reinforced the feeling of jubilation and released tears in many of those experiencing the moment. Flags soon flew from other poles in the village while other households worked to set up flags and flagpoles which had not been used for five long years.

It has been a chaotic day, leaving no time for any sort of reflection. Synnøve has been with her family most of the day, upright and proud as ever but somewhat paler than usual. Astrid now approaches Julie to say that her mother has gone to bed.

- Oh, yes. Good heavens, we should have been thinking about her today, says Julie sadly.

That evening, Julie and Jørgen are sitting alone in the kitchen. Both are so exhausted that even retiring to bed seems a challenge. Inside Julie is a mixture of chaos, joy, grief and emptiness.

- I wonder how it has all gone with Mayer, she says.

Jørgen is struck speechless.

- You're sitting here now worrying about a German? he says.

- No, she replies, feeling confused and detached from all reality. - No, I was thinking about … then I was thinking about …, and she then collapses in a flood of tears.

Chapter 10

- Why have you been crying today, Grandma? Aren't you happy now that there is peace?

- Yes, now I'm happy, says Synnøve as she lifts little Sunniva onto her lap.

- Then why are you crying?

- You can cry because you're happy, you know. There's a time to be sad and a time to be happy. Maybe you don't understand that yet, but when you're a big girl, you will.

- You are so strong, Mother-in-law, Julie says.

- I don't know how strong I am. I just know that I can allow myself to be happy now that Norway is free again. I thought the day would never come. May God bless the future.

Even though the celebrations have started early this year, 8th May is the big day. Jørgen has said that everyone who wants may come to Storvik, and the yard becomes full. The radio is placed on a windowsill, and benches have been brought from the Young People's building for people to sit on. Wives bring food, cakes, waffles and sandwiches. Each has brought her own cup and a small packet of coffee substitute. In the kitchen coffee is being prepared in the large kettle from school. After a while, a feeling that this is the National Day itself settles over the yard. There is happy laughter and chatter and small children are scurrying around with flags.

Flags are flying all over the village, there are catkins on the willows, and the birch trees all have a delicate green tinge from the tiny buds which will soon be turning into fully developed leaves. The scene is beautiful, taking in snow-topped mountains, the May skyline and the fjord.

People listen reverently to the radio. For most people present, this is for the first time since radios were confiscated. The youngest children have never even seen a radio, so they sit totally fascinated by what is happening.

Women circulate, distributing coffee to the adults and juice to the children. Synnøve also helps out with this, watched by Julie. Dressed in a long, flowery brown dress with a golden embroidered neckline and with a black shawl over her shoulders, she chats to the people she serves. Everyone here knows that her thoughts must be about her son Ivar and the fate which now awaits him. Julie notices that Synnøve is paler than usual and that she has red blotches on her cheeks, but otherwise, her face gives no hint of what she may be feeling.

Julie has always had respect for her mother-in-law, a respect which has not infrequently had difficult consequences. Now she feels a different sort of respect, for never before has she seen her mother-in-law behave with this level of dignity and pride. Just now she feels proud to be related to this strong, elderly woman.

At 15.00 the BBC broadcasts Churchill's speech, and there is deathly quiet in the yard. Even though most people don't understand a lot of what is being said, they are attentive to every word. Following the speech, jubilation breaks out, but people are reluctant to return home before hearing the news come in from London at 18.30.

There is a feeling of solemnity when King Haakon's speech comes on air. Many people cannot suppress their tears. And when the national anthem is played, everyone rises and sings along, their voices trembling with emotion, and even the strongest men taking out their handkerchiefs.

They also listen to Prime Minister Nygaardsvold's speech before slowly making their way home, but it is the prime minister's words which mark the end of this incredible day: 'Together we will make Norway a good land to live in - better than it has ever been.'

As soon as the news from London has finished, Jørgen receives a telephone call. This is from the police station, asking him to meet up at the school as soon as possible. Together with some others he is needed in connection with a task for the police and protection agency.

In the course of the past twenty-four hours, events have been moving very quickly. Myrhe has been dismissed from being mayor and Hallgrim from being a police officer and deputy mayor, both with instant effect. The former mayor is now back in post, as are the police chief and his assistant. This has all happened with such efficiency that it must have been carefully planned beforehand.

- Have you had an order from the protection agency? Julie exclaims in surprise. - Aren't you a bit old for that?
- Well, you know how it is, they need people.
- Did they let you know what it is they want you to do?

No, he hadn't learned anything over the phone. The only thing he was told was that it might be late before he returned home. However, Julie need not worry as there are no Germans in the village now. No doubt he is to be involved in a tidying-up operation of some sort.

In the school hall, several men are assembled beside the police officer and two unknown women. The women are dressed in dark clothing with brown armbands displaying the Norwegian flag. The officer introduces them saying that they are from Kristiansund.

The operation he sets out is brief and concise. They are to keep watch over Hallgrim, Gunnhild and the oldest son from Ås. The second oldest son is not affected on the grounds of his illness, and the daughters are not covered by any arrest order.

The officer says that he has already placed all NS members in the village under arrest and explains that the police have responsibility for all the villages in the area. All those arrested have had their weapons confiscated and are under guard. Those watching over them need relief, which is why Jørgen and two other men are now being asked to guard the detainees. They will be issued with weapons and must not allow the detainees out of their sight. One woman present is there because of Gunnhild so that she can be accompanied on errands of every type. Everyone is required to act reasonably and politely. The two other men present are to keep guard over the roads leading to the farm. All suspects from the area are to be taken by boat to Kristiansund. The boat is not expected to arrive before nightfall when those currently guarding them will accompany them on their journey.

- Are there any questions?
- Yes, Jørgen says, may I have a word with you privately?
- Of course, the officer says, and they go out into the corridor.
- This is a serious job you're asking us to do, Jørgen says, and it's a job we can hardly say no to. At the same time, I would rather not keep guard over Hallgrim or watch over the roads. That Hallgrim and I were childhood friends is not the reason, and anyway it's a long time since we've been friends. No, the reason is that I have a brother in town who is in the same

position as Hallgrim. That's why I don't feel that I'm now the right man to be keeping guard over members of NS.

- I'm aware of the situation, Jørgen. We know all about it. That's why I want you to take on this responsibility. None of us who know you have any doubts about what your position is. Your taking this on will confirm that once and for all.

- Does this mean that you're not going to let me off? That it's an order?

- You could put it like that. But it's an order you won't ever regret.

- So there's nothing more to be said?

- That's about it.

- And you, are you going to keep guard with us?

- No, I'll be guarding Myrhe. Between ourselves, and without this going any further, he's a bigger fish than Hallgrim.

The guards are equipped with the protection agency's armband and a pistol. Asked where these weapons have come from, the officer replies that an airdrop on Silset had arrived with weapons for Nordmøre. They know then that much more had been planned than they had previously dared to think.

Halllgrim, Gunnhild and their two sons are sitting in the main hall at Ås. Hallgrin stands up as the new guards enter the room. With a contemptuous leer he surveys this strange changing of the guard while those who have been guarding them up to now are dismissed and leave. His sons have the same expression as Hallgrim, while Gunnhild stares straight ahead, her face bloated with crying.

- There are plenty of you here, officer, says Hallgrim. But … well, you seem a bit short on soldiers.

The feeling in the room is very tense, not least for the three who are going to be guarding their neighbours. It is Gunnhild who is the most indifferent as she sits reading a magazine, but then she is not from this area.

They have orders not to engage in wordplay with Hallgrim. Instead, they should just answer politely any questions he or the other prisoners may have. Is that what they are, prisoners? Jørgen thinks, shuddering because of the unpleasant atmosphere in the room. Looked at from the outside, this situation is absurd. Here, three neighbours are sitting, each armed with a pistol on their lap, keeping guard over a fourth. And all four have known each other all their lives.

- Put those things away! says Hallgrim, pointing to the weapons. - Stop treating me like a criminal.
- We're just obeying orders, the oldest of the guards says. He is an upright man and close neighbour to Ås.
- How long is this farce going to go on?
- We just need to be a little patient until the boat arrives. That's unlikely to be before nightfall.
- Then can't we so much as lie down while we are waiting? asks Hallgrim, flushed with anger.
- Yes, you can. There is both a divan and a sofa here. You can lie down there if you need to sleep.
- What total idiots you all are! Hallgrim shouts. He is now pacing backwards and forwards across the floor. - What wrong have I done you other than trying to talk some sense into you?

His sons' eyes are ice cold. Gunnhild is sitting as she was before, apathetic and staring straight ahead. Not one of them has said a word. The hours crawl slowly by, with brief interruptions when one or the other captives need to be accompanied to the toilet. When Gunnhild needs to go she protests angrily that she wants one of her daughters to accompany her.

- It's best that I go with you, says the guard from town.
- What are you afraid of? That I'll run away? Or maybe I'll take my own life? How can you believe I'm such a coward? she shrieks.

For those sitting there it is almost liberating to see her react in this way. It shows that at least there is still some life left in her. She reacts too when Hallgrim asks her to see that the guests are served food and coffee. The men refuse her offer protesting that they've brought sandwiches. She then stands up and for a moment, becoming once again the mighty hostess from Ås.

We are not so rude that we will allow our neighbours to leave without having something to eat, she says, her voice trembling with indignation.

- But we aren't allowed anything. Those are our orders, says the eldest.

Then Hallgrim guffaws.

- Oh, I've experienced that too, he laughs, sounding remarkably cheerful. At least *we* must have some food. You can't deny us that!

Their two grown up daughters have also been seated here for the last few hours. The oldest one is tearful like her mother, but Solveig looks at the guards with the same icy expression as her brothers. She has come home from town where she is in her final year of middle school. Their youngest children who attend the local school have now been put to bed.

Gunnhild now goes into the kitchen accompanied by her daughters. When the lady from town tries to join them, she turns round, her eyes aflame with indignation.

- Don't you dare come into my kitchen! she shouts.
- Very well, says the lady from town as she positions herself in the doorway.
- Don't be afraid to eat your sandwiches, Hallgrim laughs. There is such an air of polite respect about him that all now take out their thermoses and sandwiches. Jørgen feels that Hallgrim has to exploit the situation for all it's worth, just as the other two are doing.

Hallgrim grasps Solveig's hand as she pours him his coffee.

- I hope they haven't ruined your exam chances, he says.
- No, they can't do that. Even if I have to take every subject privately. I promise you that, Father, she says and looks straight at the guards, her eyes filled with contempt.

Hallgrim continues pacing backwards and forwards over the floor, becoming all the time more enraged.

- Shame on you, coming here and taking a mother away from her poor, innocent children!

Jørgen can no longer restrain himself.

- Oh, come on! You lot have shown no consideration for either mothers or children.
- Is that really what you think, Jørgen? That you have no reason to be ashamed? I would never have thought that the best friend from my childhood and youth could ever come out on the sort of errand that you have today. Do you know where you should have been? Yes, guarding your brother. If you'd refused to come here, would you also have refused to guard him? Oh,

but there is more, *I* could have had *you* punished, but that wasn't something I could do to an old friend. Maybe you think I didn't know you had a radio at Storvik? I long suspected that you had one, and this was confirmed last spring when I saw a man cycling over to Storvik in time to get the news. But I promise you this, Jørgen, that I will never forget your coming here this evening. That has shown just how much and how little a friendship can be worth.

At around two in the morning, the men are relieved of their watch. As they walk back down the farm track, the eldest of them gives expression to what all of them are thinking.

- That must be the toughest job I've ever had to do, and I hope I'll never have another like it.

Back in the kitchen Julie, Krister, Jostein and Dreng-Anders are waiting for Jørgen to return.

- Haven't you gone to bed yet?
- We heard what you'd been sent to do, and after that we couldn't get to sleep. - Was it really so bad, Jørgen? You're looking pale.

He tells what he had experienced at Ås and how the various family members had reacted. When he recounts what Hallgrim said, Julie turns pale.

- Then he knew about the radio? Can that be true?
- Right at the end he knew. We weren't too careful by then. But I have difficulty believing that he knew about it any longer than that. I can't think that he wouldn't have reported it despite all his fine talk about old friendship. But I can assure you that it was far from pleasant sitting there listening to what he said.

- I can't help feeling sorry for Gunnhild, Julie says, her youngest child is only seven.

- Hallgrim didn't show much mercy when Torstein Sand was arrested, Anders interrupts, and nobody knows what his fate has been.

- No, we shouldn't forget what Hallgrim has on his conscience, and Gunnhild didn't exactly stand up for any of the others who were imputed.

- Helge has rung, Julie says.

- Have they arrested Ivar? And what about Helene?

- They've arrested Ivar, but not Helene. That what we expected. She is not a party member.

- But she is German.

- Yes, she is, but she is also a Norwegian citizen. That's why she was exempted.

- How did Helene take it?

- Helge says she took it very calmly.

- And what about mother?

- It has been terrible for her, Julie says, feeling the tears well up inside her. - Astrid is looking after her.

- Mother won't like that, says Jørgen. He stands, passes his hand across his face and remains there with his back towards them and staring out of the window.

Julie's heart sinks. How frequently has she seen him like this when reality becomes too much to bear?

- Where have they taken my brother? Jørgen says now that he has grasped the situation.

- Helge says that everyone who has been arrested has been sent to the middle school, though he doesn't know where they will be sent on to from there.

- Is Helge going to come home?

- No, he wants to stay with Helene. He doesn't want her left alone. And then he thought that school would soon be starting up again. But he'll be home for 17th May if someone can be with Helene.

- That's very generous of him, says Jørgen.

- Yes, I've been quite proud of him. They would be listening at the telephone exchange and needed to hear that.

Jørgen says the boat to take the people from Ås is due to arrive. He knows that many people will be waiting at the quayside. Even though he doesn't much want to, he intends going to witness the end of the drama. He asks Julie to go with him, but she cannot face it.

He goes there along with Krister, Jostein and Anders and watches as the boat arrives at the quay. On board there are guards everywhere, many in the civil defence uniform, a light anorak with armband, trousers gathered at the knee, boots and a ski cap on their head. The police officer is there and also a couple of police officers from town. There is no sign of those under arrest. They will all be down below, with no great desire to meet the welcome committee which has turned up.

The three from Ås are rushed through the assembled crowd. No one else from their family has come, only the guards. Hallgrin walks upright, glancing neither to right nor left. He is holding onto Gunnhild's arm. She has a handkerchief covering her mouth and looks as if her legs can barely carry her weight. Her son supports her other arm. Nothing in Hallgrim's or the son's face betrays what they are feeling at this point.

Not a sound is to be heard from those standing there. Through a wall of total silence Hallgrim takes leave of a village in which he was once a respected figure. Now he is leaving in the depths of disgrace. What Jørgen feels as he stands watching he will never be able to put into words.

- I have been sitting here wondering about how a man like Hallgrim could lead his family so far astray, Julie says when they arrive back and describe what they have seen. - You say, Jørgen, that Ivar has brought shame on his family. He has, and I have to admit that I wish he hadn't, but what Ivar has done is nothing in comparison to the things Hallgrim has done to his family.

Newspapers may once again write freely. *Tidens Krav,* which refused to be controlled by the Germans and was therefore suspended from all activity following the bombing, is now back on sale. In all the newspapers there is an appeal to the public to show restraint and on no account to engage in confrontation with the Germans.

'(…) Everyone must behave with dignity and consideration. It is of the utmost importance to preserve law and order. No one must take the law into their own hands. Looting and lynching are against the law, and those who break the law are punishable (…)

The Key words are: UNITY - DISCIPLINE - RESPONSIBILITY.

The Germans also print General Böhmer's appeal to his forces:

'(…) We stand here in Norway unvanquished and in possession of total power. No enemy has dared to attack us.

'(…) We expect the Norwegian people to display the same restraint towards the Germans that the German soldiers in Norway have always shown towards the Norwegians. From you, dear comrades, I expect the ideal, an attitude which deserves respect from even the worst of enemies. Grit your teeth, keep order and discipline, be obedient to your superiors, and continue to be what you have always been, decent German soldiers who love their people and their home above everything else on earth.

This communiqué, despite its bitter and sarcastic undertone, calms people down. The German soldiers are known for their discipline and obedience to orders. Nevertheless, people are horrified by what could have happened. It is said that there are more than 350,000 German soldiers in Norway. What Armageddon might have been let loose if these all revolted?

Here in the village they have not heard of any confrontations between Norwegians and Germans. All German soldiers from Nordmøre are now being sent to an assembly camp in Sunndalen. The story is told that many of the German soldiers broke down in tears when news of the surrender came.

- Is that so strange? Julie asks. - They will be just as tired of war as the rest of us and will want to go home to their loved ones.

The first days of peace feel very odd. People are living in conditions which cannot be compared to anything they have experienced before. The feeling fluctuates between rejoicing, pleasure and bitterness. Some grieve. On Sand, Torstein's wife is desperately worried about her husband's fate. She has still heard nothing from him. The dismal events at Ås cast long shadows over people there, just as Ivar's fate does over Storvik. Despite their rejoicing over their freedom they cannot forget that they have had in their midst someone who has let down their country. They are reminded of this when they go out, for despite Jørgen's steadfastness under the whole of the occupation, there are always some who make insulting remarks or come up with quirky questions. Julie can see it in Jørgen's face whenever this has happened. He becomes silent, moody and unapproachable. Then she leaves him in peace.

People cannot help wondering about the children at Ås. If everything was normal, the neighbours would have gone in to offer help, but in the present situation this is not possible. The tubercular son is having to take over the father's role, assuming responsibility for the spring sowing and all other work on the farm, while the oldest daughter takes care of all the domestic arrangements as well as being mother to two young siblings. This affects the neighbours who have to suppress their feelings, having grown up with neighbours who help each other out in critical situations. But they have also heard that the son has said that if any of the neighbours should dare to come and get involved, he will personally send them packing.

Fortunately, a serving girl and a farm boy have remained on the farm. Neither has had anything to do with NS and are said to be remaining there because of the children.

Later an older sister of Gunnhild's from Romsdal comes to look after things. This sister and her family are said to have no connection with NS, and there has been little contact between the two families in recent years.

Like Gunnhild she is very talkative and is not in the least hesitant about being seen out in public, where she frequents both the shop and the post office. Whatever Gunnhild and Hallgrim may have done, the children have already paid a high price for it, she says, and now the time has come to look after them and to carry them through this first difficult time. Hallgrim has also had the foresight to hire in a couple of adults from her home village to act as farm hands and to support the sick child. She herself will remain at Ås until just before May 17th. Then she will take the two youngest children back home with her, for they must not remain at Ås watching their friends through the window as they celebrate Norway's National Day. It is also already heartbreaking knowing that the children are being bullied at school and that other children avoid them. Adults in the village can correct this, she says looking pointedly at everyone present.

Julie is touched on hearing this. She will send Sven to play with the first-year pupil there. Even though Sven is not due to begin school until autumn, all the children in the area know each other and play together, a group of children all of different ages. However, she has not been keeping up to date and did not realise that the pair from Ås have not been part of this group recently. She thought, as many others did, that children handle these matters differently from adults and is sickened by the thought of how their parents have affected them.

Sven flatly refuses. He will not go to Ås. The other young people say it's dangerous there.

- No, it's not dangerous, Julie urges, it's no more dangerous than here in our house.

- I'm not going. The other children will tease me if I go there.

Neither scolding nor persuasion is going to work. Sven is immovable.

- Leave the boy alone, Jørgen says, he can't be persuaded if his mind is made up.

Sven rushes out of the kitchen.

- Heavens, Julie says, - I can't bear thinking how awful it must be for the children over there.

- You can't save the world, you know. And don't forget that the bigger ones came over here in Horde uniform and the one who's left there now would have gone on with it if he'd been well enough. Remember that he volunteered to fight on the front. He knew what he was doing. You should have seen his eyes and the eyes of that other fanatic from town.

- But the two young ones, Jørgen?

- They should have thought about them before getting involved in all this.

- And I don't understand them arresting Gunnhild, a mother of young children? Shouldn't that be challenged?

- Yes, I've thought that too, but then she had been heavily involved in the Horde.

Hallgrim's guards reported that if Hallgrim and his associates had to run the gauntlet of the crowds when they were arrested, this was nothing in comparison with what they had to face when they were brought out on land. 9 May was a Friday, and people were free to turn up to see the traitors. Both the pier and the route leading up to the Middle School were crowded with people. The prisoners were subjected to insults and spitting, and several of those watching had to be restrained by police to prevent them attacking them directly.

This is hatred, Julie says. Hatred, that terrible word which she hardly dares to utter. But it had to happen. So many people have lost someone close to them or have seen their relatives tortured and mutilated by the Gestapo, by Rinnan and his followers or by other Norwegian supporters. Julie understands why hatred towards the Norwegian participants is so fierce. It has been there all the time smouldering away but people have not dared to release it before.

- That's what Ivar is going to experience, says Jørgen. What he has or hasn't done won't come into it. He will be hated just because he was *there*.

The newspapers report the dreadful consequences of the war, of tortures and executions, of concentration camps and of the fate of the Jews. All this is becoming more and more unbearable. People knew that conditions were terrible, but the reality is like the worst of nightmares.

Frightening, too, are the rumours they hear about what is happening in town. Girls who have been mixing with Germans – they are known as German tarts - are having their heads shaved and are being chased along the streets. One person has seen some such girls being driven into town stark naked with their heads shaven. Another has seen a gang of youths with law-and-order armbands dragging girls along the streets by the hair before shaving their heads.

- That's frightful, says Julie, visibly shaken. - Surely that can't be legal?
- Well, no doubt those tarts knew what they were doing when they went along with the enemy.
- But that still doesn't entitle people to behave like animals. Are we no better than the worst of the Germans and the Nazis?

But Krister, who had once sat making crude remarks about these girls now comes to the defence of many of them. Certainly some were tarts in the everyday sense of the word, just as there have been tarts in every community, but most of these were probably genuinely in love with their German boyfriends and faithful to them.

- There were many young Germans who used to meet in Ivar and Helene's house that I could have been friends with if circumstances had been different, he says.

They also hear that windows have been broken in the Storvik villa. Julie shudders when she hears this. How will Helge, who is normally so cautious, tackle a situation of this sort?

Similarly, in Øra windows have been broken in Myrhe's house. This is searched by the police, but Myrhe has had the foresight to send his wife further south before the trouble began. It is said she took most of their valuables with her when she left.

A couple of windows in the shoemaker's house have also been broken, but the neighbours have prevented this from going any further. The shoemaker's wife, a quiet lady who has almost certainly done nothing illegal, remains inside and scared out of her wits while her children carry out all their outdoor errands. Myrhe's neighbours have been given the job of keeping watch over his house in order to preventing further damage. But nobody on Ås has dared to attempt to bring about damage, and nobody in the village would be likely to either.

- We can be a bit proud of this, Jørgen says, - proud that we managed to control ourselves when Hallgrim left. Even though he knew about the bitterness and cold feeling, people kept calm and showed common decency. It might be good to think of that later on.

The young people in the village and some older enthusiasts in the youth club are working flat out to prepare an entertainment for a celebration on the evening of May 17th. This party, with entertainment and dancing, has gone on for as long as people remember, and now it will be happening again after five long years. Krister is leader of the entertainment committee. They do not have sufficient time to rehearse a play which is what the tradition used to require, but they are rehearsing sketches, songs and poetry readings.

Late one evening Krister and Jostein come home after a rehearsal with their clothes dirty and dishevelled, and Jostein with a bloodstained handkerchief over his nose.

- Just look at you! Julie says in alarm. - Whatever have you been doing?

Krister says that along with group of friends they met a gang from Øra and it ended in a fight, Krister says.

- Oh, don't say that's all starting up again, Jørgen says. - I thought it was all over now, that people had learned better than to fight each other over pointless issues.

- That's not exactly how it was, says Krister. They were on their way to Ås. They said they had things to say to the girl, the German tart. They were going to help her get a more appropriate hairstyle.

- Oh, dear God, no, Julie says.

- We managed to stop them even if it cost a bit of blood and gore and a few dirty clothes. I feel quite proud that they didn't get through. We told them that they were not welcome here if they didn't behave properly.

- I take it they'd been drinking? Jørgen says.

- No, there are those among us who don't need to get drunk before they lose control, Krister says. And it was Jostein who delivered the decisive blow. He landed their leader a punch which all but knocked the living daylights out of him.

- That was because he was the yobbo who gave me the nosebleed, Jostein says, his face still flushed with anger.

- It was good you prevented them getting to the girl without her being attacked Julie says, but I suppose that's how it is now at Ås. I don't know at all how our lives will be if it's going to go on like this.

- There have always been gangs, says Jørgen, - and this rabble will have been encouraged by rumours coming from town. We should be pleased we haven't seen more of this round here.

17 May is approaching and Julie has her hands full with getting clothes ready for the family. Suits need to be pressed, shirts ironed and she is busy making a white dress for Sunniva, in a piqué material with small flowers which she has received from Helene. The house has to be spotlessly clean for the big day, the small-framed windows in the main building need cleaning and the yard must be swept and tidied. She complains that she does not know whether she can get all of it done in time.

One day Synnøve comes up to her and says she wants to visit Helene and to stay with her on 17 May. She has spoken on the phone to Helene and also to Helge, telling him that this will enable him to come home for the party and that he need not feel he has to be there for Helene.

He has done far more for her recently than anyone should expect of a young boy, says Synnøve, clearly touched.

- Would you like Astrid to go with you?
- No, there is no need for that.
- But you can't go there on your own. That would be much too tiring for you.
- Don't patronise me, Julie! Synnøve says looking her firmly in the eye.

Once again Julie is struck by the matchless strength Synnøve is displaying. She sees her face every challenge with no loss of dignity and admires the way in which she abides by the village's unwritten rule that everyone must keep their feelings to themselves. Only Astrid can know how Synnøve is when she is alone, and she is totally loyal to her mother. She says no more than she must and what her mother allows her to say.

Krister is pleased when he learns that Helge is coming home. He needs Helge to accompany the entertainment on the piano. He will be able to do some of the playing himself, but he is also going to sing and had been thinking of asking Astrid to play, something to which he had not been looking forward. Now that this problem has been solved the piano is moved down from Storvik and installed in the Youth Building, just as it was before the war for occasions such as these. Helge is so confident on the piano now that he only needs to participate in the dress rehearsal.

The children are wild with excitement at the prospect of a day which they have heard so much about. At the dinner table one day Sunniva says:

- I'm really looking forward to getting on the 17 May train.

They all laugh, Sven loudest of all.

- You are dumb. You can't *get on* the 17 May train!
- Yes, you can. The train moves off and people can get on it, Sunniva says with tears beginning to form in her eyes.
- Nobody can be so stupid! Sven says, sounding somewhat like a large adult in a small child's body. - Yes there's going to be a 17th May train, but that what it's called when people form up in a long row shouting hurrah and waving flags.

It is only now that Sunniva understands that what she has said was stupid. She slips off her chair to hide under the table. She cries quietly but cannot hide her sobs. When Julie goes to pick her up she screams and kicks, waving her arms.

Let me go. You are horrible, all of you!

- You grown-ups could at least have confined your laughter to the kid, Julie says.

After dinner Julie tries fitting Sunniva with her new dress which is by now all but finished. It is a small stubbly dress with a neckband, and with waist and sleeves edged with red lace.

- Now you're going to be a real princess, Sunniva.

She laughs as Sunniva runs round on the floor then, holding onto the skirt, spins round.

- Yes, you're going to be quite the lady, she says smiling.

Sunniva stands in front of her as Julie removes the dress.

- You shouldn't be sorry for not knowing what 17 May is.
- No, because I couldn't know about it when I've never seen it before, Sunniva says in a matter-of-fact voice. - But it was horrible of you to laugh at me.
- Yes, I understand. We grown-ups are often a lot stupider than you little ones.

On May 13 Crown Prince Haakon returns home from London with his first cohort of government members. The rejoicing in Oslo's streets where thousands have turned out to greet the crown prince and welcome him home can also be heard in those homes all over the country which have been lucky enough to receive their radios back.

These days of rejoicing have caused a delay in the usual spring farm work. People want to be free during this time, free to listen to the news, to gather or just to talk about what has been happening and what is going on now. But this is pointless. The harvest has to be prepared for, and farmers have only just managed to plant their potatoes by May 17.

On 17 May itself they awaken to a grey rainy day with a sharp south-westerly wind. However, the weather lightens up in the course of the morning, and by the time the procession sets out from the church the rain clouds have turned into a thin mist, the wind has dropped and there are even small patches of blue sky.

Anything in the village that can walk or even crawl takes part in the procession. There is no band, but everyone sings the well-known and much loved national songs. The teacher and a couple of men with strong voices lead the singing, and no one is listening out for wrong notes on a day like this. Most people have no problem remembering the words which they had hammered into them during their schooldays. Today's schoolchildren have also learned these songs, for, with the exception of the national anthem and *God bless our beloved fatherland* which they have been forbidden to sing, their teachers have taken care to see that today's children have learned the other patriotic songs. The remaining two, the most important songs, the children will have learned at home.

Children are first in the procession after those carrying the flags and banners. Their voices begin with full force as they strike up with *We little ones are a nation too,* for that is their song. The other national songs are easy to march to. Cries of Hurrah are heard all over the village where flags are seen flying above every home. All except at Ås where the flagpole is bare and there is no one to be seen either outside or at their windows. The farm looks as barren as a desert.

The old district council which is now back on its feet has decreed that from now on the entire district will celebrate 17 May together and not in groups as they had done in the past. This is to be a symbol, created in wartime, of a unity which ought to exist. The celebration is to take place in the Youth Building one year and in the People's Hall in Øra the next. This year it is the Youth Building's turn for the celebration, and the two processions will meet in the middle.

Once the serious festivities are out of the way, it is time for the children: sack races, potato races, and obstacle races. All with prizes, a pencil or a rubber, a comb, a pocket mirror - these can all be prizes. Adults meet in groups and there is no lack of conversation on days like this. From the kitchen a group of women volunteers are serving coffee and stew, buns and fruit juice for the children.

One person people are delighted to see is Torstein Sand's wife. Finally, she dares to venture out again and has heard that her husband is now in Sweden and is as well as can be expected. The whole area breathed a sigh of relief when they heard the news, for her desperation had been casting quite a shadow over people's happiness. There are so few, and they all know each other, so that any one person's happiness or unhappiness can affect everyone.

Late in the afternoon, people make their way home. Now the youth building must be prepared for the big evening celebration.

Sven and Sunniva are completely worn out after their day. At home, they feel exhausted. Sven teases Sunniva until it ends with her bursting into tears and sobbing uncontrollably.

- Come on, children, there's nothing to cry about, is there? But I'm sure you must be very tired after your day.

- Yes, it was a long way for short legs.

- What was that you just said? laughs Julie, wherever have you heard that?

- It was Auntie Astrid who said it, wasn't it Auntie?

- Yes, that's what I said.

- But that's not why I cried. It wasn't because of Sven either. I was crying because my best clothes had become dirty and I wouldn't be able to wear them for my birthday tomorrow.

- I'll wash them, and they will be just as fine tomorrow, Astrid says while lifting Sunniva onto her lap.

- No, no, I'll do it, says Julie. - Why don't you go with Jørgen to the party?

- But you'll be going there, Julie.

- No, I'll be at home with the children.

- Let me look after them tonight, Julie. That would be doing me a favour, giving me an excuse to be at home. It's … well … as things are … I … I don't want to be meeting people again today.

- Do you really mean that? But then you'll miss the entertainment.

- It's *you* who will miss what Krister has put together, and you know that I've been helping out with the rehearsals. No, you and Jørgen should go, I owe you that, and you can stay there for as long as you like.

The main hall in the youth building is decorated with flags and foliage along the walls and the edge of the stage. On the ceiling are decorations of red, white and blue crêpe paper. The auditorium and corridor outside are thronged with people. People are buzzing with expectation, laughter and loud chatter. Nobody knows what they will be watching on stage; that has been kept top secret. Even Julie has no idea.

Krister steps forward onto the stage. The public applauds, but he just stands there, a solemn figure looking until the applause dies down. He does not introduce the programme, which is what the public had been expecting, but with a serious expression in his eyes and face reads out:

A quiet crowd is moving
Though all the roar of battle,
With prayers in every tongue.
It bows before one fallen
With a cross upon his shoulder
Who speaks to all of peace.

It is not only found
There on the field of battle,
But out in all the world.
This all-embracing love
From good and noble hearts
Which now kneels down in silence.

This is the cry of man
'Gainst war and all destruction,
Praying still for peace
on earth for those who suffer,
Who knows each man's distress
And sighs to meet his brother.

This is the cry of grief
From all in pain and wounded.
This is the Christian prayer,
The cry of those forgotten.
Of all who have been harried,
The last hope of the dead.

A rainbow bridge of prayer
O'er all the world's destruction.
This is the Christian hope
That way beyond our suffering
Love will emerge victorious
For this is why *He* died.

The auditorium falls totally silent. Krister stands up with his head bowed, the curtain sweeps aside, and the choir begins:

God bless our dearest Fatherland,
Each home, each vale, each strand,
Each grove and field!
May all of these live on,
Each village and each isle
Each man and every maid
Eternally!

Here lie grave on grave,
From heights down to the sea,
They struggled on.
God bless each honest man
Who sleeps on underground,
God bless them every one
Wherever they may be.

Tears sweep through Julie in waves. She must restrain herself to prevent herself from crying aloud, but there is no stopping the tears streaming from her eyes. Nor is she the only one in the auditorium who is crying. Next to her, Jørgen is sitting, clenching his fists so violently that his cheeks turn white, and he, too, must apply his handkerchief. Julie knew that Krister was going to read a poem at the beginning of the programme and, like most people present, probably expected a national poem. But then he had chosen one by Bjørnstjerne Bjørnson, which lifted everything to a level way above the auditorium, the village and even the country.

Krister returns to the stage, steps in front of the choir and sings *Norway, my Norway* with the choir humming behind him. Julie sits amazed. She knows that he has a good voice and enjoys singing, but she had no idea this his voice was as good as this, so mature and so warm. Again, she has to fight back tears as pride in her son surges inside her. She now sees that Jostein is struggling to pull the curtain backwards and forwards. He has told her that the only thing he has any talent for is looking after humdrum details of this sort. These two brothers are so different from each other.

Next comes the lighter part of the programme. Actors have prepared various sketches based on amusing everyday events in the war. In one such sketch, a farmer receives a visit from the food inspectorate. Halfway through the sketch, a loud squeal is heard from the wings.

- Did I just hear a squeal from a pig? the inspector asks.
- A pig? No, your hearing must be at fault, the farmer says apologetically; it was the maid you heard. We've just got a new

farm hand, and he is so excitable that he chases women all over the place, scaring the wits out of them.

The room resounds with laughter after sketches like this.

Several people with good voices appear on stage during the evening. Many popular numbers are performed, some with added dramatisation.

Give me your heart, Mary, is given a seductive performance by a young father and farmer kneeling in front of a blushing young girl. Book Jensen's *Happiness Letter* is performed by a young man trying his luck as a tenor; Krister sings *The spinning wheel in the hall,* naturally with a woman sitting at a spinning wheel in the background. A group of two boys and girls performs *Jolly Bob* with sailors' collars and crêpe paper caps. As they begin enthusiastically tapping their feet in time to the cheerful melody they receive a positive storm of applause.

When the committee chairman thanks people for the entertainment, he first emphasises the opening poem encouraging people to consider all those suffering no matter which side they belonged to. He then gives all participants his well-deserved praise.

Both young and old are present when the dancing begins. Julie and Jørgen swing round on the dance floor, a little unsure of themselves to begin with. It is so long since they last danced, but it doesn't take long before they are at ease. They dance until both are out of breath and need to sit down.

- We have to admit, Jørgen says, wiping sweat from his brow, that we're not as young as we used to be.

They take time to talk to people, but both feel that they are the objects of attention. There are probably many who feel that they have little to celebrate, Jørgen with a brother who is undergoing punishment and a mother grieving over the fact. The entire village is aware that Synnøve has moved to town in order to look after her daughter-in-law.

- I have the feeling, Julie, that whatever we did would be wrong. We'd be wrong to stay and wrong if we went home.

As they stand in the corridor about to don their outer clothes, people they know approach them and say that they cannot leave yet as the celebrations have only just begun.

Julie makes the excuse that Astrid is alone at home, looking after the children.

- Then they should send for Astrid so that she too can enjoy the dancing. It's wrong for someone like her to be sitting at home.
- I'll pass on the message, Jørgen says quietly. He has not dared to have a drop of either beer or spirit in all the festivities.

On the hill leading down from the Youth Building, they meet a drunken youth. They do not recognise him, but they know that he is from Øra.

- Ah, so Storvik people are quite happy to forget about us? Well, that's only what you would expect, he says and spits on the ground.
- Huff, Julie shudders.
- Don't concern yourself about rabble like that, Jørgen says. 'Rabble' is now his favourite word when referring to such people.

The music coming from the Youth Building through the bedroom window sounds quite distant. The relaxing smells from the wet spring night outside convey once again a memory of youth, and Julie and Jørgen love each other just as they did back then. Satisfied and with that warm, secure feeling which never ceases to amaze her, Julie reclines on Jørgen's arm.

- Julie, as I sat watching Krister tonight, I knew that I had done the right thing. We can never force him into being a farmer. It's there, on the stage, that he belongs, Jørgen says with none of the usual irony in his voice.

- Yes, Julie whispers. I thought that, too. And I was so proud.

- Yes, so was I. Proud.

- I wasn't prepared at all for that introduction. I don't understand how he managed such a stroke of genius. He didn't say an unnecessary word but just let the poem do the talking. I'm so pleased that there was no applause and that the choir came in before it could happen. That was one of my best experiences ever.

- Yes, our son is certainly gifted. Just so long as it doesn't cause him to suffer.

- What do you mean?

- I wasn't very happy that in the closing lines it was *everyone's* suffering that was emphasised. Some will certainly focus on that. Then Krister was on the stage a lot. You know what people here are like. In the village, you're allowed to do well, but you mustn't do *too* well. It's a delicate balance, Julie.

- Krister will be able to handle it. And I feel a need to thank God for helping us throughout the day, to thank Him for everything.

- Yes, we have a lot to thank Him for.

The following day, the 18th, Sunniva turns five. Again in her 17 May finery she awaits the arrival of children from the neighbouring farms. They form a group of eight or nine children of ages ranging from three to nine or ten who enjoy playing together. There are a couple of younger children, but Sunniva doesn't want to invite them, for then she would have to invite their mothers as well.

- It's just infants who have their mothers at their birthday parties, she says. She has become very conscious recently about being a big girl and keeps mentioning this to Sven who is always teasing her about being a stupid infant.

Once the children have eaten birthday cake and buns, they virtually turn the house upside down.

- It's incredible how much noise little children can make, Julie says. She tries persuading them to play outside, but Sunniva will have none of it. When there's a party, they have to stay inside because that's what grown-ups do, she says. That is an argument that leaves no room for negotiation.
- She knows what she wants, that young lady, Astrid smiles.
- I wonder how she'll get on when she's older.

As the noise is about to become unendurable, as chairs are being overturned and total catastrophe is in the air, Astrid gathers the children together for games of different kinds. There are singing games and guessing games which bring the noise to a more reasonable level. She then assembles them round the piano to sing well-known children's songs, at which point they become as quiet as lambs. That someone can play an instrument as unusual in the village as a piano amazes the children.

Julie looks at them. Again she thinks how Astrid might have been shocked by the children, but then she has such a good way with young people.

That evening, once the children are in bed and the battlefield has been cleared after the party, Julie and Jørgen are sitting with Astrid and Helge over a cup of coffee and a few food remains from the celebration. Helge is about to travel back to town the following morning, and they have had little opportunity to talk to him during the hectic days he has been at home.

School started again quite quickly, he says. The NS prisoners were removed to an assembling camp out in Nerlandsdal. This was the camp where Polish prisoners had been detained.

He has a lot to say about these first days of freedom in town and the wild rejoicing, but he has also seen things which hardly bear thinking about. He was there the day Hallgrim and his accomplices were brought to town. It was horrible, he says, almost macabre, to witness their humiliation. He makes no excuse for Hallgrim and the others from Ås, but it was dreadful witnessing how his own neighbours behaved in such a situation.

Many young people from Nazi homes have now stopped going to school. But Solveig continues, she and her best friend, who is also from a Nazi home in which Solveig rents a flat. These two go round together like two peas in a pod and at least pretend to be unaffected by threats, contempt and unpleasant remarks. There is something about these two which holds people at a distance, it may be their look, but Helge is not sure about that. When a couple of boys shouted threatening remarks after them one day in the schoolyard, they stopped, looked the boys straight in the eye and said that if they did that again, they would be reported to the police for illegal harassment. So, even though no one will have anything to do with them, they are still going to get through the final middle-school examination. Apart from which, Solveig is doing very well at school.

- Oh, she will do very well, says Jørgen. - I will never forget her eyes when we were guarding them at Ås. It was not the sort of look you expect from a seventeen-year-old girl.

He says he finds it very odd that Hallgrim didn't give more of his children a good education. All of them are intelligent. Now, Solveig seems to provide him with an excuse.

The oldest girl is different. She is modest, and no one has seen any sign of her in these first days of freedom, but she is said to be a very hard worker because of the way she is looking after things at Ås.

- How is Helene coping with it all? Astrid asks.

Helene is the person he admires most of all, Helge replies. She tackles each day calmly and responsibly. The day after they had their windows broken, she went down into town and ordered new ones to be fitted. She says afterwards that it would have been more difficult to say no to her when she met up personally. How she is in herself Helge does not claim to know. But Ivar is not the only person for her to worry about. She has not heard from her parents, and Dresden was bombed to the ground in the last days of the war, as perhaps they have heard.

- Oh, goodness, I hadn't thought of that, says Julie.

They are interrupted by loud talking out in the yard, followed by a noise in the corridor. Julie pulls open the door and sees Krister irately pushing Jostein into the room. Jostein's arms are full of books.

- What in hell's name do you think you're doing? Krister shouts.

- Should we still have that rubbish by Nazi scum on our bookshelves? Jostein rages back.

- I don't give a toss if he was a Nazi, but you don't burn good literature, Krister urges. Even if it doesn't interest you, it's still literature. He was on his way to the baker to burn books by Knut Hansum, he says, turning to Julie and Jørgen. Astrid and Helge are both speechless watching this spectacle. The two brothers are facing each other like two gamecocks, both white with anger.

- Put those books back!

- Is that for you to decide? says Jostein, dumping the books onto an armchair.

- Put … them … back … now! Krister snarls, and strangely enough, Jostein replaces the books on the shelves.

- What are you trying to prove, Jostein? Krister asks.

Jostein spins round.

- Prove? he says, his voice now high-pitched. - Prove? Have you done anything else since you came home other than to prove you're a bigger idiot than anyone else? Didn't you show it on stage yesterday when you were showing off and drew the attention away from the others? Do you think I didn't hear about that? And do we know what you were up to in town when you went round with all those Germans and Nazis? Does it never occur to you that people may wonder about that? And what about the letter you got from NS? People know about that too, he says and looks as if he wants to fly at Krister.

- Sit down now and hear what I have to say, says Krister, and by now his voice is icy, a voice which is not going to tolerate protest. The others can sit down, too. This they do without a word.

- What have you done that's so great? says Krister, turning towards Jostein. Yes - you've listened to London, you've taken notes, you've helped by keeping watch, and you used to take the accumulator across town after Helge left. But what more have you to boast about? And how was burning literature supposed to help? Proof?

Jostein is about to flare up again, but Krister stops him.

- No, I haven't finished yet. Now you will hear what your younger brother and I have done. This weakling, as you call him because he is not as fond of digging in the ground as you are. You must excuse me, Father, that was not meant to undervalue farm work.

- Stop now before you say things to each other that you can't forget, says Jørgen, his face turning white.

- No, Father. I need to finish what I've got to say, though actually Helge and I had agreed to keep to ourselves what I'm about to tell you.

Krister is calm again now and tells what happened without embellishment. All of the time he was in town following the outbreak of war he had little illegal jobs to do - he now says they were little, but they were big enough. What he did was to pass on illegal papers. Some of this material was destined for the courier post, and some for illegal newspapers. These were given to him by a fellow student from a parallel class, a pleasant girl who had the papers hidden in a textbook. They had to pretend to be boyfriend and girlfriend in their free time at school as well as out of school. In fact, in some small way, this was their relationship, but it was never very serious for either of them.

When they were together so much this was inevitable, and the girl was nice, he chuckles. In free minutes, they used to sit outside pretending to be studying, and in the course of the school day they would exchange books, that textbook in which the girl hid the papers.

- This can't be true, says Julie. - Didn't you realise how dangerous this was?

Yes, they knew that, but they were lucky. Twice a week this is what they did. A couple of times, a search was carried out in which the students' bags were emptied, but this happened on days when they weren't carrying any papers. They took this to be a sign that fate was on their side. An additional factor was that Krister was the person least likely to be suspected since he lived with Ivar in a house where Germans and Nazis were daily visitors. This explains why he was chosen to keep these papers at home until the following day. And did people remember that additional job he had, as a delivery boy for the bakery, in which he would cycle out to private customers first thing in the morning? Underneath the paper at the bottom of the breadbasket belonging to one of the customers was the place where the secret papers were hidden. He didn't have to fight to get this job, although he had answered an advertisement in the newspaper. The job was his before it was advertised, he says.

- And was that the same job that Helge got? Julie asks.
- Yes, it was, Mother. Helge took over both jobs. The person who first took my place was very nervous, so I went and had a chat with my contact when Helge was about to move there. It was hardly surprising that he got the job of errand boy after a brother who had done the job well.

Julie recalls seeing them conversing in the yard on the evening before she travelled with Krister to her mother's sickbed. She now knows that Helge was being given his final briefing that evening.

- Do you realise what trouble you might have led your brother into? Julie says, trembling with indignation. - After all, you were almost an adult, but he was just a boy.

- A boy, yes, but not a weakling. And he got a girlfriend. She, too, was in the parallel class. - Was she nice enough, Helge? How was it? Were you a real item? he teases. Krister never knows where to stop when the subject is girls.

- Oh, give up! says Helge, squirming in his chair and red with embarrassment.

- Of course I was scared, Krister says in a serious tone of voice. - I was terrified when I thought he could get caught, for I knew what they could do with people like him to get them to talk.

- I don't know if I can forgive you for that, says his mother with a shudder.

- That is your business, Mother. But neither Helge nor I think that what we did amounted to much. It was tiny in comparison with what many others let themselves in for. But we had to pretend that we weren't among those who were most hostile towards Germans. This wasn't always easy when you were subject to nasty remarks.

Everyone must promise to tell nobody about this. Ivar must not get to know. However, it may be, Ivar is going to feel this as a let-down. The truth must be confined to those present here and now. Others can believe what they will.

- Do you happen to know who's behind all this? Asks Jørgen, who has not said a word in all the time Krister has been talking.

Krister glances at Helge.

- Yes, why not? Says Helge.

Right, says Krister. It seems that Yngvar Thorsen was behind everything. They will probably never have this confirmed, but Helge met Yngvar in town one day before he came home. Then Yngvar shook his hand - a real handshake it was, too.

- You are such a good person, Helge, Yngvar had said. - As is your brother.

They look at this as a type of admission on Yngve's part that he was involved and knew what the boys had done. And with his knowledge of Yngve's talent for organising, it is tempting to believe that he was at the top. But everything he has said this evening must be forgotten and never mentioned again. This is a total demand.

- How could Yngve bring himself to do this to you and to us, says Julie angrily. - I'm going to write to him, to tell him just what I think.

- No, Mother, you mustn't do that. I said just now that there is a demand that what has been said must never go beyond the walls of the room we're in now. And no one must leave before giving me their hand on that.

And this is what he does. He gets everyone to give him their hand and to swear by all that's dear and holy that they will keep quiet about everything they have come to know.

- And now, can we talk about something more pleasant? Krister says with a wry smile.

But no one feels much like informal conversation after this. Astrid goes to her room and Jostein and Helge also disappear. Krister is left alone with his parents.

- What you've told us tonight, Krister, will give me nightmares for many a long day, Julie says. - You were just so young and …

- You'll have to live with that, Mother, as long as it's just a nightmare. But think about all the young people who did the same as us, and about those who weren't as lucky as we were. I wouldn't have told you about this, but it was Jostein who urged me to do it.

- I am proud of you, Krister, proud of both of you, says Jørgen in a serious tone. - But I don't think that relations between you and your brother will be quite the same after this episode.

Synnøve returns home pale and tired following her visit to Helene and with the same red blotches on her face. She says little to Jørgen and Julie about her trip, but says the same as Helge, that Helene is admirable and unruffled.

Julie asks Astrid what Mother has said to her.

- Oh, you know, it's not great, Astrid replies loyally.

Synnøve comes in and says she wants to call a Women's Red Cross meeting. She is one of the longest-serving chairpersons of the charity and thinks it might be a good idea to set up the first meeting to follow the peace.

- Won't that be too much for you? Julie asks.

- Do you think I can't manage it? Synnøve snaps, and once again, Julie feels like a schoolgirl being put in her place.

- Oh, I don't doubt that you can, she answers. - And we'll give you all the help we can.

- I hope you will, because I want everything to be just as it used to be.

By coincidence, the meeting is arranged for 7 June. This is a new day of celebration in which King Haakon, Crown Princess Märthe, Princesses Ragnhild and Astrid, together with the young Prince Harald, are all returning home. This is why the door to the kitchen, which is where the radio is placed, remains open so that the women can share in the festivities taking place in the capital. Solemnly, they sit there working with their hands while Julie notes continual rapid glances being directed towards Synnøve and knows these are looking for flaws in her facade. She knows too that Synnøve herself is aware of this and that the most important thing for her is not to lose face in the eyes of the village. She knows, too, the real reason for Synnøve to have arranged the meeting. She intends to show them that she is still the capable Synnøve Storvik.

The following day, Synnøve does not get out of bed. She says she is exhausted after the meeting and the tiring journey to town and now just wants to sleep. She does indeed sleep, waking up occasionally during the first couple of days, taking in a little food then sleeping again.

- This is a reaction after everything that has happened, says Astrid, but one day, Synnøve awakens and has difficulty speaking clearly and raising her left arm from the duvet.

The doctor is sent for and confirms that she has suffered a slight stroke. This is not sufficiently serious to prevent her from getting back on her feet unless she undergoes a second, worse, stroke. Synnøve is really strong, he adds, and if she just gets enough peace and quiet, this can go well.

- Do you think this is a reaction to all that she's been through recently? Jørgen asks.
- No, it has probably been there for some time, though circumstances might have brought it on early.
- I understand. It has all been too much for her.
- Jørgen, you mustn't try blaming your brother for this. You've heard what the doctor said?
- And I hear what you're saying, Julie.

Synnøve gets back on her feet but this is now a very much reduced and different Synnøve. She forgets names and recent events. She repeats the same stories over and over again and forgets the food she has heated up and then allowed to become cold. She is aware of all this herself and is unhappy about it.

Oh dear, what's the matter with me? she weeps.

- It'll pass, Mother. You are just very tired, Astrid says, but everyone understands that the Red Cross meeting would be Synnøve's last public appearance.

Chapter 11

The resentment Julie has been feeling about Randi having put a stop to their friendship has in some ways blunted the feeling of missing her friend. But now she receives a letter.

This lies on the kitchen workbench for a long time before she opens it. Julie feels a strange reluctance to read what Randi is going to say after all these years. She still feels anger inside her when she thinks of the effect Yngve could have had on her sons. She can more or less accept that Krister was used, but that Helge, who was only fifteen when he moved to town and was dragged into all this, is something she is not sure she will ever be able to forgive. What is more, Krister has sworn her to silence, forbidding her to even mention this to Randi, and this creates a bar to the friendship returning to what it has been. What sustained this close friendship was the trust and confidence each had in the other. They confided in each other about nearly everything except the most intimate details of their marriages and family lives. They also discussed that there are things you do not mention except to those closest to you. There are some things in life which have nothing to do with anyone but the closest family members, and that's just how it is. But if a resentment had arisen between them, as it did with Julie following Krister's revelation, then they could have sorted it out and come through it, but as it is, it is going to sit there as unfinished business, maybe forever.

Randi's letter is brief and to the point, but behind the words Julie seems to detect a certain unease which is affecting her. It is clear that Randi has struggled with every sentence. She says that she has missed Julie during all the intervening time. Even though she was the one to break off the friendship, this was something she did against her own will but nevertheless felt compelled to do. They can talk about some of this but not all of it. If this is difficult to understand now, she hopes that it is something Julie will be able to accept one day. The only thing she wants and hopes now is that they can get back together. Her friendship with Julie was so very dear to her. Do you remember that we said our friendship could bear anything? It has now been subjected to the toughest of tests, but has it survived the test? What Randi is asking for is some sign of life from Julie. There is a lot of talk about forgiveness today. Can *you* forgive me?

Can she? Julie wonders. Forgive - well, maybe. But forget?

The reply she sends is as brief as Randi's letter, with much of the same content, but as she reads it through she realises that hers is rather more measured in tone than Randi's. She writes that she will contact Randi as soon as she has the time and opportunity to travel to town.

A concern of people in the village is that Torsten Sand is coming home. He is not as scrawny and worn out as people had expected, but then he has been to Sweden on a weight gain course, which is how he himself describes his confinement. When asked how he is, his wife replies that while there seems nothing wrong with his body, there are other concerns. He is unable to sleep at night and spends his time moving backwards and forwards between the kitchen and dining room downstairs, and he keeps her awake. This is wearing, but she hastens to say that she mustn't complain. She thanks God that she now has her husband back alive.

Some men in the village visit him, mostly to show concern, though it can hardly be denied that some are driven more by curiosity. They cannot get a word out of Torstein about his experiences. At best he may tell the odd funny story about Grini, but as to the other experiences and his spell in Sachsenhausen, about these he maintains a stony silence. If anyone mentions Hallgrim, he again says nothing, but it is then beads of sweat begin to appear on his brow, and his gaze turns dark and inward-looking to an extent that makes those who have seen this happen shudder when they later speak about it.

It sometimes happens that he can be persuaded to have the odd drink. Torstein, who was previously a totally placid and peaceful man, then changes character completely and becomes alien, aggressive and quick-tempered. One evening, when four men were sharing a drink they'd brought, he suddenly became angry and attacked one of them. They said later that there was no discernible reason for the attack. The three only just managed to restrain him by force, while the fourth escaped. They now feel that things are getting out of hand. Torstein should be very grateful that he managed to come home in one piece and should spare a thought for those who didn't have luck on their side rather than knocking down neighbours who only mean him well. There are several in the village who go along with this, but Jørgen and others see it as just an excuse for those who go along out or nosiness to tempt him with booze to try to get him to loosen up.

- They should think about what he must have seen and experienced, Jørgen says. - What sort of images he'll be storing up inside him. It's shameful.

After this episode Torstein no longer touches alcohol. As time goes on neighbours drop away, some saying that they can't face meeting or talking to him on those rare occasions when he ventures down to the shop or to the post office.

Torstein resumes his farming work, but he is becoming more and more distant from those who used to know him. This formerly pleasant man is now becoming inward-looking and morose. He no longer conforms to the people's expectations and is rapidly becoming lonely. Many say that he should just pull himself together and start behaving properly. If anyone from outside the village asks, this is what they are told.

- Torstein Sand? Oh no, he has been destroyed by the war.

Such is the reputation marking him out as different, and round here once you fail to live up to people's expectations, a huge effort is needed to recover. If Torstein had only given people what they expected, things would be looking very different now.

In the course of the early summer the first treason trials are announced. These have been set up in a temporary courtroom inside a barracks within the camp in Nerlandsdalen to enable cases to be settled quickly.

Ivar receives a sentence of one year. As what is called a supportive member of NS, he may have hoped to get away with a fine since he had done nothing to harm his fellow countrymen, but it was argued that he had had close contact with Germans throughout the occupation. In addition to this sentence he has been dismissed from his post in the bank 'for an indefinite period', whatever that might mean. This dismissal is not part of the sentence but was carried out on the bank's initiative.

How are they going to manage? Julie wonders. They have some income from renting out the ground floor in the villa, and Helene can perhaps earn a few extra kroner by taking piano and dance pupils, but this is hardly going to be enough to cover all their daily costs.

Helene has also been taken in for questioning. For a German and the wife of an NS member, this was not unfair, but because she was not herself an NS member she was freed, though with the stipulation that she must not leave town and must check in weekly at the police station.

- It's a sort of house arrest, says Jørgen. – Or at least that's how I understand it.

People had wagered that Hallgrim would receive a sentence of two or maybe three years, but his sentence was one of six years. This shocks people. They expected him to be punished for the arrests he had carried out, for his defence of NS and the Germans throughout the occupation and for having encouraged young boys to volunteer to fight on the front, but this judgement was such that there must have been much more. Could this be his frequent visits to Trondheim and reciprocal visits from there to Ås? Nor was this all. Hallgrim was ordered to pay back his entire salary as a police officer and all he had received for other public services. His position as deputy mayor was unpaid, but there were still a lot of things he was paid for.

Gunnhild is set free on grounds of the extenuating circumstance that she has underage children at home, although she is ordered to pay a fine of 1500 kroner.

The shoemaker receives two years, as does the Ås farm hand. The few small-scale Nazis in the village get away with fines. But the one who receives the longest punishment is Sigurd Myrhe who is condemned to eight years plus restitution of all he has been paid, which causes speculation about how much he may have been involved in. All those condemned are to lose citizenship rights for up to ten years, while the young lose the right to do military service and to fight for their country.

The village boils over with gossip as these judgements are made known. Ivar's verdict gives rise to a certain amount of comment, but this is drowned out by comparison with the verdicts on those of the village's 'big fish', which is how Hallgrim and Myrhe are now described. People think the judgement must mean ruin for those at Ås unless Hallgrim has been stashing away money, which seems unlikely. So far as people can see, Hallgrim has been spending quite freely. Buildings have been refurbished, and there is no sign that people have lacked anything, either for daily living or for partying. There is no way an ordinary farmer here in the village can manage to pay the sort of expenses he is now faced with. So are the people of Ås going to have to leave their houses and homes?

Everything that remains in the way of contents and valuables in Myrhe's house has now been impounded by the state. The house he lived in as administrator is the property of the Sawmill, so Myrhe's tenure of it is now at an end, which is something no one in the village regrets. The foreman in the business is currently functioning as Administrator until a new one can be found.

Those given the shortest sentences remain in the camp in Nerlandsdalen, while those faced with longer terms are taken to the former German military camp at Innland. There are barracks there for prisoners who may be serving for several years as convict workers. There will be no lack of work for them to do. They will be tidying up after the invaders of Karihola and other fortifications.

He'll now be getting a taste of his own medicine, people say, referring to Hallgrim. It will be rather different from tidying up after his guests after partying with them at Ås.

Sigurd Myhre is to serve his sentence elsewhere in the country. People say that is just as well, as they hope to see no more of him.

Strangely enough, Synnøve seems to come to life while this process is going on. One evening, she is standing at the entrance to the kitchen where Jørgen and Julie are sitting alone. She joins them at the table.

- There's something I need to say to you, Jørgen, she says, looking him straight in the eye with that old determination in her gaze. It's about your brother. You are going to have to pay his father's inheritance tax. As you know this is 1500 kroner, and that's without the interest.

- Has he written asking about this? Jørgen says, turning pale.

- No, of course not, says Synnøve tartly. How could he have sent a letter from where he is now? No, I was the one who took the initiative. You owe it to him to help your brother and Helene. I would think you owe them quite a lot, even if it's not all in monetary terms.

- And where am I supposed to get the money from? Jørgen asks sharply.

- That's your business. I'm just asking you to settle up with him. And it's now that it's needed.

- Will I need to get a loan from the bank? Is he about to bring about ruin here after all that he's already done to us?

- Do stop being childish, Jørgen, Synnøve says.

- But I … Oh hell …

- It will be all right, Julie says - tomorrow is another day.

- Do you realise that I'll have to use the farm as a guarantee for the loan? Jørgen says.

- I know, but don't forget that the farm is in my name, Julie says.

- He faces her, his face white.

- Did you have to remind me of that yet again? he says, heading for the door.

- I thought Jørgen was a bit more grown up, says Synnøve weightily.

- You know how he always reacts when it comes down to questions of money, Julie says apologetically. It will pass when he's had time to think about it. The money will be available.

- Yes, I know I can rely on you, Julie. But the money mustn't be sent by post. Whoever is going to town should take it, as it mustn't fall into the wrong hands. Well, now I've done my bit, and the rest is in God's hands.

Julie now sees that her mother-in-law is pale from the strain all this has put upon her. Heavily and with unsteady feet she takes her leave of Julie, looking once more as she has been doing recently, a worn out old woman.

Once the exhilaration over being free has begun to die down, people must get used to a new every day. They begin in a small way to take an interest in politics again. The big question now is: Who is going to govern? The Nygaardsvold government has resigned, and there is talk of a new coalition government. Soon the name Einar Gerhardsen starts appearing in the press. He is a Labour party member, well enough known in political circles, though not particularly well known throughout the country generally apart from to party members. Gerhardsen is said to be a driven politician even though he lacks parliamentary experience, and it looks as if he is going to be the most likely candidate for the task of Prime Minister in a free Norway.

On 25 July, Gerhardsen is proclaimed Prime Minister of a coalition government consisting of six representatives of the Labour Party, two from NKP, the Norwegian communist party, and seven from the middle. The proposal is that this government will remain in place until the general election in October.

The slogan then goes out: 'We won the war, and together we will win back the peace'. In the government programme it was stated that disagreements could be resolved, and it was the Labour Party which spoke most warmly about unity without the old party and class divisions. The war years had removed much of this, togetherness grew, and now it was up to each individual to promote unity. The middle-class voices were hesitant about this, their voices coming across as vaguer.

But discussions resumed once more between workers and the middle class. These were less heated than they had been previously, though it was clear that disagreements had once again begun raising their heads. In the Storvik kitchen, discussions go on late into the evening. Factions begin to show. Jørgen raises the question of whether Øra will be split off from the rest of the village as it was before the war.

- I really hope that it's not going to be as hard as it used to be and that people have learned some lessons. There are always going to be disagreements and it's good that people can talk about something other than war, and that this can become the normality we've been missing.

During summer Synnøve's health quickly declines. This does not show so much in her body apart from a stumbling gait. But she, who has always been a hard worker, having taken part in projects both at home and on the farm right up to the spring the day when she took to her bed, and who has never been able

to sit still without doing something with her hands, has now
given up on everything. This is so notable that those around her
feel they can observe differences from one day to the next. I've
done my bit, she had said on the evening she spoke about the
money Jørgen owed Ivar. It was as if that conversation put a full
stop to the work and care she had carried out both for the family
and the farm. She had forced herself to use her last drops of
energy for that conversation and to set up the Red Cross
meeting. Now she has paid her debt, both to the family and to
the village.

She loses interest in what is happening round her, and even
in the two small children who have always given her so much
pleasure. She confuses their names and calls Sunniva, Astrid,
and Sven she calls either Jørgen or Ivar. One day, she summons
Sunniva over to her, strokes her black hair and looks wistfully at
her.

- I don't know what they've been doing to your hair, Astrid.
- My name isn't Astrid. I'm Sunniva, she says and stares at
her grandmother, who has now become so unfamiliar.
- Why has Grandma become so strange? she asks. Why is
she calling me Astrid?
- She's not being strange, says Julie, she is poorly.
- But she doesn't look poorly.
- Old people can be poorly without it showing. They forget
things. Your grandma has called you Astrid because she
remembers Astrid when she was little. You're going to have to
be nice to your grandma now.
- Oh, what a lovely little girl, smiles Synnøve as she lifts the
child onto her lap. Would you like me to be your grandma, too?
- Yes, because that's what you are, says Sunniva, snuggling
up to her grandmother's breast.

Julie has seen nothing of her relatives back home since her mother's funeral. By now, she is missing them, not least her father, and she wants to meet Johanne to see how far she has overcome her difficulties. She would have loved to go back there straight away with Sunniva and Sven. Gaps in the farming year are the best times for such a journey, but she doesn't want to mention it now because of Astrid's extra burden with her ailing mother. Jørgen has completely recovered from his illness of last winter. Krister has been summoned to do National Service, but both Jostein and Helge are at home, and additional help has been hired for the farm. Astrid says that Julie is free to travel. She will go with Synnøve up to the summer farm, which she believes will do her good, and the maid will look after the house below.

Julie is to visit Helene on her way to Romsdal and will take time off to spend a couple of days with her, as this is something she thinks that Helene may need. During the time Helge is on holiday from school she is living alone in the flat.

Helene is waiting outside, ready to greet them and gives the two young children a hug.

- My, how they've grown! But Julie meets her eyes over the children's heads. They are dark with pain and sorrow, and her face looks pale and drawn.

Julie gives her a questioning look, but Helene only shakes her head. She does her best to sound cheerful and says there are newly baked buns upstairs. She moves upstairs with her arms round the children, but her movements are stiff, and her body is as tense as a violin string. At the table her concentration is focused entirely on the children. She says they must tell her about all their experiences, but her voice is so uneasy that they themselves notice it and look at her wonderingly.

As soon as they have finished eating, Julie sends the children out into the garden to play. - But don't go out onto the road, she warns.

- Helene, whatever has happened?
- I don't know if I can manage to talk about this, but now, now that Ivar is no longer here, she says, her voice breaking, you are the only person I can talk to. I believe God has sent you here today. I received this letter yesterday. An officer from the Salvation Army brought it for me. It's from my cousin, she says, handing Julie the letter from a pocket in her pinafore. - Since then, I haven't been able either to eat or sleep. All I've done is cry. And I can't even do that any longer while the children are here. Read the letter, Julie,
- But it's in German, Helene, and you know my German isn't very good.
- Oh yes, I'd forgotten that. Then I'll explain. As she had already said, her home city was Dresden, a city of incredible beauty known as the Florence of the North. In Dresden, there was a cathedral famous for its architecture and a host of other beautiful churches, museums and artistic treasures. During the whole of the war, she was happy that the city had been spared. But then, in February of this year, all that came to an end and the city was bombed. It ended in an inferno on the night of February 13 to 14. Julie must have heard about this in the news. It is not unfair to say that the whole city was devastated during that night. Explosives and incendiary bombs rained down all night long over that beautiful city. Terrible fires raged through the streets. People died because of the heat, collapsing in the street and then being turned into ash; others died from oxygen

starvation or were buried under ruins. Tens of thousands were killed, her cousin does not know how many. She lived on the same street as Helene's parents. That night she saw them both lying dead side by side outside the house in which they had lived. Where they were taken subsequently or where they were buried, she has no idea.

Her cousin says she remembers little else from that night. By some miracle, she and her little daughter managed to hold onto their lives, but she lost her two half-grown sons. Her husband had died previously on the battlefield. Both she and her daughter had suffered severe burns. These have now more or less healed, but the *other* wounds are beyond treatment.

Helene recounts the whole with a monotone voice, a voice so very controlled that Julie is unable to picture the scene as she listens.

- Helene - dear, she says helplessly.
- Now I will translate directly what my cousin writes, Helene says. 'The only thing keeping me alive now is my daughter. Apart from her I no longer have a life. And you, Helene, have lost both our dear parents. But remember now that they were old and probably died without suffering. I'm not sure I have much compassion left over for you when so many young lives have been lost. Your parents said that you have a good life up there in Norway. Be thankful for that, for the time you had with them and for their love. For us back here, everything is now meaningless.'

- If only I could help, Julie says, drawing Helene in towards her. But her body is stiff and she pulls back from being hugged.
- Not now, Julie, she says, please just let me speak.

- She had felt this deep down ever since she first found out about the bombing. During all that time, she has been grieving and weeping. Finding out the truth came almost as a relief, for it meant that she was no longer clinging to a false hope. On top of that, there is a feeling of guilt about her grieving, for what is there that her fellow Germans have not done? How many people have they killed, how many towns have they devastated? It's intolerable to think about all this, Julie.

- But *you* have no need to feel guilty, Helene.

- I doubt if anyone can understand how *that* has felt during all these years, Helene says quietly. But I can't bear talking about it anymore. I am so very pleased that you have come. The house feels very empty just now. The tenants are away on holiday. I miss Helge and am very much looking forward to him coming back. Without him, I don't know whether I would have come through that awful time after Ivar's arrest. Helge's behaviour towards me has been outstanding. I have become so very fond of your son, Julie. And of Krister and your other children of course; but after this spring Helge will always have a special place in my heart.

Julie is lying in a double bed with the children beside her. Later that night she awakens to the sound of music emanating from the loft above. It must be well past midnight as the room is dark. She rises and goes barefoot up the stairs to the loft where Helene has her dance studio. The door into the loft is ajar, and Julie stands riveted to the spot. Helene is dancing in a knee-length nightdress and with ballet shoes on her feet. Her hair hangs loosely down to her waist as she glides over the floor in the bluish half-light.

Julie steals into the room and sits down on a chair by the door, hardly daring to breathe at what she is seeing. What she is observing is Helene's grief. The music is slow and sad, spreading out into the room from a gramophone placed on a wall shelf to prevent the needle jumping because of the vibrations in the floor as she dances.

She is not as expert in music as the rest of the Storvik family but thinks this must be Tchaikovsky. It is not from *Swan Lake* or from any of the other well-known ballets, so it is probably from the Violin Concerto. When the music stops Helene glides over to the gramophone, turns the record over and sets the music going again. Even these movements of hers are elegant and form part of the dance. Helene seems not to notice that there are others in the room. But by now there is a small figure in the doorway. Sunniva has also woken up to the music and found her way here. Julie makes a sign that she must keep still and picks her up onto her lap.

- Why is Auntie dancing at night?
- Hush! Whispers Julie, I'll tell you later.

Julie sits spellbound and moved by the beauty and pain concentrated in the scene unfolding before her eyes. There's Helene, the music and the dance, and together in this strange light these create an almost supernatural feeling. Sunniva sits quiet as a mouse and equally spellbound before falling asleep on Julie's lap. Julie carries her back to bed before herself returning to the loft, to the dance and to the music.

She does not know how many times Helene has started the music up again but knows that she must have done so again and again. It is only when the soft blue light changes to a cold grey dawn that Helene stops and stands quietly with her arms hanging by her sides, her head bowed. Her heavy breathing is the only sound to break the silence before she comes running over to Julie, throwing herself into her arms.

- I knew you were here, she gulps and holds Julie tightly, and Julie can only continue holding onto her and crying along with her.

Helene's wet hair hangs down over her brow, and her night dress is clammy and cold.

- I think we'd better get you to bed now before you become ill, Julie says gently.
- Thank you for being here.
- Now you have no need to tell me anything, Julie says. - I have seen how you feel.

Exhausted and unresistant, Helene allows herself to be cosseted. Julie accompanies her to the bathroom, fills the bath, helps her off with her shoes and nightdress then ties up her hair. She rubs soap all over her and treats Helene as if she were one of her own children. She then finds a clean nightdress and lies down next to her, holding her tightly.

- Now you must sleep, my dear. And you may sleep as long as you like tomorrow.

She lies there until Helene falls asleep before stealing back to her own room, but she lies wide awake while images of what she has just observed pass before her eyes. She had not known before that dancing could express such feelings. Dancing and music together can say more than words ever can. She knows too that something has happened to the relationship between herself and Helene through her experiencing this. That Helene had the confidence to share her deepest feelings with her will be something which binds them together for life.

Sven is the first to awaken and curls up close to Julie.

- Shhh! Julie whispers - Let's just rest quietly so that your sister can go on sleeping.

But Sunniva wakes up, too, opening her eyes wide in the way children do.

- Why was Auntie dancing tonight?

- Was she dancing? asks Sven indignantly. - So why didn't I get to see it?

- Because you were asleep, says Sunniva.

- She was dancing because she was unhappy, Julie says.

- Surely people don't dance because they're unhappy. And anyway, why was she unhappy?

- Because she'd heard that her father and mother were dead.

- Were they very old? Sven enquires. Isn't it just old people who die, Mother?

- Are you and father old, Mother? Sunniva asks.

- No, Julie says, smiling, we're not so very old yet.

- That's good, for then it will be a long time before you die. Then I'll be unhappy.

- So dumb! Sven snorts.

- I could see that Aunty was unhappy, Sunniva says, looking ahead thoughtfully. The music was so sad. When I grow up, I'm going to be a good dancer, just like Aunty.

- That may be hard while we live here, Julie smiles. You can't get lessons, but you will still be able to dance in your own way.

- Do you think Auntie will dance for me? asks Sven.

- I'm sure she will, but not now. Another time, maybe. But for now we must be kind to Aunty.

It's as if time is turned back. Randi and Julie are sitting opposite each other at Randi's kitchen table. Through the open window can hear the happy sounds of Julie's children playing with Randi's youngest, the late arrival Martin.

- It sounds as if they're getting along well. Randi smiles.

So far their meeting has been a strange one. The spontaneous uprush of pleasure they always used to feel when they met has given way to a mutual embarrassment. They try to work through this first of all by talking about non-sensitive issues. They have talked about their children, their experiences during the war and how they have dealt with everyday troubles. They talk about the terrible things they have learned since news of the concentration camps reached them, and about the atom bombs, those weapons from hell which eradicated the Japanese cities of Hiroshima and Nagasaki on the 6th and 9th of the present month.

- As soon as one dreadful thing's over, another just comes along to take its place, says Randi. You find yourself asking if you knew what you were doing by bringing a child into the world.
- Hasn't it always been dangerous bringing a child into the world? Julie says. - The two of us have lived through two world wars.

And this is how they talk, discussing everyday concerns, but they also subject each other to some searching looks. Do they dare to come any closer?

- How is Helene? Randi ventures.
- How *she* is? She found out the day before yesterday that both her parents had been killed in the bombing of Dresden.

- Oh, that's terrible, says Randi. That's where she was from, isn't it? I remember you telling me that once. Poor thing, she'll be all alone now. I've had enormous respect for her recently. I've seen how brave she has been in town, walking tall among people who know no better and shouting and swearing at her. I have heard people shout 'Jerrygirl' and 'Go back to the shitty country you came from' and even worse things. She has been so much in my thoughts, and I really ought to have had the courage to go and see her, but the way things are it's too early for that. But you should know that here in town there are people who have only good things to say about Helene and Ivar.

Yngvar has expressed surprise at Ivar's sentence; he thought that he would get away with a fine. But so many strange and unpredictable things are happening now, he says. He cannot understand why Ivar has lost his job in the bank, a job he has held throughout his adult life, and in fact his only job. If this had been a public position it might have been understandable, but this was a shabby and totally unnecessary action on the bank's part, though maybe we shouldn't expect better of such people. That Ivar has to pay for his involvement with NS is both just and reasonable, but people must not lose perspective.

- You can tell Helene that I'm not the only one thinking about her now.
- She will be pleased to hear that
- But what about us, Julie? I haven't forgotten that day in the park when I said we couldn't meet while things were as they were then. Who would have thought that it would all take so long? I cannot forget the look on your face and your shocked and bereft expression as I left. That has stayed with me all these years. I still cannot tell you the reason I had to go. Maybe I'll be able to do that at some time in the future when it's all behind us.

I don't know, but perhaps you can understand that it has something to do with Ivar.

- That had occurred to me, but it hasn't been easy for me either.

- Do you think that this can come right over time?

- I do hope so, Randi, I really do hope so.

- We should be able to manage it when we think about all the terrible things other people have been through. At least we have survived.

But they cannot continue talking as the children surge into the kitchen, hot and bothered after playing out on this August day.

They join hands as they bid each other goodbye. Julie sees in Randi's eyes the same goodwill she has always felt towards her.

- Has it been fun playing with Martin? Julie asks as they return to Helene.

- Yes, and Martin and I have become boyfriend and girlfriend now, Sunniva says.

- What, already?

- You are stupid, snorts Sven. You are too little to be boyfriend and girlfriend.

- It's you who are stupid. We can at least become that when we are older.

- Why do you want to be Martin's girlfriend? Julie smiles.

- Because he has such lovely blond curls.

- Well, that's a good enough reason.

- And we have a new aunty today, Randi said that we can call her Aunty Randi. Right mother?

- Yes, and I hope you will. We'll see.

Julie was afraid that her father would have aged after her mother passed away, but he is looking better than ever. He was standing smiling on the quayside and met them as usual with horse and buggy. As they drove through the village that beautiful August evening he said that for as long as he could he wanted to keep alive the tradition of picking them up by buggy when they visited.

- You're looking as fit as any youngster, Father.
- That's down to Johanne. She looks after me so well. Then there's all the life in her kids. That keeps you young.

As they enter the kitchen at home, everything is just as it has always been: her mother's little dolls and bits and pieces on the benches and tables, rag rugs on the floor and pot plants on the windowsills.

- It's so good to be here again. But *you* have changed she says to Johanne as she takes her hands in hers.
- Yes, maybe she's become our good little girl again? their father says.
- It's wonderful to see you again, Julie says, deeply touched as she hugs her sister.

Julie watches as Johanne goes back and forth setting the table. She is still slim but is now beginning to regain some of her former chubbiness. Her face has become fuller and the wrinkles which her earlier life had caused her are now becoming less pronounced. But the biggest change is in her curly hair which now has a modern half-length cut. Julie has never seen her before without that old-fashioned bun at the back of her neck. She now looks ten years younger than she did at her mother's funeral and her laughter now rings round in the kitchen just as it used to do when she was young.

Her children are unrecognisable. The two girls are still shy, but not more so than is usual for girls of their age, and it could be that they are shy by nature. But now they open up more than they used to, taking part in conversations round the table, while the boy has become a real boy, talking all the time so that Johanne has to keep shutting him up. Sven looks up at him with huge admiration. The oldest girl has been for a year at a middle school in Molde, where she lodges with her Aunt Helga who is as vigorous as ever. Both she and her uncle had met Julie and accompanied her to the boat earlier today. The youngest girl is about to begin further education in autumn, while the youngest boy will be in year seven. All three speak with a pronounced Romsdal dialect, as Johanne now does too, having shaken off the received pronunciation she had been compelled to use as Inge's wife. She is working now as an infant teacher, something which has clearly increased her self-confidence.

The two sisters remain sitting and chatting far into the night. It is not just recent years they talk about but the whole of their adult lives.

- Did you know that Inge married again last year? Johanne asks.
- Well, he hasn't wasted any time.
- It did me good to know that, for it leaves me in peace. But I feel sorry for the poor woman he's marrying. She is still young, barely thirty, and has just had a child. I hope she'll be strong enough to cope.

The woman Inge has married is a nurse and used to do church work in Inge's parish. She was also an NS member and Johanne had met her on several occasions. She avoided punishment on account of the child she was expecting, but Inge was sentenced to three years and permanently lost his status as a Church of Norway priest. Apart from that, as a Nazi priest, he got a sizeable reduction in salary.

He lost interest in the children once he realised that they did not support him. Their father's punishment has affected them less that was to be expected since he had already become distant to them. And as far as she knows none of the children has been bullied on account of him. She says she has a great deal to thank God for. But not that scary god that Inge had tried using to break her.

- Can you understand how my life has changed from being hell to being a fairy tale these last two years?

- It's such a pity that Mother didn't know about this, Julie says. - She was so afraid for you.

- I feel that Mother sees all this, Johanne says, her voice firm. - And the strangest thing of all - I'm not sure I dare tell you this, she says, blushing like a young girl - but at my advanced age, I have fallen in love!

- What are you telling me now? Julie asks in astonishment.

- It's all very recent, so you must keep it to yourself, but I'll tell you who it is, then you won't get quite the shock that you did when I introduced Inge as my fiancé. Maybe you thought you'd hidden your shock?

- You mean I hadn't? No, you're right. You did give me a terrible shock that time. Now it is Julie who is blushing. - But please don't keep me waiting here in agony. Tell me who is the one you've given your heart to?

- It's Hans Li.

- *That* Hans? says Julie, open mouthed. - Has he come back home?

- Yes, he has come home. Home to stay. He is divorced now. He and his wife had a sick retarded child. Their son died at around the age of fifteen while he was away, and by that time the marriage was over. He and his wife separated amicably, sharing all their belongings without any kind of quarrel. He also made his wife a one-off payment so that he would not have to pay maintenance as he would otherwise have had to do where they lived. But he can tell you all this himself, Julie, as I've invited him for coffee tomorrow.

- And is Hans in love with you? says Julie smiling.

- He most certainly is, Johanne says, blushing. But they have decided to give it time. Both are adults with a complicated life behind them, and there is no reason to rush. An advantage they have is that the children are fond of him, for he has a very good way with children. The two oldest probably understand that some of this is deliberate, but it looks as if they are willing to accept it. If their relationship with their father had been better things might have been otherwise. She and Hans have also talked about the relationship between himself and Synna, and that it was her death which led him to move to the States.

- I seem to be fated, says Johanne, into taking over my sister's boyfriends, though she is smiling and her words are entirely without malice. - I just hope this will turn out more successful than my first attempt.

- I would hardly say that you and Inge were lovers. I would describe it more as a youthful infatuation.

- Describe it how you will Julie, he never forgave you for standing up to him. To mention your name was like waving a red rag to a bull. Once when he was angry with me he said that I was just like that awful tart I had for a sister. Those were his very words, the words of a priest. But that was no surprise. Inge could never bear to lose.

- You should be glad to be rid of him, Julie says with a shudder. But that you are getting together with Hans is the best news I've heard for a long time. No, I'm really looking forward to seeing him again. I suppose you know that he and Jørgen were best friends when they were at agricultural college together? For the first few years we got Christmas letters from him, but then that stopped.

- That was probably because he had more than enough matters of his own to deal with. - But you don't think it's idiotic for us to fall in love like youngsters now that we're older?

- That's nonsense! Julie laughs, - love doesn't ask about age. Even now it often happens that I can look at Jørgen and feel just as smitten as a young girl. Enjoy your love, Johanne, you deserve it.

Fate is so strange, Julie thinks lying in her old bed in the girls' room while her children sleep in the other beds. This room will always be full of memories for her. How often the three sisters lay here having whispered giggly conversations about boys and all the exciting things they experienced. It was mainly herself and Synna who chatted. Johanne, who is four years younger than them, was too young to join in but she listened to everything her other sisters talked about. And here they were again this evening like young girls talking about love. This room is strange. She feels young again every time she sleeps here. And Jørgen feels so close; she remembers lying here and writing him letters. She recalls the scent of cherries coming in through the window, her longing for him and the months they spent apart, months which felt like years. She was so young then. And she feels so young again now, her yearning for him feels like a huge hollow inside her.

Hans lights up as he spots Julie standing in the yard along with Johanne to welcome him. Tall and slim he moves towards them with brisk steps. His hair has become thinner and his tanned features more marked, but she would have recognised him wherever she were to meet him.

- How good it is to see you again, Julie he says giving her a hug.
- Oh, this is all too much for me, Julie says, reaching for her handkerchief, but you haven't changed much at all, Hans.
- Well, we are no longer young. Time takes its toll, but you haven't changed much either, Julie.
- It's kind of you to say so, but it would be strange if we hadn't changed. I was only eighteen the last time I saw you.
- And I was twenty-two, he replies.

Here, as elsewhere in the villages, it is not customary for people who are unrelated to exchange hugs, and even married people don't do it in public view. But for Julie and Hans it is natural for them to express their delight on seeing each other in this way rather than by shaking hands or resorting to the usual polite phrases. Hans has been around and learned other habits and Johanne has always accepted these with a quiet smile. She feels safe now, and Julie warms as she sees the looks Hans and Johanne exchange.

In the afternoon heat they have set out a table for coffee on the lawn. Now it is only the adults who sit round. Ingrid is pregnant and again Julie is struck by the feeling of contentment she radiates. She is also beautiful, resembling Synna more than ever on account of her dark eyes and thick blond hair. She can see resemblances between Helge and both of them. If he had been a girl, he would have been their double.

Johanne's girls are out with some friends, Sven is kicking a football behind the barn with Johanne's son, and Sunniva is enjoying playing with Ingrid's children. She now comes running towards the table and jumps onto her grandfather's lap.

- I am so lucky, she says happily, to have a grandfather here and a grandmother at Storvik.

- Yes, aren't you lucky? Johanne chuckles.

- Before I had a different grandmother here and another grandfather at Storvik, but they died. Now grandma is ill and maybe she is going to die. She is ill in her head and says all kinds of strange things, so maybe she won't die just yet. But people do die when they get old, don't they?

- Yes, that's how it is.

- Are you old, grandpa? Will you die soon?

- No, I hope I shall live for a few more years yet, Johannes smiles.

- I hope so too, for I would be very unhappy if you died.

- Stop bothering your grandfather. Run away and play, says Julie, ushering her out.

- That's a lovely little girl you have there, says Hans.

- Yes, she sometimes makes me wonder what kind of creatures I have in my house.

Conversation is relaxed round the table and Hans looks very much at home here. Julie remembers the time Inge was here, and the silence and unpleasant feelings he created around him.

Hans talks about his life in the States. His first thought had been to acquire a farm. But having given up farming back home he felt that might seem an odd choice there. He then obtained a job in a firm of entrepreneurs, which he subsequently took over. The firm did well, so when he decided to travel home he was well-equipped to set up a similar business here even after he had settled up with his wife. Now he wants to establish himself in Molde and has already come some way with the necessary paperwork. He intends to build his own house there, he says, smiling at Johanne, who blushes as she meets his eye.

As Hans is about to leave he asks Julie to accompany him part of the way home. Julie looks questioningly at Johanne, who nods in assent.

- Isn't it strange that Johanne and I have got together, and that I've become very fond of her?
- I am so happy about that.
- I hope to be able to give her a good life after all that she's been through. Both of us have seen life and know what it's all about. Has she told you about mine?
- Yes, you don't need to say anything more about it.

If Johanne had looked like Synna, this probably wouldn't have happened, he says. He experienced such a shock first time he met Ingrid; they were so much alike that it was just like meeting Synna again. Synna had, and always will have, a special place in his life. He has never forgotten her and never will. But love is not ungenerous, he says, and if you lose someone you love, you can always love again. Even if what he felt for his wife was not overwhelming love, he was genuinely very fond of her. It was probably the same for her. But difficulties wore them down, and when her son died there was nothing left. Both grieved but came to see that it was good for the child that he died before them. For he was a child and was always going to remain a child. But Hans will always have good feelings towards her and keep their friendship alive.

- And now with Johanne I know that I can love her and it's not just crumbs that she will get. Isn't it strange how life works out? That happiness should lie in wait for me all these years? And I can see that you get along well with Jørgen.
- Yes, we are happy.
- It would be good to visit you sometime in Storvik.
- You know you will always be welcome there, either by yourself or with Johanne.

She watches as they walk down the road and thinks that anyone who does not believe that fate has a hand in human lives knows nothing at all about life.

People are tired of war. Now when neighbours visit each other they are likely to be greeted with: You may come in just so long as you don't mention war.

People say they must now look forward. The country must rise again, they will build up a new existence, a new kind of life.

October 8th is the parliamentary election. As expected it's a victory for Labour, and on 5. November Einar Gerhardsen becomes Prime Minister in a Labour government. There is rejoicing in the socialist camp, while the words of Carlo Hambro, who was the mighty leader of the Right when the coalition government was formed are frequently quoted: 'For most of us it is incomprehensible that these men have taken upon themselves a responsibility which lies is far outside their competence'. This was a reference to Gerhardsen's lack of parliamentary experience. But Gerhardsen is popular even outside his own circles. He is a both a good speaker and approachable, and has five years in jail behind him, which increases his popularity.

Before the waves following the parliamentary election have died down the local authority elections take place on 19th November. Here in the village there is lively discussion before, during and after the vote, which is a big win for Labour, and where the old mayor continues on from where he left off before the war.

Vidkun Quisling is executed on 24th October, and most people think his punishment is well deserved. A joy and relief for the Storvik community is the news that Ivar is to be set free before Christmas after serving half his sentence. Nobody knows why he is being set free, least of all Ivar himself. However, he has not been given back his old job at the bank. It comes as a relief that Helene will not have to celebrate Christmas on her own, but Julie wonders whether Jørgen and Ivar will ever really get back together.

They have now celebrated the first Christmas of peace. This was a fairy tale - lighted candles, no blackout, a great Christmas celebration in the Youth Building on Boxing Day and the traditional dance party in the period just after Christmas. Traditions which have been in hibernation in the dark years have now come back into the light. Children are given sweets they have previously only heard about. When Jørgen came home before Christmas with the first oranges, a whole bagful that he had obtained by using Sven and Sunniva's ration cards, there were great rejoicings. He hid the bag in a cupboard in the hall, and the two children kept on going there just to enjoy the smell, for they were to be kept out of sight until Christmas itself. Sven and Sunniva also receive sweet rations, and they keep careful track of what these consist of: chocolate with nuts, milk chocolate with a picture of a cow on the wrapper, liquorice chocolate, which they call black chocolate and chocolate with rum-flavoured cream, which tastes quite adult and is really not very nice. Then there are raspberry drops and camphor drops, throat pastilles with a picture of a monk on the front and menthol pastilles with snowdrops on the packet, butter caramels and chocolate caramels. And even though all this is theirs they will share it with everyone else in the house, something that makes them feel proud. - It's because of us that we got so many sweets for Christmas.

It has also been a joy to have Krister home, now looking so strangely adult in his uniform. He was present for the first few days but then had to return to duty later. He said that he had been thinking about joining the German brigade but then changed his mind. He couldn't bear seeing any more ruins.

The days he was at home passed without sparks flying between him and his father. All the same, it pains Julie to see how they avoid each other. If they talk to each other at all it is with a politeness which seems inappropriate between a father and son. She can see that this relationship troubles both of them, but she also sees the pride in Jørgen's eyes when he looks at his son. She wanted nothing more than that these two could talk together until they had settled all their disagreements.

On the evening of New Year's Day, after the house has settled for the evening, Julie and Jørgen are sitting together in the warm living room, making the most of this last day of the holiday. Each is sitting in an armchair close to the stove, Julie with her legs up on Jørgen's lap. As they sit, each is nursing a small glass of brandy in their hand - Jørgen has saved the last of the Christmas ration for just this evening.

They have been talking a great deal about the future recently, sharing their stories and dreams. Jostein is beginning to be an adult. In a few years he will probably have a family of his own and will take over here. But the two younger children will still need looking after, and this is a burden which will be too much for Jostein.

- When that day comes, we'll still be young enough to make some changes. - Then it will be our turn, Julie. Then we can have a new life.

It is the Aura foundation in Sunndal that he has in mind. A great deal is going to be happening there with work for everyone who wants it.

- That will be quite something, Julie. Can you see yourself as the proud owner of a town flat in Sundal?
- You're dreaming, Jørgen.
- It doesn't have to be a dream. Not this time. In five or six years' time, Jostein will be married. We'll still be able to work, and he won't have to look after us.
- But he hasn't even got a girlfriend yet, so far as we know, Julie smiles.
- We don't know that. He's not like his brother, who carries on with girls all over the place. He's more like me. I never brought a girl home if it wasn't serious, but then it could move quickly.

Jørgen could be right about that. Jostein has never talked to him about girls in the way that Krister does, but that doesn't mean that he doesn't have a girlfriend. In the Young People's

Building Julie has seen what a good dancer he is. So maybe Jørgen's plans are not so unrealistic after all?

- Do you really think we could move away from here one day?
- Yes, I really think we could, he says confidently.

He plays affectionately with her legs and passion surges through her. His eyes look at her warmly.

- Shall we go to bed? he smiles.
- Yes, let's, she says breathlessly.

Dizzy from the effect of the unfamiliar drink and as passionate as a youngster, she yields to what she knows so well, but which also feels new every time. They know each other's thoughts and have such trust in each other that they even dare to talk about them.

- Oh, this is just so good! she moans.
- Should we not say that it's good for us both?

The next day, Jørgen asks Jostein to fetch a saw, which he shares with his neighbours. There is a pile of birch logs in the garden which Jostein and Anders intend to work on in the course of the day. Christmas having made such inroads into maintenance work, Jørgen will go into the woods himself to make preparations for the following day's work. He tells Julie that he won't be home until evening. She is making vegetable soup and will bring it out to him in a metal container, something she does when the weather and ground conditions permit - going into the wood with a container of soup or stew, food that's easy to carry.

- Will you really do that? Jørgen says brightly, and she detects something of last night's passion still in his eyes.

She stands by the window, watching as he makes his way over the snow-encrusted ground. It is clear that he is feeling good. He is walking with a youthful spring in his step, and Julie feels sure he is whistling. He always whistles when he is happy.

The day is freezing cold. Julie's clothes all date from before the war. She is wearing a pair of loose-fitting trousers she made herself for the skiing trips she and Jørgen used to treat themselves to. She has avoided using these to make clothing for her children precisely because she intends to use them for times when she has to go out of doors as she does today. On her feet she has a pair of well-used boots which Helge wore one winter until he grew out of them, and whose soles are still intact. She has on a cardigan under what for her used to be a luxurious garment. When she turned thirty-five, she had received from her parents a loose-fitting calfskin jacket with wool lining. This has now been patched and has all its seams sewn over. It feels stiff when the weather is cold, but is still warm and windproof to wear. In addition, she is wearing a knitted hat, a scarf and thick mittens, so she is well protected against the cold. Apart from the containers of soup, she is carrying a basket with cups, plates and cutlery for everyone working there. To this basket, she adds a small packet of coffee and some Christmas buns. She is aware that Jørgen has a kettle at the clearing for brewing coffee over a small fire. On her arm, she is carrying a blanket so that they can sit down. She experiences trips like today's as celebrations, as do the men she visits. It is not often she has time for pleasures like these.

The snow crunches underneath her boots as Julie makes her way along the path leading up to the workplace. The cold pinches her nose and cheeks, and the frosty mist from her mouth turns white the hair sticking down under her hat. It is a beautiful day. The sun creates patches of gold over the mountains and meadows on the other side of the fjord but has not yet reached this side. The trees are covered with a thick layer of frost. Juniper bushes along the road look like large white doughnuts. If Julie comes too close to a branch overhanging the path, needles of ice cascade over her, reaching under her scarf and turning into large drops of water down her neck.

In the woods all is as quiet as in a church. A large bird flaps into the air with beating wings, and a hare, chalk-white, darts over the path in front of her. Otherwise she hears only the crunching of the snow and the distant whirring from a saw down below. It is quiet, but is it too quiet? Julie always hears the blows from Jørgen's axe as she approaches the workplace. Follow them and you'll find me, as he always says. She comforts herself with the thought that he must be taking a rest. She knows where he is today, so she rushes forward on the ground with her pulse racing and her cheeks burning.

She inhales the smoke from the fire and breathes a sigh of relief. Of course, he will be preparing for her arrival. As she stands there in the clearing where she knows he will be, the first thing she notices is a wisp of smoke from the dying fire, looking something like a mirage in the cold air. Then she sees *him.*

He is sitting in the snow in front of a pile of logs with his legs extended in front of him. His head is resting on a stick behind him. The top buttons of his shirt are undone, his hand is thrust into his chest and is resting on the bottom buttons. His other hand, enclosed in a mitten, is resting on his lap, and then the terrible certainty strikes her. *She has lost him.*

She remains standing in front of him, unable to move, letting go of everything she has been holding in her hands and rapidly taking in every detail around her. The soup container with the lid falling off, the hot liquid sending a cloud of steam into the clear air, the intense smell of the soup, that of the newly chopped logs and of the fire, the wood in the background, and *she sees him.* The picture becomes fixed as a huge scream builds up inside her, but the only thing she hears is an animal growling in her throat before it all breaks out.

- Jørgen! No! Jørgen!

She kneels beside him, leans in towards him and emits heartrending sobs as she calls out his name again and again. She rages, screams, weeps, and in all this, is aware of a voice inside her saying that she *may* do this, that she *may* let go and express all of her pain without restraint. Here there is no one to hear her. She will later be surprised about this, that such a thought should occur to her in the middle of the most frightening experience she had ever had to endure.

Afterwards she cannot understand how she managed to lay him out on the blanket she spreads out on the snow. She finds birch twigs to place underneath where his head will rest. His body is still soft as she lays it out on the blanket with his arms across his chest; she looks for a long time into his glazed eyes before closing them, but there is nothing she can do about his half-open mouth.

All the time she is doing this she talks to him.

- I have to leave you now, Jørgen, but don't be afraid. I will soon be coming back for you.

She then runs away, runs, trips and gets up again until she stops out of breath in the quiet of the wood. Why ever is she rushing? Jørgen is gone, and no one can help him. While she walks through the wood with all its winter covering, the thoughts which will not leave her are: Jørgen is gone. How can she protect the children?

She reaches the farmyard and goes over to Jostein and Anders, who are sawing logs.

- Stop what you're doing! she says, pointing to the saw.
- What was that you said? they ask above the noise of the saw.
- Stop!

The silence is everywhere when the saw stops. Jostein and Anders stare at her.

- What is it, Mother? Has something happened?
- It's your father, she manages to say.
- Has he been injured? Jostein asks nervously.
- No, he's not injured, she says in a voice as weak and fragile as that of a child. - He is lying out there, dead.
- Dead? gasps Jostein, his face pale.
- Yes, dead, she says, collapsing into his arms.

She is trembling, her body shaking as Jostein holds firmly onto her. A thought suddenly flashes through her mind. *She* must not give way. She must fight for those who are left behind and must begin at once. She owes this much to Jørgen.

She breathes in and exhales a long, trembling sigh before releasing herself from Jostein's arms. She is now filled with a strong sense of calm as she stands in front of them. Anders is standing with his arms by his sides and looks as if he is frozen to the spot.

- We'll have to bring him home. He can't lie there in the woods all by himself. They will get out the long horse-drawn sledge.
- I don't suppose you will want to come, Mother. The two of us can go and fetch him, says Jostein helplessly.
- No, I want to be there.

Astrid has now come out onto the veranda. She has been watching them through the window.

- Julie? she says.
- Jørgen is dead. I think his heart has given way.
- Oh, Julie, Astrid weeps and holds her close. - Yes, Julie says, - but now we have to think about the youngsters, we don't want them frightened.

Sven is at school, and Sunniva is on a neighbouring farm playing with a friend.

Julie asks Astrid to contact Sven's teacher so that he can stay with him until evening. This teacher has a son of Sven's age, and he often goes there to play. She can ring the neighbouring farm to see if Sunniva can remain there until evening. She must also make sure that the children are not told of Jørgen's death. The adults need to ensure that the children are kept indoors and away from the windows until they bring them home. The children may be told that their father is ill but not that he has died. It is Julie who will break that news.

Julie has placed a leather sheet over the sledge and a pillow for Jørgen's head. He is lying there just as she left him. She now sees that his face looks peaceful apart from his half-open mouth but detects a look of worry and surprise in those stiffening features. What were you thinking about when you felt this happening, Jørgen? she wonders. Were you worried about us?

They cover his face and body with the blanket and carefully pack support around him. Julie and Anders sit one on either side, keeping hold so that he does not fall off the sledge at the sharper bends while Jørgen uses the reins to steer from behind.

Astrid, with help from the maid, has moved a divan down into the lounge where he can be laid. A nurse has already arrived to help with preparing the body.

Julie asks if Astrid has told her mother that her son has died.

-Yes, Astrid says, she cried, but I'm not sure how much she understood.

Synnøve is seated on a chair in the kitchen with tears streaming down her cheeks while rocking backwards and forwards.

- Oh dear, oh dear! she says.

Julie helps with preparing the body. She only wishes that this was something she could do alone.

In Storvik, the flag is flying at half-mast. At first, people thought this was to mark Synnøve's passing and were deeply shocked upon hearing the news of Jørgen's death.

The children, fortunately, seem unaffected. Sven has reached the stage where he may know a little of what death means.

They have already had their evening meals where they were staying, and Julie now takes them straight up to their bedrooms to get them ready for bed. Sven gives Julie some enquiring looks, but Sunniva chatters as usual about the games she has been playing and the food she has eaten, which is better than what she gets at home.

Julie sits on the edge of the bed with her arms around them both. Everything inside her trembles at what she now has to do.

- I have to tell you that something sad has happened.
- Is there something wrong with Father? Someone said that he was poorly.
- Father is dead.
- But you said … you said … gasps Sven and clings to Julie crying, and then Sunniva too begins crying.

She is perhaps the one who understands this least, while Sven is inconsolable.

There is nothing Julie can do but to hold and comfort them, but her own body, mind and will all conspire together to create an intolerable pain. She mustn't cry, she mustn't, must not.

She sits with them until her crying stops, then puts them to bed and sits at their bedside.

- Is Father in heaven now? asks Sunniva.
- Yes, Father is in heaven, says Julie and her tears well up once more before she regains control … And I am sure he can see that you are sad. It is right to feel sad, but he may feel sad if he sees that you are too sad. He doesn't want his children to be unhappy. Can you manage to think about that?
- I'll try, says Sven.
- I will, too, say Sunniva.

Julie sits there until they fall asleep. Then she turns off the paraffin lamp on the dressing table and sneaks out. Once out in the corridor, she leans against a door behind her. Her legs will hardly bear her weight. How did she do? Did she manage to find the right words?

- Help me, God, she whispers. And if you can hear me now, Jørgen, you too must help me. Hear me.

Jorgen has now been laid in his coffin. This took place while Julie was looking after the children. After all has become quiet Julie goes in to him.

The cold hits her as she opens the door. The candle she is carrying in her hand sends flickering shadows over the ice-cold room and the man lying there while she fumbles her way over the floor to light other candles. She wraps herself in a warm blanket and sits down beside the coffin.

Someone has left a hymnbook in his folded hands and removed the band round his face. The candles behind him are burning with steady flames, their light bestowing on him a somewhat distant, majestic look.

Yesterday evening, Julie sat with her legs on Jørgen's lap as they planned a future together. They made love. So close and intimate were they that she can still feel the warmth. How is she to deal with that now?

She feels within herself a hollow emptiness, a loneliness beyond all measure, and yet as unreal as a nightmare. At the centre of this emptiness is this white-hot burning pain, and the only thought which fills her is that she has lost him. Her body is shivering from the cold in the room, but most of the cold comes from within herself and from the cold of his body. She feels no repugnance at this but knows that she must be here with him to take her farewell in this way. She cannot bear him lying alone in this cold.

She sits with him until the candles burn down, and Astrid comes into the room.

- You should go to bed now, she says gently. - Try to sleep. You're going to need all your forces now.
- Yes, I'll go to bed, she replies obediently.

Her children are sleeping in the double bed. She gets in beside them, feels their warmth, and sleep swallows her into a merciful darkness.

From early morning to late evening she drives herself throughout the next days. Jørgen must have a worthy burial. Mechanically she gets through the work of doing what is expected of her and saying what is expected of her, but all the time she feels that it is someone else doing it all. She, her real self, is still held somewhere in a paralysing unreality. Sometimes she sees fear in Sunniva and Sven's eyes. Then she lifts them onto her lap and holds them tightly into her.

- This is going to be very good, all of it, she whispers.

She is also aware of Astrid's worried look.

- You mustn't drive yourself too hard, Julie. There are many people here to help you.
- What? Am I driving myself too hard? she says.

The hardest thing is seeing Synnøve sitting in her chair weeping and repeating No, no to herself. One day, Julie's patience runs out.

- Mother-in-law, stop it! she cries, I can't bear it!

Synnøve looks at her with an expression so alive and alert that a feeling of horror sweeps through her before Synnøve continues as before.

Is it possible, Julie wonders, that she understands what is going on around her, or is this just something she has imagined?

Each evening she lights the candles and sits with Jørgen in the cold room which is gradually becoming filled with flowers and wreaths.

As time goes on the feeling of revulsion over his cold body which she had experienced on that first evening disappears. Pictures from their life together crop up. Some are good, others painful. When the memories are painful, she asks for his forgiveness. But most memories are good. Then come the smiles.

- Do you remember that, Jørgen? she says.

These hours spent with him gradually bring with them a strong sense of calm. This calm carries her through these days and also clarifies the reality for her; it fills that empty space inside her and enables her to feel warmth and care for those around her.

Her father has now arrived along with Johanne and Hans. Hans gives her a hug, as he did the last time they met.

- I didn't think I would be coming here for an event like this, he says.

Helene and Ivar arrive on the evening before the funeral. They will be staying in the cottage. Julie doesn't dare think about how this is going to feel for Ivar. All the unfinished business between himself and Jørgen and that first meeting with his mother once she had retreated into her own world?

The worst will be meeting Krister. He is standing ashen-faced in the corridor when she meets him. He drops his travel bag to the floor, whereupon Julie pulls him, her grown-up son, in towards her. His whole body is shaking with crying. She leads him into the living room, sits down on the sofa with him and places his head on her lap as he sobs in a manner which leaves her in pieces.

She strokes his back and hair.

You don't need to say anything, Krister. I know how you're feeling. But you must never - never, do you hear? - feel guilt. Your father loved you and was proud of you. It's that you have to remember.

- I just can't …. he weeps.

Yes, you can, she says gently. - All of us have to get through this. We owe Father that much.

She does not know where she will find the strength to do this, but in witnessing her son's pain, she knows more than ever that it is she, and she alone, who will have to carry them through this.

- Do you want to look at your father?
- Yes, please.
Once again, she lights the candles in the room.
- Here we are. Can you sense the peace around him?
- May I be here on my own, Mother?
- Yes, you may, she says, leaving the room and closing the door quietly behind her.

The three oldest sons carry their father to the grave together with Ivar, Hans and their nearest neighbour, who has been a good friend of Jørgen's right from childhood. Julie walks behind the coffin leading the two young children, and behind them Synnøve is supported by Astrid and Helene. The funeral procession is huge. The entire neighbourhood and many others from the village have turned up to accompany Jørgen to his grave.

Today is as crisply cold and fine as it was on the day when Julie found him. The sun decorates the mountains with gold just as it did then, but today, the flags are flying at half-mast over a district in grief. The hymn singing sounds crisp before it spreads across the hamlet. Julie hears it clearly, but it's as if she's looking at pictures, pictures which will stay with her forever. But she is feeling unsteady and is unable to feel the ground under her feet. What she will remember most about today is Krister's and Ivar's fixed and inflexible expressions at the graveside.

Immediately after the funeral, her grief casts a shadow over everything round her. She frequently wonders what it was that drove her to the woods that day. It is nightmarish to think what might have happened if Jørgen had been in the woods with Jostein and Anders. She imagines a terrifying scene in which they drive back home with him, dead. She thanked God it was she who found him and that she had that time with him alone, that she was able to express her grief with him then. She still does not know how long she was lying next to him in the cold wood while she raged, screamed, cried and called out his name, but she knows it was that which kept her from going under.

Everyday life now takes over. During the day she gives herself over to work. At night she lies awake while thoughts whirl and go on whirling around in her head. How is she going to achieve all the things required of her? What is the future going to be like? In the end these thoughts fill her days and nights. It's the first thing she thinks about when she wakes up in the morning, and it is still with her as she falls asleep at night. Occasionally she sees her reflection in the mirror and feels she is looking at a stranger. She becomes angry and agitated with the children, with Jostein who is bearing a grief he cannot quite grasp, and with Astrid, whom she just wants to help. There seems to be nothing she can do about any of this.

One day, after Julie has been more than usually unreasonable towards her, Astrid blows up:

- Julie, you'll just have to pull yourself together. Here we are, all of us trying to help you. But I'm getting to the end of my tether. Look around you! Look at your own children who are so unhappy and fearful that it's a terrible sight. And do you see how Jostein is feeling? Julie, you're not the only one who's lost someone. The children have lost their father, and are they now to lose their mother as well? I have lost my brother, and there is a certain old woman who has lost her son and knows she has. It's soon going to be too much for me, Julie.

Julie then bursts into tears.

- Don't you understand how afraid I am about the future, Astrid?
- Yes, I do understand. But you must accept the help I want to give you and be a proper mother to your children. Maybe you think I'm being hard, Julie, but this needed saying.

After this she tries to pull herself together, but it is Sven who awakens her.

One day he arrives home from school, sits down on a chair still wearing his outer clothes, and looks at her with pain and defiance that cuts right through her.

- You lied to us, Mother.
- I lied? she whispers.
- Yes. You said it was only old people who die, he says, giving her a look so direct and so wide awake that she gasps.
- Did I say that?
- Yes, you did, and it's just lies and nonsense.

Just lies and nonsense comes also as an echo from Sunniva who has been sitting drawing and is now eagerly following what is happening.

- Because now I know that people don't need to be old to die, Sven says. - Father is dead even though he wasn't old. You could die, Mother. We can all die if we become ill.
- But you're not afraid that I'll die, are you? she says, trembling as she lifts him onto her lap. Can't you see that I'm healthy?
- Father was healthy, too, and he still died.
- No, she says - he wasn't healthy. He had a bad heart. It wasn't easy to see, but that's why he died. But my heart is healthy, I'm healthy, all of us are healthy, so none of us is going to die. And do you know what we're going to do now? Sunniva and I are going to get dressed, and we'll all go to the seaside. There's something I want to show you.

She takes them down to the sea, to the rock where she and Jørgen used to sit. Easter is approaching, spring is here, and she has not seen it before today. She takes off her coat, spreads it out over the rock so that Sunniva and Sven can sit there without freezing, and embraces them both. The springtime sun is already spreading warmth, and the waters of the fjord are a bright blue; there is a smell of sea and shore and the gurgling sound of water as it trickles down between melting patches of snow.

- What were you going to show us? Sunniva asks.

- I wanted to show you this rock and how good it is just to sit here looking over the fjord. Your father and I often used to sit here and talk about important things.

- What was it you talked about? Sven asks.

- Maybe we talked about you, Julie smiles. - We talked about all the good things we wanted for our lives. The last thing your father wanted was for you not to be happy.

- Do you think he can see us? Sven asks.

- Is it possible to see us all the way from heaven? Sunniva wonders.

- Yes, you can be sure that he can see us and is looking after us, Julie says confidently.

She remains seated there, staring ahead of her into the distance while her gaze takes in the blue spring day. She feels Jørgen as close as if he were sitting there with them and hears the words he often used to say when the world was at its most difficult for them both. We'll get there, Julie, we'll get there if we help one another.

- What have you been thinking about, Mother? Sven asks.

- No, was I thinking?

- Yes, you were, because when people are looking into the distance as you are doing now, that means they're thinking.

- Shall I tell you then what I was thinking? she smiles. I was thinking that we'll get there if we all help one another. So shall we try? Shall we try to help one another?

- Yes, Mother, we shall.

Chapter 12

Easter 1947 is just around the corner. More than a year has passed since Jørgen died. That they have come through everything in that year as well as they have is in no small measure down to Jostein's efforts. Adult and with a natural authority, he has taken over Jørgen's place as head of the farm. He has organised the harvests, the slaughtering of sheep last autumn and the timber business, just as Jørgen did. In the spring after Jørgen died, he passed his final school-leaving examination as a private student in Kristiansund.

Krister is expected to be home for a visit at Easter. When he had finished his military service he offered to live at home for a year, but Julie rejected the idea. She said that he had already lost enough time and must now get down to study before it's too late and he loses heart. He was at home until the harvests were over then travelled to Oslo. He still had some money left which he had saved during the time he worked for his grandfather, and said he could get an extra job in addition to his studies. Julie would not suffer economically because of him.

However, he had not been in Oslo long before she received a letter from him saying that he had obtained a job as a general assistant at the National Theatre and that he would try to enroll as a pupil there. This is what I want, Mother, he wrote, to become an actor. And if that is what he wants, what more can Julie do than support him in this?

Helge, too, has finished school. Once he had completed his second year, Julie tried to persuade him to go on to high school, which was now a possibility, but this was not what he wanted. He would take the school leaving examination before deciding what to do next. He says he will live at home for a year, something which is something Julie cannot say no to. Jostein will be off to the military in autumn. She will then have to rely on Helge and Dreng-Anders and as much extra help as the economy will permit. They are very fortunate to have Anders. He is approaching seventy but is a full-time worker and knows the farm inside out. This will work out so long as Astrid can give Julie a helping hand, but Synnøve is demanding more and more of her time both by night and day.

Working days are both long and burdensome for Julie. Just the weekly wash takes an entire day. Water has to be taken to the washhouse, clothes scrubbed on the washboard, whites have to be boiled before being scrubbed, and the wet clothes must be brought down to the stream where they are rinsed in cold water. In winter this is particularly unpleasant.

Saturdays are dedicated to cleaning the house, when Julie gets down on her knees and scrubs the wooden floors. Then there are all the daily duties. Meals have to be prepared, dishes washed, clothes repaired and ironed, the cows are to be fed three times a day when they are in their stalls, and then there is milking both morning and evening. Fortunately, Jostein has begun to help in the cowshed when he can find the time. He has no qualms about milking, which is something new in the village. Men don't normally show their faces in the cowshed unless there is an extra tough job which women cannot do by themselves, problems with calving or something else requiring a man's strength. For a man to sit down beside a cow to milk it is something of a sensation, but Jostein just ignores this. This is work, like any other work, and he learned milking at an agricultural college. In Autumn, electric lights are to be installed on the farms. Electricians are already busy fixing them. That will be the time to get machines for milking, Jostein says. Looking after the cowsheds is going to be too hard for Mother to do on her own.

Work can be made lighter for farmers who don't just want to hang on to the old ways now that two businesses have been set up for the hiring of machinery. It is now possible to hire someone with a tractor to do the ploughing, harrowing and mowing in fields and meadows. While this costs money, farmers can save by hiring fewer workers.

Jostein discusses topics of this sort with Julie and shows delight as he makes plans for a new and more modern type of farming. He appears so adult and enthusiastic that she can forget he has just turned twenty-one. Even though their conversation is mainly about work and money, she nevertheless feels that she has become closer to him during this time. But when it comes to personal matters, he does not allow her into his world. He then behaves just as before. If she is bold enough to raise some such topic, he backs off and becomes cautious and distant, and she has to recognise that this is just how he is, so very different from his siblings.

Julie has always been a night person, but even so, she has never had a problem getting out of bed. She does not need much sleep and comes to life when the others have retired. After Jørgen's passing, she has adopted the habit of sitting up for an hour, often more, in which she deals with personal matters. Sewing and mending clothes, finishing off some knitting, writing letters and even such luxuries as reading; alternatively, she may sit by the stove with a cup of coffee and simply allow her thoughts to wander.

She has come to depend on these evening breaks. It is then she can savour the quiet of her tidy, warm kitchen and that little portion of a life which is hers alone and which gives her the strength to meet the coming day.

She always has a book by her bedside and cannot sleep without reading a page or two.

Reading in bed keeps her thoughts at a distance, and she always reads until sleep takes over. But sometimes, this strategy fails. There are nights when thoughts and images whirl around and keep her awake for hours.

The intolerable pain following Jørgen's death has now diminished, but the grieving and yearning after him is always going to be with her. She often talks about him to her two youngest, hoping to keep his memory alive for them.

In these night hours, she thinks about Jørgen and about their life together, but mostly about him and what his life must have been like here on the farm.

During the difficult years they had spent together, he often said that she despised him. Did she really do this? She denied it at the time, but as she delves into herself now, she thinks that maybe this was not too far from the truth.

Now, with the benefit of hindsight, she sees that she was fighting by her own rules and that when they took over the farm he lost a great deal of that youthful spark which he had about him in the first years they lived together. Those painful years, as she now calls them, when they lived together like two strangers wore them both down. This is undeniable, even though it is a great pleasure to reflect that they got together again later. They had Sven and Sunniva and rediscovered each other as they were when they were young. Nevertheless, she can understand Jørgen's sense of defeat during these years: Krister rejecting his inheritance, Ivar, who in Jørgen's eyes had brought shame on the family and the family in Kristiansund, which fell apart. She now understands what he meant by broken chains. Painfully she sees what life did to him. He came here and was subjected to his parents' wishes. Later, he became subject to her own will, and for Julie, this was the most painful consideration of all. For she now sees that she had been forcing through her own wishes in the case both of the children and of the most important decisions for their lives, while Jørgen was becoming less and less visible as the years passed. But what else could she have done? And if she allows these thoughts to take over, then she knows that she will go under because of the pain.

Julie beams as she meets Krister out in the yard, and he is not afraid to give his mother a big hug in public.

- It's so good to come home. Have you remembered the herring balls, Mother?
- Oh yes, there is a whole pan of them waiting for you.

Herring balls with fried meat, bacon and turnips are his favourite dish, and Julie always takes care to have these ready for him when he comes home.

She jests around him, serves his food and, seeing that he does not lack anything, feels a real warmth at having her son back home again.

- Oh, I see the favourite has retured, says Jostein sourly. He is dressed in his weekend clothes, is freshly washed and has combed his hair.
- Are you off to enjoy yourself? Krister says.

- What's has that got to do with you? says Jostein and bangs the door behind him as he leaves.

- Huff, can't you so much as look at each other without quarrelling? Julie says disappointedly.

- It would seem not. - But please don't blame me. It will pass in time. Isn't that what they say in the village? Is Helge not at home?

- No, they are off meeting with friends at Kjell's. You can go too if you want, but I don't think that will please Jostein.

- I'm not so sure. Jostein goes his own way.

- What do you mean by that? Julie asks sharply. - His own way?

- Oh, forget it! That was just something I said. You know how I'm always in the wrong with Jostein? But I don't want to go out tonight. I have so much to tell you.

- That's lovely for me, Krister. By the way, a letter has arrived for you, she says, handing him a thick envelope with an Oslo postmark. The address on the envelope is in neat, girlish writing. - It must be something important, coming from Oslo and being addressed to you here.

He glances at the letter and puts it in his pocket.

- Aren't you going to read it?
- There's no hurry.
- And you're not going to tell me who the letter is from?

Yes, he will tell her that, but first, he wants to talk about the theatre.

He says he was overjoyed when he landed the job. To have a foot in the door, to soak in the feeling, the smells, and the electric atmosphere before the curtain goes up for the play. He has already been on stage a couple on a couple of evenings as a cover for someone. It was only a tiny role, just a couple of lines; he was on stage for barely a minute.

He is having lessons from a highly respected actor at the theatre. He mentions this actor's name to Julie, and it is one she recognises. What he is currently working with most of all is his language. He needs to get rid of his Nordmøre accent. He is also having singing lessons and will be having dancing lessons later, but all this is expensive, and he must be careful to keep an eye on what he can afford.

- Your father would be so proud of you now, says Julie, but she immediately regrets it as she sees a shadow flit across his face. It seems that he cannot bear to hear his father mentioned.
- What about that secret letter, then? she says coaxingly, whereupon his face lights up.

Yes, she will find out about this, too. Perhaps she remembers him writing to her about a girl he was in love with during the short time he spent in Oslo back in 1944. This was a young actress. They broke up, or rather, he broke off the relationship with her when he came back home. He decided to do this because of the distance and the fact that he did not know how long he was going to be at home. This girl now has a job in the theatre as what you might call a minor actress. She may not have an outstanding talent, but there's a place in the theatre for people like that. When they met each other again, the feeling was the same as before, and now they have become an item.

- Her father is a banker in Oslo.
- A banker? My, what fine people you're mixing with now! she says and once again she wishes it was something she had left unsaid. For, like an echo of her own words, she hears the scorn

in her mother's voice when she first told her about Jørgen and
his family: Banker, my goodness!

- Mother?

- Oh, forget it, Krister. Tell me about your girlfriend.

- Yes, he will, but she must promise not to get too excited
over things which are not worth getting excited about.

- No, why should I do that?

- First he must reveal that Eva, which is what she is called,
is a little older than he is. Five years, in fact, though he never
thinks about it.

- Well, that could be a problem, says Julie, trying not to
sound too sceptical. - But it's probably all right. You have
always been a bit older than your years.

- The other thing is that she is divorced and has a year-old
son, Krister says, looking enquiringly at her.

- Divorced? says Julie. - And she has a son?

- Yes, Krister says, and before his mother can go on, he will
explain how all this came about.

After Krister broke off their relationship and came home,
Eva threw herself into the arms of a man she was not in love
with. It was a relationship which had consequences. She was
forced to marry the man, for that was what both sets of parents
wanted. They took out a separation order even before the boy
was born. She now lives at home with her parents and the boy.
Her parents own a large villa at Smestad. In the garden, there is a
small guesthouse. It is this house he has told her about in his
recent letters. He is now renting it.

- Do you mean that you're living in the same house? Are
you telling me that you are living together?

- To say we are living together is putting it a bit strongly, he says. - Of course, she pops in to visit her boyfriend. Come on, Mother, we are modern people, aren't we?

- Modern people? Julie says and cannot hide her concern. Have you thought about what you are doing with your life and what responsibilities you might be taking on? An older woman and one with a child?

- But we're not married, he says desperately. Marriage hasn't even been mentioned between us.

- So much the worse, she says. Have you thought about how it would be if the relationship came to an end, just like every other relationship you've ever been in? It might not be so simple this time if you are living off her father's goodwill.

- I won't be living off his goodwill. I'll be paying to live there.

- Can you be so sure about that? Will you be paying the full rent for a house like that?

- Good heavens, Mother, you're making all this sound as if it's the end of the world.

- Yes, maybe I am, she says, exhausted.

- Mother, he says comfortingly. - Her father believes in me. He believes in my talent. He is on the board of the National Theatre and is a man of culture. He was the person who put in a good word for me when I got the job there.

- Yes, and I suppose he'll put in a good word for you when you sign up as a pupil?

- How can you say that? Do you think I got in there on something other than my own abilities? Besides, who these days say no to a little extra help?

- Well, you know best whether you can look yourself in the eye.

- Look me in the eye? What a moralist you are, Mother!

- Isn't that a bit like cursing your mother?

- No, that's not at all what I meant, but you have to accept me as I am. Don't create me as you want me to be. And if Eva and I should marry, then you'll have to accept that or just leave the whole thing alone.

- You need to understand, Krister, that the things you've told me tonight have given me no pleasure. It has been tough for me since your father died, and without Jostein I would not have come through it. You have to realise that no matter how much you disagree with each other, Jostein has been a tower of strength to me.

- And I haven't been? Is that what you're saying? Jostein is clever and always has been, says Krister bitterly. But just remember this. I'm the one with the right of inheritance here. If he now has the farm, it's me he has to thank for that.

- What are you saying? says Julie in shock. - Have you come back here to claim that right? Are you going to repeat to your brother what you've just said to me?

- No, you're quite safe. I will never come back here as a farmer, but I am so fed up with Jostein and his pretentious ways. By the way, do you know where he is tonight? I don't suppose he's told you that he's at Ås visiting his girlfriend.

- What! At Ås? she gasps, her body turning numb.

- Yes, that's what I said. And don't tell him I told you. Let him tell you himself.

- Is it Signe you mean?

- No, it's Solveig. Jostein and Solveig have had their eye on each other for as long as I can remember. They didn't dare do anything about it during the war years, but they've been together ever since.

- And I've been the last one to find out about it?

- Yes, it would seem so.

- But when they're so young? Don't you think it'll come to an end? she says and hears the desperation in her own voice.

- I can't see that happening, says Krister.

She remains seated, staring straight ahead. How could she have been so blind? Solveig is in her first year of teacher training in Levanger. She passed the entrance examination with flying colours and began last autumn. She did the same with the school leaving examination in the first days of peace. Locally people talk about how capable she is, not just academically but also in her work on the farm, both outdoors and in. She now realises that Jostein became noticeably quiet after Solveig left in autumn. He came home early from dances and stayed at home rather than going out with the other young people. But tonight, he was going out to meet her. She had presumably returned home for Easter. How was Julie going to take it if this turned out to be serious and if she should become related to people from Ås? She had been looking forward to Krister coming home, but now he has brought chaos into the life she has so carefully tried to create recently.

- Go to bed now, Krister, she says. - You must be tired after your journey, and now I need some time to myself.

- I didn't want it to be like this, says Krister unhappily. You mustn't destroy the time we shall have together.

- I won't, she says.

She remains seated, incapable of doing anything as her thoughts whirl around inside her. Krister has found a woman older than himself who, on top of that, is both divorced and a mother; Jostein may now land her with a daughter-in-law from

Ås. Is it, then, so strange that she feels everything she cares about is slipping away? The worst thing is that she has seen in Krister something which she cannot bear to see and which she must thrust right out of her thoughts. Has she not seen a cynicism in him tonight? And hasn't she noticed this in him before? The question which she knows can shake her to the core: is it she herself who has brought him up to be like this?

Helge arrives home happy and smiling. But he is taken aback when he catches sight of Julie.

- Are you still up? Aren't you feeling well?
- No, I'm not ill. There are one or two things I just need to think about.
- Maybe Krister has been telling you about his women?
- There is that, but it's not just Krister who has things going on. Have you heard about Jostein and Solveig?
- Yes, he says sheepishly - I do know about that. Has Krister been talking about it? He shouldn't have done; Jostein should have told you himself.
- I won't mention it to Jostein before he chooses to tell me. So all I need now is for you to run off with a woman.
- I can promise you that I'm not going to do that. There's so much I want to do and to find out about life, so I'm not going to tie myself down to anyone, not for a long time anyway.
- That's good to hear. I'll just say this one thing, Helge. When you were young, there were many difficult conflicts between my mother and me. I then decided that if I ever had children, I would never get mixed up in who they wanted or who they married. Tonight, I met myself at the door. I would never have believed that the decision I took then would be so difficult to stick to.

Easter passes without any further confrontations. Helge goes up to the summer farm with some friends. Krister spends the night there a couple of times; otherwise, he takes day trips there with Jostein, and so far as can be seen, they behave as most brothers do on such occasions. Julie never mentions again to Krister what they spoke about the evening he came home. She can no longer bear talking about this but is also afraid that her anger will run away with her and that she may say some unforgivable things. She knows Krister sufficiently well to know that it doesn't help trying to talk sense into him. The only thing she can do is hope that the present relationship will come to an end, just as all his other escapades with women have.

Nor does it look as if Krister wants to raise the subject again, and both avoid being alone together. This puts a damper on the pleasure of having him at home, and for the first time she feels a sense of relief when he goes.

- Mother, I'm an adult now. Can you please remember that?

Krister is now far away, well beyond her reach and influence. She must simply hope that he is adult enough to assume responsibility for his own life. It is harder to have Jostein around and to keep quiet about what she has found out about him. But she has not uttered a word to indicate that she knows anything about his relationship with Solveig. Nor does she comment on the fact that she heard him coming home in the small hours throughout the whole Easter period. In one moment she comforts herself with the thought that both of them are still young and that such youthful passions pass. In the next, she reflects that Solveig is eighteen or nineteen, the same age she was when she met Jørgen. But the very thought that she could acquire a daughter-in-law from Ås turns her cold. Hallgrim is still in prison. Jørgen kept guard over him the night that he was arrested; is it so strange she feels unwell at the thought that this connection might continue? But if it is difficult to talk sense into Krister, it will be totally hopeless in the case of Jostein. Unlike Krister he shuts himself away totally if she so much as tries talking about his personal life. And as long as he does not mention Solveig, she can neither say nor do anything, but now she understands why he was overcome with delight when he found that he was called to join the military at Steinkjer in autumn. Steinkjer is no great distance from Levanger. Now that Solveig has gone back to college he stays at home when the rest of the youths are out dancing or having fun at the weekends.

- You shouldn't work so hard that you are too tired to go out with the other young people, she suggests.

- I'm a bit tired of their celebrations, he says.

- But isn't it natural to have a bit of fun when you're young?

- Maybe, but I'm fine as I am.

She doesn't know how Jørgen would have taken this. She imagines how furious he would have been. He would probably have shouted and slammed doors until the house shook. He would certainly have given vent to his anger and disappointment. She cannot do this; she just remains cold and shut in. She wishes that she was more like Jørgen, that she could rage and get rid of the intolerable anger and bitterness gnawing away inside her, but instead, she reacts by becoming irritable and angry at those around her and by being unreasonable and obstinate. She often used to reproach Jørgen when she thought his language was too strong. He said the Lord would forgive him when he saw that he had good reason for coming out with the occasional oath. She could do with some of that forgiveness now, but that is not how she is made.

One evening, just before Whitsun, Jostein is sitting with Julie in the kitchen. They chat hesitantly, and her whole being tells her that he wants something from her. She sits there with some knitting, trying to focus her mind on this while waiting for what is to come.

- There's something I need to talk to you about, he says finally.
- Yes, I thought so.
- I hate asking you for money, but I need a few kroner. I didn't think I was going to need it. You know that I've been doing some work in the woods but this has not brought in as much as I thought it would. With all the other things that need doing, there won't be time to spend on this any longer. It's not a huge amount I'm asking for, maybe a hundred kroner.
- Well, that seems affordable. Is there anything in particular you need the money for?
- Yes, I'm going away to Whitsun.
- Going away? Where to?
- To Levanger.

Julie feels a chill ripple through her; her heart thumps against her ribs, but she manages to remain calm.

- So you're going to visit Solveig, am I right?
- You know about that? he says, blushing furiously. - Has my brother been spreading gossip?
- Nobody has been spreading gossip, Jostein, but there are some things that just can't be hidden.
- Yes, he says and looks at her defiantly. - All right, yes, it's Solveig. We are thinking of getting engaged.
- Engaged? You mean with a ring?

- Yes, with a ring. I can afford the ring myself, but I need some money for the journey, and a little bit extra for food. Have I not earned the money, Mother?

- This is not about money, Jostein. My question is whether you know what you're doing. Getting engaged? Aren't you a bit young for that?

- If I'm old enough to take responsibility here on the farm, then I'm surely old enough to get engaged, he says defiantly. - There's no need for you to tell me why you're against it. I know that well enough. I didn't come here to listen to a lecture either about Solveig or her family. No one needs to remind me of what Hallgrim and his children have done, but they're already paying the price for that. And Solveig doesn't need to suffer any more than she has already.

- But you wouldn't expect me to lie and say I'm happy about what you're doing?

- No, but I expect you to accept it and to treat me like an adult human being. The past year has not been an easy one, and Solveig is the only person I've been able to share things with. She's the only one who knows how my life has been here on the farm.

- You have us, Jostein, you have me. And don't we talk to each other?

- Yes, but have we ever talked about the things which matter to me?

- There's nothing I'd rather do, but you've never given me the chance.

- And have you asked yourself why, Mother? There are the others, and I'm not talking here about Sven and Sunniva, for they need you more than ever. It's Krister and Helge I'm talking about. You've always thought more about them than about me.

- No, Jostein, that's not true, she says.

- Is it not true? Yes, they're clever, my two brothers, and they have highfalutin interests, just as you have. You've emphasised how praiseworthy they are. This is not going to get any better now that you're dreaming of Krister becoming a great actor. It will be the same with Helge, whether it's in music or in something else you care about. Where have I stood in all this? Yes, I've dug the ground, as Krister so kindly put it once. But that's not something you can boast about in the village, is it?

- Now you're being unfair, Jostein. That you and Krister are different is not something I can do anything about, but do you think that gives me pleasure? And doesn't Helge deserve what you've just said about him. Hasn't he offered to stay here while you do your military service? Doesn't he contribute here too?

- Yes, and that's something I'm grateful for.

- Well, it's good to hear you say that. And am I not proud of you? Do you know how proud I have been of you, not least in the year that's just gone?

- Yes, I know that, but that's not what I'm talking about. After …

- After your father died; that's what you mean, isn't it?

- Yes, it is. I could always talk to him.

- You miss your father, don't you? she says gently, tears welling up inside her.

- Yes, I do miss my father, says Jostein, his voice too becoming hoarse with tears. He stands up, wipes one hand over his face, and then goes out.

Stunned, Julie remains seated. What has he just done? What has she done with this, her child?

The conversation is never mentioned again, but Julie gave him the money he asked for. It has also left a deep impression on her, Jostein working in the woods during his free time to earn money for his own purposes. Jørgen had once done the same thing before being forced to go begging to his parents. But that's not how it should be, she thinks disappointedly. That is not how she should relate to her own son.

- I shall be staying with Solveig, of course.
- You'll be staying with her? But doesn't she just have a little flat?
- Yes, but then I don't take up a lot of room!
- Yes, but …?
- Mother! he smiles resignedly. - What sort of times do you think we are living in? he says, which makes her blush. Exactly as Krister had done.

When she was young, it was the young people who blushed with embarrassment when situations like this arose. Now it's the parents' turn to blush, she muses.

Julie casts a last glance over the coffee table she has set out in the living room. She had dreaded the first time she had invited her mother-in-law here to Storvik. This time she is dreading even more having her future daughter-in-law here. The table is laid for three, the two young people and herself.

She has rarely spoken to Solveig since she was a girl. Like all the others from Ås, Solveig has stayed at home except for arrangements in the village. Julie has seen her occasionally in the shop, maybe exchanging a couple of words with her, and has been impressed by how such a young girl seems to be tackling the difficult situation which has befallen her family. She has also heard rumours about how capable Solveig is.

Hand in hand, the two of them come into the living room. Jostein is tall and powerful and radiates an adult seriousness. He has curly red hair, and she is struck by how much he looks like Jørgen. She now sees that he is going to look more and more like him as the years pass. By his side Solveig looks small and frail, her medium-length blonde hair in a feast of curls round a serious face with what many would call over-refined features. Her gaze meets Julie's as she grasps Julie's outstretched hand.

- You are very welcome here Solveig, and I sincerely hope that you will both have a happy life.

She was afraid that a certain mood would settle round the table at this first meeting, but she could have spared herself the thought. Certainly, she is aware of Jostein's watchful gaze on her throughout the meal, but Solveig speaks freely and openly. She speaks about Levanger, about her college and describes some episodes from there. Her descriptions are so real and alive, and she laughs with a high, trilling laughter.

But Julie sits there with the feeling that here something is being buried. If everything was normal, she would be asking how Solveig's family are, but this is something she hardly dares to bring up. At the same time, she is aware that not to bring it up would offend against public decency, so in the end, she summons the courage.

- How is it with people at home, Solveig?

It's fine now, Solveig says looking at her with a gaze so cool and direct that Julie must hold onto herself not to look elsewhere. Anders has now been released and come home, which has been a huge relief for her mother, though she will not be fully herself until her father has served his sentence and come back to the farm. But it looks as if they are going to manage financially. Signe has been to business college and now has a good job in Trondheim and Terje will soon be well again. He has been declared free of infection but must still go for treatment for some time into the future. What he will do after that is uncertain, but for the time being he will remain at home, and she says that work on the farm is doing him good. The two small children are also doing well, she says.

- Oh, by the way, Mother asked me to say she will soon be inviting you over for coffee, she adds.

- Then you must give her my best wishes and thank her. That will be nice.

When they have gone, Julie feels confused. She is not surprised that Jostein is obsessed with this girl. Blond and pretty and with a slim, lithe figure, she looked so attractive in that simple short-sleeved cotton dress with a wide belt round the waist, her arms and legs a golden brown colour. It came as a relief, too, that Solveig was so open and easy to talk to. But was she not just a little too bold? Julie wonders. Would it not have been more natural in this, a first meeting between a mother-in-law and daughter-in-law, for her to have been a little more reserved in her behaviour? Was this a game Solveig was playing in order to deal with a situation which, because of the circumstances, must in fact have been difficult for her? Or maybe that is just how she is, naturally fearless and bold? But Julie is left with the very uncomfortable feeling that during this meeting with her daughter-in-law-to-be, she was the youngest person there. This is a feeling she tries hard to shake off. She must not be so tense. Ought she, with a long life behind her, feel inferior to a nineteen-year-old girl? But in all Solveig's openness, she had still felt that there was a reserve: a clear signal which was saying: go this far but no further.

There is one thing she promises herself, that it will not be
her responsibility when it comes to Solveig settling in here on
the farm, and she has a long time to prepare for that. Jostein has
said that there can be no question of a wedding until Solveig has
finished her teacher training. She has three years left, three years
in which Julie can really get to know her. And in that time most
of the local gossip about the people on Ås will have died down.

Solveig mentioned economy. This must have been a concern
on their farm. How was Hallgrim able to meet his enormous
expenses? Now people are claiming that a fund has been set up
by the Nazis for helping their members. People ask if it can be
this which has rescued Ås from his financial responsibilities.

The village boiled over with gossip when Jostein returned
from Levanger with a shiny gold ring on his finger. Julie was
quite aware of the symptoms: the familiar experience of
conversation breaking off when she enters the shop or the post
office or when this or that person cannot resist asking the
question:

- Has Jostein become engaged?
- Yes, once a child has grown up, isn't that what happens?
she answers with a smile.
- They say Solveig's clever and is at college, so there's
going to be no shortage.
- Yes, Solveig's a lovely girl, Julie says. They mustn't think
they can get her to say anything to Solveig's disadvantage. - She
is going to be a lovely daughter-in-law.
- They say that she's a hard worker. But is she thinking
about being both a farmer's wife and a teacher?
- I think that's for the two of them to decide, Julie replies
abruptly.

Jostein comes back from accompanying Solveig back home and looks searchingly at Julie.

- Well, you carried that off nicely, Mother.

- Yes, and why shouldn't I? Solveig came through it well too, didn't she?

- Oh, yes, Solveig, he smiles. I never feared for her not managing it.

- Jostein, Solveig is a lovely girl. I will do all I can to support you. The most important thing for me is your happiness.

- Do you really mean that? he says, wiping his hand over his face and making as if to leave.

- Stop that now!

He spins round in the doorway and looks at her in surprise.

- Stop what?

- No, it was just … no, it was nothing.

- OK, he says and is out of the room.

Julie cannot bear seeing this gesture which she associates with Jørgen. That awkward wiping his hand over his face to indicate that he is feeling embarrassed, whether out of desperation, because he's fed up or even because he's happy. She hadn't noticed until recently that Jostein does this too. Has he inherited it from his father, or has he learned to do it by imitating how Jørgen used to behave? Whatever, it's a shock for her every time she experiences it.

Julie feels that all the village's eyes are on her as she makes her way to Ås for an afternoon coffee with Gunnhild. This is going to be their real trial by fire, the one she has dreaded more than anything. That it's an ordinary working day means that the meeting is unlikely to go on too long, and it's good that Sunniva and Sven have been invited to play with the two youngest of the Ås children.

Gunnhild has been isolating herself on Ås ever since the war ended. She has not been seen in the village, either at the shop or the post office. Julie has caught the odd glimpse of her when she has been passing either to or from town, no doubt to visit Hallgrim. She has not appeared in Ås since that notorious Christmas party back in 1940. Julie noted that Gunnhild was present in the churchyard with Solveig and Terje when Jørgen was buried, but they did not come to Storvik to take part in the service.

What had Julie been expecting, a woman broken and destroyed? No, Gunnhild is just the same as ever, a little thinner than before, but that suits her. Like Julie, her face is marked by worry and hard work. Her face is now showing wrinkles which she did not have earlier, but she has preserved her proud bearing and her blond hair is as shiny as ever, combed away from her forehead and held in place with slides behind her ears. Quietly, and with a proud self-confidence she welcomes Julie to the farm and does not mention a word about how long it is since they last met.

Jostein has not been invited. It is harvest time and he has not much time for events of this sort. No men are to be seen, they are out in the grounds, but Solveig is present. A coffee table has been set out in the living room for the three women and the children. Once again Julie feels some relief that the children are there requiring her attention. This makes it easier to keep the conversation going, for it is clear that Gunnhild is much more reserved than Solveig. Solveig talks just much as she did that first time she visited Julie. They talk about their children and everyday things, women's talk, as the men like to call it.

The atmosphere immediately becomes rather more tense when the children have finished eating and ask to go outside to play. Hallgrim has not been mentioned. Should Julie seize the initiative and ask how he is, she wonders anxiously. She realises that to leave without acknowledging his existence would be an unspeakable rudeness and hopes that Gunnhild will mention him.

- I have to say that I think the world of your Jostein, Gunnhild says. That's a fantastic boy you have there, Julie.
- I could say the same about Solveig.
- How are you dealing with everything Jørgen was involved in? asks Gunnhild.
- Well, you know, it has been quite hard. Without Jostein I don't know how it would have turned out. But I don't suppose it's been easy for you either?
- No, but at least Hallgrim is still alive.
- How is he?
- I hope he can come back with both life and health intact, Gunnhild says, and a tremble in her voice reveals how she feels before she continues.

Before Julie can say any more, Sunniva comes in crying her eyes out and saying that the boys have been horrible to her. This gives Julie the opportunity to break off. She says she will go out and reprimand them.

- Yes, I would think that you, too, have enough to do.

Julie feels that she is floating on air as she makes her way down the hill from Ås. The worst is now over. True, she has still to meet Hallgrim, but that cannot be any worse than it was facing today. Now at least she has been to their farm. She knows too what Jørgen would have said if he had been with her now. That the boy has done a good job, those would have been his words.

- I'm looking forward to Jostein and Solveig getting married, Sunniva says as she hangs on to Julie's arm.
- You are?
- Yes, because they'll have children, and then I'll be their Auntie.

Solveig now pops in almost every day. She enjoys coming over when they are about to have their evening meal. She always accepts the offer when Julie gratefully invites her to share their meal, and before Julie has found tableware, she will have found it herself with great alacrity and a sense of being perfectly at home. With equal alacrity, she will help Julie to clear the table, to put the food back in the cupboard and she will help with the washing up. Julie cannot help noticing how quickly and efficiently Solveig works, but she finds herself fighting a gnawing sense of displeasure as Solveig seems to be taking her familiarity with things for granted in what is, after all, her own kitchen. She feels ashamed of this thought when she recalls the suspicion she was met with by Synnøve when she first came here to the farm. She must never become as Synnøve was then. She has at least learned that much from what happened.

Another thought she is struggling with is how it is all going to be once Jostein and Solveig are married. She has decided that at that point they may take over the farm, but what will this be like for her? Sunniva and Sven will still be at school and need her for several more years. But how are they all going to manage economically? She hopes that there will be something for her to do on the farm. There will have to be even if she moves into the cottage, but she cannot expect Jostein to make provision for everyone. And what about Astrid and Anders? Then there's Synnøve, who may live for several more years as she is physically so strong even if her mind is affected. What Julie is currently thinking is that she may take in sewing, but now for payment. There is still time for her to think about this, but she must be prepared before that change takes place.

Julie has been invited to Hans and Johanne's wedding in August, and Johanne asks her to bring Sven and Sunniva. As is usual in farming communities, they schedule all events of this sort either before or between busy farming seasons, usually round midsummer in late June or in August before harvesting begins.

She is not sure she can afford the time to go, however much Johanne may want her to. But once again it is Astrid who comes to the rescue. Yes, of course, Julie must go to her sister's wedding, she says. The girl helping with the harvest this year is so very capable and can help with preparing food for the farm labourers and help Astrid in the cowshed. They have ceased working on the summer farm now that they have begun to supply the dairy with milk. This has come as a great relief as it saves them from the tiresome tasks of separating and churning. What they do now is to place the large milk bags to cool in the stream before men carry them up to the ramp where they are picked up each day by the milk lorry. An effect of this is that money arrives in the post each month, which feels like a great step forward. Now, the cows graze out in the meadow after having been in the cowshed and the forest pastures during early summer.

Jostein has said that Solveig may come to help out while his mother is away, but Julie says that she is already needed where she is. Apart from this, Julie feels resistant to the thought that Solveig and Jostein should be going round as if they were married already. This is not what she wants, for people gossip enough as it is, but she does not mention this to Jostein.

This time she will again stop off at Kristiansund on her journey north and will look up Randi on the way back. As time has progressed things have become easier between them. Randi paid her a surprise visit a few weeks after Jørgen's death. She said she would rather do that than go to the funeral. Her visit and the warmth from her friend's presence comforted and helped Julie over a difficult time. The disagreements between them melted away and were trifles compare with Jørgen's death. Now their relationship will soon be back as it was before, and will become even closer as time goes on.

Ivar meets them on the pier that day, to the children's great delight. But Julie sees a new Ivar, one who is almost unrecognisable, pale and stooped with no trace remaining of that childlike enthusiasm which was once such a significant part of his nature.

After all the horrors of war have been revealed, Ivar is now having to live with an intolerable burden of shame, Helene says. Jørgen's death and the unfinished business between them have also affected him. He rarely touches his violin now, playing only at home when Helene persuades him to play for her. He has been offered a chance to begin playing again in the symphony orchestra but has turned down the offer. He has also been offered back his old job in the bank as from autumn, but this, too, is an offer he turns down. Things have been from hand to mouth and very tight in the past two years, but despite this he is not looking forward to going back, Helene says. He is happiest now with a paintbrush in hand, working away on his beautiful watercolours. But if she suggests that he should think about mounting an exhibition, he refuses. He is an amateur and does this for his own pleasure.

Helene is holding a dancing session for young girls in the loft when they arrive. Julie sneaks into the room with Sunniva, who stares in fascination at the young girls as they move across the floor. But when Helene asks her to get up and take part, she is overcome with embarrassment and hides behind her mother's skirt.

As so often previously Helene and Julie are sitting together after the others have gone to bed. Julie is tempted to pour out to Helene all the problems Krister and Jostein have given her recently.

- I'm sure your boys will get by. Isn't the question whether you will be able to accept it?
- I'm ashamed of finding it so difficult to accept the relationship between Solveig and Jostein. You mustn't think that this is just because she's Hallgrim's daughter, even though you understand that this has not been easy. It's no secret that for you, Helene, the relationship between us and the people on Ås has been poor ever since the start of the war, and even longer than that. No, there are other things I can't quite put my finger on. Solveig seems so very strong.
- Need that be bad?
- No, I'm the one who am too tense.

- If it should all go so wrong that the two of you cannot get on, you can always move here with the two little ones. We rent out the downstairs flat, so why can't we rent it out to you?

- Move here? Can you see me as a town lady?

- Need that be an impossible thought? When Jostein marries, won't you still be too young to move into the cottage? There is a need for people like you here in town. Business and private customers alike will be grateful to have someone with your dressmaking skills. You'll have more than enough to do. Your children will get the education they need, and you'll still be close to them.

- No, we mustn't get carried away with our dreams, Julie laughs. That's not going to happen, even if the thought is very tempting.

Johanne and Hans are to have a civil wedding in Molde on Friday. The ceremony will be private with only the essential witnesses present, Johanne says. Afterwards, they will have dinner on their own at the Alexandria where they are to spend their wedding night, she says, blushing like a teenager.

- I am so happy for you, Julie says, clasping her sister close to her.

The wedding feast will take place on a Saturday evening. Hans has invited all the adults in the hamlet to a dinner dance in the Youth Building. This should not be seen as an attempt to play Bør Børnson or the so-called rich Norwegian American. For a start he is just so happy that he feels the need to share his happiness with others. But this will be more than just a wedding party for him. It will also be a reunion. He will be celebrating coming home to friends of his youth, to old and new friends and acquaintances. He is really going to let go, he says. And

Johanne, that formerly cowed priest's wife for whom most earthly pleasures were sins, nods her total agreement.

Julie slumps down in a chair by the table where her father is sitting.

- Are you having a good time, Julie? he asks.
- Oh, yes, says Julie, hot and breathless. To think that I'm dancing again here in the Youth Building with all its good memories, an old person like me!
- You didn't look in the least old when you were doing that waltz. And just look at your sister! Did you ever think you'd see her again on a dance floor? Can you remember how she loved dancing before Inge arrived on the scene?
- Oh yes, I remember that, Father.

The sky is lightening in the east as she walks home with her father. There are still many participants in the party who don't want it to stop, and Johanne and Hans must stay until the very end.

- Now let's have an ever so little drink, Julie, says her father as he takes the fine cognac from the cupboard. *Skål* for a wonderful day, Julie. I can't remember the last time I felt so happy. I think our family needed something to celebrate after all we've been through,
- Yes, isn't it really good that there are still things to celebrate in the world? It has been good for me, too, Father, to feel real pleasure again, to feel truly alive.
- You still have a life ahead of you, Julie. A life with a lot to give.
- Do you think so, Father?
- Yes, I do. You've had your share of difficulties, just as Johanne has. Now's the time to enjoy the good things. Johanne

seems to have them for now. One day it will be good again for you. Things are looking up for us all.